SHE LOVES ME...

Time to get dressed. Time to leave. She had been a beauty, oh yes. He looked around the room. Nothing was out of place. Then he took his white carnation and began the ritual which would ease her passing into heaven. "She loves me, she loves me not. She loves me..."

He touched her adorable parted lips with his forefinger and then kissed the glove. Debbie would now belong to him always.

"Good night, Sweet Princess," he whispered as he closed the door. Could he stop? he wondered. No. He'd just begun.

Avon Books are available at special quantity discounts for bulk purchases for sales promotions, premiums, fund raising or educational use. Special books, or book excerpts, can also be created to fit specific needs.

For details write or telephone the office of the Director of Special Markets, Avon Books, Dept. FP, 1790 Broadway, New York, New York 10019, 212-399-1357. *IN CANADA:* Director of Special Sales, Avon Books of Canada, Suite 210, 2061 McCowan Rd., Scarborough, Ontario M1S 3Y6, 416-293-9404.

I'll Be Wearing A White Carnation

JUDI MILLER

AVON
PUBLISHERS OF BARD, CAMELOT, DISCUS AND FLARE BOOKS

I'LL BE WEARING A WHITE CARNATION is an original publication of Avon Books. This work has never before appeared in book form. This work is a novel. Any similarity to actual persons or events is purely coincidental.

AVON BOOKS
A division of
The Hearst Corporation
1790 Broadway
New York, New York 10019

Copyright © 1985 by Judi Miller
Published by arrangement with the author
Library of Congress Catalog Card Number: 84-091243
ISBN: 0-380-89586-2

All rights reserved, which includes the right to reproduce this book or portions thereof in any form whatsoever except as provided by the U.S. Copyright Law. For information address Avon Books.

First Avon Printing, April 1985

AVON TRADEMARK REG. U.S. PAT. OFF. AND IN OTHER COUNTRIES, MARCA REGISTRADA, HECHO EN U.S.A.

Printed in the U.S.A.

WFH 10 9 8 7 6 5 4 3 2 1

For my brother Alan, who gave me a gift subscription to *The New York Review of Books* for Christmas

"SWF, 28, sensitive, sensual, and sometimes scintillating computer programmer desires to meet smart, sweet, successful male counterpart who likes good conversation, has sensational sense of humor, and lots of *joie de vivre*."
—*The New York Review of Books*, Box 10462

"I am an invisible man. No, I am not a spook like those who haunted Edgar Allan Poe; nor am I one of your Hollywood-movie ectoplasms. I am a man of substance, of flesh and bone, fiber and liquids—and I might even be said to possess a mind. I am invisible, understand, because people refuse to see me . . ."
—Ralph Ellison, *Invisible Man*

PROLOGUE

He stood stark still, watching silently, his toes curling into the shag rug. He knew he should put on his clothes and go, but he wanted to look at her a while longer. Standing at the foot of the bed, he studied her exquisite feet. He hadn't noticed before, but her toes were painted a shocking pink. He should have sucked her toes. It was too late now.

His eyes traveled slowly upward. The blue sheets had silky, damp butterflies on them. One of her slim, white arms was flung recklessly across the pillow, and one hung limply over the side of the bed. He looked at the creamy hands—and the delicious nails—that had clawed his back. No woman had ever done that to him before.

The pillow still covered her face, the little vixen. Well, he wouldn't disturb her just yet, but he did want to kiss her goodbye. Not that she would forget him. Slowly, methodically, he got dressed. White shirt, white underwear, black socks, gray three-piece suit. In the reflection of the lamplight shining in her window, he put on his new red-and-black Cardin tie. Then he took out his handkerchief and wiped off all the surfaces in the studio apartment—even the wineglasses, which he put in the sink.

The full-size bed occupied an alcove in the L-shaped studio. Parquet floors gleamed between area rugs. One was Oriental and had a big stain in a corner. He stooped to study it. Nope, that was there before he entered her life.

1

Then he went back to his lover. Gingerly, he lifted the pillow with his elbow, careful not to touch it with his hand. What a pity. Her raspberry mouth was twisted into a scream. He turned to his attaché case and took out a black glove, which he put on his right hand. Then, leaning in, he took his thumb and forefinger as if to chuck her dimpled chin. Tenderly, he closed her mouth. One bright, violet-blue eye was open, rolled upward, gazing at the ceiling. He smiled indulgently and left it that way. Her rich, lustrous hair fanned out like strawberry lace over the pillow.

She had been a beauty.

With his gloved forefinger he touched her lips and then touched his own. Kissy-kissy. Time was running out. He had to leave. A smile ran slowly, crookedly, across his face, and little tears dotted the corners of his eyes. His face felt crinkly, plastic. He didn't want to leave. He put on his black overcoat and plucked the flower in the lapel.

"She loves me, she loves me not, she loves me, she loves me not, she loves me . . ." The white petals fell like snow. But she loved him. Of course, he had known all along.

Pausing for a deep breath, he imagined himself a forest animal trapped between one world and the next. Straightening up, he prepared to leave. In the case he placed what was left of his boutonniere. Then he took out a wig and slipped it on. Blond curls tickled his forehead and the back of his neck. Next he popped on a pair of studious-looking black horn-rimmed glasses made out of window glass.

He flung on a green tweed scarf and put his black bowler hat in the briefcase. Then he took out a big Macy's shopping bag and put the attaché case inside it. He would have to stop in a rest room somewhere and change clothes all over again, or someone in *his* apartment might become suspicious.

He smiled. It was going so smoothly. He wasn't

2

even nervous. With her help he had stolen the one thing from her apartment that might have mattered. At the door, he looked once more at her soft whitish-pink body sprawled almost obscenely across the bed. She had laughed at the jokes he had rehearsed in front of the mirror; she had turned up her eyes and looked into his, the little flirt. She had been his lover and he hers. Certainly, she would never have another. They were entwined forever in eternity. His heart swelled with love for her. He kissed his gloved fingers as if tasting again her once-ripe lips.

"Good night, Sweet Princess," he whispered shakily as he blew her a last kiss and let himself out of her little apartment. She would sleep a long time. She would sleep forever.

CHAPTER ONE

Debbie felt a flutter of excitement like she did when she came upon a good floor at Bloomingdale's. She put down her glass of red wine and cleared away the dinner dishes. Her tongue glided over her lower lip as she reached for the manila envelope. Tonight she would make her final selections. It was like shopping for a man. She giggled. *The winner, please.*

She lifted her long, strawberry-blond hair back in a clump and went into the bedroom for a barrette to fasten it back. Then, businesslike, she spread out the letters on her little dining/living-room table. Twenty-three replies to her first ad. Not bad. And she had only run it once in *The New York Review of Books*, an intellectual newspaper that achieved a secondary notoriety for its classy personal ads section. Very few singles read the book reviews in it. Very few read the books.

There were many ways to answer the personals or run ads. The *Village Voice* was good, too. And *New York* magazine. A few other places, and then there were the national magazines. Face it, it was the thing to do. Though Debbie Greene wanted to be first, wanted to be where it was happening, it had taken her six months to get up enough nerve to run an ad. At first it had seemed so . . . desperate to her. But what was she supposed to do? Either take action or leave it to fate. Fate was slow. And she went through boyfriends fast.

It didn't seem to matter that she was attractive,

successful, sharp—all those things. Because she was a teacher. Not exactly in the mainstream of socializing. So if the new "in" way to find Mr. Right was by advertising for him—so be it. Better than a well-meaning friend or relative fixing her up with a "nice boy" who was a loser, then apologizing to the person who fixed her up because she didn't want to marry after the first date. Forget it. Besides, after all the talking to herself, Debbie decided it might be fun.

Rolling up the sleeves of her Club Med sweat shirt, she studied her ad. After clipping it out, she Scotch-taped it on a piece of white paper. She lit a cigarette and reread the ad.

SWF, 32, teacher with Masters, vivacious redhead, looking for fun-loving partner. Must be successful, have great sense of humor, want the Good Life. Smokers okay. Photo appreciated . . .

Debbie sat there debating. Some of the other ads were better. Hers wasn't that great. She picked up *The New York Review of Books* and scanned it.

Attractive, ebullient businesswoman, slim, financially secure, witty, seeks her mirror image in a gentleman who dresses well, knows good food and wine, is fond of absorbing chatter, and likes a mature-minded woman. Must be 40–60. Send me your photo and I'll send you my phone number and address. NW area . . .

seemed better. But there were always the weird s that made you wonder.

SJWM, psychotherapist, 45, seeks pretty, outgoing young woman, slender and tall, who is not afraid to be feminine and enjoy the earthly pleasures. Would you like to sunbathe in the nude on my boat with me? Photo please, with handwritten reply, and only if you are 18 to 21 . . .

Hers seemed staid in comparison. But it got to the point. She wanted only a certain type of man. And though she had been to Smoke Enders, she still couldn't quit. So, having a man around who was going to kvetch about her constant smoking would be a pain in the ass. It's just that the others seemed more clever somehow. Oh, well, cleverness had never really been her strong suit. Anyway, it was too late now.

She just didn't want a lot of creeps answering the ads. Especially not her first time. She was tired of baby-sitting for misfits. She longed for someone like herself, who had drive and ambition and who was, God help us, normal—and who wanted, one day, to marry and settle down. She wanted to sit on the other side of the PTA experience. She was thirty-two years old. Time wasn't exactly on her side anymore.

She picked up one letter. She knew it was destined for the wastebasket.

I'd like to be teacher's pet. And I like a lady who likes fun. If you're into sharing your fun with more than one, give us a call. Maybe you can teach me a thing or two. I'm home during the day, but you'll never catch me at night. The name's Nick. P.S. Would have sent a photo, but I'm fresh out of them.

His phone number was scribbled on the bottom.

Debbie laughed and then shuddered. *Blecchhh.* The handwriting was so sloppy she couldn't even read it, either. Well, you just had to stay away from the offbeat types. They might be a little dangerous. This *was* going to be fun, she reassured herself. Everyone was doing it. Not just in New York. All over.

One down, twenty-two to go. She came upon an envelope with just a business card. Somebody had warned her about that. Married. A business card meant no home number, no letter, no nothing. Unless you were into married men. Forget it. Debbie had tried that once. Then there was the envelope with nothing in it but a card for Ultimate Experience Videotape Dating Service. She debated a moment, then walked across the room and wrapped a rubber band around it with the rest of her business cards. Two down, twenty-one to go.

She was concentrating so intently on weeding out the potential Mr. Right from the definite Mr. Wrong that she almost jumped when the telephone rang. As she picked up the phone, her silver bracelets jangled. She let them slide off her wrist onto the rug and sank into her imitation velvet couch.

"Well? Should I buy a dress? Have you found Prince Charming?"

Debbie crinkled up her tiny, freckled nose and laughed. One man had once said she had a "Great Gatsby" laugh. When she laughed, it reminded him of the tinkling of money. His. Debbie had read the book for a course in college, but she still didn't understand what he meant. She stopped going out with him. Other people had called her laugh infectious. She liked that better.

Her friend Candice was calling, Debbie thought, to get a vicarious thrill. She didn't have the nerve to answer an ad or run one of her own. If Debbie succeeded, Candy would try it.

Debbie went over to the little dining table where her letters were spread out like a game of Solitaire. The long cord on the phone followed her like a snake.

"I've gone through these twice. Two were . . . forget it. I like five. But, listen, five out of twenty-one is not bad. And twenty-one decent replies to one ad is fantastic. Don't you think?"

"Yeah, I guess so. Do they send pictures?"

"No, not really. A few did, but I can't always tell

what he looks like with the picture. It's usually just a small snapshot. I'm better off judging from the letter. That way I can tell what his personality is like."

"I would want the picture."

"Well, look, I'll meet them in a restaurant or a bar or someplace. A public place. I mean, I'm not letting a stranger in my apartment."

"What's the difference, Deb, they usually get in sooner or later. And if they pick you up, you can just get your coat and leave. They're not going to open the door and mow you down with a machine gun. I am not going to live in fear. It cramps my style."

"Listen, I'm the one who's running the ad. Don't talk about bravery."

There was an awkward silence.

"So what did you get?" Candice asked.

"Okay, of the five I like, a man who produces documentary films and lives in Brooklyn; a salesman for a sportswear firm who just wrote, 'Hi, you sound great. I'd like to meet you'; and then there's a lawyer who is self-conscious about his hair thinning and loves redheads. And a man who owns a health-food restaurant and sent a picture of him with his dog. But it's too blurry and small to make out which is which."

"Take the lawyer. What does he look like?"

"No picture."

"Read me his letter."

"Oh, c'mon, run your own ad!"

"Okay, maybe I will. Do you really think it works?"

"I don't know. But it's a way to go out. Everybody else is doing it. Better than sitting home and watching Merv Griffin."

Candice gulped silently and said goodbye, then went over to the TV and turned up the sound on Merv.

Debbie hung up and went to the big oval mirror in her main room. She teased her coppery hair with her fingertips and then realized how foolish she was being. Candice was right. Take the lawyer. She wasn't selecting a husband. Just a date.

Lighting a cigarette, she walked her phone over to the couch. In her hand was a letter. She dialed the number, but when the phone rang, she lost her courage. She wanted to hang up and forget it. One ring, two rings. Maybe he wasn't home. This was stupid. She didn't have to do this to get a date. And then someone answered.

"Hello?"

Debbie felt her mouth go dry. She had never called a man for a date before. Did this mean she had to pay?

"Hi," she said, recovering. "I'm Debbie Greene. Or Box Number 12701 from *The New York Review of Books.*"

There was a noticeable pause.

"You're Bob, the lawyer? Or do I have the wrong number?" Oh, God, this was so embarrassing. How many box numbers had he answered? She should hang up right now.

But then he cleared his throat and said, "I'm sorry. I was working on some briefs when you called. So how are you, Debbie? You sounded terrific in your ad."

Debbie smiled, crossed her legs, and took a drag on her cigarette. He sounded nice after all. Better to play it cool. She couldn't act the nervous role and tell him it was her first time and that she was, truthfully, scared shitless.

"I liked your letter," she said. The letter sat on her couch like a tiny throw pillow. She picked it up.

"Read it to me," he said.

For a moment she wanted to ask, Why? Do you write so many that you forgot? But there was such a warm, playful quality in the tone of his voice, she decided not to be paranoid. " 'Dear Teacher with Masters,' " she began, reading his letter to him. " 'I have a weakness for redheads, especially vivacious ones.'" She stopped, feeling more relaxed, her courage building. "Do you really?" she asked him.

He laughed. "Yeah, I do."

Then she laughed, continuing to read his letter. "'Actually, I have a weakness for anyone lucky enough to have hair. Mine is thinning out. And I'm only thirty-four. But I make up for it by being overly attentive and considerate.'" Debbie smiled. "Do you?" she asked, teasing just a little.

"Absolutely," he replied.

"'I'm a lawyer,'" she read. "'Married once to another lawyer, a law-school mistake. No children. But I would love to have some.'" Debbie had liked that part. It meant he was looking for a commitment. "'I play tennis, like to go to films and plays, and am a gourmet cook. I'm sure a vivacious redhead like yourself will have many, many replies. Maybe when you narrow it down, you will include me in the many you chose to answer. I'd love to meet you.'" Debbie had been touched by that last part. If there was one thing she couldn't stand, it was arrogant, macho men.

"I really liked your letter, Bob," she said, hoping she didn't sound too much like a personnel manager.

"Actually," he blurted out, "the truth is that this is my first time doing this. I'm a little nervous."

Debbie let out a squeal, and all pretense was gone. She sat up straighter out of her slouch and practically sang, "So am I! This is my first time, too."

"Isn't it funny how lonely people can be in New York City? You think it's supposed to be so glamorous and you're supposed to be so busy and involved, and you feel like a failure just because you had to answer an ad just to meet someone nice."

Debbie felt butterflies in her stomach. Not every man talked that honestly. He sounded so sensitive and nice. And normal.

"They say it's better in other cities," he continued.

"Houston, Atlanta, Boston, Phoenix. Easier to meet other singles. But I don't know. There's something about the City I like, though. Are you originally from here?"

Debbie was instantly alert. She had been so enrapt in what he was saying, she was momentarily at a loss. "I'm from Great Neck, Long Island."

There was a pause. She didn't even get to ask him where he was from before he said, "I have an idea. Let's continue this conversation in person."

Debbie lit another cigarette.

"Would you feel better if we met in a public place? I mean, like a restaurant or a coffee shop?"

Debbie let out a deep, but silent, sigh of relief as she exhaled smoke. What fantastic insight this man had.

"Yeeeees."

"Name the place."

"Well, okay, there's a little restaurant in my neighborhood called Jimmy's that has a jazz combo that comes in every weekend. We could meet for a drink. But I don't know if you like that kind of music."

"I love all kinds of music. And let's make it dinner. What about Friday night? Are you free?"

"Perfect. Jimmy's is in the middle of the block between Eighty-first and Eighty-second on Columbus Avenue. You can't miss it."

"I'll see you there. Say . . . around eight?"

"Fine. But wait a second. I don't know what you look like. How will we recognize each other?"

He laughed. "That's right. Well, I have a black hat and a black raincoat. No, I've got it. I'll be wearing a white carnation."

She had to laugh, too. It was a cute touch. When she hung up, her face was flushed; she felt like dancing around her apartment. It had worked. And he sounded so fantastic. You never knew. Maybe this was the start of something big.

* * *

He hung up the phone and smiled. It had never been this easy. You just picked up the phone and there was a woman on the other end who wanted to go out with you. Without even knowing who you were. And this one was sharp, he could tell. Probably beautiful, too. A vivacious redhead. She had chosen his letter. And it was her first, so he didn't have to compete with all the rest. Competition and rejection. He hated it. Unless she was lying and she said that to everyone.

His newspapers and magazines were piled on the floor under a paper plate and an empty tuna-fish can. He lifted up the papers, and the fork that was sticking upright fell on the carpet.

Riffling through stacks of *The Village Voice*, *New York* magazine, the *Learning Annex*, which took ads for free, and a *Metropolitan Almanac*, he found—on the bottom—copies of *The New York Review of Books*. After a moment, he found her ad. It was circled in red. With a magic marker he sketched over his red circle and expanded it into a heart. Debbie. He had forgotten to ask her last name. He admired her, he really did. It took spunk to place an ad in the personal section of a paper. He couldn't do that. He could only answer them.

Rolling over in bed, Terry Morrison hugged the other pillow. Thursday, March 18, it said on her night-table clock. Who needs it? She didn't want to wake up. She lay buried nose-down, thinking about her odd dream. She and Bob had been swimming in the warm, greenish-blue waters of the Caribbean, naked. At night. They had jumped and splashed like dolphins. They had been so free then. Why is it that honeymoons were easily forgotten? Nobody really remembered them when the marriage was over.

The alarm went off. Seven A.M. sharp. No exit. She reached out, still not looking, and pressed the button. She used to reach across his body, and if he had to get up at seven, they would set the alarm for six. But that was long ago. No Caribbean now. Today she was lying alone in a bed in an apartment in Queens.

Terry rubbed her eyes. She could hear the steady pinging of rain on the outside half of her air conditioner. A regular weather announcer. Rain. Again. She flung the covers off and sat up. Terry always slept in the nude. Only with Bob had she worn those frilly, lacy, sometimes itchy nightgowns—because he had wanted her to. She switched on the radio, keeping it low. She gazed longingly at her pack of cigarettes and gold lighter on the night table but realized she didn't have time for a smoke.

She grabbed a pink terry-cloth robe from a boudoir chair and went into the bathroom. After her shower, she dried off with a fluffy towel, then put on scented deodorant and Chanel No. 5 behind her ears and between her breasts. Wrapped in her robe, she clogged into the kitchen. Grapefruit juice would get her started until she got to work and was able to have her morning coffee. Then back to the bathroom.

On the shelf above the ivory, shell-shaped toilet seat was her makeup. Foundation. Powder. Mauve eye shadow. Violet eyeliner and mascara. Blusher. Lipstick brush. She combed through her short, black curls, but there was no time for a nail-polish touch-up.

In the bedroom she selected a pair of camel-colored pants and a cream-colored blouse. She reached over to the dresser for her gold watch and put gold earrings in her pierced ears. Then she slipped her hand under the mattress and brought out a .38-caliber Smith & Wesson revolver, which rested in a shoulder holster. She fitted the holster under the left arm.

Terry checked her leather shoulder bag. Cigarettes and lighter. Department I.D. Keys. Lipstick. A pocket pack of tissues. Small, black leather case containing her detective's gold shield. Wallet. Another leather case with spare bullets. Sugarless gum. Heavy, steel-plated handcuffs.

She debated about wearing a scarf but decided against it. She put on a tweed blazer, went into the kitchen, wrote eggs on her shopping list, then returned to the bedroom and made her bed. She left one table lamp on in the living room. Expensive, but when you lived alone, it was easier to come home to.

When Terry pulled into the big driveway-parking lot of the Twentieth Precinct, between Columbus and Amsterdam Avenues on Eighty-second and Eighty-third, she found a collection of unmarked cars of every color and description. Terry drove her own car to work. She grabbed her bag of danish and coffee and slammed the door shut. Another crazy-weather March. She looked up and saw a swirl of gray and white clouds as thick as an oil painting. No doubt the rain would soon turn to snow.

Inside the precinct house, she waited in front of the two elevators, which were both stopped on the third floor. All she could think of was coffee, a danish, and her first cigarette of the day. She took the elevator up alone. When she got to her floor, she waved and murmured "hello" and "good morning" to the men at the desks. Bernie Moskowitz, who was on the phone, glanced up and smiled. He was her "angel," "rabbi," "godfather," whatever, on the force. He was one of the few men she knew who genuinely respected and trusted women detectives.

The short, pudgy detective who had been promoted over the years to sergeant detective was her superior officer. He had worked on the Ballet Killer case a few years back and helped to capture the maniac who had killed some of Lincoln Center's most beautiful young ballerinas. Terry wished she had been on that task force. The man had murdered eleven ballerinas and was holding the twelfth hostage when they captured and killed him. Moskowitz was partnered with

Lieutenant Frank Fazio, now detective zone captain of the Fourth Homicide Zone, which included the Twentieth Precinct. Both men had opposed department protocol because they felt they were right. Moskowitz had been a nobody then, just a sergeant. He made the bureau on that case.

She was just starting to take off her raincoat when Moskowitz looked up and said, "Don't bother. Homicide. You're catching. Seventy-fourth Street between Broadway and Amsterdam. Woman's body found. Been dead for a few days." Terry looked at the bag with the danish and coffee. Great. Just the case to start off the day. She looked around for her new partner, Charlie, but he was out.

"C'mon," Moskowitz said. "We'll cover it together."

She followed him out of the precinct house. In her boot heels, which probably made her about 5'7", she didn't know if she was the same height or a little taller than Moskowitz. Outside, Terry pulled her raincoat closer around her. She had been right. Bits of snow the size of rice were falling. Winter had returned on a mid-March morning.

She ducked into an unmarked blue Plymouth and cut, with her fingernail, a tiny triangle in the plastic cup, so she could drink while riding. Moskowitz climbed into the passenger seat.

"Your ex called about ten minutes before you walked in."

Terry tried not to show any emotion. They had separated six months ago, and just lately it seemed he had second thoughts. She didn't. "He's not my ex, Bernie, you know that. We're just legally separated."

He shrugged. "Well, it's none of my business, but I think he misses you."

Bernie Moskowitz stared out the window. Maybe he shouldn't have said that. He wondered if he'd feel so protective if Terry were a man. Probably not.

Sometimes it was just hard to know what to say to Terry. But she was one of the best detectives he'd ever had.

Terry parked next to the apartment building, and they ran quickly through the falling snow. After ringing apartment 4D of the old building, they were buzzed back. Terry took in the whole building as if she were a camera. It was a walkup. No doorman here to answer her questions. As they ascended the stairs, she heard a downstairs door quickly slam shut. At the top of the fourth-floor landing, a police officer stood outside 4D, leaning on a balustrade. His arms were folded across his chest and his ankles were crossed. "Some of 'em you don't want to see. This one you don't want to smell."

Terry took a second to inhale and brace herself for whatever waited inside that door. Moskowitz went first. There were two other officers in the studio apartment waiting for the detective in charge to take over. Terry wished she hadn't eaten half of that danish.

"How long?" she asked.

"The heat comes up pretty strong here," an officer replied. "My guess is a coupla days. Nobody's seen her for a while. But they sure did smell her."

Terry could feel waves of nausea surging to make her dizzy. It was routine. A naked girl with red hair sprawled across a bed with a pillow on her face. But it took a little getting used to, even though she did this kind of thing every day. The men felt ill, too, when the stench first hit their nostrils, but they wouldn't say so. Cover-ups were Tums, chewing gum, throat clearing. No one could smoke or touch anything at a crime scene.

Moskowitz walked around the apartment, and Terry opened the small spiraled notebook she had brought from the car.

"Name?"

"Laura Frank," an officer said.

"Who found her?"

"Super."

"Where does she work?"

"Don't know yet." He shrugged. "She was suffocated, Detective." Terry looked up. She didn't know the man. He was a uniformed officer. Then he said, "Block away when we got the call."

As-phyx-i-a-tion. She printed because her handwriting was execrable. With a large caseload she could forget a detail.

"Any signs of struggle?" she asked.

"Not any we can see. Maybe on the man," the officer said. "Looks like rape to me."

"Marks on body?"

"She was found with a pillow over her face, Detective. That's how she was suffocated. No bruises we could see." Terry noted the slight twinge of impatient sarcasm. She didn't know who the man was, but she didn't like him.

Moskowitz shouted across the room. "Two wineglasses in the sink. They look dry. Should be dusted here." He walked across the room and whispered in her ear, "You okay, Princess?"

Terry realized she had been scowling. She nodded and said, "Better call for a crime scene unit."

"I did that," the officer said.

"What is your name?" Terry demanded.

"Yablonsky." For some reason he had an irresistible itch to add a prim "ma'am" to that.

"Officer Yablonsky, the detective who is in charge calls for the crime scene unit."

Yablonsky blinked. "I was just trying to save time."

He had never seen a lady homicide detective before. And what a looker this broad was. Oh, he knew how she had earned *her* gold shield. That was easy.

The door opened as if on cue, and three men comprising the crime scene unit came in. They started flashing pictures immediately. Now the focus was on the dead woman. Terry didn't have to prepare herself for this one. No one had put a blanket over the corpse. There were no ugly gashes. The limbs were still attached. No ancient, withered body had been violated here. For Terry it was almost worse.

The woman on the bed was beyond attractive. She was beautiful. A natural redhead. With the photographers clicking away, the scene appeared almost pornographic. Suddenly embarrassed for the dead woman, Terry wanted to take off her raincoat and cover the body.

One man was vacuuming. Spotting something odd on the parquet floor, he halted the others and, stooping, examined it.

"Something has fallen here. Looks like yellowish snow."

Everyone leaned in and peered at the floor between the chair and the bed.

"Delicate," said Terry. "There's a cluster of them. Have them sent to the lab. You know what they look like? Dried-out flower petals. Very dried out."

"Naaah," Yablonsky muttered in a low voice. "It's probably shredded paper."

"No fingerprints on the wineglasses," yelled a voice. "Looks like they were wiped."

No fingerprints. This wasn't a routine case in Terry's mind anymore. A clever murderer knew how to eradicate fingerprints. She studied the apartment a while longer, making amateurish sketches in her notebook. Typical single woman's apartment. A studio. But the ubiquitous pull-out sofa was missing. Instead, there was an *L*-shaped alcove. She had placed a double bed and dresser there. The apartment was bright and perky. The parquet floor was dotted with fluffy shag rugs. There were framed watercolors, unsigned. Terry wondered if the girl had painted them herself.

Moskowitz stood in a corner by a desk, looking at some papers. The kitchen sink was clean except for the wineglasses. The garbage pail was empty but for a clammy Hefty bag. Only the material on the desk puzzled him.

There was a knock on the door, and Terry turned.

The officer outside stuck his head in. "Next-door neighbor. Thought you might like to talk to her."

Terry stepped outside. There was a woman wearing a bathrobe. She was crying. Terry clicked her ball-point pen and drew a line in her notebook. *Neighbor,* she printed carefully.

"Your name?"

"Mrs. Dorothy Panachek," the woman said shakily.

"Mrs. Panachek, did you hear any unusual noises coming from this apartment?"

"It's been pretty quiet these past few days. Except for the smell. The smell was awful. So I called the super, and he called the police. We thought maybe something bad had happened." The woman continued to cry.

"How well did you know Miss Frank?"

The woman sniffled in. "Not very. She was a single girl. You know how they are. She kept to herself."

"Did she have a steady boyfriend that you know of, Mrs. Panachek?"

The woman looked away. Then she looked at Terry, avoiding her eyes. She shrugged. "I don't know. What do I know? I'm not a busybody to spy on my neighbors. You can imagine how I feel. Living alone. To wake up to something like this."

Terry nodded and took down her telephone number. She couldn't interview this woman properly now. Time-consuming, but she'd wait and then come back. She had a hunch Mrs. Panachek might have a little more to add when she was calmer. Terry walked back into the studio. The stench assaulted her again. Moskowitz looked up. He was standing at the desk.

"Here's something," he said. "See what you make out here. On this desk there's an open file with letters from men—and they give descriptions of themselves."

A little before dark, he left his apartment for a walk. He had to get out. Move around. It was snowing. He could see the white polka dots falling in the light of the street lamp. Some rowdy teenagers were having a snowball fight on the corner. He crossed to the other side of the street. He had to walk. The story was in the paper.

It was a magical, gingerbread city spread with powdered sugar. He felt very close to the stars and the moon. Walking helped him resolve a very important question. He sighed deeply, and his breath caught in a little cloud in front of him.

When he had seen it in the paper, so small on page four, he became nervous. Laura Frank. Her name seemed to stand out in bold type, though it actually wasn't. He had waited for his door bell to ring, but no one had come. He asked himself, Should I stop now? They'd never discover it was him. He had been too smart.

The glistening snow falling on this mid-March night would soon stop. Next month it would mostly rain. The month following would be sunshine and spring. Everyone would forget how lovely and precious this snow had been. They would forget the moment, because there's no way to stop it in time.

Yet being with her had been like this moment. And he could stop it. He could remember and savor every delicious detail. In this way he had the power. The other women bested him. Women had always done that. The bright kind, the beautiful ones, the outright bitches. Could he stop? Should he? He smiled, feeling reassured. He was the only person in the world at that moment. Only he knew he was the person they wanted. Quickly, he looked around. Then he picked up a fistful of sugary snow and flung it wildly into the dark space.

Stop? He hadn't yet begun.

CHAPTER TWO

The Weight Watchers meeting was over, and everyone had signed out. The third floor in the big office building was empty now. In her bag was a "before" picture. She had proudly passed it around like she did every week. She remembered what the lecturer had said about the kinds of fish Weight Watchers could eat. "If it swims, it's yours." Then she didn't know what else to think about. He was late again. Here she was waiting in the dark. Standing alone in a shadowy doorway on Broadway with no one around didn't give her a thrill.

Taking out a tiny pocket mirror, she studied her face, though it was hard to see in the dark. It gave her a sense of self. She cleared her throat and then hummed something she had heard on the radio sometime during the day. She slipped the gold-cased mirror in her bag and tapped her foot, turning her body so she faced uptown toward Lincoln Center.

Then she froze. She heard sucking, kissing, vile sounds, and a taunting voice that crooned, "Hey, baby." Phyllis didn't turn around. Her stomach muscles contracted; her eyes took on a steely glare. She became a breathing mannequin. Fifty-seventh Street and Broadway was dark and lonely. Nobody was around. She might be raped or killed in a doorway and no one would even notice. Even if she began to scream, what good would it do? It might anger him.

"Hey, baby, c'mon."

Phyllis whimpered silently, paralyzed. What about her anger? How ugly and demeaning that whining sexuality was. And frightening, too. If she turned around she might be facing some punk, sneering, his knife ready to plunge into her if she didn't give him what he wanted. What *did* he want?

She cringed against the wall, burying her face in her coat collar and knowing somehow he was coming closer. Unable to stand it any longer, she screamed, spinning around and frightening the man. He turned and fled but not before reaching out to touch her face.

A second later she heard footsteps running toward her. "Where were you?" she screeched, and flung her arms around him. "What took you so long?"

"What happened? I saw you waiting, and then I heard you scream. I couldn't see," he said.

"Oh, Marty, someone tried to attack me."

"Phyllis, don't wait here. Next time wait across the street in the bookstore. What's the matter with you?"

She was still trembling from the experience.

"Don't worry about it, Phyllis. It's over, okay?"

Phyllis stared at him incredulously. It wasn't okay. He made her feel as if she had done something wrong.

"Now, where to?" Marty asked brightly. "There's a great little Italian restaurant around here. A little linguini in clam sauce, some Italian bread, oh, and the rum cake. . . ."

Phyllis ran her tongue over her teeth, as if there were a delightful crumb of rum cake still lurking. "Fish," she said with shaky authority. "I thought we could go to the fish place near me." For dinner she could have four ounces of fish, a small baked potato, a vegetable, and some salad. Tonight she could also have a small glass of white wine.

"That's where you want to go, Phyllis?" Marty said, unable to conceal his agitation.

She nodded, maintaining control. They would have the dinner she wanted. Later he could have what he wanted. Marty said nothing but gave her his arm, pulling her from the dark doorway. They headed toward the bus stop. Phyllis wished just once they could take a cab. Instead, they waited for the Number 7 bus and got a transfer slip to Thirty-fourth Street where they would catch the crosstown bus. He made a decent living. But his clothes! Plaid sports jackets were not classy. They had met at a party a year ago. Right away he knew she was a loser. But he was sweet. Not many men liked overweight women.

When they got off the second bus, they walked a few blocks and entered the restaurant. Phyllis slipped out of her coat and draped it on the back of the chair.

"You look different," Marty said.

"I put a red rinse on my hair, and I lost two and a half pounds this week," she replied proudly. "A grand total of thirty-four pounds since I started last year. Everyone applauded."

"I liked you better before," Marty confessed sadly. "You don't have to lose any weight. All these things. First Weight Watchers and then that night course in public relations. You think this will make you happier? You're a nice girl, Phyllis. I liked you the way you were when we first met. Don't go changing."

Phyllis glanced almost savagely at the waiter, who brought a basket of warm rolls and took their orders. She had just ten pounds to lose before she went on maintenance. But Marty made her so angry at times, she just wanted to binge. And when that feeling came over her, she was powerless. Glowering, she watched Marty rip off half of one roll and slather it with soft butter. Her eyes lingered on the yellow square seeping into the soft, white inside of the roll.

"So, what's new?" she said, wrenching her eyes away, fighting to replenish her willpower. "I haven't seen you in over a week, Marty." She would ignore what he had told her, although his unasked-for advice was a constant source of irritation. The funny thing was that a few months ago, it would have upset her that he *didn't* approve.

"Nothing much. There's an opening for a supervisor in credit. I'll probably get passed over. Why get my hopes up?"

Their salads came. "You just don't believe in yourself. I think you can do it."

Marty wiped salad dressing from the corner of his mouth with his little finger. "I believe in myself," he said, chuckling. "I also believe in not rocking the boat. The guy who gets the promotion could also get fired. Then where does he go? There are a lot of risks to being a supervisor. I'm just an ordinary, average, nice guy, Phyllis, but I do believe in myself. And I make a good living."

Phyllis looked away. She had always liked Marty. He was also convenient. He wasn't her idea of her one true love, but he was safe. Unfortunately, her weight loss had created problems. She wasn't even sure she liked Marty. She was getting more confidence in herself. That must be it. She knew he was staring at her, expecting her to volley back in the game. She got no support; she gave him all the support, and he pretended he didn't want it. Forget it. She switched, instead, to playing the coquette, a role new to her and one she would never have dreamed of applying for thirty pounds ago.

"Would you ever answer an ad in the personals or put your own in?"

He gave her a blank stare.

"Oh, Marty, those ads. Everyone does it. The *Village Voice. The New York Review of Books.* You know, DWF—that's divorced white female—wants to meet . . . or SBM, single black male . . . you know."

Their dinners came, and Marty slowly poked at the trout with his fork. He speared a piece, then said with his mouth full, "I wouldn't do that, Phyllis."

"Why not?"

He said slowly, almost angrily, "Those people are strangers. It's dangerous."

Phyllis put down her fork and, her hand shaking a little, reached defiantly for a no-longer warm roll. She slathered it with butter. Stuffing it into her mouth, she said, "I just might try it, Marty. Don't be surprised if I do." She hadn't dated anyone else since she met him. "I'm changing," she continued, unable to stop. "Millions of people answer the ads." She looked at the piece of roll in her hand and suddenly put it down. "Until you reach out—at least make an attempt—*everyone's* a stranger."

One leg was crossed over the other. A notebook rested on her thigh. She looked like a secretary taking dictation. It was a delicate situation. Terry was sitting in a room of the Milford Plaza, a glittery hotel in the heart of the theatre district. It was Friday morning, almost a week after the murder. She was talking to Mr. and Mrs. Frank. They had flown all the way from Denver to bring their daughter home. Like a war casualty.

Terry spoke in soft, delicate tones. She had a good interviewing technique. It was razor-sharp, designed to trap a liar, but today she knew she had to change her style. She asked quietly, sympathetically, if their daughter had any boyfriends.

Mrs. Frank, a small-boned, pretty woman, whose face, under her graying red hair, gave the impression of mild surprise, thought a bit.

"Oh, I'm sure. Nothing serious. But she wrote home about one or two. Laura never had difficulty dating," she said. "She is . . . was . . . a very beautiful girl. Why she had to run that horrible ad . . ." She dabbed her eyes with a tissue to dry the well of tears.

"Laura was engaged when she went to art school. But that broke up. Gave up her artwork, too, and seemed happy being an office manager. Always thought she had talent, myself," Mr. Frank said. His eyes couldn't look directly at Terry. He seemed to be studying the rooftops and billboards outside the window. He sat with his hands folded in his lap like a choirboy.

Terry knew she wouldn't learn much, but she had to talk to the parents. For herself, she asked, sickeningly, the next question—knowing what the answer would be.

"She . . . your only child?"

The response was barely audible. "Yes." Their voices were strangled.

Terry figured there wasn't too much a girl like Laura would tell her parents about her life in New York City. Suddenly Terry got angry. Like many cops, she believed in capital punishment. The bleeding-heart liberals who thought we were threatening civilization—well, just let them sit across from poor Mr. and Mrs. Frank. Let them go with her one day and interrogate the mindless cretins who committed these horrible crimes. But that was what bothered her about this case. She didn't think it was mindless. She had a hunch this murderer was different.

Terry stood up. Mrs. Frank's lower lip trembled, as if she were reluctant to part with a friend who had come to the funeral home. Mr. Frank's eyes looked watery. The medical examiner had released the body to the family to be flown back to Denver. The autopsy had shown death by asphyxiation with intercourse beforehand. After Terry left, the Franks could leave for home with their dead daughter.

"I shouldn't say this," Mrs. Frank almost whispered. Terry still had her notebook open. "But I thought lady cops—I mean, detectives—were, well, husky and unattractive. You're beautiful."

It was a statement she was used to. Ordinarily, her answer would have been brusque.

27

"I'm just average-looking, Mrs. Frank. It's because I'm a detective and a woman that you think so."

Her stock answer for shutting everyone up. But she knew it wasn't altogether true. While she didn't flaunt her femininity, she wasn't going to hide it. She was a woman. That was her strength, and she never tried to pretend she was a man.

She left the Franks and walked down the hall to the elevator. What a waste meeting with Laura's parents had been. Those letters they had found would tell a better story.

Terry came back to the Two-oh, a deli sandwich in her bag. Her gray metal desk was about two inches away from Moskowitz's. She went right to the file of personal letters. After unpacking her sandwich and coffee, she started reading. She had heard about the personal ads. People were advertising for dates or mates, and they were finding them.

She thought what an ego-booster this must be for a woman who ran an ad. Instant popularity! All a woman had to do was reply to the letters, and she automatically had a date. Several.

One man had written, "I'm nice, attractive (see photo), and available. Why should you choose me? I'll tell you why. I loved your ad, I drive a nice car, and I have a good job in an ad agency. I'm generous, almost to a fault, I'm athletic and in good shape (5'11", muscular build, don't smoke or do drugs), I'm intuitive, I like poetry and classical music . . . and I'd like to take you to dinner one night."

The guy was a bullshit artist, Terry thought. But the letter was appealing. She would have picked him. His name was John; Laura had put a little red check in the corner. John might be the man who had killed her.

Terry wondered, though. If the murderer had been clever enough to wipe his fingerprints, she doubted he'd leave evidence like this around. In fact, *had* the killer come from the ads?

She looked up and saw Bernie Moskowitz stepping out of the elevator. He was carrying a small paper bag which she knew contained his coffee. His wife insisted on packing his lunches. Terry had tried them. Chopped egg and sardine. Thick slices of brisket. Delicious.

"The lab called this morning," Moskowitz said, sitting down. He reached in his drawer for a tin foil square. "Those dried-out things on the floor you thought were flower petals? They were from a white carnation."

"A white carnation?" She was watching him eat the sandwich.

"Yeah." He looked up. "Bite?"

"Chopped liver and onion?"

"Yeah."

He handed her the sandwich, and she took a small bite. "I just had lunch," she said. "White carnation, huh?"

That was unusual, Terry thought. There was no vase of wilted, dried-out flowers. Maybe the killer had taken the flowers. Maybe he had brought one in as a gift. If she had time, she would interview the florists in the area. She sighed. Then again, the petals could have been stuck to the man's clothing and fallen off. They might have been from a flower thrown away the day before Laura was murdered.

Her phone rang. She didn't know sometimes how she could recognize her extension with most of the others jangling at the same time. She snatched it up.

"Twentieth PDU. Detective Morrison speaking."

"I'm looking in from the window opposite your building. I have a telescope. No, wait, don't cross your legs."

Terry's heart stopped for a beat until she recognized the voice. She frowned. "Have you gone mad? You've got to stop calling me. Does this kind of thing turn you on?" Her hand shielded her mouth in a futile attempt at privacy. She could almost hear Bernie's eyeballs shifting her way.

"Theresa, have a heart," the man pleaded. He was standing at a pay phone and rolling another coin between his thumb and forefinger. In case she broke the connection.

Terry lowered her voice. There was no humor in it. "You don't understand: We are about to be divorced. It was your idea, too!"

The wind threatened to rip off the phone-booth door. His partner was making wild signals for him to hurry. Bob Morrison, standing in a graffiti-decorated phone booth on Tenth Avenue didn't know how to say he had changed his mind. Terry was his wife. She would always be that. When it came to her, he had never been good with words.

"That doesn't mean we can't be friends," he said in his best Irish-cop voice.

"We're not friends," she said through clenched teeth. "Talk to my lawyer." Then she added, in spite of herself, "What's wrong? Something wrong at the precinct?"

"No, just my usual load. Sodomy of a six-year-old by his stepfather, a ten-year-old girl raped by her father, forced entry, rape and murder of a young widow while her two children were forced to watch. And you accuse me of being a lousy lover. I miss you, Ter. Screw the divorce."

Terry gulped. She could smell the onion wafting from Moskowitz's direction. Her coffee was lukewarm. She missed him, too. But it was hopeless. He worked nights, she worked days. He wanted a child. Above all, she wanted to keep doing the job she loved. They had been over and over all this. Everything had changed as she rose in the department. Life with Detective Robert Morrison was not always perfect bliss. Not a marriage you would write up in

McCall's, that's for sure. Anyway, she wasn't in love with him anymore.

She wanted to say, "One thing I never accused you of was being a lousy lover," but this was hardly the time or place. "Take care of yourself, kid."

"So, what are you working on?" he persisted, ignoring the horn, the flapping door, and her obvious dismissal of him.

She sighed. "The usual. And an interesting case. Young woman suffocated. Left a pile of letters men had answered from the personal ads."

"That's interesting. I answered one of those myself."

"Before we were married or after?"

"Oh, c'mon, Terry, loosen up. I was joking."

Terry grimaced. She had been married to the man for eight years. He wasn't joking. "I have to go, Bob," she said abruptly. "Take care." She hung up on him. Terry got up from her desk, but for a second she didn't know where she was going. The ugliest homicide case would be easier to face than to examine her own confusing emotions.

"Hi, you must be . . ."

The young woman wearing a tan raincoat turned around. She looked at the white carnation, then peered into his face. She was pleasantly surprised. He had a cute smile that made his eyes crinkle. She liked his black overcoat and the black bowler hat. She tapped the flower lightly and said, "Aha, you must be Bob. Oh, God, I hope I'm right."

He laughed and held out his hand. She shook it, noticing again the engaging, friendly smile. She saw the tiny separation between his two front teeth, the glistening, almost-black eyes. He really wasn't bad-looking, after all. From the way his letter was worded, she imagined he might be.

He followed her into the restaurant and scurried to pull out the chair for her. She thought that was sweet. When they were seated face-to-face, she leaned in and whispered, "Is this really your first time?"

He smiled. Again that boyish grin. "Oh, well, second," he admitted. "But I'm still very new at it."

She saw no reason to lie with this nice man. "I was terrified to do this."

"I can see why. You're probably in a slump. I can't imagine your phone not ringing."

She liked him. "You look like a lawyer. And your hair isn't thin at all. Your letter made you sound almost bald."

He patted his head self-consciously. "One day. You don't look like a schoolteacher."

"No? What then?"

"More like a model."

She started to protest, loving every minute of it.

He looked at her as if appraising a painting. "That red hair. That's natural?"

Debbie smiled. "Oh, yes. It's natural. I got it from my Grandmother Greene. Old carrot top, that's me."

"You know what it reminds me of?" he asked, leaning closer.

"What?" she whispered conspiratorially, playing the game, not knowing the game.

"It looks like the leaves when they turn reddish-gold for the fall. Around late October in New York. Before they dry up and fall away to float down the drains."

Debbie blinked. Her lips came open a bit as she stared raptly. Such a way with words. Well, lawyers were verbal. She could imagine him interrogating a witness.

"What kind of lawyer are you?"

"Municipal bonds," he replied.

"Oh."

"Your hair. It reminds me of my mother. She had red hair."

Debbie leaned back and emitted a soft but knowing "Oooohh, that's sweet."

Debbie sometimes annoyed her friends. When she tried to be warm but obviously didn't mean it, she sounded phony. She could make a compliment sound like a cross between "To be sweet is to be a loser" and "The next time you have to go to the bathroom, raise your hand."

Bob was delighted. He didn't like sweety-sweet girls. The hint of bitchiness in Debbie's voice excited him. He loved the way she took a strand of that long, cherry-licorice hair and twirled it around her finger. Then he looked up. The waitress was standing over their table, pad poised. They both ordered the London broil and a small bottle of wine.

They tried to talk above the jazz piano and the crashing of the drums, but they were too near the combo. So instead, they just exchanged smiles. Debbie thought then how wrong she had been about the personal ads. Bob was sweet and gentlemanly. She should have taken the plunge months ago.

The restaurant was packed now. The bar was a cluster of people all trying to capture the bartender's attention. After dinner, they could hardly find the waitress to get the check. They wriggled out of the jammed, jabbering room just as the cornet was bleating a solo. They burst into the cold, misty night laughing. As they walked to Debbie's apartment, Bob took her hand. Debbie liked the feel of his hand in hers. It was so natural, without being provocative.

"No doorman?" he asked critically when they reached her apartment.

"No, but the buzzer system is excellent. The West Side has really improved. Come on in. Make yourself comfortable."

Debbie wanted to have another glass of wine with him or make some coffee and talk a little longer. A good-night kiss would be nice. She never slept with a man on the first date. It never worked out.

She'd let him stay a while longer before telling him she had to get up early. On Saturday mornings she liked to jog in Central Park.

Any minute now her friend Candice would call. Long ago they had made a pact. Any date with a stranger, a real stranger, one would call the other at an agreed-upon time. Debbie checked her watch. Ten-fifteen. Candy was supposed to call in about fifteen minutes.

She would only say, when Candice called, one of three things. "I'm so glad you called. I'm in a lot of trouble at work." That was a Number One and meant: Call the police. Neither had ever used it. "I'll call you right back." That was the norm. Number Two: It was supposed to help to get a guy to leave. Most couldn't take the hint. Or there was Number Three: "I can't talk now, I have company." Which meant: Boy, did I score. Call back in the morning. Late. Debbie had never given that signal with a man she didn't know. Only a lot of Twos. But she didn't foresee any trouble persuading Bob that she needed a good night's sleep. He was so sweet. He would be easy to get rid of.

Candice Klein hunted in her change purse for a quarter. Good thing she had one, or she'd have to grovel for change from the man behind the desk in the service station. The man who kept ogling her, his tongue sliding over his lips. She put a quarter in the pay phone, cupping her hand over the receiver for privacy. The quarter didn't go through. She tried again and again.

"Phone's out of order," said the burly man, smiling, obviously enjoying this.

"Well, you could have told me that before," she said angrily.

"Didn't see ya."

My ass, thought Candy.

"There's another rest area after the next exit."

She glared at the man with the bulging eyes. And shuddered, too. There was no one else around. She just wanted to get into her car and drive out of Westchester County. It was so lonely and desolate, she might as well be in the sticks. Almost ten-thirty. She had promised to phone Debbie. Oh, well, maybe she wasn't in yet.

Debbie brought in a glass of wine for Bob and a cup of Sanka for herself. He sat at the other end of the couch, legs crossed.

"Mind if I smoke?"

"Don't be silly," she replied, fetching an ashtray. She lit a cigarette for herself.

Bob's black overcoat was draped across a chair near the couch. Debbie noticed it and rose to hang it up. Bob motioned for her to sit down. "Leave it. I have to go soon."

Debbie relaxed. He wasn't a heartthrob, that's for sure. That was her problem: She fell too fast for the wrong ones. And then had neurotic relationships. It was refreshing to meet a man who wasn't trying to prove himself with intellectual macho, didn't talk endlessly about how his ex-wife screwed him, or how indispensably dazzling he was in his career. Still . . . something seemed to be missing with Bob. He was shy. That was it. Well, she'd just have to get to know him better. He was sitting quietly, smiling at her.

She returned his smile and glanced casually at her wristwatch, her customary warmup to a polite comment about the lateness of the hour.

"Say," he exclaimed, "do you still have the letter I wrote?"

She nodded.

"Would you mind if I looked at it?" He half-laughed, blushing.

Just the letter and then she'd have to tell him to leave. It would be nice if her phone call came. She had always been on time for Candy. She rose and went to her little bedroom. Where was her file? Oh, yes, in the night table. She couldn't show all of them to him. After taking out Bob's letter, she stuffed the file in the drawer. As she turned, she saw him standing in the doorway, one hand flat on the doorjamb as he leaned against it, blocking her path.

"I'll take that," he said playfully, snatching the letter, not letting her pass.

"C'mon, Bob," she said, feeling tired. But he wouldn't let her pass.

"C'mooooon," she sang, hitting the high note of the octave and sliding down.

He wouldn't budge.

"Stop fooling around," she said sharply, summoning her classroom voice.

He shoved her. She fell on the bed, then scrambled to get up. "If this is a joke," she exploded, "it's not funny." She began to get up off the bed, but he pitched her back, slapping her. She looked up, confused, into his enormous, intense eyes.

"What do you want?" she whispered, her anger turning into fear.

"Lift up your dress and take off your panties."

Debbie tried quickly to adjust her mind to panic. A second ago this man was sitting on the couch sipping wine and shyly smiling at her. Maybe if she did what he wanted, nothing bad would happen. She started to weep softly as she gingerly picked up her skirt and peeled down her panty hose, snagging them with her fingernails. She threw them aside in a little ball. Breathing in gasps, she pulled down her panties obediently. Oh, God, where was that phone call?

Candice walked up and down the highway kicking up loose gravel with her high heels. The dumbass at the station could have told her her tire looked flat. She had been trying for ten minutes to flag someone down. The cars just whizzed by as if they didn't see her. Nice. This was the last time she'd drive all the way to Westchester for a dinner party.

Just then, a van pulled close and slowed down. A man with a crew cut and a toothy smile rolled down his window. "In a jam, little lady?"

Candy groaned silently. Well, she had no other choice. She climbed into his van and looked directly at him. "Could you take me to the nearest phone?" He grinned and nodded, stamping the accelerator. "My husband's expecting me," she said smugly.

Her eyes were shut tight to blot out the shame and panic. It was a nightmare. She was naked now and so was he. Okay, so she'd submit, and he'd rape her and then leave and she'd bolt her door and take a thousand baths. Tears welled at the corners of her eyes. How could she have been so dumb? Such a sweet guy? The man was a pervert. Now the tears were making her contacts sting. *Oh, God,* she prayed, *please help me stay sane.* His body was heavy on top of her, and his thrusts were ripping her apart. If she cried, her contact lenses would feel as if she had soap in her eye.

Debbie held her breath. She thought of a beautiful summer's day she had spent near a serene lake making love to a man who had treated her body like a finely tuned instrument he had the good fortune to play. The vision faded as Bob ground his body faster. Debbie began to match his breathing. Her arousal, however, didn't stem from passion. It came from pain and anger. Why was she submitting to this animal? Although pinned under his weight, she had to stop him. Humiliated, she discovered within herself a rage she didn't know she was capable of.

Scissors. Yes. In her night table. She could stab him in the back. Her arm was stretched almost to the drawer. She just had to reach a little more. The drawer was slightly open. Her fingertips touched the scissors. She could do it, she could—

His hand found hers and clamped down. Panic bubbled in her throat as she tried to scream. One contact lens had slid out of place and was causing such pain that she felt her reason slip away. Her mouth opened to cry out, and her lips felt cloth. The pillow . . . oh, God, no . . . she couldn't see . . . couldn't breathe. She dug her fingernails into his neck and let them slide down. Please God, let it be over. Laughter . . . he was laughing. Wasn't funny . . . couldn't breathe . . . God, why me?

Satiated, Bob collapsed on top of her. She was still. His head rested on her sweet pillow. The thrashing she did with her hips when she tried to save herself . . . that was the yummy part. But this was absolutely delish, too. The euphoria. As if time had stopped. Words . . . words would ruin it . . . no words could explain this feeling.

And then it was time to pull out. Time to get dressed. Time to leave. She had been a beauty, oh, yes, with that perfect piece of orange cotton candy. He sang a little as he dressed. He'd have to go around and wipe his fingerprints off everything, but . . . just then, a shrill jangle murdered the perfect serenity. He froze.

The phone rang and rang. He stood still, holding his breath, reminding himself that the telephone couldn't see him. Then, finally, it stopped, and he breathed easily. He had to finish. Time was flying. Fingerprints wiped, all dressed, coat, too warm for the scarf, hat in briefcase, blond wig, fake glasses, briefcase in shopping bag . . . the damn phone again. Annoying. Like a baby squalling. Just won't shut up. Farewell, euphoria.

He looked around the room frantically, trying to shut out the noise. Nothing was out of place. Then he took his white carnation and began the ritual that would ease her passing into heaven. "She loves me, she loves me not, she loves me, she loves me not, she loves me . . ." At that precise moment he knew she was his forever. He remembered the ashtrays and went to the bathroom to dump them down the toilet . . . carefully . . . wearing gloves now. Then everything was in order but for the final kiss from Prince Charming.

He tiptoed into the little bedroom as if he were afraid of disturbing her. With gloved hands he lifted the pillow and peek-a-booed in. She looked lovely. He touched her adorable parted lips with his forefinger and then kissed the glove. He looked once more at the precious fiery triangle that guarded the entrance between her legs. Before he put the pillow back in its place, he felt a sincere pang of regret at having to leave.

"Love 'em and leave 'em, Bob," he said aloud, knowing what he had to do. Once more the telephone rang, piercing his world like an intruder. Bob looked angrily at his watch. Twenty minutes to twelve. Mustn't let anything annoy him. Enjoy. He would remember this moment always. Debbie Greene was forever lost to them. But she would belong to him always.

"Good night, Sweet Princess," he whispered, blowing a kiss from the front door. His hat was tipped rakishly to the side. Even as he closed the door he could hear the phone ringing again. To an empty apartment.

At midnight Candice toyed with calling Debbie one more time. But it was stupid. Maybe she had come home early and just disconnected the phone. But she would be alone. Debbie never, ever slept with a man on the first date. Or maybe they went for a walk or to a movie or out for a drive. He probably never even came back to her apartment. She reassured herself by deciding to call Debbie first thing in the morning. Meanwhile, she was waiting in a gas station, in early spring weather that had a definite bite to it, for her car to be returned. It was dark, and she was miles from home. She had her own problems.

Dear Benjy,

Here it is springtime in the north. Glad to see all that snow melt away for good. Had a date with a redhead last night, Benjy. She was some beautiful doll. You know my weakness for redheads. And she went for me, too. Like a ton of bricks.

Remember in eighth grade when I was chasing that little redhead—what was her name?—and I got in all that trouble at school? Even when her family moved away, after the incident, I wrote her every day. Then the post office returned the letters with "Address Unknown" stamped on them.

Do you think, Benjy, that they moved away because I liked her too much? They all had red hair. Just like you-know-who. Take care of yourself, you hear? I'll be down real soon to pay you a visit.

The Swinger

CHAPTER THREE

The City was awash in a pinkish-gold glow, and he could see the bright ball of sun peeping from behind gray clouds. Across the street was a deli, but it wasn't open yet. He had walked all the way down from Times Square—not quite certain why he had come so far in the pitch-black night. Letting off steam, he supposed.

When he realized he was on Eighth Avenue and Twelfth Street, he gave in to exhaustion. Might as well hop the IRT subway uptown. He always had to be one step ahead. Underground was safe during the day. The streets were safe at night.

Walking to the subway station, he mentally reviewed the five new letters he had written last night. He chuckled and then started hiccuping. He loved the ads.

He had his favorites like:

SBM, 24, desires full-figured woman, 50ish, to share erotic pleasures . . .

Married NJ housewife seeks discreet companion for mutual understanding . . .

And there were so many more. He laughed behind his hand. No one saw him. No one was around except for a few bums and winos sleeping it off in doorways. He didn't like to look at them. Dirty old men, unshaven, with their flies half-open.

You took your chances, though, when you answered one of those ads. Sometimes the women called. Sometimes they didn't. It was like playing the lottery. And he had won twice. Two dates. Though he had never seen either again. But that was the way he had planned it. He laughed heartily, and a drunken, toothless bum staggered up, hand out. Shaking his head, he walked faster, not wanting to face the shadowy man. Not wanting to acknowledge his existence.

If he ever used his real name, it would all be over with. He signed the letters with pen names. *Noms de plume.* John for John F. Kennedy. He always felt JFK was still living. Tom for Tom Paine. He forgot what *he* really did, but his last name was a hoot. He rubbed his eyes and massaged his temples. Tired. He was so tired. Then there was his favorite, Bob. A nice, friendly name. And you could spell it the same way backward and forward. He never made much of last names. Just any old things. No one ever remembered surnames, anyway.

But his real identity. Only people who had known him for years and years knew the name on his birth certificate. Those were the people who could catch him.

He looked up and squinted. The sun was rising, almost shining. He was hungry. He hadn't eaten all night. Maybe a pizza place was open. He could use a slice or two with mushrooms and anchovies. He'd go to an all-night joint right now so he'd miss the changing shifts and banging pails and wet mops. He hated that ammonia smell when he was having breakfast.

Walking down Fifth Avenue swinging a paper bag holding a corn muffin, Marty squinted at St. Patrick's Cathedral. The sun was spilling over the domes and spires of the majestic church. One day he would have to go inside. He had this same thought every day as he passed by. And the same decision:

not today, I haven't got time. What luck. Having to work on a glorious Saturday like this. He could be sitting in the park watching all the beautiful girls jogging, their little noses turned up, trying to catch the first rays of spring sunshine. Pretty soon it would be the season of no coats, no bras. He smiled, and a passerby smiled back.

Approaching the windows of Saks Fifth Avenue, he wondered if that awesome store would ever not be there. It was his boss. His paycheck. Saks Fifth Avenue was a tradition. Forget about the stores it spawned in the suburbs all over the country. It would never be Saks Fifth Avenue. Even if it moved to Columbus Avenue, it would still be known by its original name. A classy place to work. Only a certain type of woman shopped at Saks. Others were afraid of it.

It was half-past ten, and the store was already filling with avid shoppers. He crossed down the aisle that led to the information booth and the escalator behind it. A girl behind one of the cosmetic counters winked at him. He turned quickly to see who she was flirting with, only to realize she was looking his way. He grinned but looked down so no one could see him. Then he shook his head, marveling at his stupidity. She must have winked, if she really did, at someone else. Or maybe she had something in her eye.

When he walked into the credit office on the eighth floor, he saw that someone had made coffee. Pretty soon people would line up in the other room. He dealt mostly with people who loved to buy but couldn't pay the bills. Charge-account customers. That wafer-thin, brown-and-beige plastic rectangle could get a lot of people in trouble. Usually women. He dealt with infuriated husbands, slippery business managers to whom Saks must be the least of a client's debts, or embarrassed working girls who thought of the credit department as an indulgent father who would let them slip by. Marty rarely did.

And he never raised his voice. He was good at his job and he enjoyed it. Marty was at the computer when someone said there was a phone call for him in the back.

Phyllis Samuels sat trembling in her Murray Hill apartment. She prayed her voice didn't sound too bright or healthy. Never, ever in her whole life had she done anything like this, though she was sure it had been done to her many times.

"Marty, I have a bug," she said when he finally came to the phone. "I can't go out tonight." Her lips were in a pout, eyes shut tight as if she expected to be punished for telling a lie. Even as she said it, she began to feel ill.

Marty smelled rejection. But, how could it come from Fat Phyllis? That was why he picked her, because of her obvious availability. But he had logged enough years of dating to suspect that she was lying. That she didn't want to spend the evening with him.

"I'll come over," he said earnestly. "What should I bring? Won ton soup? You could have that. Or Häagen-Dazs? Do you want some ginger ale?"

Unconsciously, Phyllis licked her tongue over her lips. God! Talk about smothering someone. Couldn't she even be sick? And then she reminded herself she wasn't.

She stared out the window toward Third Avenue. At her bird cage with no bird, at the tiny round table covered with a blue cloth, at the multicolored sweater she had been knitting. She fixed her gaze on one object. The yellow fringe at the end of her paisley window shade. Too bad, Marty Loomus. She was going to do what *she* liked. In fact, she wondered if in her whole life she had ever done that.

"Thank you, Marty, but I don't want company or . . . food. It's just a virus. I'll probably pull the phone and just rest."

Marty looked out the window. The sun was passing behind a cloud. She was trying to get rid of him.

Everything had changed. He had warned her not to make herself over. That never worked. You were what you were. He gulped and thought of his untouched corn muffin, which suddenly had the appeal of sawdust. He had the oddest notion he was losing her.

"C'mon, Marty, I'll see you as soon as I'm better." Damn him. He was making her feel guilty.

"Uh-huh," he said dully. Then, "Okay, Phyllis, take care of yourself." The hostility in his voice was unmistakable, and he knew it but didn't care.

"Yeah, you, too."

Marty slumped in his chair and started to cough.

"What's wrong?" Phyllis said, on guard.

"Smoke. Someone's smoking, and the smoke is blowing my way," he stage-whispered. "They're not supposed to."

"Well, move. Listen, Marty, I have to go to the bathroom. I'll talk to you next week."

"Yeah."

She hung up. He looked out the window, squinting. The sun had disappeared behind a cloud. Well, that was prophetic. To be rejected by Phyllis? Impossible. She had been so grateful in the beginning. Maybe she actually was sick. Now, of all the inappropriate times. He reached in his pocket and took out a little box. Glittering within was a tiny diamond engagement ring.

Phyllis put on a cha-cha record and danced and leaped wildly around the room. Downstairs someone banged up. Bravo! She had done it. She had outgrown Marty Loomus. Now for adventure.

She had placed an ad in *The New York Review of Books*:

> SWVF wants to meet gentleman who likes the good life, dancing to the wild beat of Latin music, mushy poetry, baseball, quiet afternoons in the

park. Effetes or intellectuals need not apply. Curvy, big, brown-eyed, redheaded imp is waiting.

She had collected about fifty replies so far. And *The New York Review of Books* brought such classy men. Letters were still coming in. They all wanted to know what the *V* in SWVF stood for. It stood for . . . voluptuous. She needed to lose a few pounds before going on maintenance, but she wasn't fat. Curvy, she thought, and still losing. All her friends at Weight Watchers thought her ad was terrific. Only one person she couldn't share this with: her once, practically best friend, Marty.

She had picked ten "live" ones from the letters. So far she had called only one. But he was so nice, she decided to go out with him that night. She should be happy. The only thing preventing that was the guilt she was feeling about Marty. She sensed he knew she was lying to him. Rejection. Did she know about rejection? She wrote the book. But she was doing something about her life. And it was *her* life. Heck, why should she feel guilty about him? He only took her out once a week. He didn't even care about her. Why not have fun?

Terry heard the phone, but she couldn't steady her hand to insert the key in the door. She supposed it would stop just as she got in, but she was wrong. It was eleven o'clock on a Saturday morning, and she closed the door, leaving her laundry basket in the hall outside.

"Hello?" she spurted, slightly out of breath.

"Hi, Ter, like to join a few of us lowly policewomen tonight?"

Terry recognized the voice. It was Camille, a policewoman she had worked with in Brooklyn on the Tenth Homicide Squad. Camille, belying her delicate name, was a tall, big-boned woman. Camille's invitation seemed appealing. A bar in Queens right near her apartment. Terry agreed to go.

Maybe her old friend was right. She should socialize. Get her mind off her problems.

The phone rang again. Terry fantasized about buying an answering machine. "Hi, there. This is Terry. I'm at home right now, but I don't feel like talking to you. Or anybody. I just need some peace and quiet."

So much for fantasy.

It was Moskowitz. "I just got word. There was another one. Same exact M.O. Personal ad letters. Girl had red hair. Asphyxiation. Intercourse before. Even got those flower petals before they were vacuumed. Just a few. Fresher than before."

"Should we go in?" Terry asked. It wasn't unusual for a cop to work off-duty on a case that was interesting. Sometimes you could find out more. But you ended up a workaholic, a slave to your job.

"Wait until Monday, Princess. She's not going anywhere. There's nothing we can do now. She was found this morning. Died last night. Her girl friend had an extra key. Went into the apartment. Sure enough, she found her friend dead. Name was Debbie Greene. And the girl friend confirmed it for us: The man with her last night came from a personal ad she had placed."

Terry felt disoriented, out of synch, as if she wanted to swim to shore but was being carried out to sea by the undertow. She longed for relaxation, desperately needed it. Yet she wanted to go in and work on this case. Why? Because it was fascinating. And because, for good or ill, she identified with these two women, the victims.

Terry hung up. Suddenly, she felt chilled. So her instincts had been right all along. The killer wasn't routine. He had struck again. He might be a mass murderer hitting through the personal ads. Was there some woman dressing right now to meet a man who had answered her ad? She wondered. Was there a man preparing at this very moment for that date? Knowing that tonight he would kill again.

Phyllis assessed herself in the mirror and made an ugly face. She had planned to wear her aqua dress with the long sleeves and the tie belt. But it just hung there like a sack. It was miles too big for her, but instead of making her look slim, it did quite the reverse. She tried to think quickly. Jeans and a turtleneck? Nah. Not on the first date. Besides, her new designer jeans were just a wee bit too tight. Then she remembered. A black wraparound skirt and a white silk blouse. Perfect.

There wasn't much time left. Powder had spilled on her bureau. Her aqua dress lay in a puddle over her bed. Phyllis's hand was trembling as she tried to brush her reddish-brown hair. Then the door bell rang and she froze. She shut her eyes, crossed her fingers, and prayed for help. He was here. She had to be calm, not show her panic. Shakily, she walked down the narrow hallway. She commanded her lips to smile, then she released the chain lock. She had to be brave. This is what she had worked for for so long.

CHAPTER FOUR

The woman sat slumped, one knee crossed over the other. She had begun to cry again. Terry paused, looking at the floor, until this fresh spasm was over. The woman was wearing a black dress and tinted hose to match her black pumps. She wore no jewelry except for a gold watch. She had just come from the funeral of her good friend, Debbie Greene.

It was a dismal, rainy Monday afternoon. Terry looked quickly around the apartment. A large studio on Second Avenue in the East Seventies. All she could think about was spending one-third of your life in a bed that rolls up during the day. Terry lit a cigarette. She had already gone over all the letters mailed to Debbie from *The New York Review of Books*. She had made no discriminating check marks like Laura Frank. Candice Klein's story did not match the facts. Terry had counted twenty letters, not twenty-one. None from a lawyer. The lawyer Candice said Debbie had dated. The man who killed her.

Candice sniffled and sat up straighter. If she had been on time with that stupid phone call, maybe Debbie would still be alive. She shouldn't have let her friend go out with a complete stranger. It was all her fault. Oh, God, she didn't believe it. They had tickets for a Broadway show this week. And then coming over with a bag of bagels on Saturday morning and ringing and ringing . . . because she knew that Debbie would rather die than break her rule.

She never slept with a man on the first date. So why didn't she answer her phone or her door bell?

Something was wrong. As a precaution, she had a spare key. Just in case Debbie locked herself out. Or when her friend went away, Candy took the mail and watered the plants. So she let herself in. "Debbii-iieeee?" she had yelled. Another thing. Debbie never slept late on Saturday morning. She was a jogger. But Candy noticed the bedroom door ajar, and she could see a bare foot. For a second she wanted to leave. What if there were two naked bodies lying in bed? Maybe Debbie had broken her rule. And then she started to scream and she couldn't stop. Oh, God, there was only one. It was Debbie's and she wasn't asleep. She was dead.

Terry waited for the woman to compose herself. "Miss Klein . . ."

"Candice, please," she said weakly.

"Getting back to the letters. You say she received twenty-one answers to the ad in *The New York Review of Books?*"

"That's correct."

"But we only have twenty letters. Did she throw any away?"

Candice shrugged. "I don't know." Then she started to cry again, blotting her nose with a wet tissue.

"And this lawyer you say she went out with. There is no lawyer in the file of letters I have. Is it possible that the man didn't come from the personal ad?"

"I don't know," Candy replied. "I told her to go out with the lawyer, and that's who killed her." Her voice cracked slightly. "Nothing is right anymore. Nobody is safe. The personal ads. Everybody does it. Why her? Debbie was such a sweet person—oh, you should have known her. Her parents—you know what Mr. and Mrs. Greene said?"

Terry framed her mouth into a silent "What." But she didn't particularly want to hear this part.

"They said that the rain this morning was God crying, and that the maniac who did this terrible thing should be made to suffer just as poor Debbie did. An eye for an eye. Castrate him and then kill him."

Terry left the apartment. Getting into her car, she looked up and saw the curtain part and a dark-haired woman wearing black. Terry shook her head. If she were Candice Klein, she wouldn't stay alone today.

More rain. Not in torrents but a steady, cold drizzle, which did nothing for you if you already felt low. Terry turned on the windshield wipers. She thought of the man she had met at that bar in Queens on Saturday night, Donald Phillips. She liked him. He was a businessman, owned a dry cleaning store, and did very well. His brother was a cop in Albany. He said he understood. Did he? He said he'd call and they could go out to dinner. Would he?

The apartment smelled unmistakably of chopped meat and onions. Terry wondered if Mrs. Panachek was making some kind of goulash. Her stomach growled. She hadn't taken time for lunch.

Mrs. Panachek offered coffee. Terry declined.

"Look, I live alone. I'm a widow. My daughter lives in Toronto, and she wants me to come and live with her. I don't want to get involved."

Terry nodded. "How well did you know Laura Frank?" she asked.

"Not at all. Not a passing hello, even, from that girl. Single girls. They have no time. Especially a beautiful girl like that."

"Did she have many boyfriends that you noticed, or was it just one special guy?"

The woman shrugged. "No, not one. They came, they went. I didn't keep score."

"Did you notice anyone that night?"

"What night?"

"The night she was killed," Terry persisted.

"I only know when they found her."

"She was found on Thursday, March 18, but she was murdered five days before. So that would be Saturday, March 14?"

Mrs. Panachek shook her head. Her lips were pursed together resolutely. "No. Nothing on Saturday. My bridge group meets on Saturdays."

Terry nodded and looked at her watch. This was turning out to be a time-eater. She half-rose when she saw Mrs. Panachek close her eyes and heard her murmur, "Oh, my God, yes." Terry sat down quickly.

"Saturday night. I was taking out the garbage to the incinerator room. It was late. Do you know what time she . . . the thing happened?"

Terry looked at her opened notebook hastily. The time of death provided by the medical examiner's office. "Between eleven and midnight."

"I stayed up late that night. Later than usual. Yes, that was Saturday."

Terry leaned in. She locked the woman into a stare. "Mrs. Panachek, what about that incinerator room? You saw someone?"

"I don't want to get involved. It might be dangerous."

"Mrs. Panachek, a murderer is loose."

The woman shrugged. "Well, as I came out of the incinerator room, there was someone waiting at the elevator. It wouldn't seem significant except he went back to her door and tested it, you know, to make sure it was locked. Be sure it was safe."

Terry was scribbling furiously. "What did this

man look like?" she asked, enunciating each syllable.

"Well, he wasn't too tall, wasn't too heavy, wasn't too thin."

Terry sighed. "Color hair?" she asked.

"Oh, blond. Blond, curly hair. And he wore black-rimmed glasses. And a black coat. He also carried a big Macy's shopping bag."

"Anything else?" Terry looked up.

"One other thing I won't forget. He was smiling. Real happy, that one was. Listen, take it from me, that girl was no innocent young thing. Like I said, they came, they went. And if she was raped, so why didn't she scream out? Our bathrooms connect. I would have heard."

"You said you were out late," Terry reminded the woman.

"Oh, yeah."

"Could you come in for an ID if we find this man?"

Mrs. Panachek hung her head and then said, dully, "Of course. If that's what I'm supposed to do." She was thinking that after the goulash was ready she would write her daughter a nice, long letter.

They called him Reep the Creep. A crime reporter who haunted the precincts smelling out stories. He didn't write for *The New York Times* or the *Post* or the *Daily News*. He didn't write. He sold information to the dailies and to the sensational checkout-counter tabloids. Reep the Creep wasn't considered a legitimate journalist in the eyes of most cops. Lenny Reep sold news like some people sold belt buckles off wooden stands on the streets. He was a vendor. Sometimes he sold the same scoop to more than one eager buyer.

Pulling into the Two-oh parking lot that afternoon, Terry thought dismally, "Oh, no, the Creep. He's got wind of this case."

She stepped briskly out of the car. He was immediately at her elbow. "You can't keep it from the press, Morrison."

"I don't intend to, Lenny." She looked around. "But I don't see any reporters here."

"Word got out. You got another single lady murdered because she ran an ad for a man. That's good copy."

"You sicken me, Reep."

"But you can't deny it. You're the catching detective, right? Must be terrible seeing those single women lying around, naked, dead, just because they got lucky, huh?"

Everything about the man turned her stomach. That corned beef sandwich she had had for lunch was beginning to repeat. So was the pickle.

"We don't know if those women were killed because of the ads they ran," she said defensively.

"Oh, aren't we being cautious, Lady Detective? It's quite a coincidence, isn't it? At least, if this story breaks, other innocent girls won't be found dead. They won't run an ad. They'll stay alive. And if it's *not* coming from the ads, what's the harm?"

Terry looked at the man and shrugged. "Yeah, Reep, you're right, what's the harm?"

She gave him some information about the case and then watched him walk to his car. Instinctively, she knew that even if this case appeared on page one of the New York dailies, it wouldn't be a tragedy. Departmental policy dictated withholding select information. In this case, the police held one fact in reserve. The flower petals were confidential information. During interrogations, suspects could thereby be taken off-guard with the question: "What did you do with the white carnation?"

* * *

That same Monday afternoon, Marty called Phyllis at work. The switchboard operator said she was out. But when he phoned her at home, no one answered. He felt alarmed. Maybe something really was wrong with her. Maybe he had imagined the rejection. Maybe . . . there were too many maybes. Phyllis Samuels had never been hard to reach. Her telephone was never busy for long periods of time. She was usually home. She didn't have that many friends.

Maybe something really bad had happened.

Or wasn't it just possible that her phone was unplugged? Probably she had done this on purpose to drive him crazy. Knowing her, she wasn't sick at all, just sneaking around going to the movies and binging on pastries and junk food. He knew Phyllis.

If he wanted to buy another engagement ring he'd probably have to pay twice the price. That had been a good deal, but he'd returned it. Phyllis had picked a bad time to act up.

Terry and Moskowitz decided to stop for drinks at the Titanic, the favorite watering hole of the Two-oh. Columbus Avenue was blossoming with chic bars and restaurants, but this old place was the hangout. Vinnie, the owner, was one of the reasons. Gossip columnist, psychiatrist, bartender, chef, and friend. Vinnie, with his rotund figure, wasn't hard to spot.

"How ya doin', gorgeous? Those legs are wasted in those pants," Vinnie teased, coming over to the partners. "What'll you have? First round is on me." They both thanked him and ordered, then plunged into the case that was on their minds.

"Candice Klein still puzzles me," Moskowitz said. "She swears Debbie Greene went out with some lawyer who answered her ad."

"Think she's lying?" Terry asked.

"Do you?"

"No. For what reason? Something happened to that letter, though." Two detectives approached them. Terry could almost hear them breathe down her back. "Hey, Morrison," one said, "you hear the latest joke about the female cop?"

"Sure Willie, I told it to you yesterday. Remember?" That silenced him.

She hated cops like Willie-Boy, her nickname for him. Why did she have to take his gaff? She didn't get promoted by giving away "favors" the way rumor had it. She was good. She was a second-grade dick, and she got her gold shield for merit.

Willie-Boy tapped her on her turtleneck and said, "Very good, Morrison. I'll have to remember that one." Then he and his companion ambled to the bar.

Terry watched Moskowitz brush away air with his hand. "Ignore it," he said softly. She tried, but every time it happened, the hurt and anger lingered. She was just as good as any of them. And a better shot than most. Even now she went to Rodman's Neck in the Bronx just to practice her shooting. She wanted to make sure she was perfect, not merely good.

Suddenly, she was aware that Moskowitz was speaking.

"The man Mrs. Panachek described—did you have an artist's sketch made?"

"Yeah. It'll be distributed to all the precincts. Maybe we'll get it on the air. But I couldn't pin her down to real details like the size of his nose and the color of his eyes."

"But she'll come in for an ID?"

"She said she would. You know, something is bothering me."

"What's that?"

"In the Laura Frank file, now that I remember it," Terry said, "I think there's a snapshot that fits Mrs. Panachek's description. A blond man with curly hair. Not wearing glasses, but then people take them off when they have their pictures taken."

Terry was still babbling excitedly when she realized Moskowitz had tuned out. He was looking past her shoulder—watching someone approaching. She saw who it was.

Moskowitz stood up. "Well, kiddo, gotta get home. See you first thing."

Her eyes followed him, in a telepathic plea for him to stay. No such luck. He had deserted her.

Bob Morrison slid into the booth opposite his soon-to-be ex-wife.

"Can I get you another drink?" he said amiably.

She shook her head.

"What brings you to the neighborhood?" she asked sarcastically.

The waiter took his order. The jukebox was playing. There was chatter punctuated by loud crescendoes when groups of cops started arguing or joking. Terry studied this man she had lived with for eight years. Did she ever really know him? She tried to look at him objectively. By anybody's standards, he was a handsome devil. The twinkling eyes, the quiet charm, the little-boy grin. She doubted whether he had been faithful all those years.

She became businesslike. "Look, Bob, what's the point? We're both paying divorce lawyers. We split up a perfectly good house and we each have apartments. I think we can be friends eventually, too. But right now you're becoming a pest, Bob, you know that?"

Terry lit a cigarette.

Bob looked at her with the yearning eyes of a puppy. "Yeah, but I miss you, Ter. I want you back."

"Are you in league with Willie-Boy to torment me?" she said through clenched teeth.

"Where is he? Tormenting you? I'll beat him up."

Terry laughed, then she looked to the ceiling in silent prayer for help.

"Do you really think it will work, Bob? For two years we haven't seen each other. You worked a day tour, I worked nights. Then we switched tours. But that wasn't what broke us up. It stopped working when I made detective, and you know it. Better find a lady who's not a cop." She wondered if she meant that.

"Aw, Terry, we could patch it up. I don't want a divorce."

"Listen, Bob, you'll get over this. Women get hurt first and men adjust. Then, after a while, women adjust and men fall apart." She smiled at him.

"Who said that?"

"An article in *McCall's.*"

"Oh."

"I got married when I was too young, Bob. Just a baby."

"Ter, you were twenty-six."

"Well, I went to college and then right into the police academy. Look, I just want to be left alone. No hassle, no more fights. I want to be single."

Bob's face fell. "So that's it."

"I can't just stop work and have a baby. That broke us up, too, you know. And now I'm thirty-four. You don't want to wait forever."

"Terry. It doesn't matter."

"Oh, c'mon, you know that's an issue. Neither of us would have time to spend with a child."

"This is the issue, Theresa. You know what you are? A workhorse. You don't care about anyone or anything except making it. The beautiful but tough cop. Your ego, Ter, that's all you care about."

Terry stared at him, physically recoiling from his attack. "That's exactly why I want a divorce. You think you know me, Bob Morrison, but you don't. And I'm too much of a lady to give you a rundown of your faults. Just let it be." He got up, flung some bills on the table, and stalked down the aisle between tables. She sat there, shaking slightly with suppressed fury, and finished her drink for appearances.

CHAPTER FIVE

On the other side of the Titanic, the long bar was beginning to resemble any happy-hour celebration in Manhattan. Except the men all wore raincoats and outnumbered the women about nine to one. Captain Frank Fazio spun around on his barstool.

There was one big difference about making captain, he mused. As a lieutenant at the Two-oh, he had been one of the guys. Now they showed him so much respect, he didn't even get a decent hello. He couldn't figure out the last time he heard some really foul language come his way. No sergeant would stop and tell him a dirty joke. No one bought him a drink, except for Vinnie. Well, he couldn't complain. He drained his glass. Good life, good pay. He was bored.

Yes, he was a zone captain now, in charge of the Fourth Homicide Zone, pulling in the Nineteenth, Twentieth, Twenty-third, and Central Park Precincts. His office was now uptown on the East Side. He was higher in rank than his former boss, Captain Bill Hogan, head of the Ballet Killer task force. Hogan had the intuition of a gnat and had blocked his path every step of the way. Forced him to go against the department to capture that maniac. Someone had to. Well, Hogan had never received those promotions he coveted above everything else. He had just slinked back to Manhattan South. Fazio and Moskowitz, who was just a sergeant back then, had solved the case almost single-handedly. Had they failed, they wouldn't even be walking a beat today. They'd had been scrubbed out of the force. But when they collared the Ballet Killer, they became heroes. Fazio was proud of himself. His wife Connie was, too. He liked being a captain, enjoyed his privileges and pay. But something was missing.

He sat at the bar, raincoat on, knowing he should go home, debating the wisdom of another drink and watching the crowd. He had seen Moskowitz leave. Good man, Bernie Moskowitz. Didn't make them like that anymore. Detective Morrison was okay, too, he supposed. Maybe he was just an old-time cop, but he wasn't crazy to have women on the force. Those were his feelings—and the feelings of a lot of the men. He wondered who the man was who sat down with Morrison and then left so quickly. Didn't know him. Didn't know much about Morrison.

This case of theirs interested him, though. The personal ads case. Two identical killings so far. Interesting M.O. Red hair, suffocation, letters. Could be a mass murderer like the Son of Sam or the Ballet Killer. Yes, indeed. Well, he was going to see that they got a task force for this case. A task force would keep it safe, meaning in the Twentieth Precinct. Otherwise if a third murder was found somewhere else, they would lose it, and this could be a big one. He would speak to the Chief of Detectives about it. He had pull, and everyone trusted his hunches. They had made a good beginning. Why lose it? Frank Fazio stared into his empty glass, finally admitting the truth. He wanted some action.

Terry drove for a while until she had cooled down. Driving always calmed her. Soon she'd go home and make something to eat.

The rain had stopped and she rolled down her window. It was that personal ads case that occupied her thoughts now. They would send out a sketch of the blond man to the post office and other precincts. And there was something else. Oh, yes, the snapshot in the first file. She had to check that. Was it the same man?

Spots of dizziness swam before her eyes, and she realized she needed to relax and just go home. She headed back toward her apartment in Queens. Honestly, if she were single, she would be afraid to go out of the house. Especially with what she knew about the City. Then Terry felt a rising moment of panic, an unreal sense of déjà vu. She *was* single now.

The phone rang six times before he burst through the door and picked it up.

"Hello? Is this Bob?"

"Bob? Uh-huh."

"You answered my ad. I'm a little late getting back to you. I placed the ad about a month ago. It keeps running continuously."

"Oh, yeah."

"Well, I'm Doreen. I ran an ad in the *Voice*." She giggled. "I liked your letter. Wanna get together?"

"Sure. When?"

"I thought tonight. If you're free. Is that okay?"

"Oh, yeah, fine."

"What's the name of your brokerage firm?"

"My firm? Oh, Sullivan and Shawn. Do you want to meet in a public place?"

Again that shrill giggle. "I've been running ads for years. Just come up to my place and ring the buzzer. It's 167 East Thirty-fourth Street."

"You don't want to go out first? I could meet you somewhere."

"No, just come on up."

"I love redheads, Doreen. Have a weakness for them, you might say."

"Oh . . . that's nice."

"What time should I come over?"

"As soon as you can. Now. Monday is my day off."

After hanging up, Doreen wondered if maybe she

should have told him. Especially if he had a "weakness." Her mind was a bit fogged. Her ad had been running continuously, and so far no one really cared. Should she have warned him? Now she was going to open the door and he would see she wasn't a redhead. Not anymore.

Marty tried Phyllis one more time. His heart sank lower with every ring. No answer. The trouble with Phyllis was that she didn't know how to reject. She just left him dangling. Tomorrow he'd try again. If she didn't answer, he'd go to her door and leave a note. Demand to know if they were through or not.

He closed his eyes and leaned back, comforted by knowing the solution. Then he opened his eyes, breathing hard with anxiety. A yes-or-no answer would leave him too vulnerable. No, he'd have to play her game. Phyllis had control now. Gee, he wished she hadn't lost all that weight. The first time they did it, she practically thanked him. Now he wondered if she was counting calories in bed. He missed the old, timid Phyllis. It was a loss.

The apple-green pants ballooned out and became tight around her ankles. He could see her legs through it. In fact, he could see through Doreen Stewart. Brown hair or not, she was a bitch.

He had to admit that when he saw that short, curly brown hair, he didn't know what to do. He wanted to leave. It was still early evening. He could make new plans. But in two seconds she had him inside, and the door was closed.

"I thought you were a redhead," he admitted. He wanted to be polite, but underneath, his anger was surging.

"I am a redhead. But I was helping it along and straightening it, and then the hairdresser said, 'Doreen, if you want to lose your hair in the sink, keep dyeing it.' So, I took the color out and had a perm. Just recently. I couldn't change the ad. I wanted to meet you because you sounded so sweet. So I lied. Actually, my hair is still kind of reddish, um, you know where." Her giggle was more like a whinny.

"Oh," he said, pulling out a pack of cigarettes.

"I'll let you smoke one, and then that's all. I don't approve. I quit three years ago. I'm an obnoxious reformed smoker."

She scampered up to locate an ashtray. "It was cramping my style, not to mention my career."

"What do you do, Doreen?"

"Didn't you read my ad?" She giggled again, and he wondered if she had been a pony in another life.

"I teach," she said proudly, not waiting for a reply. "Exercise classes—at several health clubs. Fancy ones. So I need my wind." At that, she jumped up and swiveled in jerky motions. Then she kicked her leg, almost putting her pointed toe through a lamp shade. She giggled again and sat down. "You know, aerobics and stuff like that."

He stared at her, fascinated, as if she were a movie.

"My ad said, 'I'm a very physical person. Let's get physical.'"

"I envy your freedom. I mean, your hours. I need the security of that paycheck."

"Why?"

"I send money home."

"Oh, that's adorable." This guy, she thought, has just the right set of values.

"Let's go somewhere and have dinner," she said merrily, with visions of embarking on a great adventure.

"In a minute. I'd like a little more wine. I have to unwind. I work long hours."

"You must," she said, nodding to his briefcase on the chair.

"What do you want to eat?" he asked. "Italian, Chinese, French, Greek . . ."

She stopped him. "Oh, whatever, wherever."

"Say," he asked mischievously, "do you still have my letter?"

"Letter? . . . oh, you mean—that. Why?"

"I'd like to see what I wrote," he said sincerely.

"You write so many you forget?"

"No." He smiled boyishly at her.

"Oh, all right." She slithered toward the kitchenette.

Her letters were spread out over an open copy of the *New York Post*. She whisked his from the top of a large batch, not allowing him to see how many letters she had. Seventy-seven so far. Her eye spotted a small headline in the paper. Funny, she hadn't noticed it before. "SECOND SINGLES MURDER." She scanned the small article. From the personal ads? She hadn't heard anything on radio or television. They were always sensationalizing the singles world. Personal ads were safe. She was living proof.

He was putting on his raincoat and hat when she came back into the room. "Ready to go?" he asked pleasantly.

She smiled brightly. "I'll get my raincoat. It's a little chilly."

"Yeah, you'll need it." He was opening the door.

She turned to face the closet when he shut the door quickly and grabbed her from behind, spinning her around, kissing her.

"Hey!" she protested. It came out twisted. His hands were on her lips, roughly puckering them, controlling her mouth. Then he forced his lips on hers and ripped her gauzy apple-green top with one movement.

One hand still covering her mouth, he dragged her toward the couch. She made a muffled sound, but he was more powerful. Oh, God, she thought, this man is going to rape me. Then she saw the newspaper article in her mind's eye. But, no. That happened to other people . . . oh, God, no . . . this . . . couldn't . . . be happening. . . .

She blew away a wispy strand of hair that was threatening her eye. Damn elevator was out. And today of all days. It was a quarter after six on Tuesday evening, and Phyllis Samuels was running late. Just three flights up, but it seemed like a mountain with the two bulging grocery bags she was carrying. At the top of the landing, she caught her breath, screamed. One bag slipped and fell to the ground.

Marty jumped up from the lower step of the stairwell. Instead of writing a note, he had decided to wait for her.

"I'll pick it up, Phyllis. Oh, you had eggs. I guess they broke."

"Marty," she said menacingly, "what . . . are you doing here?"

"I was worried. I haven't been able to reach you in two days."

"What are you . . . my mother?"

"Phyllis, c'mon. Is this how you want to end it? Can't we talk?"

Phyllis picked up the undamaged shopping bag and dragged the wet one to the edge of the door.

"But why is it I never hear from you except once a week before our date? We don't see each other a lot, Marty. It's not a real relationship." There! It was said.

"I can give more, Phyllis. I was thinking the same thing. I should give more." He couldn't tell her about the engagement ring he had returned Saturday.

She ignored him. "I'll have to go back and get new eggs."

"You're not sick," Marty said carefully.

"I *was* sick. Now I'm better."

"You took days off."

"Yeah, I have four more sick days coming this year." Her voice was slipping into hostility.

"Where were you? I kept calling."

"Marty, I had the phone unplugged. What's the big deal?"

He sucked on his lip.

She turned the key in her door, remembering the four delicious days and nights she had spent so far with Raoul, her lover. All she had to do was advertise and there would be more. Marty watched her hungrily. She thought, My God, he's going to get emotional over this. Shit. She felt sorry for him.

"Listen, Marty, want to come in for a drink? I have that apricot brandy you like." Stupid question. He was already in.

He felt confident now. She'd ask him to stay for dinner. Phyllis was a great cook. Sometimes she would make dinner, and they would eat in her apartment instead of going out.

She handed him a tiny tumbler of the warm, amber liquid, which was definitely not legal on Weight Watchers. Then she began unloading her groceries, taking inventory, while he watched. Olives on the side. Bread on counter. She made the best garlic bread in the world. Diet margarine, second shelf; low-fat milk, top shelf; grated Parmesan on the middle shelf; salad greens, below. She'd make the salad first. Raoul would get there around eight, and time was rushing.

"Marty, I'm having a friend over for dinner." Her head was in the refrigerator.

"Sure," he said, choked for a moment. It might be a girl friend, he reminded himself. But he knew it wasn't. "Saturday night, then, Phyl?" he heard his voice say—the words sounding detached, seemingly arising from someone else.

He had never called her Phyl before. She wanted to say "Yes, okay," but she clamped her mouth shut.

"Sometime next week is better," she said, her eye on a cucumber. "Give me a call."

He swallowed the lump in his throat.

She put the tomatoes on the lower shelf. Hardhearted Hannah, sure. The *Cosmo* Woman. Oh, yeah, even better. She felt like crying. "Seeing other people," she said cautiously. "Sometimes that's what a relationship or friendship is about. Letting the other one grow. Giving them space, you know?"

"You just said I didn't call enough."

Phyllis sighed. Great. She had to do her nails, iron a top, make the salad, bake the eggplant parmagiana—and he was holding her up.

Finally, mercifully, he said, "Well, I guess I'd better go. You seem busy."

They did a cat-and-mouse pas de deux to the door.

"Go out with others, Marty. If we're meant to be, we'll be," she said, opening her arms like some newly shrunken guru. She managed a final goodbye. He replied mournfully, "I'm a one-woman man, Phyllis."

"What?" she asked as the door closed.

Marty found his pride. "You're a smart woman, Phyllis."

She leaned her head against the door for a second. Nice of him to pay her a compliment. She couldn't remember when he had. But everything would be different now. She thought of Raoul.

Fat Phyllis the Victim was a thing of the past. But she wasn't sure if Marty was . . . yet. He would stick like glue. And then she started to cry, in spite of herself. For his rejection. For his pain. Because *she* had felt it all her life. Well, he'd have to accept her terms. She dried her eyes and started to giggle through her tears. She wondered what kind of woman Marty would take out. She pictured the two of them getting a transfer and finding seats on the bus.

Marty had been walking. He couldn't remember

exactly where he'd been. But it was nine o'clock and he felt better now. Darkness was beginning to smother the City, and the shadowy twilight had deepened into ink. He could barely see the green statue of what's-his-name sitting in Herald Square. There was usually a crown of squirming pigeons nestled on his head. What's-his-name was watching Macy's out of the corner of his eye. Macy's was in bed for the night. Bed. He didn't want to go home. To be alone. Not just yet.

He had made an ass of himself. Not cool. Phyllis had the upper hand now. Why did she have to lose all that weight? She was nicer the old way. He could control her. Phyllis made the mistake of changing. Well, she'd suffer. Ultimately. She'd become one of those skinny, overalert, always made-up, gorgeous Princesses. God, did he know them! He saw them every day at Saks.

A noise. He looked up. Nothing. Just a drunk who had slumped off his bench and lay there on the ground. His bottle rolled out of his hand and clunked against another bench. Marty watched it roll back the other way. Phyllis. Now he had to ask for a date in advance, he supposed. Now she'd expect a lot of . . . foreplay. And her hair. That brassy red. Without saying anything, she'd put a rinse on her nice brown hair. Odd. He had been attracted at first to Phyllis because she was fat and easy and grateful. And she had that mousy brown hair that hung in bangs. He couldn't figure it out. Lately, he liked only redheads. Slim, gorgeous redheads. Except for that one. Good old Doreen. But she had been right. Her hair was red in the place where it mattered. He started to laugh. He laughed until tears welled in his eyes. "Hey, pal," he called, waving his hat to the statue. "I'm going to be famous like you are. Only no one knows who the hell I am, either."

Then when he could hardly breathe from laughing so hard and he was half-falling off the hard bench, he started to cry. He didn't want Phyllis to go away. Women were always going away. He only liked it when he *said* they could go. Then he knew they would be his. Forever.

Dear Benjy,

I would call you Dad, but we never were that way, were we? Just pals. You can't answer, so what's the difference? Now it's my turn to give you what you deserve. I called all the way to Florida to see how you were. But if you could talk, you would have a lot to say, I bet.

I'm still a lady-killer. Three so far. Two had red hair. The third was a close runner-up. I'll make you proud of me yet. But only you will know who I am. And a lot of good that will do.

Love and Kisses,
Your son,
Martin Robert Loomus

CHAPTER SIX

At eight the next morning, Terry was at her desk in the Twentieth reading the *New York Post.* Monday evening, after her distressing reunion with Bob, she had driven home and had a brandy, longing for an evening of relaxation. But later in bed, she found she couldn't sleep. It was Bob, damn him. He had upset her. Maybe another glass of brandy. Then she realized it wasn't him at all. It was that snapshot in the Laura Frank file.

In seconds she had pulled on jeans and a sweat shirt. Somewhere in the Laura Frank file she had seen a snapshot that fit Mrs. Panachek's description. A blond, curly-haired man. Getting into her car, she reflected that that was a fairly unusual description. Tall, dark, and handsome; red hair with a freckled face, wavy hair and a mustache; but blond, curly hair must be in the minority. That would mean the man looked a little like Harpo Marx.

When she reached the precinct, she stalked in, oblivious to any stares from male detectives on the night tour. At her desk, she took out the Laura Frank file. She sifted through the letters until she saw it. The letter she had remembered with the snapshot paper-clipped to it. Handwritten, not typed. That was better, easier to trace. She unhooked the small picture and stared at those blond curls. The man was smiling. He had signed his name, Bob.

Maybe that's how she had remembered it all so perfectly.

Quickly, she scanned the letter for other clues.

I'm a free spirit, too. I'd like to find a soul mate as well, but it would only be a bonus. I'm independent, happy with myself, and entirely self-sufficient. I sense you're like me.

I'd really like to meet you. I always think you can tell more about a person if they take the trouble to write a letter. Are you up to the challenge? Here is my box number. I am in the process of getting a divorce, so I've taken a box number until I get an apartment. I'd love to meet you.

Terry had driven home a happy woman. She would sleep well. There was a picture they could give to the media instead of a sketch. It was a beautiful chunk of the jigsaw puzzle. Blond Bob had rented a post-office box. It had a number, and he had filled out forms.

When Terry came out of her reverie and looked up from the paper's coverage on the blond suspect, she immediately realized that something was wrong. The precinct room was too quiet and still. Like a ghost town. She looked around quickly and had her answer.

Standing at the door was Zone Captain Frank Fazio, and right next to him was the chief of detectives, a spare, hollow-cheeked man. Sitting at her desk, looking up at the captain, he appeared taller than he was.

Fazio raised his hand to silence the room, and every detective talking into a receiver hung up immediately. "We're forming a task force right here at this precinct," he said. A few faces looked downright puzzled. There was no big case they knew of that merited taking over a floor, putting in phones, and stripping personnel from their precincts.

Terry's heart sank. She knew. She was a cop. She

had trained herself not to cry, but tears of frustration threatened to roll down her cheeks. Her case. The one she had come so far with would be taken away from her. She'd never make the task force. Fazio wouldn't put her on it, and she knew it. If her name was Detective *Robert* Morrison, yes. But Detective Theresa Morrison, not a chance. She began doodling on a note pad so no one would read her face if it gave her away.

Frank Fazio was scanning the room. Actually, he didn't think it would be a good idea to lift too many detectives from the Two-oh. They couldn't spare that many men. Fazio wanted a task force of twenty-five to begin with. He always trusted his hunches. This would be another big case. He needed key people. Maybe three men from the Two-oh and the rest from other precincts, other boroughs.

"Moskowitz," he said firmly, staring at the sergeant detective who had helped him in the old days. "Task force." Moskowitz's jaw dropped. "For that case you're handling, you know, the personal ads case. The Lonely Hearts Killer." Fazio liked that. There, the case was named. It would sound good in the papers and on radio and television. Catchy, and it fit. Terry screwed up her nose. She didn't like the name because it was a put-down to singles. Furthermore, Moskowitz got on the task force and she wouldn't.

"Turk," Fazio said.

"Yo."

"Take over for Moskowitz. We'll move the force upstairs. You know the old space we used on three." Fazio and Moskowitz exchanged glances. Terry slumped a little in her chair. She wasn't part of the club, that was for sure.

"You, Yablonsky," Fazio shouted.

Terry looked up quickly. Who? She met the mocking eyes of George Yablonsky. He seemed to come out of the woodwork. "Just promoted to detective and he lands on a task force," Fazio said. "Well, he found the first body." Terry bit her lip.

Finally, Fazio asked, "Who was catching on this case?"

Terry's lips felt flash-frozen. Before she had a chance to speak, Moskowitz answered. "Morrison, Captain. Morrison was the catching detective."

Fazio looked at Terry as if seeing her for the first time. "Okay, Morrison, task force and that's it from the Two-oh." Terry's face remained impassive, and she was afraid to breathe.

Fazio and the chief were heading toward the elevators. Terry looked up and saw a man standing over her. Her partner, Charlie "the Hawk" Hawkins, was extending his hand.

"Good luck, Ter. They'll probably give me just an ordinary man to work with."

"And that will make your wife happy," said Terry, acting very businesslike. She was cleaning out her desk, stacking notebooks, putting pens in a rubber band—trying to adjust quickly to this turn in her life.

"I'll be back, kid," she said to Charlie, touching his shoulder.

"You'd better. We hardly got a chance to know each other."

Charlie and she had been assigned to one other just a month ago. He had inherited his nickname, "the Hawk," because of his protruding beak. He was reputed to be something of a ladies' man, always dressed in cashmere turtlenecks, soft leather boots, custom-made pants and sport jackets. Precinct gossip had it that Terry and the Hawk must be sleeping together. They loved to feed the fire with smiles or gestures. In reality, and to most detectives who knew them both well knew, Terry was still shaken over her separation, and Charlie was devoted to a gorgeous Italian wife who would never let him out of her sight.

"Take care of things for me," she said flippantly.

She noticed out of the corner of her eye that Detective Yablonsky was enrapt, witnessing their exchange. From a distance she couldn't make out whether he had eyes; he seemed always to squint in order to see more. And his mouth. Was it always twisted into a scowl? He made her nervous.

Holding her raincoat and balancing her stuff, Terry walked toward the elevators. Just as she was about to step in, Charlie ran up to her. "Phone call, Terry." Terry started to turn. "It's Bob."

She stepped back into the elevator. "Tell him I'm not there. Tell him I went to the ladies' room. Tell him I'm out on a case." While the doors closed, she said to herself, "Tell him to go to hell."

The lined wastebasket was full of blond curls. The man put the scissors down and, without blinking, plugged in a cheap electric razor he had just bought in Times Square. He proceeded to shave off all his hair in two-inch strips. When he was finished, he stared at himself in the mirror. He looked like a man on death row. That made him shudder. No, maybe he looked like one of those Hare Krishna people. Maybe he could join them. Anything to get out of this mess.

The *New York Post* was spread out on the single bed. It was the first edition. Thank heaven for the stabbing of a rock star on page one. His story had been delegated to page three. "SEX KILLER ANSWERS ADS." And there was his picture. He was wanted for questioning in the killing of Laura Frank. He was a suspect. He had never even heard of Laura Frank.

Even the letter and his handwriting. My God, she was just another ad with a box number. Oh, why did he have to send that snapshot? Why? He went back into the bathroom and looked at his pinkish skull in the mirror. Some of his courage returned. The fact was, he didn't have blond, curly hair anymore. He had a head that was freshly mowed. He stared at it in awe.

Wandering back into the tiny hotel room, he tried to remember what name he had used in writing that letter. Tom as in Tom Paine. John as in John F. Kennedy. Bob? He had to walk over to the newspaper to check. Oh, yeah, Bob. That was his favorite pen name. Because it was the same in any direction. None of those names were anything like his real name, which was a lulu. He couldn't remember all of that, though. He was running away, but he couldn't recall from whom or what. All he remembered was his first name, which struck him as rather odd. Krueger. Though he had no identification, he guessed his age to be about thirty-two. He wasn't exactly sure who he was at the moment, but he would bet money that he wasn't the man they were looking for.

Quickly, he glanced around the room. Time to move on. Mustn't forget anything. He put his khakis, T-shirts, and underwear into his plaid duffel bag. In a gray plastic garment bag went his navy suit and shirt and tie. That's what he wore on dates with girls from the ads he answered. Let's see . . . who were they? There was this girl named Sally . . . something. And one more. Oh, yeah, that girl who worked in the health clubs teaching exercise. Doreen. The peppy one. He couldn't remember her last name, either. Just wasn't much good at last names.

He'd never answer another ad again, that was for sure. What puzzled him was that someone had seen him coming out of this Laura Frank's apartment. But it hadn't been him. Or had it? Sometimes he couldn't remember from day to day where he had wandered or who he thought he was. He sat down on the green plastic chair, and a lump of stuffing dribbled onto the dusty linoleum floor. Looking out toward Eighth Avenue, he began to cry. Large sobs shook his body. He was so tired of running. What did they want from him? And if he had killed those girls, he didn't mean to. He didn't plan it or hate them or anything. He touched his bare head. It calmed him down. Whether he murdered those women or not, he had to find a new hiding place.

He'd check out and then have a slice of pizza over on Times Square in one of the clean places. He hadn't eaten anything yet. The bed was made, so he hadn't slept in his room. That was another thing that bothered him. He didn't know if he had found a bench to sleep on or if he had slept at all. He couldn't tell the difference.

He did know he had money, because he had found it in his pocket when he arrived in New York. But that would run out soon. He'd have to get a job washing dishes or maybe working in a pizza parlor. He'd like that. One of the clean places.

Spirits up, he gripped the case and slung the garment bag over his shoulder like a sack of laundry. Then he remembered. He had left his toothbrush in the bathroom. Whoops. Hair. Good thing he had double-checked. He overturned the plastic-lined wastebasket and watched his hair spill into the toilet, a sea of blond curls. Then he flushed it away and said goodbye to his old self. Whoever that was.

Picking up his gear, he left the room, completely forgetting one other thing. The new electric razor that was still plugged into the wall.

In the lobby a man was lounging on one of the dusty parlor chairs, sleeping it off. The day clerk was reading a newspaper when Krueger approached the desk. He reached toward the cubbyholes, but Krueger waved his key like a little flag, reminding him he was going, not coming.

"I'm checking out. Room 702."

"Phone calls?" he asked.

"No."

Looking up over the glasses perched on the tip of his nose, the clerk thumbed through the register.

"It's only Friday," he said. "You're paid until Sunday." He lifted his eyes accusingly.

"I-I-I—have to . . . something came up," Krueger managed, taking a little step backward.

The room was beginning to rock and sway. The desk clerk was screaming at him, but he couldn't hear the words. His mind exploded, and he saw only the man's mouth, which seemed to bark at him like a dog.

"Hey, son, didn't you used to have a little more . . ." The clerk touched his own bald dome. "I mean, weren't you . . ." Krueger stared at him. Then he spun around and ran out. The clerk shook his head. "No?" he said to himself. "Must be someone else. Well, I thought . . . oh, well, they come and go." And soon he was engrossed once again in the page-one story about the rock star who had been stabbed.

Two patrolmen from the Seventeenth Precinct stood in the lobby of the East Side apartment building. One, a six-foot-tall, muscular officer with a tattoo on his arm, was picking his teeth with a matchbook cover. His partner was studying the pebbles in the plastic floral arrangement. "Look, real rocks and fake flowers," his partner quipped in a heavy Brooklyn accent.

The big officer grunted. They were waiting for the super to appear with the key to an apartment. An old woman weighted down with a plastic shopping bag full of groceries hobbled up and asked, cautiously, "Any trouble, officers?"

"No, just routine. Answering a 911 call from a concerned neighbor. Nothing to worry about."

"Oh, good." The woman disappeared into the elevator.

The super entered the lobby. He was a short man with a round belly and a bushy mustache. In his hand was a big ring of keys. All three entered the elevator—the two knights in blue with guns bulging from their middles, and the short man who was hung over from two nights of steady drinking.

As they stepped onto the eighth floor, a door popped open, and a woman in a flowered duster rushed out to meet them.

"I'm Yetta Perleman, her next-door neighbor. I'm the one who called. Haven't seen her in three days and that's not like her. She always stops in to say, 'Hi, Yetta, how are you,' you know? Okay, that's okay. But at the mailbox this morning, I happened to see for myself that the mailman couldn't stuff her mail into her box. It was spilling out! She hasn't picked up the mail."

"Maybe she went on vacation," the tall cop proposed.

"No, no. I know what you think." Yetta was shifting her weight, dancing a little in her effort to express herself. "Whenever she goes on vacation, she gives me her plants and the key to take her mail." She shook her head emphatically. "Oh, no, something's wrong."

The super fitted a key in the door of the next apartment. The officers and Mrs. Perleman waited. Nothing happened. Then he tried another key, this time getting down on his knees. Still nothing happened. "Nope," he said finally. He stood up. Everyone was looking at him. "She's changed locks. That must be it. So the key is somewhere else. In a box. I forgot to add the new key to the ring."

"Look, this isn't an Agatha Christie whodunit," the big cop bellowed. "Do you have the key?"

The super nodded. "Yeah, sure. Thing is, I hardly ever open the tenants' apartments."

The shorter cop walked to the elevator to press the button for the super. He looked at his watch. There was, come to think of it, a case exactly like this one last week. A neighbor complained because a woman was missing. Nobody'd seen her for a few days. Found her reeling drunk in a sleazy bar near Chinatown. She couldn't even remember her name. A closet alkie. Big waste of time—just like this one was going to be. This girl was probably shacking up, having the time of her life, and here they were, cooling their heels while some super who barely understood English was looking for a key that probably didn't exist.

Reep the Creep was waiting for Terry as she stepped out of the elevator onto the third floor. Toothpick in his mouth, hat shading his eyes, he was standing there, leaning against the wall.

"Let you in the building, did they?" Terry asked. Like finding a cockroach walking over your lipstick she thought.

"Got a bone to pick with you, Lady Detective," Reep said menacingly.

"You have no business being here, Reep."

"Going to yell for help, Lady Detective?"

Terry looked into the vast room and saw Fazio supervising the arrangement of the desks. Men were setting up phones. He was right. She couldn't yell for help.

"Could be another Son of Sam, huh?" Reep said. "Or even another Ballet Killer case, huh?"

Terry looked him in the eye and said quickly, out of the corner of her mouth, "What do you want, Reep?"

Lenny Reep replied just as quickly. "Why'd you give that picture to the papers without letting me know first?"

Terry groaned. "Who has the time? Who the hell are you!"

"I could have gotten you bigger space, more coverage, Lady Detective. You screwed yourself."

Terry began to walk away. "Who cares?"

He grabbed her arm. "Look, this is a big case. You scratch my back, I'll scratch yours."

Terry stopped, not believing this conversation. "Is that a threat, Reep?" She knew he would never stop

Moskowitz this way, certainly never Fazio. As a woman, she was fair game for his power fantasies.

That thought made her angry. "Get out of my way. I don't owe you anything. It's not even my case anymore, so get lost, Reep."

Lenny Reep threw back his head and laughed softly. "I think I know what it is you're holding back on this case. What it is the newspapers don't know about. I could leak it anytime I want."

Ten minutes later, the super was back on the eighth floor apologizing. Mrs. Yetta Perleman and the two officers were waiting in strained silence. He inserted the new key in the door. The momentum of emergency had evaporated by now. Everyone wanted to get this business over with and leave. When the door opened easily, it was Mrs. Perleman's scream that was heard down the hall.

The bigger of the two patrolman strode over to the body and took a small mirror out of his pocket. With a handkerchief he lifted the cushion and looked into the wide-open, accusing stare of the woman. He held the mirror to her mouth and then took it away, saying almost as an afterthought what everyone suspected. "She ain't sleeping."

The moment of shock had passed. Now it was time for action. "Take that cigarette into the hall," he said to the super, who had lit up. It was a crime scene now. There had been a homicide. Nothing could be touched or disturbed.

"Can I use your phone?" he asked Mrs. Perleman, who nodded vigorously, her knuckle stuffed in her mouth. She couldn't take her eyes off the pale young woman lying naked, sprawled on the couch, who had just last week sat in her kitchen eating freshly baked coffee cake. She shook her head and knew she wouldn't be able to sleep for a month.

As if on cue, they all stole one last look at the

couch. At the woman who lay still, her arm flung across the back of the couch.

As they walked down the hall into Mrs. Perleman's apartment, her chatter continued nonstop. She offered them water, coffee, tea, seltzer. She offered information they hadn't even asked for. "She was so attractive. I used to say, 'Doreen, stop pfutzing around and get yourself a man, get married.' But no, she went out with a different one every night." Mrs. Perleman stood in the kitchen shaking her finger at the two cops. "Maybe that's what happened. She used those personal ads—where you advertise for a man. And you know what I think? I think she got into trouble."

The bigger officer dialed the Seventeenth Precinct. He reported a homicide, asked for detectives, and gave them the address. "Neighbor noticed she hadn't been around for a while," he said. "Found her on a couch, dead, naked, cushion over her face. Neighbor says she had a lot of boyfriends. Ran those personal ads." As he said it, a click went off in his brain. Familiar.

At the Seventeenth Precinct, a lieutenant got the information and signaled two detectives to go out on the call. Then a click went off in *his* brain. He glanced at a memorandum on his desk. Task force. At the Twentieth. He scanned it more carefully. And as the two detectives were putting on their raincoats, he yelled out, "Hey, you two. Forget it. Not our case." He took out his directory and thumbed the pages until he got the number for the Two-oh.

Near Times Square in the Roy Arms Hotel—so called because both the *a* and the *l* had dropped off the sign years ago and had never been replaced—the day clerk was eating his lunch. Sardines and onions slithered out of thick slabs of pumpernickel bread and onto a very dated copy of *Playboy*. Rosa, one of the maids, wheeled up her white-cotton bin, now almost depleted of bar soap and white towels, whose fluff had flattened into a sandpaper finish.

"Got something for you," she said in her broken English, reaching into the pocket of her housedress.

The clerk didn't look up.

"Hey, you, here." She handed him an electric razor with the cord wound around it. He grunted and took it, absently.

"Room 702," she announced. "I coulda kept it for my brother-in-law, but I thought someone would catch me, you know."

The clerk put his sandwich down, took the razor, and walked into the little room abutting the front desk. He tossed the razor in a box labeled "Lost and Found." It wouldn't be there long, though. When he turned his back for a minute, someone would steal it.

With not all of their task force team assembled, Terry and Moskowitz were sent out together on the first call. Terry couldn't fail to notice that Fazio was almost jubilant when the Seventeenth Precinct called. Any doubt about the validity of this task force was now squelched. Here was another murder. Terry had scrutinized Captain Fazio's face. She had the oddest feeling that he was enjoying all this. It was almost as if he had been waiting for another mass-murder case.

When they strode into the building on Thirty-fourth Street, they looked like any couple off the street. Moskowitz was wearing a navy suit and striped tie. Terry wore a plaid skirt, boots, a velvet blazer, and a white blouse with a bow. Only one thing distinguished them from a typical Manhattan couple: They flashed gold shields to the doorman.

When they approached Doreen Stewart's door, the police officer in charge took one look at Terry and said, "I'm sorry, miss, you'll have to leave. This is a police crime scene." Again, Terry presented her badge. The officer gaped at her.

While Moskowitz was in the corner talking to the other officer, she took out her notebook.

"Name?" Terry began.

"Doreen Stewart."

"Where did she work?"

"Taught exercise classes at a few of the better health clubs in Manhattan. We're checking."

He was looking Terry up and down, though his head didn't move an inch. A homicide detective that looked like a fashion plate. What next? He wondered who she had slept with to get her gold shield.

"Who found her?" Terry continued.

It was a few seconds before the officer realized he was being asked a question. He felt like he was in school and made to perform for a lady teacher. He didn't like it.

"Neighbor called 911 and said the girl had been missing for a few days, and we responded to the call. Super had the key."

Their conversation was stopped by the crime scene unit, which appeared at the door. Terry was reminded bizarrely of the Three Stooges. A medical examiner materialized from behind them. She thought then that if the chief medical examiner ever appeared, it would signify a real headline-breaking case. So far they just had a task force.

"Don't vacuum yet," she requested one of the men on the crime scene unit. Then she got down on all fours and raked her fingernails through the rust-colored carpeting.

"Lose a contact lens?" one of the men quipped.

"Looking for the petals," she murmured, her face down.

Moskowitz came to her rescue. "Part of the M.O. in this case. Killer's been leaving flower petals. Lab said they were from a white carnation."

The men were impatient to begin shooting. "Can we just take a few shots," one asked Terry, "without your ass in the picture?" She stood up and brushed off her skirt.

The man with the small vacuum that sucked up hairs, fingernail parings, and other potential clues said kindly, "I'll be careful. If I see anything, I'll let you know."

The medical examiner had carefully removed the cushion from the victim's face, and Terry felt a rush of disappointment. The hair wasn't really red, not by a long shot. It was a warm brown with honeyed highlights, perhaps. But the pubic hair. That was reddish. She thought they were looking for a man who had a sick weakness for redheads. Now they were looking for a sick man who would kill any woman. Would she be blond next time? Maybe a black woman?

"Got any aspirin?" she asked Moskowitz.

Moskowitz shook his head knowingly. "Look at it this way. The first two were redheads. This one isn't, but she comes close. At least he does it the same way every time. Rapes them and then snuffs them out. Probably does it all at once. Gets off on that."

They both stared at the body as the flashbulbs popped. Again, Terry was overcome with that queasy feeling she had learned to identify as embarrassment. She and the naked body were the only women in the room. Just because Doreen Stewart was dead somehow didn't make her pose any less suggestive. She longed to go over and clamp the dead woman's legs together. She looked precisely like what she was: a victim.

An aqua-colored phone rested on a little shelf in the foyer. Terry turned away from the scene and walked toward it, on the lookout for an address book. There was nothing she could see. Then she drifted into the kitchenette. A dried-out tea bag lay in a brown puddle on the counter. She looked in the sink. Two perfectly clean wineglasses. Probably also clean of any fingerprints—as before.

Then she spotted them on top of the tiny table. A stack of letters. Terry couldn't see them clearly. Her arm ached to touch them, but she knew she mustn't. Bending over, she looked for a date at the top of the newspaper, which she could see was the *Post*. Monday, March 22. Two days ago. Was that when Doreen Stewart was raped and suffocated?

Noise in the main room of the small apartment. A chorus of male voices overlapping. She stepped quickly into the doorway. No one was paying any attention to her. She knew that she should wait until the letters were dusted, but she just wanted one quick look. With her forefinger and thumb she lifted her skirt by the hem and toppled the pile of letters so she could see them. That way she wouldn't destroy any fingerprints, and she would have her answer.

She saw the letters were addressed to a box number. Some were handwritten on lined paper or stationery. Others were typed. There were quite a few. She gave a short gasp when she saw it: the handwriting, the paper clip, the photo. Hungrily, she snatched this one letter, not bothering to shield her hand with her skirt. The same smiling, curly-headed blond.

Just then a harsh voice said, "Why, detective, are you touching something on a crime scene unit?" The officer she had interviewed before stared at her. He was standing with his arms folded across his chest. She didn't reply.

They stood quietly like that, posing, until, after what seemed like an eternity, he stepped away. She clumsily put the picture back under the paper clip, using her skirt as a glove. And then she noticed the signature on the letter, and her heart sank. It looked exactly like the letter in the Laura Frank file. It was handwritten and invited a reply. There was a post-office box number. But it wasn't signed Bob. It was signed John.

* * *

The night clerk at the Roy Arms was late. The day clerk frowned. He would have to wait for this man because he couldn't leave the damn desk unattended. The overtime wouldn't amount to anything much, either. It was six o'clock, and the news was on. The tiny, almost-ancient black-and-white television set rested on a high stool. Sometimes he could watch a whole program uninterrupted. There wasn't much action at the hotel during the day. The hookers didn't really start coming in until around midnight.

He reached forward to adjust the snow and wavy lines. Then he took an old shoe that rested on the counter and smacked the set. Six o'clock. That bastard had better show up soon. He should have been on the subway by now, going back to Yonkers.

". . . has been reported on Manhattan's East Side. Police have established a task force to track this man, now being dubbed as the Lonely Hearts Killer. This is the third death believed to be committed by the same suspect, who reportedly rapes and then suffocates his victims. Two other young women"—the pictures flashed across the screen—"have been murdered in this way. Laura Frank and Debbie Greene. The third victim's name has not been revealed to the media at this time.

"Police are looking for a man with blond, curly hair who is wanted as a suspect." The picture stayed on the screen. "If you know the man or his whereabouts, please contact the special number"—the number flashed across the screen several times—"that has been set up by the police department."

The clerk blinked at the telephone numbers. He couldn't think, and he was never much for numbers. But that picture. He had a good, long look at that photo. He looked at his coffee, which was flavored with whiskey during the day. No, he wasn't drunk, and there was nothing wrong with his brain, either. With slow, deliberate movements, he went to the lost and found box. Son of a gun. The electric razor was still there. He was right. Because he never forgot a face. The kid on TV with the curly locks was the same as the bald monk who left the razor. The dumb kid was a celebrity. His picture was on television and everything. The fucking cops, though. What dummies. They were looking for the right face—but the wrong hairdo.

CHAPTER SEVEN

Marty's back was to the people lined up at the credit windows. He concentrated very carefully on pouring his coffee. He ripped open a little sugar packet and watched it sprinkle into his paper cup. Twirling the light brown liquid with the skinny plastic stirrer, he tried not to smile. Then he took a paper napkin and cleaned up his little area, a small shelf space in back, crumpling the soiled napkin and crushing the stirrers in his hand. He stood by the wastebasket, knowing it was time for him to face the line of customers, but he couldn't turn around just yet. Marty was shaking with silent laughter.

Thursday morning at ten o'clock and customers and employees alike were talking about the young woman who had been murdered on the East Side. People were carrying tabloids that screamed "SINGLES SEX KILLER ANSWERS AD" and "ANOTHER LONELY HEARTS MURDER."

He walked toward his line and overheard a conversation between two employees behind him.

"What's M.O. mean?"

"Modus operandi, the method of operation."

There was a low whistle. "Some method," a man said. "I answered a few of those ads myself."

And another female voice. "Pisses me off. Everything I like is injurious to my health. Cigarettes. Salt. Booze. Red meat. And now some killer is running around stopping all my fun."

"He's like herpes on the singles scene," someone else said, and they all agreed.

Marty took his place at the window. The young woman next to him asked, "What do you think of all this, Marty?"

He straightened his tie and looked directly into the eyes of the woman. He cleared his throat. "I think answering personal ads is dangerous. Even if there were no"—he searched for the words—"killer, well, then, you would still be going out with a stranger. A perfect stranger. Not like, say, if one of us in the office went out with another one."

The woman turned away and gave her undivided attention to her next customer. She stole a look at Marty. He was busy, too. For a minute she assumed he was fishing for a date. He was a pussycat and all that, so she didn't want to be placed in the position of rejecting him. She wasn't good at rejecting. But face it, Marty Loomus was the last person she would want to go out with. He was just so colorless.

Terry passed Martin Van Buren High School and slowed down, looking for the house. She was in the Floral Park section of Queens, not too far from her apartment. Other members of the task force were talking to Doreen's co-workers at the health club, manning the phone for leads on the blond suspect and tracing and interviewing every man who had written to the women.

She parked her car. She got out and squinted at a house that looked like a quintessential suburban home. On a patch of green there was a circle of shrubbery, a garage at the end of the driveway, and a small child's red wagon blocking that. A solid mass of drapery covered the front window. Terry walked slowly up the front path.

She rang the door bell. No answer. She lifted the heavy brass knocker and let it fall against the door a few times. No answer. Then she noticed a quick movement to the side of the shrubbery. A little boy's head stuck out and then pulled back and completely disappeared. Terry retraced her steps and noticed the living room drapes move and then snap back. Someone was home.

She walked back up the front steps. Just before she pressed the bell again, the door opened a crack, and a woman's face peered out at her. "What do you want?" came a hollow voice.

Terry showed her shield. "Detective Morrison. I'd like to ask you a few questions about your daughter, Mrs. Stewart."

The door opened a little more. The woman sighed, and a sob slipped out. "I thought you were a reporter. I don't want to talk to any reporters."

Terry nodded sympathetically.

"Well, come in, then. My husband and my two daughters are at St. Hedwig's making arrangements for a special mass. Anthony's home with me." She indicated the little boy who was now in the room. "He doesn't understand. Anthony, go play. Outside."

Terry was willing to bet there would be no help here, as there hadn't been with the other parents. They seemed to have a different idea of how their daughters lived in Manhattan. The shock was compounded when they found out their girls had been living like grown-up women.

"Doreen was a good girl . . ." Mrs. Stewart began, brushing away a lock of gray hair that had fallen in her eye. The fingers of her right hand drummed on the polished mahogany end table.

"We found a number of letters from men. Personal ads . . ."

Mrs. Stewart nodded to indicate she knew of Doreen's activities.

"Apart from the personal ads, did Doreen have any special boyfriend?"

"No."

"Any old boyfriend that might have been angry or jealous?"

"I don't know."

"She never spoke about that area of her life?"

"Oh, yes," Mrs. Stewart exclaimed. "She talked about those personal ads all the time. I didn't like the idea of that, you know, I never did. But she seemed to get so much fun out of it. She was always so high-spirited, you see."

"When was the last time you talked to your daughter?"

Mrs. Stewart, who had been almost unbelievably stoic, suddenly burst into tears. She rose, plucked a tissue from a box, then gently blew her nose. "The day she died. Just a few hours before. I talked to her on the phone. For the last time. Before her date."

Terry looked at the woman sharply. "Mrs. Stewart, did she actually say she had a date? Were those her exact words?"

Mrs. Stewart nodded.

"Did she give a description of him?"

"Oh, no, nothing like that. Only that it was the seventy-seventh letter she'd received. I remember the number: two sevens. And that she was going out with him or he was coming over, I don't recall which right now." She began to weep again. "Doreen wasn't a very scholarly girl. She just had fun. So we all learned to tune her out a little. She dated so many young men. She was just twenty-five. Didn't even live out half her life." Mrs. Stewart was crying so hard, her last sentence was almost unintelligible. Terry looked away, studied the carpeting, and waited.

"Mrs. Stewart," she said when the crying had subsided, "I know this is difficult, but I want you to think for a moment because it's so very important. You said she received seventy-seven letters. You made a mistake, I think. We only counted seventy-six."

The woman shook her head stubbornly. "No, seventy-seven. If it had been seventy-six, I'd've thought of that song, 'Seventy-six trombones led the big parade,' and I didn't."

Terry regarded the woman with a solid feeling of déjà vu. Just like that dark-haired friend of Debbie Greene's, Candice Klein. The story didn't match. The files in each case were short one letter. It couldn't be pure coincidence, could it?

The task force was culled from Manhattan detectives, Bronx sex crimes, Brooklyn homicide, the Queens D.A. squad, and even some retirees. In less than a week they were operable, with Fazio at the helm. Moskowitz acted as Fazio's deputy when he had to attend to other duties. Every member of the task force considered it a privilege to be working on the assignment.

That morning Fazio was presiding. He was explaining the psychology of the pathological versus the psychotic killer.

"The shrinks will tell you there is a difference. That the pathological killer murders for enjoyment while the psychotic kills because it's an extension of the illness." Fazio slouched against a chair and relit his cigar. "They overlap, is what I've found. As for this Lonely Hearts Killer, try to read the mind of a sick man and figure out his motives. Then you will have his next move." He cleared his throat and took a sip of water from a glass on the desk behind him. "His next move is obvious. He'll kill again. He's making headlines."

Fazio looked at his watch. God damn! There weren't enough hours in the day. Even so, he felt exhilarated. Spring never smelled sweeter. To have two manhunts in a career; well, that was nothing to complain about.

"The phones are important," he said. "Any lead

coming in that sounds halfway decent, follow up on it. Go to it, gentlemen and lady. . . ."

There was soft laughter from all but Moskowitz.

"She's in Queens with the victim's mother," someone offered.

"Well, then, gentlemen . . ."

As Fazio surged out the door, he brushed past Detective Bob Morrison. Fazio recalled that he had seen this face somewhere before, but he couldn't remember where.

Morrison found Moskowitz talking to another detective. "Hi, Bernie. Where's Terry?" Moskowitz excused himself and walked across the room to the handsome first-grade detective from the Sixth Precinct.

"She's out," Moskowitz said.

It had been no trouble for Bob Morrison to learn that Terry was part of the task force. He just called, said he was her husband, and someone told him why she was no longer at her desk.

"Listen," Moskowitz said, his face matching his red crew cut, "it's none of my business, but sometimes women need to be left alone. Terry's got a shitload on her mind these days. She was catching on this case, you know. She has quite an interest in it. Look, Morrison, like I said, it's none of my business, but I see the gaff Terry takes, and she's a damn good detective. Now you're on her back. You know, either shit or get off the pot. If you're divorcing her, don't keep bugging her this way."

"I didn't ask for psychoanalysis. I just want to know how to reach her."

Moskowitz looked down. He could hear one of the men calling to him. "She's through tonight, and then she has her days off. But I don't know if she'll be home or anything," he said quickly. "She might work off-duty."

"Oh, I'm sure she will," Bob said sarcastically, possessively.

Moskowitz watched the man stalk out. Maybe he had said too much. But when he saw two people who were so obviously in love and couldn't make a go of it, it saddened him. He worried about Terry, he supposed, in a protective way, though he knew she hated it. A woman like that, so beautiful she made heads turn, so competent she had risen to second-grade detective with a gold shield, so sensitive every insult from one of those cretins made her stronger and yet vulnerable . . . what good was it? He often thought Detective Theresa Morrison was the loneliest woman in the world.

Her head rested back on the seat; her hand was on her forehead and her eyes closed. A passerby stopped for a second, debating whether to knock on the car window to see if the woman was all right. But Terry picked up her head and looked straight ahead. She was just resting her eyes. Summoning enough energy to get out of the car, lug her bag of groceries, walk into her apartment building and . . . what? She was exhausted. Drained.

After she had finished interviewing Mrs. Stewart, she'd returned to the station house, and she and another detective had talked to men who had written letters to the dead women. Most were frightened, some appalled. None claimed to have gone out with any of the victims. All the men they talked to had alibis, and none fit the description of the suspect. They had many other suspects to interrogate.

What was giving Terry a headache was those missing letters. One from Debbie Greene's file and one from Doreen Stewart's. Was there one missing from the Laura Frank file, too?

When she plopped her grocery bag down on the carpet and shut the door, the phone started up. Terry rushed to pick it up.

"Hi, this is Don Phillips. Doing anything tonight?"

Terry looked at her bag of groceries, took off her holster, and fought a self-waged battle. Why him? Why now? Yet, what really mattered if she didn't begin to make a life for herself? Perhaps if she showered and had a drink, a good, stiff one, she could reanimate herself. Maybe it would make her forget about the case.

"Oh," she said casually, like any other career woman, "I just got home from work."

"Why not dinner? I'll pick you up at your place." Instantly, his tone became flirtatious, intimate.

Terry mimicked his intonation. "Why not? Sounds great. You know where I live, don't you? Come over around eight."

When she replaced the receiver, she sank into a chair. She sat, exhausted, unable to think, let alone move. Then she willed her body into motion, picked up her groceries, turned on the radio, fetched Scotch from the bar, and went into the kitchen for some ice.

The Titanic was just starting to fill up with people from offices along Broadway and the Lincoln Center area and with cops who had finished their tours. Bob had driven all the way uptown on a whim. Maybe Terry would stop in for a drink. Funny, he thought, after all the arguing over the inability to match their schedules: They had the same tours now that she was on the task force. Just like any other couple off work. They could be together tonight.

He sat at the bar and dipped his hand in the wooden bowl, fishing out some pretzels. Then he turned. His shoulder brushed against someone. He looked into the deepest, greenest eyes he had ever encountered. They were fringed with black eyelashes.

"Are you a cop?" a red-gashed mouth inquired, the voice blurred with a surfeit of liquor. "I love cops."

Bob looked away. "I'm not a cop," he said. Months ago, before Terry left, he wouldn't have said that. He would have considered himself lucky; like any deserving, good-looking detective, he'd have fed the young lady's illusions for a few hours. He wouldn't have recalled her last name—if he'd ever known it—and he would have gone home to his wife.

He wondered if Terry suspected his short, harmless affairs. Probably. But never had she said anything. What the hell. Screwing around went with the territory. Some broad had asked him what his wife did, and he had replied that she was a detective. "Oh, and does she play around, too?" came next. He couldn't answer. He doubted it, though. That question made him ponder, for the first time, the unfairness of her position. Cops' wives didn't play around. And he would bet that Terry had never cheated in all the time that they had been married.

He toasted himself silently for his stupidity. Because now she could cheat. She could even remarry when the divorce was final. And he was sitting here, free as a bird, free to pick up any women he wanted—and he wasn't interested. He didn't want another woman. He wanted Terry. And if he could get her back, he would never stray from the fold again. He would change.

His eyes peered into the mirror below a line of glasses facing the bar. He saw a golden head with a shock of hair that kept falling across his brow. The lights were bright over the bar, and what he noticed next depressed him. Even from that distance, he could see strands of silver. No, it wasn't a reflection. It was gray hair. Today was his birthday. He was thirty-nine, and he had no one to celebrate with.

He ordered another drink. He was what he was, a cop, but he could bend more than a little. It wasn't his fault. He was a man. Terry minded what she called his macho thinking, but she would make mincemeat out of a weak guy.

Why did he realize all this now? he wondered. The answer: because it was too late. It *was* his fault. He had wanted Terry to be a wife. Well, damn it, he was realizing that's what she was. And more than just a wife. There was nobody on the force he could talk to the way he could her. She understood him because they were alike.

He paid the bill. Green-eyes gave him one last smoldering look. Maybe it wasn't too late. He now realized what his course of action must be. He had to go to his wife and tell her he loved her. That was why he wanted her back. That's what women wanted to hear.

Two warm brown eyes shone behind glasses. Terry somehow couldn't take the adoring stare of Don Phillips. Instead, she looked around the restaurant—a homey, family-run neighborhood place in Queens.

Terry willed herself to concentrate on what her date was saying. Not especially easy now because all day long her job required concentration, analysis, deciphering. She sat up straighter and fingered the floating gold heart suspended from a chain over her cashmere sweater. The heart had been a Christmas present from Bob. On one corner of it was a tiny chipped diamond.

Their dinners came, and she studied Don. He was divorced, had two children he adored. A decent guy. No heartthrob, though. Terry realized that in many ways she was a prude. She was square enough not to have cheated on Bob even when she discovered his infidelity. Nor would she easily go to bed with *this* man. It wasn't Don Phillips's balding head that turned her off. It wasn't his wide-eyed enthusiasm, which seemed so incredibly naive in a man of his mid-forties. She didn't mind that he talked about his two little girls all the time. Maybe she had to get to know him a little better. But it was just that she felt so lonely when she was with him.

"Tell me," he said, rolling spaghetti around a spoon. "When did you first decide to be a cop? I mean, Dawn, my youngest, wants to be a doctor, and she's only seven. Where did she get that from? I don't know."

Terry found it hard to eat and respond to interrogations. "When I got out of college, I didn't know what to do, so I entered the police academy. Then it took only a few months to get through."

Now, why did she lie? she wondered. She promised her mother she would go to college, and there was dad's insurance money. She had majored in history for the hell of it, and she hadn't gone for a teaching degree because she knew all along that she would be a cop. And that she would one day be a detective. Just like her dad.

"And how long did it take to become a detective? This is fascinating. I talked to my brother in Albany, and he said it's very unusual for a woman to become a homicide detective. And you're what? Second-grade? What does that mean? I forget."

Terry gulped, began to speak, had too much in her mouth, swallowed air, and had a choking spasm. Her face was pink with embarrassment until she was in control again.

"Are you all right?"

Terry nodded. Suddenly, she felt very tired.

"In 1977, the chief of detectives assigned nine women to homicide squads, and I was one of them. I became a detective early the next year. It took a while longer to earn my gold shield. In answer to your question: I became a policewoman in 1968. Ten years." Hardworking years. Which would have been easier if she were a man.

"Are you carrying a gun now?"

She raised her hand. "Don . . ."

"Oh, I'm sorry. Am I asking too many questions? It's just that you're so different, so exotic, so—"

Terry yawned. "Maybe I'll skip dessert and coffee and call it a night. I'm sorry, but I had an unusually rough day."

"Of course, I know you must've. All I did all day was fill out dry-cleaning slips."

"And I bet you're good at it," Terry said, stifling another yawn.

It would take less than ten minutes to put on some clothes. The bakery was still open. Phyllis scanned the shelves from memory. The assorted butter cookies were to the right. The luscious, whipped-cream confections were in the refrigerated window. The flaky croissants were to the left. Right smack in the middle were the big chocolate and mocha cakes and the pies—apple, cherry, blueberry. She thought she'd go mad if she didn't get a fix. A jelly doughnut would do. Phyllis shuddered. She was like an alcoholic, and she felt another binge coming on.

Everything had been wonderful. Raoul had been so attentive. He had left Wednesday morning, chucking her under her chin and promising to call. Now Friday was here, and a long weekend loomed before her. Nothing to do and no one to do it with. He hadn't phoned. No one had prepared her for this kind of pain.

Out the door—and the penalty was probably two or three pounds. Instead of being the Weight Watchers darling, she would be so ashamed, she wouldn't go to the next meeting. She didn't want to eat all those things, and she knew she didn't. But if she filled herself up, maybe the pain would go away.

There was only one way out. She looked at her phone, then picked up the receiver. She'd just have to call Marty.

"Marty? This is Phyl."

This wasn't the call he wanted. But it would do.

"Marty, I really want to apologize for the shabby way I treated you." Phyllis gulped. She could taste a chocolate eclair. She closed her eyes and imagined sinking her teeth into a cloud of whipped cream. "How have you been? What's new?"

"Fine. Nothing too much is new."

Phyllis felt awkward. He sounded stiff and standoffish. "You're angry with me, aren't you?"

"I never get angry, Phyllis, you know that. You want to go out? Is that what you want?"

She could tell by the strident tone that he was hurt. "Look, Marty, why don't you come over for dinner tomorrow night? I'll make garlic bread."

Something told Marty to beware. He had almost a sixth sense about these things. So, she hadn't truly rejected him. Or she had tried but realized he was the best. And more importantly, a tiny little voice inside his head warned, Save Saturday night for a Princess. Phyllis didn't matter anymore. Once he had bought a ring for her, but that was in another life.

"Not Saturday night, Phyllis. What about Sunday night?"

Phyllis couldn't believe it. "Sure, Marty, whatever you say."

Later on, she thought how wrong she had been about him. He didn't waste any time. Had them all lined up for Saturday night. It was one thing to be rejected by a man like Raoul, whom she adored, but it was goddamn humiliating to get kicked in the ass by Marty Loomus.

She shrugged. Well, what the hell! Her confidence was just at a low ebb, that was all. Marty was just an insurance policy, someone to have around when real dates weren't available.

She grabbed her coat. As she stepped into the elevator, she thought she heard a phone ringing. Was it her apartment? Should she run back quickly? It was hard to tell. But the odds were against her, she thought as she rode down.

Phyllis Samuels was on Third Avenue biting her lip, debating between a trip to the bakery or a little jaunt to the ice cream parlor. She was no longer in possession of her rational mind. And the phone in her apartment had stopped ringing.

* * *

When the pink Impala pulled up in front of her apartment, Terry felt even more vulnerable because she was so exhausted. She simply had no idea of how to act on a date. It had been so long. He was actually getting out of his side of the car and coming across to open the car door for her. Just as he had lit all her cigarettes and helped her on with her coat. She, who could approach a darkened alley, both hands on her gun, and yell, "Police." She who had used the gun—though so far she had never been forced to kill anyone.

She felt like a schoolgirl. What if he tried to kiss her? That thought nauseated her. She thought of the naked bodies sprawled in front of the men at the crime scene unit. The women who wore nothing but pillows or cushions to hide their faces. She wouldn't invite him up to her apartment.

As he opened the passenger door and Terry set her heel on the street, she tensed. Her senses were alert.

"Is something wrong?" Don Phillips asked.

"Shh, I'll get back in the car and then you just squeeze in. I don't have my gun."

"My God," Don said. "You mean something, someone's out there after you? Oh, my God."

Terry carefully began to fold herself back into the car when she heard someone calling her, saw a figure emerging from the parked cars.

"Oh, my God," Don said weakly, trembling, trying to stuff himself into the car.

"Ter?" came the voice.

"Oh, shit. Never mind, Don, it's okay. No danger." Terry thought briefly of an appropriate science-fiction title, "The Thing That Never Left." Reddened with embarrassment, she made the introductions.

"Don Phillips, this is Bob Morrison." The two men shook hands.

"Your brother?" Don asked, looking from one to the other.

"Her husband," Bob replied with a Cheshire grin. Terry wondered how much he had had to drink. Then, suddenly, whether it was the hour or her fatigue or her wacky sense of humor, she lifted her hand to her mouth and turned away. It just struck her as so funny, she was afraid she might start to laugh. Her one and only date, and *he* shows up, stepping out of the shadows.

"Soon-to-be *ex*-husband," Terry amended. "I told you the first time we met. Remember?"

"Oh, yeah, sure," Don Phillips replied. "Well, it's getting late."

Good-byes were understandably brief.

On the street, Terry watched her date's car pull away and then faced Bob. She began screaming at him, unleashing fury that wasn't satisfied without physical expression.

"Now look at what you've done. A perfectly nice man. He took me to dinner. I'm entitled to date. We're legally separated. I'm not asking alimony, so why are you following me like this? I never came out from the shadows when you were out with one of your . . . ladies. Does it make you happy to make me unhappy?"

"You didn't like him; I could tell," Bob said matter-of-factly. "Not your type. Too soft."

Terry was enraged.

"Go away! Go far away! I don't like you! I don't love you! And I don't want you at my door when I come home from a date!"

A voice boomed from one of the apartment buildings. "Lady, will you shut up, or do I have to call the police?"

Bob started to snicker. He grabbed Terry by the arm and yanked her toward the sidewalk. They stood facing each other. Terry looked ready for a boxing match. Bob looked sad.

"I just came by so you could wish me a happy birthday. I spent my birthday alone."

"It's not until tomorrow."

"What?"

"Your birthday is tomorrow, you asshole."

He looked bewildered for a second. "I thought it was the twenty-sixth."

She shook her head. "Our anniversary is the twenty-sixth. Of January. Your birthday is March twenty-seventh."

"I got drunk for nothing."

"I'm tired, Bob. Have we finished this round?" What a character! He would never change. But she dared not smile. Right now, standing in the spring darkness seeing him so vulnerable, she felt a desperate need to maintain her anger. Quickly, she turned to go inside.

"Ter?"

"What?" She spun around impatiently.

"What I came to tell you is that . . . I love you."

He stepped forward, put her arms around his neck, and kissed her under the lamplight. For a minute Terry forgot everything but his impassioned kiss and the familiar curves of his body. She forced herself to remember the brutal fights and their insurmountable differences.

"Happy birthday, kiddo," she said, squirming, releasing herself. She walked briskly away so he wouldn't see her tears.

At that moment, in a studio apartment on One Hundred Sixteenth Street, skirting Columbia University, a young woman reached for her phone, then abruptly yanked her hand away. She had vowed to make this call, and she would if she could compel herself to dial. It was nerve-wracking. One call a week, she promised, or she'd never get out of the house. Bars were out.

She had advertised in *The New York Review of Books* and had received twenty-seven letters. Really, she shouldn't be so terrified, because she had already been out with one fella. He'd been okay, though not intellectually her equal. Martha Wychzensky was a librarian at the Mid-Manhattan Library. She did not own a tube. She did not read the *Post* or the *Daily News*. She read only the Sunday *Times,* and she concentrated on the Book Review and Arts and Leisure sections. She scanned the rest with less interest. Since she hadn't told anyone that she was running an ad to get men, she had no idea that what she was doing might be dangerous. She merely considered herself a coward for not doing it better.

It just wouldn't do to sit behind her desk at the library, repeatedly answering the same boring questions. Librarian. There was a stigma to it, as if she were shy, retiring, intellectual. She *was*—but she longed to break free of this imposed role and become the adventurous soul that resided deep inside. So she turned to *The New York Review of Books*.

Martha had worked for several days on her ad before she felt it was ready.

LIBRARIAN WHO IS NOT A NUN seeks intellectual hedonist for romp through life. I have the strawberry-blond hair of a cherub on the Sistine Chapel, the soul of Dostoevski, the serenity of Aristotle. Won't some Adonis try me? I.Q. above 140, please. Photo appreciated.

Even now she loved her composition. It had been so much fun to create. She should have added: the courage of a mouse. She looked at her kitchen clock. Soon it would be too late to call. In a few minutes it would be ten-thirty.

She picked up the letter. What impressed her was that, though he was a computer programmer, his hobby was reading the classics. The man loved literature. Martha lifted her hand. She had to meet this one. He said he just loved redheads, too. Buoyed by her silent pep talk, she began to dial. It wasn't a matter of life and death, just a phone call.

"Hello?"

Martha's mind went blank. "Hello?" Then her robotlike librarian voice seized control. "My name is Martha Wychzensky, and you answered my ad in *The New York Review of Books.*"

Marty smiled. All the waiting paid off. It made sense to have patience. He was still good. Good? He was the best. Still the one they wanted. He stuck to the time-honored scenario. Mustn't play easy to get.

"What?"

"Aren't you Bob? I'm the librarian who's not a nun. I have strawberry-blond hair . . ."

"Oh, yes." His throat became dry and constricted. Time to turn on the charm. "I loved your ad. That one really stood out."

Martha relaxed against her high-rise bed and twirled the fringe on her throw pillow. "Do you ever go to the Mid-Manhattan Library?" Dumb question. But she had to know if he'd be a waste of her time like that last Neanderthal was.

"Oh, yeah, I go there on my lunch hour just to sit and read." Marty was trying to figure out which library it was. Was it the one on Fifty-third Street? No, that had a funny name. Donnell, that was it.

"I work on the fifth floor. Maybe we've met."

"Maybe."

"Wouldn't it be funny if you were one of the ones that keep asking the same questions over and over?"

"What questions are those?"

"Where's the rest room, where's the pay phone, can I have change for the photocopy machine?"

They both laughed, though Marty didn't quite grasp the humor—if any. He just responded to her musical giggle and laughed along. "Hey, Martha, why don't we get together? Would you like that?"

"Sure."

"What about tomorrow evening?" He was sitting

on his heels, perched on his worn couch, ready to explode with euphoric energy.

Martha took her time deliberating. On Saturdays she usually cleaned her apartment and listened to opera records. This Saturday night she was supposed to have dinner at her aunt's place on Eighty-second Street. She would much prefer to have her personal ad date on a weeknight. Somehow there was too much intimacy attached to a weekend. But this man sounded special, and she wasn't wild about Saturday dinner with an aunt who couldn't hear half the things she said, anyway.

"Okay. Why not meet at this place near me?" She never allowed the men to know her address. Not until she was sure she could trust them.

"Sounds great to me."

"There's a restaurant on Broadway that's not too crowded. Why don't we meet at eight and have a drink. The Jewel Box—it's on One Hundred and Eleventh Street, near Amsterdam Avenue."

"It's a date." No need ever to buy this one dinner. She liked him already. He could tell. "Oh, wait a second. How will you know me?"

"I forgot to tell you: I have a red beret I can wear."

"Oh, don't do that. In this warm weather? Hey, I have a great idea. I'll be wearing a white carnation."

After a search, he found her ad. With a red magic marker he drew a plump heart around it. Red hair. She was a winner. It didn't matter if she had a face to stop a clock—as long as she wore a garland of crushed apricots.

His black bowler rested on the card table in the main room. The weather was warm now. It would look odd to wear a hat. His briefcase . . . well, that could be explained. He needed his wig and glasses. But he wouldn't wear a hat.

He ran to the mirror and smiled. Suddenly, he was Bob. The man the voices had created to perform destiny's dirty work. All he needed was a white carnation. These women found him attractive. As Marty, he couldn't do it. As Marty, he had been invisible. He wasn't invisible any longer.

Dear Benjy,

I used to call you Dad, but I never meant it. Sylvia made me call her Mother. Do you think that, had she lived, that beautiful red hair of hers would have been ghostly white now? I mean ghastly. I could call you dead, whoops, I mean Dad, but my spelling is so bad.

There's no end to all the redheaded girls I can get into trouble in New York City. They love me. They call me up and ask for a date. They even run ads for me.

I hope you like the charming place I have chosen for you. Just remember, I pay the bills. I hope the people who take care of you are swell. God knows they're paid well enough. Take care.

Your Mistake,
Marty

CHAPTER EIGHT

In Miami that day it was hazy, the air hanging close. Yet all along the shore, people covered themselves with suntan oil anyway because, behind the haze, the sun was intense. They swam, they dived, they walked on the beaches.

In a small nursing home someone had callously named Avenging Angel, no one would ever swim or run or dive again. Most patients couldn't even apply suntan oil. They didn't have the use of their arms.

Benjamin Loomus would have been wearing a frown on this lazy Florida morning, but his face muscles didn't work anymore. Years ago he would have grumbled about the lousy weather. Now he couldn't even open his mouth or turn his head or move his arms or legs.

A chubby black nurse entered the large ward, chuckling over a joke someone had just told her. She came over to her favorite baby and, with her two big hands, shifted his body so that he faced the television set in the center of the floor.

"How are we today, Mr. Loomus?"

Benjamin Loomus blinked his eyes. One blink meant yes, and two blinks meant no. He was seventy-six, and he had suffered a massive stroke, which left him paralyzed except for his eyelids. He blinked once for yes to satisfy her; but if he'd enjoyed the privilege of speech, he would have told the meddlesome bitch to take her patronizing attitude and shove it you-know-where.

The moist Miami air lingered like mist on the few tiny plants lining the window ledge. They were covered with dust. The nurses rarely had time to tend to the plants, and the patients certainly couldn't.

Annie, the black nurse, was one of the few who remembered to water the plants. She also looked out for Mr. Loomus. She often said, "That poor baby is the worst one." So she paid him special attention. Sometimes she washed his snowy white hair, taking great effort to bend his nearly unbendable body toward the sink as gently as possible. She shifted him regularly so he wouldn't get bedsores, and she included him in her prayers.

Benjy would have frowned every time she ministered to him or made her life miserable if his mouth muscles worked. If he could speak he would have claimed that life wasn't worth living. He had nothing. No one. His wife, Sylvia, had passed to her reward as soon as they had moved to Florida. She had saddled him with a half-witted son who wasn't even his—or hers, for that matter. He had tried his level best to straighten the boy out. Now this. What thanks did he get? Marty had dumped him in this godforsaken home and trotted off to New York City.

The son had been Sylvia's idea. She wanted a son and heir, and they couldn't have children. She said someday the boy would take over their grocery store in the Bronx. But, no, the ingrate wanted something else. The grocery store wasn't good enough. He had to take a course in computers. They had made a whopper of a mistake, as far as Benjy was concerned. Years ago, when the real mother came banging on their door begging to have her son back, they should have handed the kid over. For free.

"Now I got time for my favorite baby," Annie was saying. She dragged a chair to his bedside and reached into the pocket of her uniform. "Two letters from your son. Came almost together and ain't that nice?"

Benjy hated the little bastard. He blinked his eyes—twice. But Annie didn't notice. She continued her recitation.

"Every month he sends a check to keep you here." There was nothing for little extras, but then there was nothing Benjamin Loomus needed. "Your son writes that it's spring . . . and the snow has gone away . . . oh, and he had a date with a redhead." Benjy moaned inwardly. He wasn't starting that again. That's where all the trouble had begun. "I guess they hit it off real well . . . and looky here, Benjy, he says, 'Remember in eighth grade when I was chasing that little redhead, what was her name?' " Louise Suzanne Richer, Benjy supplied silently. " 'and I got in all that trouble at school.' " Raped that girl, you damn fool, how could I forget? You weren't even thirteen. " 'Even when her family moved away, after the incident, I wrote her every day. Then the post office returned the letters with an address unknown stamped on it.' " They had to move away because the little girl was too humiliated to arrest you, and you were too young to be taken seriously. " 'Do you think, Benjy, that they moved away because I liked her too much?' " Annie looked up. "Hmmm, your son sure is a romantic at heart."

Benjy blinked two quick no's, but she didn't see him.

"Oh, and he says he'll be down real soon to see you." Who cares, thought Benjy, and why couldn't she just read the letters to him without the constant analysis and commentary? He wasn't going to come down to Florida. Marty never spent money.

"Now, here's another letter, Mr. Loomus."

Who cares? Use it for toilet paper, he railed at her silently.

One of the other nurses was calling Annie. She looked at the huge clock on the wall. It was getting late. She promised she'd relieve another nurse during her break. Quickly, she scanned the letter, filtering out what she thought the poor baby didn't need to hear. "He says he called to see how you were. Now ain't that kind?" In silence, she skipped to the end of the letter. Then she said, "My, my, your son sure is partial to redheads, Mr. Loomus. He says he's a lady killer, and that he wants to make you proud of him."

Benjy stared without blinking as she got up. Still in his line of vision, she tossed the two letters into a wastebasket and walked into the hall. She certainly wasn't going to tell the poor man what she really thought: that on top of all his other problems, his son was weird.

Benjy lay there staring straight ahead. A lady killer? That didn't sound like Marty. Marty was always afraid of females. Except for that time when he raped that little redheaded girl.

With hat in hand, he walked through the doors of the Twentieth Precinct. To his right were potted plants and a memorial plaque honoring officers who had died. Everywhere posters proclaimed community activities. The wall tiles were Halloween colors: pumpkin, black, red-orange. To his left was a huge room with a long desk. He knew from watching movies that this was where they brought criminals to be booked. In fact, a teenage hood, his wrists shackled behind him, was being led in there now.

As the man entered the precinct room, a policewoman asked, "Can I help you?"

"I have some information you want," he said out of the side of his mouth.

The officer gave him the once-over. They got a lot of loonies in this neighborhood, but he didn't look like one. She saw a squat man with a balding head and hair that spurted out like fringe over his ears. He was twisting his cap in his hands.

"The Lonely Hearts Killer. I saw his picture on the television. I know who he is."

"Oh," she said, "that's upstairs. The task force for that case is on the third floor. Look. Take the elevator over there and go on up."

By the time the elevator opened on the third floor, the task force had been alerted that a man was coming up. As Ronald Tischler, day clerk at one of the sleaziest hotels in New York City, walked through the door, every eye appraised him. Every muscle tensed to reach for a gun in case there was trouble.

Ronald approached the first desk. "I saw that man on television. The one you're looking for. The blond with the curls. Only he ain't curlied anymore, so you're looking for the wrong man."

Detective George Yablonsky stared at the man in front of his desk. "Sit down, Mr. . . ."

"Tischler. Ronald Tischler. I'm the clerk during the day for the Roy, I mean, Royal Arms Hotel. This man stayed at our hotel. He looked like the picture on television. Only when he checked out, he looked like a different person. I didn't even know who he was. You know why?"

Detective Yablonsky shook his head, mesmerized.

"Because he knew he was wanted, that's why. Sure, I read detective stories, I watch TV. He shaved off all his hair and then he didn't have curls. He didn't look like the suspect. Forget the blond curls. Look for . . . bald. As in Telly Savalas and Yul Brynner, know what I mean?"

"What's his name? What name did he sign in at the hotel?"

"Theodore Roosevelt."

Again Detective Yablonsky stared at the man, discerning whether he was a fruitcake or not. Ronald Tischler sensed this. He hastened to explain. "Obviously, it was an alias. Listen, that hotel, we don't care if they register as King Kong as long as they pay for the room. Hookers dignify it, really."

Yablonsky leaned forward. "Just exactly when did this man check out? Where did he go? Did he leave a forwarding address?"

"A forwarding address? Listen, you think anyone in that hotel gets a letter? They don't stay long enough. Besides, most of them, I don't think, can read."

"How long did *this* man stay at the hotel?"

"I don't know exactly, but you can look at the books. I only know that he left the day the murderer's picture was shown on television." Ronald Tischler wiped some moisture from his upper lip. "Earlier in the day he left. Without his hair. And" —he pulled something out of his pocket—"this is what he used to shave his head. A maid found it in his room."

It was difficult persuading Ronald Tischler to leave. He seemed to be expecting something more. But he agreed to come in for an ID if they needed him. Yablonsky examined the razor, realizing the fingerprints were probably totally obliterated by now. Captain Fazio should know about this. He glanced around. Everyone was out in teams to interview men who wrote letters answering personal ads, and to talk to the families of the girls. Someone had phoned in to state that they had spotted a redhead in a bar the night of the second woman's murder. That was Debbie Greene. Moskowitz had gone to interview the waitress who thought she had seen her.

Fazio was off-duty and probably at home. Yablonsky calculated that this would be a good time to score points. He never thought of himself as just another cop. No, he had his sights set high. A big career in the department. All the way to the top. This task force would be a starting point. Captain Fazio liked him. He dialed Fazio's home in Brooklyn, confident he was justified, positive that here was something solid.

"Hello?" A woman's voice. Yablonsky figured it

was Mrs. Fazio. The captain was known as a family man.

"Listen this is a . . ." He wanted to say emergency, but Yablonsky was a man who chose his words carefully. "This is a detective from the task force calling. Is the captain home? Something important has come up."

"I'll get him."

Captain Fazio was on the phone immediately. Yablonsky identified himself first, then gave the details.

"The clerk says the man was a real weirdo, kept to himself, didn't have a job, just a drifter. Thought I'd send a couple of men to the hotel, then cover Times Square. Maybe he moved to another flophouse."

Fazio ignored the fact that Yablonsky was subtly taking over. This was their first real lead. "Yeah," he said. "Send as many men as you need into the Times Square area. Good work, Yablonsky."

Frank Fazio sat down with the cold beer and turkey sandwich his wife had brought him. His mind was spinning. The thought of those young women lying naked, their lives snuffed out because of another one of those twisted maniacs, was enough to cool his appetite. One more murder and this would be a sensation, though. The commissioner would expand the task force. The dailies would sensationalize it. The mayor might even use persuasion to stop publications from running those ads. He took a swig of beer and bit into his sandwich. This might be the biggest case of his career. And all because he had had a hunch. Tomorrow he was off, but he'd go to Times Square with the men and work like any other cop. Every minute counted in finding this man and stopping him from taking another woman's life.

CHAPTER NINE

Between Friday and Saturday morning, twenty men had been added to the task force, code-named Valentine. Early on Saturday, a brisk, blustery morning, four teams of officers and detectives penetrated Times Square. They passed pizzerias, souvlaki stands, porno houses and peep shows, drunks and old ladies rummaging through garbage on the curb. The morning after the tricks had been turned and the neon lights had blazed, the street was sleeping late.

Somewhere in the City, in another flophouse, in a furnished room or on a park bench, was their man. No one believed that he had the wherewithal to get out of town, but they were also checking trains and buses. Later, much later, if need be, they would go to the airports. Fazio was giving the orders now, and he believed this man was scared. Very scared. He was probably in a similar hotel in this vicinity because he didn't have much money.

Armed with photos and the police artist's revised sketch, the teams would canvass the City until someone recognized the face.

Yablonsky and his partner approached yet another seedy-looking hotel that resembled all the others. Wearily, they walked in the doorway.

A man behind the ubiquitous front desk looked up. "Can I help you?"

Yablonsky showed his ID for the hundredth time,

or so it seemed. "We're detectives," he said when the impact of his shield didn't register.

The clerk nodded. This one's hair was white, he had steel-framed glasses, and one of his suspenders was slipping off his shoulder.

Yablonsky dug out the glossy picture of the suspect with a full head of curly blond hair once again. The man pressed his glasses closer to his nose and looked at the photograph respectfully. Finally, he said, "Nope. Never seen him around this hotel."

"What about this man?" The other detective, his partner, Noonan, presented the police sketch of the same man but with no hair. Noonan noticed that the sketch was growing a little ragged around the edges.

The man nodded. Yablonsky, his excitement mounting, was about to ask questions when the desk phone rang. The clerk explained, somewhat laboriously, what the rates were and cautioned the caller that it "ain't the St. Moritz, you know." Yablonsky exchanged impatient glances with Noonan. Click.

"About the picture . . ."

The clerk nodded.

"Then you know the man with the shaved head?"

The clerk nodded. "Nope, ain't never saw him neither."

"Are you sure?" Yablonsky said, controlling his anger.

The man nodded.

Yablonsky stood there, firmly planted on the threadbare carpet. Damn it, the man kept nodding. Maybe he knew something and was holding back. Yablonsky drew Noonan aside. "But he keeps nodding," he whispered.

"Forget it. Maybe he has a nervous tic. I've seen that before. He's an old man."

"Shit! This is the closest we've been."

"We need a break," Noonan said as Yablonsky looked hopefully behind, only to find the clerk still nodding at some papers on his desk.

* * *

The waitress was applying iridescent pink polish to her toenails. Her name was Sally, and when she wasn't waiting table at Jimmy's, she was auditioning for singing and dancing parts.

"You see, Detective Moskowitz, I take acting lessons at Herbert Berghof Studios, so I'm very observant. I would know exactly the people you're talking about, except you have no idea what a mob scene it's like at that place on weekend nights. The redhead I remember. She stands out; she had been there before. But the guy with her. There must have been someone, but I draw a blank."

Moskowitz, now off-duty, hadn't stopped at the precinct first, so he didn't have the artist's sketch depicting the suspect with no hair. He showed Sally the old picture, since, presumably, that's how she would have seen him.

"Yeah, yeah," she said, puckering her lips and creasing her forehead. "I've seen that picture in the dailies. Yeah, could have been him. Sure. But it seems to me, now that I think of it, blond curly hair would have left its mark. See, that's distinctive. I would even have registered that it was a colorful table. A redhead and a blond, know what I mean? Are you sure she was with a man?"

"She was murdered that evening," Moskowitz explained. He was wondering how much a busy waitress could observe, even if she did have the total recall she boasted.

"Listen, it's horrible," she said, shuddering. "I wish I could help you more, but like I said, the man she was with didn't leave an impression on me at all. I guess it could have been the guy in the picture. I mean, if you say so, but I think I would remember him. He looks like Harpo Marx."

"How busy is it on a weekend night?" Moskowitz asked.

"You wanna know how busy? Our instructions

from the boss are to get 'em in and get 'em out. Don't let anyone sit at a table too long. I'll tell you the truth. I saw her briefly. But the man she was with doesn't stand out at all. Blotto. Nothing. Like invisible."

The window was open about six inches, and the torn, dusty curtain billowed in the evening breeze. Krueger was staring up at the ceiling. His arms were crossed over his chest, his shoes were on, and he was lying flat on his back on the lumpy mattress. At night when it got dark and the lights of the City beamed like fireflies on an August night, red stripes would flash across his room from a blinking neon sign. He didn't mind.

Nevertheless, he would have to change hotels again. He felt he had been recognized, even though his habits were almost foolproof. He was virtually unknown to the day clerk; he snuck past the night clerk—only emerging after midnight and then usually to an all-night supermarket. He never, never made any noise in his room. If there were people in the corridor, he would wait for hours to go to the bathroom at the end of the hall.

Late last night he had crept out, hat on his head, wearing sunglasses. He had passed a newsstand, seen the headlines, and stopped, unable to move, or breathe. "SINGLES KILLER STRIKES AGAIN." Then there was his picture. His picture! He had burrowed his head in his jacket like a sleeping turtle. He noticed the caption under his face. "She wasn't really a redhead!" The temperature was in the mid-seventies that night, but as he bought a paper, he kept snuggled in his jacket.

Hugging the darkest corner of the streets and avoiding the lights, he arrived in the lobby, jacket collar pulled so high, he looked headless.

In his room he sat before the open window reading—partly from the dim desk lamp and partly from the blinking lights. Her name was Doreen, poor kid. Yes, he remembered her. He had worn his suit, and they had gone to a restaurant. She talked and he listened. Why did he have to kill her? Pounding his fists on the window ledge, he silently wept for the woman. Then he picked up his head. How could he have killed her? He had been holed up in this room all the time and never went anywhere except to buy cans of baked beans or Chef Boy-ar-dee.

But he *had* gone out with Doreen. Wasn't that some time ago, though? Now she was dead. Was this some kind of plot *they* had invented to trick him?

From now on he had to be even cagier. No more mistakes like the one involving the vendor who had sold him the newspaper. That man had seen him. Oh, everything was hopeless! If the police didn't find him, *they* would.

He scratched his head. Damn, it was starting to grow again. Thin ringlets of blond hair were sprouting on his scalp like weeds. And he had left his razor back at that hotel. He couldn't afford to buy another. Besides, someone might recognize him.

His stomach rumbled. His food supply was meager. Cold beans and spaghetti. Potato chips made him too thirsty, and they were too noisy to eat. He'd have to get a job soon because his money would run out. But he couldn't wear a hat to work. On the other hand, he would need money to buy a razor. If he told them he had ringworm, they wouldn't hire him. It was a mean, vicious circle.

Exhausted, he flopped facedown on the bed and buried his nose in the pillow. It scratched his cheek. He dreamt. He was sleeping on creamy satin pillowcases monogrammed with chocolate-brown silken threads. He used to rub his finger over the tiny, little bumps. Terrified, he awoke with a start. He looked around, forgetting where he was and not being able to remember his dream.

* * *

Walking down the steps of the hotel, Yablonsky and Noonan were arguing easily.

"C'mon, relax, let's have coffee," Noonan was saying.

"I say we break from the Times Square area and start branching up and down. Tenth Avenue. Let's go as far as that."

"You figuring on working all night?" Noonan asked, lighting a cigarette nervously.

"Yeah, if we have to. I think we should go up one street, say Fifty-fourth, and all the way down until we cover every hotel on every street from east to west."

Noonan choked on some smoke as he inhaled. "Good idea. Like to share it with the department? We're supposed to stay in Times Square."

"But we'll be working on our own time," Yablonsky said impatiently.

Jabbing the air with his cigarette, Noonan countered, "Oh, no, *you'll* work on your own time. I'll work off-duty if there's a good reason. But I need sleep. I'll be better to the department tomorrow if I sleep tonight." The man was trying to solve the whole case himself, Noonan thought. Wanted that collar, lusted after it. He found the lead, and he'll find the killer.

Yablonsky looked at his watch. They had been walking around all afternoon like rookies pounding a beat. Quitting time would be close to four.

"Suit yourself," Yablonsky said. "I'm off now and I'm off tomorrow, and I'm going to find this guy."

"Whadda ya mean . . . single-handedly?"

There was no answer. Yablonsky was already halfway down the street. Noonan stared at his back, shrugged, and headed for the car.

Most buildings leave out the thirteenth floor. The building on Fifty-seventh Street had included it. On this floor was the office of *The New York Review of*

Books, one of the original innovators of the personal ads. The offices were a potpourri of clutter. Walls were covered with posters, work orders, and clippings. Computers occupied space in almost every room. The men and women who worked at *The Review* weren't your average nine-to-five office people. They were special, and they knew it.

In the conference room, the classified ads editor, a woman with a cultivated voice, was conducting a meeting. With her were a young man from *The Village Voice* and a young woman from *New York* magazine. Here, then, were the Big Three in Manhattan personal ads. They were trying to reach an equitable decision.

Artie, the *Voice* man, was turning a pencil up and down rapidly. "The first killing was from an ad in *New York,* the second came from here, and the third from us." He looked thoughtfully at the two women on either side of him. "You know, I remember that lady, Doreen Stewart, and her continuous ad. She came in and placed them herself. Used to hang around." It was quiet for a few seconds while they silently convinced themselves that there was no reason to feel guilty.

"You know I've had a call from the mayor's office," said Louise, of *New York* magazine, "and those detectives are always buzzing around. They all want me to discontinue the personals."

"That's the point, Artie," agreed Regina, from *The Review.* "I think we have a moral obligation to stop running ads, refuse to run them. Don't give this killer an opportunity to strike again. Take away his weapon."

Louise nodded.

"I'm not sure," said Artie. "Anyone who doesn't want to answer the ad has the option. It's called freedom of choice, the First Amendment, remember? Freedom of the press?"

"The *Voice* would lose a lot of money if you stopped the personals," Regina said bluntly.

They were all silent for a moment until Louise commented, "We could take a vote."

"We already know the outcome," Regina replied. "Two to one. I would feel better if this were a unanimous decision."

Artie frowned. "I just don't appreciate being told what to do by someone I don't even know. Our paper is being controlled by this crazy Lonely Hearts Killer."

"I resent that name," Regina said. "It casts a bad light on personal ads."

Artie laughed and sputtered at the same time, then wiped his mouth. "A bad light? What do you think killings do?"

"Listen, Artie, that's my point," Louise said, leaning into the table earnestly. "If we pull out now, he won't be able to murder. If we stay, we'll look bad for a long time afterward. It's like products. After one person gets botulism, the public is afraid to eat that brand. I say we withdraw and come back when it's safe."

"Look," Regina said. "We're losing already. We hardly have any ads anymore. Our people pay almost a month ahead of time. They're already calling up and asking for refunds because they've reconsidered."

"And you're allowing that?" Artie asked.

Regina shrugged. "What can we do? The situation's out of control. Better to lose a little money than foster bad public relations."

"What about the men who run ads?" Artie asked.

"They're scared, too. It's like a panic," Regina said.

Artie flipped his pencil in the air. "Okay, then. I give up. We'll stop running ads as of tomorrow. And we'll publish a statement right on the front page."

"Good," said the women, almost in unison.

"No more ads," Regina said.

"Until the killer is caught," Louise said quickly.

Artie groaned. "Which won't be overnight. These things sometimes take months or years."

Regina stood up, and the meeting was over. "There are going to be a lot of disgruntled singles," said Artie.

"Yeah, but at least they'll be alive," Louise mumbled.

Martha studied her reflection in the mirror. Something was missing. Rummaging in her dresser drawer, she found a thin, reptile-looking belt. It worked! A perfect complement to the turtleneck jersey and the plaid skirt.

Her freshly washed light red hair was swept up over each ear with tortoiseshell combs. Again looking in the mirror, she slicked on a light tangerine lipstick and blotted her lips. She had told her aunt she was coming down with a virus. This was more fun than having greasy lo mein. And Bob had sounded like a dream come true. So soft-spoken. So gentlemanly and considerate.

Grabbing her raincoat and checking her bag for her keys, she slammed the door and double-locked the top. Almost skipping down the steps of the walkup, she hummed a tune from one of her madrigal records. Her hair flying behind her, she ran down the front steps of the apartment building—engulfed by the lovely spring evening. This was her favorite season. A time for rereading all her Eastern philosophy books. Spring meant rebirth.

Walking up to the restaurant and looking through a small cluster of people, she spotted the white carnation right off. Like something out of an historical romance, she thought. She pictured herself in a windblown skirt and a wide-brimmed hat held by a ribbon around her neck. She would fly through the heather to greet her lover, who would kiss her hand and give her a bouquet of white carnations.

"Hi," she said, approaching the man. "You must be Bob. I'm Martha."

Terry wandered aimlessly around her apartment. She was too exhausted to go out, too restless to stay in. A dozen times she fought the urge to go into the precinct and work. There was so much to be done. One minute away from her work, she felt, gave the murderer an edge.

Maybe Moskowitz was at the Two-oh. No, he was off. She turned on the radio, but it was too late for the news. No, the case was quiet. Someone would have called if there had been new developments. She paced around the living room restlessly. Now she could use a call from that guy—what was his name? Oh, yes, Don Phillips. What the hell, her timing always seemed to be off. She thought of her soon-to-be ex. Tonight was his birthday. She smiled again about his confusion. That was so like him. He might just be endearing if he weren't causing her such grief. Who was he celebrating with?

She thought again of the discrepancy between the number of letters the two dead women left behind and what others said they had received. That continually agitated Terry. Tomorrow she'd say something, have it followed up.

And there was that statement of Candice Klein's. What was it? Candice had talked to Debbie on the phone Wednesday night before she was murdered on Friday night. One day in between. How did she have time to write to the killer's box number and have him call back in one day? The blond man had a box number. He would have had to go and pick up her letter. Very strange. She'd have to tell them that, too. Yawning, she leaned back in her recliner and shut her eyes. There would be time. Might as well rest. The case was obviously quiet.

* * *

He gripped the edges of the bathroom sink and sobbed with joy. Lovely—oh, so exquisite! She had departed clutching his back as if he were a liferaft adrift in a turbulent sea. He thought for one ecstatic moment that he might stay awhile in her apartment. To stop time. But what was the use? Her soul had now risen, and all that remained would be her decaying body. But he could take his euphoria with him, hold on to it to savor.

Water. He was so thirsty, but he didn't want to bother with a glass. That meant more fingerprints to wipe off. Bending his head under the faucet, he ran water into his mouth, pretending to be under a bubbling brook in some green glade where his Princesses dwelt.

He used his handkerchief to wipe prints off the sink. Then he returned to the main room. His blond wig was secured, his letter was in his pocket, his glasses were on, and his hands were gloved. He slipped his briefcase into his Macy's shopping bag.

It was time for the ritual. He plucked his carnation from his lapel and tossed petals recklessly until they fell like snow. "She loves me, she loves me not, she loves me . . ." Lovely, fragile Martha with her cupid face. One leg was half in her black tights, and the other dangled over her high-rise bed. He walked over to her clenched fist and opened it gently. A tortoiseshell hair comb tumbled to the floor.

Blowing kisses, Marty whispered ardently, "Good night, Sweet Princess." This one had been special. But he couldn't let the others know. They might get jealous.

Looking quickly right and left, he confirmed that the hall was empty. He skipped lightly down the steps, imagining himself decked out in top hat, white tie, and tails—like Fred Astaire.

Still euphoric, he then noticed that the moon was full. A yellow balloon. He opened his mouth and inhaled the perfumed air of spring mixed with the garbagy smells of the street. Nothing like New York.

It was close to midnight. His wig itched, but he couldn't risk taking it off. Everything must be perfect. In a split second he knew everything wasn't. Something was missing. His flower was gone. He turned back, running, and then stopped. He rested the briefcase on his knee and opened it, frantically searching. He recalled putting it back in his lapel after the ritual. Maybe he had dropped it. On the steps? In her apartment? Did it drop somewhere where it could be found? He stood in the middle of the street panicking, not knowing what to do. He had dropped his flower.

A passerby gave him a strange look. He walked faster. So they'd find a little white, all-crushed-and-stepped-on carnation somewhere! So! It was only a flower. He had never read anything in the papers about his white carnation petals. How could they know from a flower? Anyway, the police were looking for some blond curlyhead. He stopped short. Then he snatched off the wig and hurriedly stuffed it into the briefcase. Mustn't get nervous, he reminded himself. Mustn't wear the blond wig. That's what they're looking for.

Walking slower now, he began to relax. Why was he worrying? Everything would work out. Eventually, they'd find their suspect, the guy in all the papers, and when they did, he'd be free. One day somebody was going to get wise to that. And then he could ask for anything he wanted. Even the moon.

CHAPTER TEN

It was ten A.M. when a grimy, exhausted Detective Yablonsky arrived in the lobby of the Globe Hotel on West Twenty-eighth Street. His breath was sour and his face unshaven. Officially, he was off-duty. This was the fifty-second hotel since he had left his partner. After every three interviews, he stopped for coffee. He was running on raw nervous energy and a caffeine high.

All the hotel lobbies and desks were a blur. All the little men who peered at him asking, "Room?" looked alike.

"Room?" the little man behind the desk asked.

Yablonsky pulled out his ID. Then he placed the photograph on the desk. "Ever see this man here?"

"Nope," the clerk replied. "Can't say that I have."

Yablonsky's right hand swooped up the photograph and, just as quickly, his left hand slapped the sketch on the desk. "What about this one?"

The clerk looked quickly from one to the other. "Are you kidding? That's the same guy. Wait a second, I'll ask."

He disappeared inside a room, and a disheveled man returned with him. "This is my brother," the first man said. Yablonsky looked at the tall, wiry man and the pudgy, squat clerk who had looked at the pictures. "He's the night clerk. I'm the day clerk. We own the hotel. He was catching a few winks on the cot in the back room."

The tall man rubbed his eyes and scrutinized both

the sketch and the photograph. "Hmmmm," he said, scratching his chin.

"Did you see this man check in?" Yablonsky pointed to the artist's sketch.

"Think so. Yeah." He turned to the wooden cubbyhole boxes. Yablonsky was afraid to breathe. This couldn't be it. He was so accustomed to uninterrupted disappointment.

"Key's out. I didn't see him leave, though. He wears a hat. He's probably up there now. Room 909. You a detective, huh? Well, we don't want no trouble. You want something from him? Get it quietly . . . he ain't no murderer or anything like that, is he?"

Yablonsky wasn't even listening. In one second his painful fatigue had lifted. He fumbled in his pocket for change. He picked out a quarter and ducked into one of the booths in the lobby. Thankful that the phone was in order, he dialed the Two-oh. He would never put this on the radio.

Waiting for someone to answer, he looked toward those elevators. He would be going up to the ninth floor soon. He had the man cornered. He would make this call and ask them to get a warrant. That would take about an hour.

Nine floors up, the man Yablonsky wanted rolled over in his sleep. Dreamless and peaceful sleep. He had abandoned Times Square and was thrilled to find at four in the morning that the window of this new room opened onto a residential street. There was even a tree encircled by a broken-down little fence. True—the medicine cabinet was hard to pull open, the furniture was sticky, and the room smelled of accumulated dust. But that little tree was growing just for him. It meant a lot. Because this would be his prison for a while.

Then the dream started. He was at home—a small boy with a Buster Brown haircut. She was there. She was wearing a white dress with a blue sash, and her long, straight blonde hair flew out behind her. He was chasing her down to the boat basin, and she was squealing. "I'll tell my governess!" But he knew she wouldn't. He wanted to kill her, and then she was all grown-up and her blonde hair became the blue sash, and it just kept unwinding. It was a blissful dream.

Within an hour, forty men were standing in the lobby of the tiny Globe Hotel. They were waiting for the warrant. One car was parked almost on the curb and threatened to knock over a fragile little tree encased in a rotting fence.

Officers carried radios at their ears; detectives had their guns at the ready; two paramedics waited in the lobby. But there was silence. When the warrant came, it was rushed in, passed from hand to hand with no ceremony. Carefully, Yablonsky strode to the elevator. It opened, and a resident walked out, his mouth open. He was advised to get out of the hotel fast. Yablonsky and another man rode up on the elevator. Other officers were climbing slowly up the stairs. Someone was coming out of Room 914 and was signaled by a detective to go back in his room.

Stealthily, guns drawn, Yablonsky and his backup man approached the door of Room 909. The elevator was bringing up two more men, guns poised, who would stay in the hall. The rest of the men were swarming up the steps like ants on a hill. Yablonsky rapped on the door.

"Police. We know you're in there. Open the door."

There was no sound from behind the door.

Yablonsky knocked again. "Police!"

"Maybe he went out, and they just didn't notice downstairs. Maybe he doesn't hand in his key."

Yablonsky knocked harder. He was feeling the exhaustion of this agonizing wait. He was also feeling fury. If the man wasn't in there and he saw all the cops in the lobby, forget it. A trickle of sweat rolled down the side of his face to his neck. His fist raised to knock again, and he whispered hoarsely, "I heard something. He's in there."

At the same time, someone commanded, "Break in." Yablonsky, in an explosion of anger, knocked the flimsy door off its hinges and, when it fell, walked over it.

"Oh, Jesus," he said. "Somebody get him before he kills himself."

The suspect was crouched on all fours on the windowsill, poised to jump into his beloved tree and too frightened to let go of his perch with his hands. When they invaded his room, his hands were covering his ears, his feet were wobbling, and he was screeching and sobbing at the same time.

The West Side had more than its share of restaurants and bakeries. This morning Terry double-parked her car with the motor running, ducked into Zabar's, and got a danish to go. As she drove up to the Two-oh, she noticed it was jammed with cars. More men must have been added to the task force.

In the lobby she was met by Reep the Creep. He gave her a dirty look and snarled, "You're going to get it, Lady Detective." Maybe she should say something about these threats of his. In her opinion, he was walking a thin line between sanity and insanity.

The third floor looked like a police convention. Groups of detectives and officers were clustered, deep in conversation. A thin film of smoke hung over the room like a droopy cloud. There was one thing wrong with the picture. Terry knew all the men, and they were on the task force. There were no new men added. She dropped her bag on the desk. She was no longer hungry. Something big had happened. And no one had bothered to call her.

She spotted Moskowitz. She didn't say anything.

As they tried to weave toward one another, her body language inquired: What? Where? When?

"They have a suspect," he answered. "The one whose picture we've got. He shaved his head." Moskowitz indicated Yablonsky, who was surrounded by detectives.

"He found him."

"Where?"

"In a cheap hotel."

"But how?"

Terry listened wide-eyed, to the explanation.

"Yablonsky, working off-duty, went a little further downtown, found the guy in the sketch, got a warrant, and picked him up. Nuttier than a fruitcake, but they all are."

"Why didn't someone tell me?" Terry asked icily.

"Don't get upset, Princess. There wasn't time. It all happened so fast."

"I'm not upset."

Moskowitz recognized that tone of voice. In a sense, he couldn't blame her. But if she were a man, no one would have called her. It wasn't her case anymore. It belonged to the task force, and everything was escalating. "Everyone's in there. The chief, even the commissioner. They're interrogating him now." His voice became low. "Listen, I don't like that schmuck, Yablonsky, any more than you do. But you've gotta admit that was a good piece of work."

"My hero," Terry muttered under her breath. Moskowitz didn't catch it. She had her own personal doubts now, as to whether the blond suspect was the one they wanted. Even though she had supplied the picture.

Terry went over to the table where the coffee maker was. She took a styrofoam cup from the stack. She put it under the spigot and got two sooty drops. "Anyone making more coffee?" she shouted to a room full of men. No one was listening to her. Okay, she'd make coffee. She picked up a bag of coffee and then put it down. Oh, no, she wouldn't. Let one of the goddamn men do it.

In a tiny room down the hall, the suspect sat with both hands pressed on the table. His eyes were wide, and he was staring over the heads of his interrogators. He refused to answer any questions.

Zone Captain Fazio was smoking a cigar. His raincoat was on. The commissioner, a sour-faced, mammoth man whispered, "Can't you say something? I'd at least like some answers before you dump him in Bellevue."

"Did you kill Laura Frank?" a detective asked for the third time. He might as well have been talking to the wall. Fazio watched the suspect very carefully. Maybe he was deaf. "Anyone know that sign language for the hearing-impaired?" he asked.

No one answered. One man left the room. He couldn't take it. Yablonsky, who had arrived for his triumph, only to suffer through this scene, was now aware that he had been up for twenty-four hours. The overhead lights were crackling in tiny swirls in his eyes; he had a sore throat; and he was suppressing an impulse to beat the man with no hair to a bloody pulp.

"That's enough," Fazio said of the current interrogator. "We won't get anything this way."

"Should we try force?" someone asked.

"Bring in a shrink?" someone else suggested.

"No. I have a better idea," Fazio said. "Is Detective Morrison on this morning?"

No one knew.

"I think she's here. I'm pretty sure I saw her," came a voice from the back of the room.

Fazio had a hunch. The man looked so pathetically helpless that maybe he would talk to a woman.

Maybe a woman's touch would get him to open up. It was worth a try.

Two minutes later, Terry found herself in the interrogation room, face-to-face with the formerly blond curly-haired man who might have raped and murdered three women.

The first thing she said was, "Are you hungry?" Her tone was warm and motherly.

The suspect nodded, looking at Terry slyly. Fazio smiled, and if his arm had been long enough, he'd have patted himself on the back. Terry began to feel better about this. She had obviously been brought in because it was her case. She was the catching detective.

"What would you like?" she asked sympathetically.

There was a hush in the room as the suspect spoke his first words. "Two slices of pizza, one with mushrooms and the other with pepperoni, and a 7-Up. Large."

Fingers snapped. A door slammed.

The man stared at Terry. He felt comfortable with this lady, though he wasn't sure why. Maybe her voice: It was friendly, accommodating.

At that very moment, a car with its siren on was racing to the nearest pizza parlor. The driver had orders to buy a whole pie and a six-pack of 7-Ups.

"What's your name?" she asked, as if they were meeting at a high-school social.

"Krueger," he replied through tight lips.

"How do you spell that?"

Ten detectives wrote the answer in their notebooks.

"And your last name?"

"I don't know."

"You forgot?"

"Uh-huh."

"So, Krueger"—her voice was warm but businesslike—"did you kill those women? Are you the man the police are looking for?"

Krueger No-name looked at the kind, beautiful lady, gazed at the ceiling, and did a poor imitation of a young Marlon Brando agonizing over the right word. Then he burst into tears.

It was a tough question. Which was the lesser of two evils? He had to be smart. Then he made his choice.

"So what if I did?"

"Did you?" Terry asked, carefully observing the man's body language.

"I did. I killed Laura Frank, Debbie Greene, and Doreen Stewart."

"Why?" Terry asked.

He rolled his eyes to the ceiling and shrugged.

In the back there was a whisper. "You know, he reminds me of Berkowitz—you know, Son of Sam. He couldn't care less."

"Did you hear voices?" Terry asked. Someone touched her lightly on the shoulder. "Save that for the shrinks." Terry recognized the voice of Captain Fazio.

"And what about the white carnation, Krueger?" Terry asked quickly, hoping to throw him.

"What about it?"

"What did you do with the white carnation?"

"I ate it," he said simply.

"Why did you—"

Fazio interrupted Terry. "Okay, get him his food and take him over to the hospital. Read him his rights. And do it very slowly. Not that he'll understand . . ."

The room started to empty. Terry stared long and hard at the thin, tall man who seemed so lost and lonely. His eyes lit up when they rushed in a whole pizza for him, but then, just as quickly, they became dull again. As the room emptied, Terry studied the man again and saw only a frightened boy where a murderer was supposed to be.

At the press conference later that day, the commissioner spoke into the cameras. "The man, known only as Krueger, seemingly a transient in our City, has confessed to killing Laura Frank, Debbie Greene, and Doreen Stewart."

Krueger had been taken to Bellevue Hospital with around-the-clock police protection. The task force would continue to interview witnesses and other suspects, and the department would not consider the case fully closed until the loose ends had been tied up and further proof could be gathered.

Captain Frank Fazio smiled into the cameras. No one could accuse him of doing a half-ass job. The man was not proven guilty yet, and he would not let the media get carried away. The task force would still be working, though with reduced staff, to check and double-check. The fact that he personally believed this man to be the killer wouldn't affect the continuing investigation.

Terry watched from the steps as a mob of newspaper and television reporters descended upon the men. When she could get within earshot of Fazio, she tapped him on the shoulder.

"Wonderful job you did there, Morrison. We couldn't get him to talk at all. It needed a woman."

"Captain, I was wondering if we could talk about the case. I think there are some questions you ought to ask this man. Like the letters, captain. With two women there is this discrepancy on the letters. . . ."

"Later, Morrison. You'll stay on the task force. Everything will be cleaned up."

She could see that his attention span had lapsed. The chief was motioning for Fazio to come over. Terry's mouth dropped open. At the chief's side was the mayor. She didn't need a psychic to tell her what was in everyone's mind. The case was almost completely closed. Suddenly, the male voices became unbearably repugnant, and the cigar and pipe smoke began to burn her nostrils and make her eyes water. She was left out of the club again.

Everyone believed Krueger Somebody had raped and suffocated three attractive single women who had run personal ads. Maybe he had. But she wasn't buying it. All of her intuition said that man couldn't kill a fly.

Martha's aunt clutched the big pot firmly with one hand and rang the street-level door bell with the other. There was no answer. A woman holding the cumbersome Sunday *Times* under one arm shifted her weight and inserted a key in the front door.

Martha's aunt slid in before the door slammed shut.

The woman turned. "My niece lives here," she said sweetly, by way of explanation. The woman said nothing.

Martha's aunt was appalled. Such security. She wasn't sure it was safe for Martha to live here. Two o'clock and Martha hadn't answered her phone all morning. Well, she was good and worried, her the only relative Martha had in New York. Made some nice chicken soup for her. Couldn't blame her for not answering her downstairs buzzer. One never could tell who was ringing, and unless you expected someone, it was best not to answer. How many times had she told Martha that, and yet, ironically, today, she needed Martha to buzz her in.

Walking up five flights was no great joy. Her soup was sloshing in the pot, and she had to stop and rest at every landing. When she finally reached Martha's door, she gingerly set her big pot of cold soup on the floor and knocked once. Then twice. Nothing. She put her ear to the door. No noise. She might be sleeping, poor dear. Such a glorious day; this was no time to be a slugabed. Looking cautiously first to one side of the long hall and then to the other, the old woman took off her shoe and banged on the door. Simultaneously, she called, sotto voce, "Martha? Are you there?"

A door opened down the hall, and a head peeped out. Martha's aunt replaced her shoe, picked up her soup, and walked toward the stairs.

The old lady figured she would just keep phoning her niece. After all, maybe she just went for a stroll in Riverside Park. She wouldn't be with a young man, would she? No, Martha kept to herself. If she went out with men, she wouldn't spend her Saturday nights eating Chinese food with her old aunt.

The floor where the task force was housed looked liked the day after a hurricane. White styrofoam coffee cups were everywhere. Ashtrays had been forgotten in the commotion. A few detectives were still on duty, following up on the aftermath of the investigation.

Terry was sitting at her desk. Her hand shielded the note pad she was writing in. She had been making notes but suddenly changed to idle sketching.

She had a sixth sense about people creeping up behind her.

"Nice depiction of a carnation," the voice said. "I always said you were a talented artist." She covered the paper with her arm and turned around sharply.

"What are you doing here?"

"Oh, c'mon, Terry," Detective Bob Morrison chided, "knock it off. Why aren't you out celebrating with the others?"

Terry felt like snarling a quick "None of your business," but she held her tongue. She had been caught at her most vulnerable.

"Listen, let me take you out to dinner or buy you a drink. Why not?"

"Because I have work to do."

"Oh, Terry, why do this to yourself? Give yourself a break. Everyone's loaded. They won't know you stopped to celebrate."

"You know I can't do that, Bob," she said wearily. "With the men you wouldn't notice it, but I'm the only woman homicide detective on this task force. I can't do it. Besides, I do have work to do and I don't want to drink and I'm not hungry."

Bob cocked his head. "Bullshit. I know you. Something's wrong. Somebody else got the collar, that's it. Your ego couldn't take the trouncing. Your little case was pulled out from under you." Bob moved to the front of her desk and stood over her. "Or is it some other reason you're holding down the fort like this? I know you too well, Theresa Morrison."

She said nothing.

He slapped his hand on the metal desk. "You think he's not a valid suspect."

Bob noticed one side of her mouth curve slightly upward. And then he knew. He was right.

She looked at him and knew what he was thinking. That she was a tremendous egotist. Just like him. She really felt that the wrong man had been nabbed, and she was frightened. Frightened for the next victim if she was right. But she wouldn't explain this to Bob. Before she might have. Not now. He would use it against her. He wasn't her best friend anymore.

"Terry, can't we talk this over?"

She turned away, offended. She thought he meant the case. Bob Morrison meant their relationship. He wanted to tell her he had made mistakes and he wanted to change. But what was the use? Suddenly, he was tired of fighting her resistance. Terry guarded her notebook, thinking he might have seen her notes.

She heard him walk away without a word. She wanted to stop him but couldn't. What she had planned was too dangerous to share with anyone.

Bob punched the elevator button angrily. What further proof did he need that she was totally turned off by him? She ran away from him that night. She turned him away today. She wouldn't even have a drink with him. Hands in his pockets, he stepped into the elevator. Maybe he should give up.

Terry continued her sketch of the carnation. That bothered her. They were going to leave it at that. Just a schizo response, such as, "I ate it," and they would dismiss it until a battery of shrinks could rewire his head and get some real answers. She couldn't let it pass. Then she noticed that her drawing was smudged and watery. And she realized a tear had dropped on her paper. Why did he have to keep popping up at the wrong times? Damn you, Bob Morrison, she whispered fervently.

At ten after six the door bell rang. Phyllis was standing in front of her television set, a big wooden spoon in her hand. She went to the door and opened it to Marty, who was smiling shyly, almost apologetically. He had his hands clasped behind his back, and for a silly second, Phyllis thought he had brought her flowers or something. But then he unclasped them, and they hung at his sides. Marty would never spend money unnecessarily. He was assured of getting his free dinner and staying the night.

"We're having Cornish hens," she said simply.

Marty stepped in and took off his coat. He inhaled the rich, homey cooking smells that filled the little apartment. Phyllis, when she was fat, would have made a good mother. Now that she had trimmed down, it wouldn't work. He had been wise to return the ring. All that unpleasantness had happened for the best. Besides, she would find out about the others and nag him to be faithful to her.

"Look," Phyllis said. He joined her in front of the small TV. Marty saw a man, his back to camera, handcuffed, being led away by a circle of police officers. The announcer was saying that the Lonely Hearts slayings appeared to be over with the capture of this suspect and that all the singles of the City could breathe easier now.

Phyllis smiled to herself because she had been a bit frightened to call all the men who had written responses to her ad.

Marty smiled, too, because soon they would discover Martha with the laughing eyes. He was the only person who knew the truth besides the blond-haired suspect. They had the wrong man.

"Which salad dressing?"

Marty spun around. "Huh?"

"Oil and vinegar, Russian, or blue cheese?"

Marty didn't answer immediately.

"Hey, you okay?"

"Yeah, sure. Just thinking of something else, that's all." He smiled broadly at her. She watched the boyish grin dimple his cheeks and light up his whole face. When he smiled like that, which wasn't often, he was almost attractive.

"Oil and vinegar," he said.

Phyllis was tossing fresh-cooked string beans with a pat of diet margarine. "Hey, any luck yet, Marty?"

Again he stared at her, hardly comprehending, but her back was to him and she didn't notice his confusion. Luck? What luck? She didn't know anything.

But of course.

"Oh, that," he said. He shouldn't have told her. "Uh, no, it's hard to trace someone like that."

Phyllis added a sprinkle of croutons to the salad.

"Someone like that. Really, Marty. Searching for your natural mother is serious. Nobody yet, huh?"

"Nope," he said.

It sounded like an impossible job and so pathetic, too. Phyllis knew where her real mother was, and there were times she wished it were the other way around. She wished she had been adopted like Marty.

Turning off the oven and pulling out two golden-brown hens, she said optimistically, "Well, I'm glad this killing business is over." Her back was still to him.

"Now you see how dangerous it is to meet strangers," he said.

"I suppose you're right," she answered. Tomorrow night she would start calling again.

The office had emptied. Terry sat alone with half a tuna-fish sandwich still in a brown bag. She was making a map of the City with the help of the Yellow Pages. She had turned to the listing of florists. She would stop in shop after shop and inquire if any man had bought a white carnation. If Yablonsky could do something off-duty, so could she. And she knew she was on the side of justice. He had just been a slave to his drive.

She had even bought a white carnation herself. It didn't shed easily. You had to rip off each petal one by one. So whoever had left the white petals had deliberately torn them off. Odd. And with the third murder—nothing. The crime scene unit, with their vacuums, hadn't picked up any petals at all.

And the missing letters. Wasn't it just possible that the killer was taking the letters? She yanked the other half of the sandwich out of the bag. When she became preoccupied like this, she forgot to eat, and she lost track of the time.

Time. She looked up. It was one o'clock in the

morning. No wonder nobody was around. Yes, she was going into business for herself. Off-duty. No one would know. Did Yablonsky ask permission when he worked after hours? Hell, no.

It was dark and still when she left the precinct house. There were only a few cars parked by the side of the building. As she pulled out of the driveway and drove down the street, she didn't notice that a car, careful to keep a distance, was following her.

CHAPTER ELEVEN

Those who were off-duty made it a point to attend the special meeting Fazio had called for seven A.M. Monday. Captain Fazio was discussing the case, the suspect, and the work that still needed to be performed by the task force.

Two-thirds of the force would be trimmed off like excess fat and sent back to their departments where they were sorely missed. Terry tried to stifle a yawn when she learned she would still be assigned to it. Captain Fazio had recognized her as the catching detective, but then turned her into a cleaning woman. Yes, she would take care of the shitwork on this case, gladly. It would help her with her own private investigation.

"We need all the witnesses who testified that they saw the suspect," Fazio was saying, reading from a list. "That's number one. Have them come down. Get ahold of a blond wig like the one he wears in the picture. . . ."

Terry's mind clicked off. It was an old trick of hers, sleeping while awake. She tuned in fast when Fazio said, "And, Morrison, I want every one of the men interviewed who wrote letters and haven't been talked to." Terry groaned inwardly, but her face remained impassive.

"Wait, you'd better not go alone," Fazio continued. "Franzoni!" He indicated an overweight, balding detective with thick lips. "You and Morrison are partners. Clean up those loose ends. Any man who sounds the least bit suspicious or *off* in any way, bring him in." It was taken for granted that during a manhunt you collected a spiderweb of assorted criminals wanted for other crimes. You also got a lot of nut jobs that were better off the streets for a while.

Terry rose to go and met the dark eyes of Detective Yablonsky. He was not looking into her face. He was staring midway between her collar and her belt. She did not look away or look down or blush, she just stood up. Next it would be the familiar put-down jokes. He was a killer, that one. Though she hated herself for it, she knew she would enjoy seeing him fall. She would absolutely adore it. She grabbed her raincoat and joined her drab partner for a boring day's work on a dull investigation.

"Stop the presses!" Artie yelled. It was early morning, and the cup of wake-up coffee he had been drinking had spilled all over the front page of the *Daily News*. "LONELY HEARTS KILLER BROKEN." Someone else had brought in a *Post*. There were squeals of joy over the headline: "GIRLS, IT'S SAFE TO RUN ADS AGAIN. KILLER FOUND."

Uptown on Fifty-seventh Street, all the staffers of *The New York Review of Books* were gathered in the tiny cluttered room where the ads were taken. Someone raised a coffee mug in a toast. Through the clamor, one could hear a steady drone issuing from a man with a phone to his ear. "SWF . . . comma, attractive . . . comma, sometimes stunning . . . comma, bubbly . . . comma, sometimes effervescent . . . yes, that's seven words so far, miss, yes . . ."

In the midtown area near Second Avenue, *New York* magazine's phones were busy. Calls were taken and promises were being made to call back. "What is the expiration date on your Visa card?" "Can you call back in about an hour? There's no one free to take your ad." "No, I don't think you can use *that* word in an ad."

One woman staffer leaned over and confided to another, "I still wouldn't run an ad. It happened once and it could happen again."

In an office in an elegant high-rise building, two young women were talking about the captured man.

"He just wasn't that cute. I certainly wouldn't have dated him."

"No? I think with his hair he was very attractive. And you know, when they're crazy, they can be charming. Like Dr. Jekyll and Mr. Hyde."

The other young woman shuddered involuntarily. "I'm glad I'm still with my parents, even though they don't live in the City. It's not only cheaper but safer that way."

On West Twenty-third Street, a construction worker with a bright yellow hard hat drew a sleeve across his gritty forehead. "And all the time I figured you for the killer, Scanlon." The other man looked up from his newspaper. "Oh, yeah, Numb-Nuts, well, I don't have to answer an ad for it."

And almost directly across town in a room all to himself, Krueger sat talking to a serious young man with horn-rimmed glasses and a spic-and-span white coat.

The young doctor stared at Krueger, fascinated. He had listened to many criminals who had stopped at Bellevue, but not many were like Krueger. He was trying to probe and find just what the last name was. He knew, of course, that this was a case of amnesia, but there was something else. He kept revealing so many moods, so many sides to his personality. Captivating. The man was positively captivating.

Krueger leaned in. "You know, I have a secret I'm not telling."

"I see," said the psychiatrist. "And how do you feel about that?"

* * *

When her scream ricocheted down the hallway, the doors flew open as tenants rushed to help. Chicken soup flowed in rivulets over the carpet and inched its way across the floor. Martha's aunt sagged, and as a crowd gathered, someone rushed to support her.

There were two patrolmen, the super, and the landlord of the building, all of whom had to supervise as Martha's aunt had ordered the lock broken after repeated attempts to reach her niece. A neighbor gave the woman a glass of water, but devoid of strength, she couldn't manage to hold the glass. It toppled from her hand and crashed to the floor. That was when the patrolmen ordered everyone out.

Everyone moved away from the body that was unbearable to look at. At two o'clock on Monday afternoon, Martha Wychzensky resembled something from a horror movie. She was lying naked, half-off, half-on the bed. Her mouth was open in protest; her eyes were cold marbles. The breeze from an open window had blown the fringed pillow onto her bare breast, where it lay seductively draped.

Terry sat in her car with her long list and scratched off another name. She was off-duty, and it was close to five o'clock. She was going on a hunch that the killer was from Manhattan, mainly because he didn't strike in other boroughs or in the suburbs. And if he bought his carnation in the suburbs and brought it in with him, it might be a little risky, or the flower would wilt. And, she assumed, there were more singles in Manhattan who were likely to answer the ads. Not brilliant reasoning but the best she could do when she had nothing to work with. It was an impossible chore. You needed a whole task force to canvass all the florists in the Yellow Pages.

Next she would visit the florist across the street on

Lexington Avenue. Did he or she remember selling one white carnation to someone? A man, maybe?

The sales clerk in the last florist shop had said, "Certainly we sell white carnations. Every day. Just last week we outfitted a whole wedding party. Happens all the time. One of the ushers picks them up usually." Terrific. And the florist shop before that had a fussy proprietor who wanted to help but couldn't remember what he had for lunch that day.

Two cars behind Terry on the other side of the street, a man sat grinning from ear to ear. It was a good idea to follow her. Oh, yes, he came up with good ideas.

She was visiting florists, and he knew she was off-duty. Well, he'd just sit and bide his time until she did something revealing or went somewhere else. But Lenny Reep knew what she was doing. She was continuing to investigate that case after hours—because she knew something, and whatever she knew had to do with flowers. He would find out. This must be what the department was holding back. There was always something they withheld from reporters so that they could maintain exclusive information. When he had told Terry he knew her secret, he was bluffing—hoping she'd slip. Now maybe she would.

Terry, Lenny Reep observed, was already coming out of the florist shop on Lexington. Face half-buried in a newspaper, Lenny Reep noticed that she was now sporting a flower on her blazer. Looked like a white carnation.

She was getting into her car. He stayed behind his newspaper with two holes pricked through it so he could see. He'd have to wait a second before he pulled out of his space and continued to follow her. No use her catching on. This was a shrewd lady, and she might just try to outfox him.

Terry was on her way to Candice Klein's apartment, the woman she had interviewed just less than ten days ago. She parked her car, unaware that as she stopped, a car drove slowly around the block and then parked down the street. She got out of her car, went into the apartment building, and buzzed.

It was a different Candice who answered the door. No mourning clothes. Terry noticed the bright blue knit dress and gold slippers. Music was playing, and there was a vase of marigolds on the coffee table.

"Seems like just yesterday," Candice said, her accent unmistakably Brooklyn in origin. "Come on in."

Terry didn't take out her notebook. She would remember whatever Candice had to say. Besides, it might inhibit the young woman.

"I thought they caught the killer." Candice lit a cigarette and passed Terry an ashtray. "The little twerp. I hate to tell you what I'd like to do to him. But he's bonkers, funny-farm material, what can you do? He wouldn't know the difference, anyway. So what more do you want to know, Detective—"

"Call me Terry," she said conspiratorially. "I was wondering if you could recall the night when Debbie called you about those letters. You see, we only found twenty letters, and you said she got twenty-one."

"Oh, that again," said Candice. "Like I told you. She got a letter from a lawyer."

"And what else can you remember?" Terry asked softly.

"Well, I've been thinking about this. See, Debbie said he had thinning hair. I remember that. But then again, the man on television had almost no hair. I can't see Debbie going out with that kind of man. But then again, she didn't have a picture."

The man on television had blond curls, which he shaved off after he killed the women, noted Terry silently.

"Also, I remember Debbie's ad. The wording, I mean. It said she had red hair, and I think he said that he liked redheads. I just can't remember. Do you have the ad? One lady wasn't a redhead. I do remember reading that in the *Post*. She had brown hair."

Her hair was brown, but there was a definite red pigment. There was something odd with that one. She'd have to check it out, Terry mused.

"I guess, though, he dug redheads," she said, her mouth curling into a snarl.

"Yeah," Terry agreed. What was the old saying? Opposites attract. When his hair grew out, it would be blond. Why did he dig redheads? she wondered.

Terry suddenly had one of her headaches that was not going to be cured by two aspirin. She stubbed out her cigarette and leaned forward to be closer to Candice.

"Just between us, if there were a Bible, would you swear to what you just said?" God, she couldn't believe how unprofessional that sounded, but she had to improvise under the circumstances. "That there was a letter from a lawyer and that he had thinning hair and was her date for the night?"

Candice gave Terry a severe look. "Debbie was my dearest friend in the world," she said in a choked voice. Then she jumped up and ran to the bookshelf section of the wall unit. She came back with a Bible, closed her eyes, and put her hand on top of it. "I swear I'm the telling the truth," she whispered passionately.

At six o'clock, two detectives from the Two-oh's dwindling task force were sent out on a call. The call was outside the perimeters of the precinct, way up on One Hundred Sixteenth Street. As an ambulance pulled out, the medical examiner drove into a parking space.

Crowded into the apartment were three men from the crime scene unit, two detectives, the landlord, the medical examiner, the super, and, of course, one very naked dead woman. The pillow with the tassels had been removed and was about to be dusted. The woman's eyelids had been shut, and the crime scene unit had found the white petals.

"Been dead over twenty-four hours," the medical examiner said.

A detective shooed the landlord and the super out the door and peered into the hall. People were standing and talking, some were smoking, all were horrified, but none wanted to leave. The detective shut the door on the noise.

Suddenly, his eyes fell on a crumpled tissue on the floor. He walked toward it. No, it only looked like a tissue. He reached down and picked it up, then dropped it like a hot coal.

The second detective joined him. Everyone stared at the floor. There on the carpeting lay a white carnation.

"Put it in a bag for fingerprinting," one of the men said.

"If you don't get the florist's fingerprints," said another.

Or mine, thought the embarrassed detective.

At six-thirty, Marty had just gotten home from work. He had walked crosstown on Fiftieth Street to the IRT subway, then taken the local train downtown and home. Walking through the quaint little side streets, he passed small town houses that were historical landmarks. He always took the same way home, never varied. He could probably get to his rent-controlled studio on West Fourth Street blindfolded.

The tiny Tensor lamp was still shining on his table and the arm of his threadworn couch. Stacked high on an end table were his precious magazines and newspapers with their telltale red hearts. He had once told Phyllis that he lived in a typical bachelor apartment. She seemed satisfied never to enter it.

They used her bed. In fact, since he'd lived here, no one else had ever set foot in the apartment.

The window was open. He had no curtains, and the window was partly covered with a worn baby blanket. He began collecting sticky glasses and mildewed tuna-fish cans—not because he cared about cleaning up, but because he had to do something. Lately he didn't feel as if he really lived there. There was nothing to do at home anymore except answer the phone. All the action was outside. At home he heard those voices, pressing him, demanding that he kill again. Maybe if he could find his real mother, the voices would stop nagging him. His head began to throb, as it often did at home, and he pressed a fist to his forehead to relieve the pain.

Must think of something pleasant, he instructed himself. Then he remembered the idle talk at work. The women who manned the credit portholes had been discussing the capture of the killer. "Oh, yes, I would go out. Now that it's safe, I would run an ad," one woman said. But others disagreed. Most said they would not answer or run a personal ad for a long time and were even afraid to go into bars to meet men. Marty had enjoyed that interlude today, even though he pretended to ignore it. He had made people fear, just as he had always feared all of his life.

A shrill ringing filled the room. He was confused for a split second. Under some newspapers was the phone. At a service center, he had exchanged his old black phone for one that was fire-engine red. Now it was the hot line. Had he gotten lucky?

Or unlucky. It might be un-Fat Phyllis again. Or it might be a . . . wrong number. That possibility terrorized him. Strangers. He hated strangers invading his privacy. On the other hand, it might be the next Princess.

He sat on his couch.

"Hello? Is this Bob?"

"Uh, yes." He cleared aside three *Playboy* magazines, a yo-yo, and an opened box of chocolate chip cookies.

The voice on the other end suddenly speeded up and ascended an octave. He loved this part.

"You sent me a letter in answer to an ad I took out in the *Voice* and, um, I'm calling you."

He didn't answer yet. He was enjoying her insecurity and embarrassment.

"You are Bob, aren't you? You have thinning hair and you're trying to quit smoking and you like redheads. I have curly red hair."

"Oh, yes, I remember your ad now." Red hair. God, it drove him wild. Sylvia, his adopted mother, had had red hair. She didn't live long enough for it to turn white. Once he had snuck into the bathroom and saw the tight little red curls between her legs. He had been very young, but he remembered. She struck him for looking. Sylvia's eyebrows had been red, too. But she never let him get that close. Except when she was slapping him with the back of her hand for his own good.

The voice now seemed to slow down with relief. "Well, I picked you. You're a dermatologist, right? Should I call you Doctor Bob? I just love doctors. Where's your practice? Are you affiliated with a hospital?"

"I work in groups. Teams of doctors that go every day into depressed areas. I enjoy it."

"Where did you go to school?"

"In Switzerland, actually. I had a scholarship."

"Oh? How interesting. You must ski."

"Only in the winter. And you, what do you do? I don't even know your name."

"Oh, I'm sorry," the voice said. It was lower now and more relaxed. "Heather. Heather DeVito. My mother is Irish and my father's Italian. I'm a little of both."

"Heather. That's a pretty name. What do you do?"

"I'm a lawyer. A new one, actually. I just opened up my own practice in Brooklyn."

He was immediately on guard. "You live in Brooklyn?"

"No, I live in the East Seventies."

"Have you run any ads before, or is this your first?" he asked.

"Have you answered any ads before, or is this your first?" she countered.

He rolled back on the couch and laughed. Feeling an uncomfortable bulge, he reached behind him and discovered a half-eaten bologna sandwich. He threw it on the floor. "I like that," he said. "Answering a question with a question." He was progressing. He knew just what to say. As Marty, he would have clammed up. As Bob, he was a prize date. And they were his for life. For after life. For always.

"When would you like to go out?" he asked.

There was a pause. "Well, actually I thought we could meet in a restaurant or coffee shop, you know, just for a drink or a cup of coffee. Earlier in the day would be better, what with all those . . . oh, well, forget it—that's over now."

"I understand perfectly, but I'm also a gentleman. Hey, I'm a doctor, remember. Make it in the evening because of my schedule, huh? Why not?"

"Okay," she relented. "You sound nice."

"Tomorrow night? Are you busy?"

"Um, no, I don't think I am. I guess I'm free. . . ."

"Then tomorrow night it is. I won't take no for an answer." He wanted that euphoria so badly. The voices were driving him again. And this one would be a sweet victory. They would blame the last one on the blond veggie. Sure, he knew that. But this one—there was no question. It would throw the City into an uproar.

He'd have to write Benjy about this one. Someone must be reading the letters to him because he had left instructions. After all, he was paying all the bills. He was in control. He'd think up some clever clue to drive the old man out of his withered skin. Dear old Dad.

"I know a nice bar in the East Seventies," she was saying. "It's near Seventy-fifth on Third Avenue. A pub, actually. Forget the name. It's between a record store and a drugstore. You can't miss it."

"Okay, is seven o'clock okay?" he asked.

"Yeah, I guess so."

"Fine. See you there. Wait a second. How will you know me? Hey, I've got it. I'll be wearing a white carnation." Nowhere had the papers given away his little secret. They hadn't found his ritualistic petals. Lucky him. Because that was the best part. And Heather DeVito would now be added to his harem of Princesses.

Detective Ralph Ronzini rang the bell about six times that evening before he was buzzed back in. Taking the elevator downstairs, almost tripping over a tricycle, he knocked on an open door. A man in an undershirt answered. Detective Ronzini showed his shield to the super.

"More cops," said the man. "Ever since that Laura Frank murder, that's all I've seen. I can't tell you any more than I already have. We had trouble renting the apartment, but we finally unloaded it."

"No, I didn't come about that. It's Mrs. Dorothy Panachek. She was the woman who gave us an ID on the blond man. I keep ringing her bell and no one answers. I've been trying to get in touch with her. Do you know if she's away."

"Gone."

"I beg your pardon."

"Gone, I said. She packed up and left shortly after the murder. Said something about going to live with her daughter."

The detective got out his notebook and his pen. "Where did she move to?" he asked.

"Toronto."

The detective who had been primed to write down the address looked up into the man's face. "Toronto!" From inside came the sound of a TV news report. "Whereabouts in Toronto? How can we reach her?"

The man held up his hand signifying he didn't want to get involved. "Can't. She left no forwarding address that I know of. She said she didn't want to be bothered by this no more. Just said she was finally moving to Toronto to be with her daughter. And she was gone. Sold her furniture pretty fast, too. I bought a couch."

Detective Ronzini replaced his notebook and clipped his pen onto his pocket. He felt slightly nauseous. Forgetting to thank the super, he made his way toward the elevator and up and out of the dank basement. No one was going to like this newsflash. Mrs. Dorothy Panachek was their star witness, and there was no way in the world they could subpoena her in Toronto. Even if they could find out where she went.

Nine dirty, nearly empty, cardboard containers danced across Captain Fazio's desk like spots in front of his eyes. Some had an inch of muddy coffee, others were substitute ashtrays, and a few were crunched in the middle and lay on their sides. He was thinking of ordering out for more coffee.

The sound of the phone he had just slammed down buzzed in his ear. He drummed his fingers on the desk. The star witness gone. Just like that. He couldn't believe the news.

The doodles on his note pad were looking angrier and more grotesque as the day went on. The latest would have mesmerized a shrink. And that reminded him. He picked up the phone, dialed, and got an immediate answer.

"Dr. Winfield's office," a voice whined into the phone.

"Is he around?" Fazio asked, twisting a cigarette between his fingers.

"Whom should I say is calling?"

"Captain Frank Fazio. The New York Police Department."

The subtle change in voice, as always, was a source of amusement to him. This voice grew practically seductive when it recognized who he was.

"He's on his way to see Krueger now, captain. Can I take a message?"

"Tell the doctor that I'll want to arrange to have the suspect come down to the Twentieth for police interrogation if that's okay with Bellevue. And to let me know."

"I'll give him the message."

He hated to leave a message, but he had no other choice. You could never find a doctor when you wanted one.

Gripping the red-hot phone tightly, Marty dialed the next number on his list. It rang out his rejection over and over. Finally, he put the phone down softly. She wasn't home. He paced around the room.

Then he sat down on the couch and picked up the phone again. Then, dutifully, he began to dial again.

One ring, then two, and then a lady answered. His tongue felt dry, and his lips stuck together.

"Hello?"

Every time he did this, he momentarily lost his nerve. Yet it must be done. Again and again until he found her.

"This is Martin Robert Loomus. That's not really my name. I was adopted. The adoption agency gave me your name. Freeman. This is Mrs. Freeman, isn't it? And you live in Brooklyn?"

"Yeeeees."

"Well, are you the Mrs. Freeman who gave birth

in 1950 to a little boy?" A sob rose in his throat as it always did.

There was a harsh laugh for a reply. Then a sputter and the nasal, rather rough tones of a very ballsy lady saying not what he wanted her to say but, "Is this some kind of joke? Halloween was in the fall, boychik."

"I-I—only thought you might be the Mrs. Freeman who—"

"And you thought wrong." Again the merciless cackle. "Listen, sonny boy, in 1950 I had my hysterectomy. I'm not your mommy. I get all kinds of crazy phone calls, but this one takes the cake. You get off on this, sweetie-putz?"

Marty grimaced. Silent tears stung his cheeks; he brushed them away. Then he sucked his thumb, whimpering softly.

"No, this is legitimate," he said, gaining control, using the voice he used at work.

The woman's voice became softer. "So, this is how they do it. Listen, kid, take my advice. Count your blessings. Be happy with what you got. Don't go looking for happiness from a woman who's a stranger. You think she's going to be elated to hear from you?"

Marty hung up the phone quietly. He slumped back onto the couch and brought his list closer. Carefully, he checked off her name. The next name was in the Bronx. He could have been born there. Because he and Benjy and Sylvia had lived in that little house on Dereimer Avenue before they moved to Miami Beach after they sold the grocery store. He hadn't gone back to the old neighborhood since. Taking a deep breath, he dialed the next number, his finger pointing to a Mrs. R. F. Freeman. He had to be careful, though. Sometimes a man answered.

Dusty sunlight filtered through the metal bars. Pretty soon it would vanish and night would creep in. The man known to the world as Krueger walked restlessly in his cell. It wasn't as nice as a hotel room, but it was safer. And he didn't have to run as much. His stomach told him dinner would be served. He didn't have a watch, but he knew that dinner here was earlier than he was accustomed to. And it was always hot food.

He padded back to his bed and sat. He touched his head. More blond ringlets were sprouting every day. For some reason, everyone seemed delighted that he was going to have blond curly hair again. Pretty soon he could twist a curl around his finger.

He bowed his head. How could he be thinking of anything nice when he was so ashamed. At first he had fought the doctors. He had told them he hadn't murdered those women, but now he agreed. They explained to him very patiently that he had memory lapses—fugues, they were called—and they were still trying to help him. He couldn't account for time. He had not been himself. He had killed those ladies. It was good that he was locked up so he couldn't do more harm.

He wondered what they would do to him. He stuffed his fingers in his ears. Would he be shot by a firing squad? Or be strapped to an electric chair? Or would he spend all his days in a place like this? That wouldn't be so bad. Maybe with the help of those pills that looked like M&M's he would someday remember who he was. Once upon a time, he had to have a last name.

Suddenly alert, his head jabbed into the air like an animal in the wilderness. The big key was turning in the door. Instinctively, he shrank back. But it was okay. A big black man in a white costume came in. On his belt dangled a collection of keys, which he wore like a prize. They jangled to his syncopated walk, and Krueger liked to snap his fingers to the rhythm.

"How you doin, baby?" the man said, setting down the tray.

Krueger was silent. He picked up his spoon and dug into hot turkey and string beans and potatoes. For dessert there was a treat: chocolate cake. He would save it for later.

He was so lost in his meal that he didn't hear the key turn in the lock a second time after the orderly left. When he looked up again, he was facing the black horn-rimmed glasses of the young man he had talked with the day before. The man carried a newspaper under his arm.

The doctor smiled at Krueger and urged him to go on eating. "I'm sorry to interrupt your dinner hour."

"I think I remember my name," Krueger said, licking his spoon.

"Yes?" the doctor said, leaning in hopefully. He was sitting across from Krueger on a chair. Krueger sat cross-legged on his bed balancing the tray on his knees.

"Yes?" the doctor said again. Krueger had become silent. Possibly another lapse.

Then Krueger looked up as if the doctor had screamed "Fire!"

"My name is Krueger Doe," he said solemnly. It had come to him in a dream last night. Green pastures, a girl with long blond hair, and a little doe that had crept up to be stroked. He was the doe.

"As in John Doe," the doctor said helpfully.

Krueger nodded.

Dr. Winfield nodded back. He wondered if this new name might indicate another personality. He felt that Krueger was possessed by multiple identities.

When Krueger had licked the spoon again and all his fingers one by one, he carefully wrapped the chocolate cake in his napkin. Dr. Winfield offered him the paper. Krueger flinched, and a tear rolled down his cheek after he read the headlines. On the front of the *Daily News* it said: "ANOTHER MURDER RE-

VEALED." And the *New York Post* boasted a stunner: "LONELY HEARTS KILLER FOUND TOO LATE." A librarian. He had killed a librarian with long red hair. And he couldn't remember it. Everything was becoming murky. Krueger flipped through the papers. He was a speed reader, and in a minute or two he had absorbed all the gory particulars of the terrible crime he had committed.

He brushed away his tears. The poor woman. He hadn't meant to kill her. Or anyone. Why couldn't he remember anything?

The young psychiatrist was watching every move of this strange man. Getting him a paper was a good idea. The murder was made more dramatic that way, and he wanted to evaluate Krueger's reaction.

Could this patient have killed four women, using only his hands as weapons? Of course. It was Dr. Winfield's personal diagnosis, and one that he was very proud of, that Krueger was inhabited by multiple personalities. Winfield wondered which self or selves did the killings.

"Getting back to the secret you said you had," the psychiatrist began smoothly, "can you tell me a little more?"

Sometime after dawn on the following day, the last of March, a hundred-dollar bill passed quietly and quickly from hand to hand on Central Park West. Lenny Reep quickly withdrew his hand and replaced it, empty, in his pocket. The other man slouched back, stretched his legs, and crossed his ankles. He put his right hand casually behind his head and kept the left hand in his pocket, fingering the bill. Reep knocked his companion's elbow.

"C'mon, cough it up," he said roughly.

"Boy, could I get in trouble for this," the man said.

"You didn't have any trouble taking a hundred bucks."

"Okay, okay. Let's start with the first case. Laura Frank."

"I don't give a damn what the names are. Just give me the information."

The young man, a lab assistant, nodded. "There were some petals found on the floor. The second murder, same thing, not quite so dry. The third murder nothing, and now this."

"Now what?" Lenny demanded.

"The whole flower. They found the whole flower on the floor. The petals had been analyzed, but this—"

Lenny almost shoved him off the bench.

"Will you stop being dramatic and tell me—"

"They found the petals in the other murders, but this time they found the whole freakin' flower. A white carnation."

Lenny sat upright, his body very straight. "A white carnation," he said softly. Son of a bitch. He whistled low. She was wearing a white carnation when she came out of that florist shop.

It was easy to figure out. The lady detective was conducting a one-woman task force. She obviously was going against the department. Because she didn't believe the man they had in Bellevue was the killer.

What a story! "LADY DETECTIVE FIGHTS NYPD FOR JUSTICE." This was a winner. Especially if he peddled it to the right reporter. He could sell out of state, maybe, or to some magazines.

Oh, yes, that stuck-up lady detective had better watch her step.

"Princess!"

Terry turned. "Hiya, Bernie, how's it going?"

"Where are you off to? We miss you downstairs. Pretty soon you'll be back where you belong, huh, kiddo?"

"Yeah, Bernie," Terry said, but her smile was thin.

"Tired of the case, huh?"

Terry forced a laugh. "No, I'm fine."

Bernie looked at her. Terry had lines under her eyes, and her face looked drawn. Probably Morrison was giving her a hard time. Well, it wasn't any of his business.

"Got all the shitwork on this case," he said sympathetically. "Well, it will all be over soon. They just brought him over in an ambulance." A mob was assembling on the third floor.

Terry sighed. She knew. Lately, she felt so irritable and impatient. No, she wasn't getting enough sleep. She was leading a double life.

"Just between you and me," Moskowitz said, leaning in closer, "I think this wraps it up. The medical examiner determined the time of death at around eleven o'clock on Saturday night. We got him Sunday."

"It could have been someone else," she said testily.

"I doubt it, Princess. I think the shrinks have been helping him open up. He's more coherent. Knows every detail of the case. Ask him anything. Even the spelling of the woman's name, which I can't do."

Terry shrugged and looked around the room, avoiding his eyes.

"Terry, you're carrying a personal grudge too far. I know you don't like Yablonsky, and I can't say I blame you. . . ."

Terry raised her head and began shaking it. Moskowitz stopped talking. "Bernie, it has nothing to do with Yablonsky. I don't think that fruitcake in there killed those women. It's that simple. I interrogated him, remember? I don't believe he did it."

"Sure, Princess, everyone's entitled to his own opinion? But why not relax? Everyone else, including Captain Fazio, believes we've got the man."

Terry nodded. "I know."

"And that man is in there spilling his guts. Not like the last time when he just stared blankly across the room."

Terry shrugged. "Radio, television—"

"He's in a solitary cell over there."

Terry looked at her mentor and friend, the man she most admired in the department. The only man who really took her seriously as a good detective. Why couldn't he take her seriously now?

"Bernie, you have to admit there are flaws in this case. The follow-up was never thorough."

"I thought that's what you were doing."

"I know, but, see, the letters . . ." What was the use? Detectives and officers were jamming the floor, and even as they talked, she got bumped off balance by the pressing crowd. Soon the reporters would congregate downstairs like caged lions waiting to be tossed meat.

"I gotta go," Terry said, her voice barely audible. Then she stepped out into the hallway, leaving more than a few men's heads turning to stare after her.

When she got outside, Terry leaned her head against the side of the building for one second. Then she pulled away and climbed into her car. How could she go against the whole department? For a moment she wondered if they were right. Maybe she was the one who was going Looney Tunes. A one-woman crusade, and why? For her ego? Was Bernie Moskowitz right about her personal vendetta against Yablonsky? Or against most of the men in the department for the hard time they gave her?

Terry took Columbus Avenue downtown. So involved was she in her thoughts, she failed to notice she was being followed. When she parked her car at the corner of Broadway and West Thirteenth, she still didn't notice a blue car pulling up a block behind her. Behind the wheel was a familiar but repugnant face.

Entering the glass-enclosed *Village Voice* building, she went up to the counter and asked for the head of the personal ads department. She was told that any of the staffers could help her if she wanted to run an ad. Terry showed her gold shield.

Artie Weinstock materialized immediately. He was wearing a *Voice* T-shirt, darkly tinted glasses, and a weary smile. He was tired of the police who constantly came around to ask questions.

"I'm trying to find the original ad that Doreen Stewart, the third victim of the Lonely Hearts Killer, placed in your paper."

Artie nodded. He hadn't supposed she was there to collect for the Policemen's Benevolent Association. It was unusual to see a female detective, especially one that was a real knockout. Personally, he didn't like cops at all.

"I'll have to go to the back files. That's probably the easiest way." People were beginning to line up to run classifieds. "It will take a while, though," he added, indicating the crowd. "You came at a hectic time."

Terry could see the man was busy, but she couldn't afford to back down. That was the trouble with being a one-woman department. She couldn't wait.

"I'm in a hurry," she said with natural authority.

"Okay," he said. "You know, I remember her. She came in several times. Spirited and friendly. That's how I know who she is. Was. Brassy-looking, though. Flame-red hair."

"Red hair? She had red hair?"

"Oh, yeah. Listen, this will take an hour or two."

"Never mind," Terry said hurriedly.

"I beg your pardon. I thought you—"

Terry smiled. "No, no. You just told me what I wanted to find out. That at one time she had red hair. It's possible that she put that in her ad."

"Oh, yeah, she did. Because she took out the red

and came in and wanted to change the wording, and we couldn't do it."

She thanked him and left.

Ten minutes later, a man approached him. Artie didn't like the look of this character with wet lips and protruding eyes. He was asking what the lady had wanted.

"I don't know," Artie said finally. "She's a detective."

The Creep smiled and extended his hand. "I'm Lenny Reep." The two men shook hands. Artie could feel a bill pass into his hand.

"That woman who came in here. She's not a detective. She's impersonating one. Got that? Now tell me what she wanted."

The woman at *New York* magazine shouted into the phone, using her hand as a shield against the noise. "Could you speak louder?" All around, her phones were ringing, and the din was giving her a major headache.

"I'd like to place an ad."

"Okay. Can you read it to me slowly?"

When the woman had finished counting the words, she said, "Eighty-four dollars."

The voice on the other end said, "Fine. When will the ad run?"

"Oh, next week. Now I need your credit card number."

"Visa," said the voice. "3213 126 014 876. The expiration date is 6-86."

"Thank you," the woman crooned into the phone. "And your name as it appears in the card?"

"Theresa," the voice said carefully. "Theresa L. Morrison."

Martha's aunt squinted. They had taken her to St. Luke's-Roosevelt Hospital. They said she had had a slight heart attack. As she woke up, she could see a man and a woman approaching her bed. The woman was beautiful. Martha had been beautiful, too. And now she was gone.

Her eyes shut tightly, blocking the horrible scene. When they opened, she peered back at the two faces hovering over her. She didn't like the round moon-face of the man, so she looked up at the woman.

"Yes, dear?" she said.

"We'd like to ask you some questions," Terry said.

"What's that? You'll have to speak up. I'm a little hard of hearing."

"Are you next of kin?" Terry said a little louder.

"Oh, no. Martha has a family. They're in Cleveland, Ohio."

"Did Martha have a boyfriend?"

Martha's aunt was shocked. "No! Martha never went out with men."

"She was raped," Terry said bluntly, hoping to speed this up.

"She told me she had a virus," the aunt said, whimpering.

"She ran a personal ad for a man," Terry continued.

"Oh, dear."

"When was the last time you talked to your niece?" the male detective said, speaking for the first time.

The old woman lay silent, her eyes rolling toward the ceiling. Then she shut them.

"When was the last time—"

"Shhhh," Terry said. "She's sleeping. They probably gave her something. We'll have to come back."

"Yeah, but—"

"What can we do?" Terry said. She wanted to be rid of him. Wanted to work on her own case. She would stop for a bite and then keep investigating florists. Why didn't anyone else care about this aspect of the case? They had found the whole white carnation.

When they returned to the car, he noticed a pink plastic shopping bag resting on the car seat between the two detectives.

"Go shopping?" her partner asked amiably as he maneuvered the car out of the parking space. "I suppose it's rough for a woman on this job. You have to shop in bits and snatches." He smiled, not really looking at her but through her. The hot shiver of fury that usually ran through Terry with a remark like that wasn't there. The man wasn't being caustic, and he wasn't even insulting her. He was sincere. Terry had encountered this type before. He was treating her like a wife.

"Yeah, ain't that the truth," she said, peering out the window, a half-smirk lifting her mouth, moving the crinkly plastic bag closer to her side. She smiled but not at anything he said. Inside her pretty, bright plastic bag was a red wig.

At exactly seven o'clock, Heather stood in front of a bar near Seventy-fifth and Third Avenue. Everyone had warned her not to go on this date. But Heather had advertised before. It was better than nothing. How did women lawyers go about finding eligible men? She didn't have time. She was too busy building her law practice. Besides, her intuition about people was uncanny. She would know while they were having a drink, and if something was out of whack, she'd just excuse herself to go to the ladies' room. She'd used that ploy once or twice before. After all, these men didn't know her last name or her address. She would sneak out.

Downtown on Eighth Avenue, Marty, wearing a black three-piece suit with a red-and-black striped tie, dashed into his favorite florist. He was frantic. He had taken the subway after work and had gotten trapped underground because there was a fire in the station ahead. Then he had to run home, shower, and change. Now he was late.

"A white carnation," Marty blurted, plunking two quarters on the counter.

The man looked up and smiled. He was wrapping a bouquet of flowers for a customer.

"I said now!" Marty shouted.

The florist, a mild-mannered man with a gold earring in one ear, looked up at him as if evaluating the situation, then excused himself from the waiting customer. The florist and his wife prided themselves on their relationship with their customers and on being a friendly place to get flowers and plants in the Village.

Marty grabbed the flower from the florist without saying anything and ran out. Outside, he raised his hand in an unfamiliar gesture. He would have to take a taxi. He looked at his watch. Ten after seven. He hoped she was still waiting there.

Uptown, Heather frowned at her wristwatch. He was late. She paced for a few minutes. Had she been stood up? Maybe he'd had an accident.

She stopped in front of a health-food store and studied the display jars of natural peanut butter. She moved to the lingerie shop on the corner, careful to keep watch. As she stared at a pink satin nightgown, she decided to wait only ten minutes more. Maybe all this personal ad stuff was a little premature in light of that horrible Lonely Hearts business. But Bob had sounded so sincere.

At twenty after seven, Heather moved to a bookstore window to peruse the titles of the week's top-ten bestsellers. She would give him three more minutes. That would make it an even half-hour.

Marty looked at his watch. The taxi was one block away, and traffic had suddenly become bumper to bumper. Marty watched the meter go up once when the cab was stopped and then blew up. "Damn it, let me out. I can walk faster!" He reached into his pocket and paid seven dollars and sixty cents. Then he pulled out a pocketful of change and carefully extracted a quarter and a dime for a tip. When he looked up, it was into the red face of the cabbie, who held his hand on the lock button of the back door. "You call this a tip?" he said.

Marty stammered. He didn't know what was wrong. At the same time, a young woman with a briefcase was knocking on the window. The cabdriver said menacingly, "I've had 'em all, but you take the cake. Now get out." The impatient young woman scrambled into the cab barely a second after Marty got out. Taking out a cigarette, he began walking fast. The cigarette was crucial. He had to be Bob. Couldn't afford to arrive as bumbling, humble Marty. He brushed off an imaginary piece of dust from his pocket and, finally, at almost seven-thirty, got to the bar. There was no redheaded woman. He looked. A woman who had been standing in front of the hardware store was approaching him. She came closer. It must be her. His next love. His eternal Princess.

He saw her hand brush away her coppery hair, and she looked as though she might walk past the bar. He stepped in front of her. The young woman gasped.

"You must be Bob," she said. "White carnation and all."

"I'm sorry I'm late. I—uh, my last patient gave me some trouble." Luckily, his tongue was nimble. For a panicky second he had forgotten whether he told her he was a doctor or a stockbroker.

"Oh, that's all right," Heather said, taking in the cut of his three-piece suit, his boyish grin, and his clean-cut looks. There was a pause, and they both seemed to know it wasn't entirely comfortable yet.

"Listen, I owe you," he said. "Keeping a beautiful redhead like you waiting. How about dinner?"

She laughed. "Okay." Actually, the first date was supposed to be only a drink, but he was so suave—and besides, he was a doctor. "Hey," she said, "don't say redhead that way. Remember what happened before they caught the killer?"

He was slow to pick up on what she meant. When it was clear to him, he hit the air with his hand, laughing, "Oh, yeah, I see what you mean. Nah, might as well forget that. It's all over now."

He put his hand on the small of her back and guided her across Third Avenue. "It just so happens one of my favorite restaurants is close by. Now, where exactly is it?" He spotted a small, lamplit doorway that proclaimed Chez Vito. "Oh, there it is," he said. He had never seen this place before.

"Sounds great to me," Heather said.

They walked down three tiny steps into a cozy French restaurant, most likely a lot of people's favorite restaurant. It was in a converted brownstone. Each table had a mauve tablecloth, pink napkins, and a slender, glass vase with one red rose.

"What made you decide to be a doctor?" Heather asked when they were seated.

"I wanted to help people. What made you decide to be a lawyer?"

"I like to help people."

They ordered, and he suggested a bottle of wine. "I don't usually do this on the first date with the ads," she said, her eyes sparkling.

"Hey, you know, you remind me of someone," he said ingenuously.

"Who?"

"Oh, an old flame. Someone who's gone now. She had red hair, too. She was a teacher." Yes. Debbie Greene. They would meet each other soon.

"Ever been married?" she asked.

"Once. But we were too young. We lasted for about a year, then got divorced."

"What was her name?"

"Phyllis. Have you ever been married?"

This topic was becoming a source of embarrassment for her. "No. Never." Then she looked up and laughed. "Someone told me I should invent a husband. Say I've been divorced. After all, I'm thirty-two. It sounds like something's wrong with me."

He shrugged. "What's the difference?" Almost magically, two plates of food slithery with rich sauces appeared in front of them. Marty wanted desperately to drown it all with ketchup, his favorite of all foods, but as Bob, he didn't dare.

"I never do something this elaborate when I first meet someone from the ads," Heather felt she had to say. Her eyes lit up at the lovely dinner and sparkling wine.

"Forget it. I can afford it," he said, almost amused. "I want to make up for being late. Besides, I'm a doctor."

Heather began to calculate silently, all the while making conversation. She would let him take her home and even come in if he wanted—but only for a half-hour. She would try to make a second date then.

He paid the bill with cash, and Heather was surprised. She expected an M.D. to use a credit card.

"May I walk you home?" he asked casually.

She nodded.

He would cut a lock of her hair this time, and all the rest of the times. A souvenir. His fifth Princess. Soon she'd join the others, and before tomorrow the life that raced through her would be held in a capsule in heaven for him alone.

"It will probably rain tonight," she said. "I hope there's good weather for the weekend. I'd like to get my bike out."

"Are you from New York, by the way?"

"San Francisco."

"And your parents are living?"

"Of course. What a question."

They approached the high-rise building where she lived. He was silent and said nothing when he noticed the doorman. Heather thought he must have a lot on his mind. Doctors were very smart.

He spoke only after they got out of the elevator and she let him in her apartment. When the lights were switched on, he could see the glittering view from outside her window. There was a blanket of navy blue studded with diamond lights and a fat arc of twinkling stars. Marty blinked. It was a bridge.

"What a view," he said, almost breathless. "Like living in an airplane."

Heather had disappeared behind the louvered doors into the tiny, windowless kitchenette. When she emerged, she held two glasses of chilled white wine.

"Say," he said after a while, for it was getting late and he had to go to his dumb job at Saks the next day. "I was wondering, just out of curiosity, do you still have my letter?"

Heather looked at him and shrugged. "Yeah, I think I do. It's somewhere. Why?"

"Could I see it?"

"Sure. I think I left it in the bedroom." She disappeared through an archway. It was a roomy apartment. Marty got up slowly, putting down his wineglass. He'd have to see that they were wiped off. God, it was Debbie all over again. He licked his lips; the prospect of euphoria was so delicious.

Heather came through the archway holding the plain white stationery. Marty approached her. They would go to the bedroom.

"Yoo-hoo, I'm home. Hope I'm not interrupting anything!"

He spun around as if a ghost had entered. Closing the front door of the apartment, a tall, very attractive brunette came over to him and smiled. "Sorry. I didn't expect to find anyone home. I'll go into the bedroom so I won't disturb you two." She stuck her hand out to Marty. "I'm Heather's roommate, Eileen."

Heather was moving toward the kitchen. "Don't be silly. Why don't you join us? I'll get you a glass of wine." Marty looked from one to the other as if he were watching an invisible tennis match. He had been framed.

Angrily, he looked around. And then he remembered in his haste that he had forgotten his briefcase. Everything was different now, though. He didn't have to do that anymore.

"Listen," he said abruptly, "I really have to be going. It's getting late."

"Oh, I did interrupt," Eileen said guiltily.

"No, I was leaving," he said politely, employing all his control.

Heather followed him to the door.

He looked at her and wanted to weep, to take his face and bury it in her orangey hair.

Heather closed the door and leaned against it. "I liked him."

"I hope I didn't ruin it. Sorry about my timing."

"This one's special. He's a doctor. And he seemed interested."

Marty slumped against the wall of the elevator. A little speaker was emitting staticky Muzak. A love song. He began to sob. On the twelfth floor, someone got on. He couldn't see who it was through the flood of tears, but he heard a gruff, masculine voice say, with a trace of disgust, "Hey, you all right, buddy?"

Marty didn't look up. His stomach wrenched in agony. He ran past the man and staggered out of the building. The rain had started, a quick thundershower. Head down, bucking the gusts of wind, he ripped off his sopping white carnation. He cast it into the street where it slid along the curb and rode into the gutter on a river of muddy water.

Dear Benjy,

You know what a smash I've always been with the ladies. Well, I'm the one everyone wants. That's right, Lonely Heart. I'm the big man in New York City. A real ladies killer, if you know what I mean.

But you won't tell anyone. Of course not. You can't. And you told me I wasn't that smart. It's such a relief to know I'm fooling you now. I'm smarter than New York's Finest. If I were there, I'd bring you a bouquet of white carnations.

Your Loving Fake Son,
Martin Robert Loomus,
originally known as
Robert Martin Freeman and
The Brides of Frankenstein

CHAPTER TWELVE

Terry was exhausted when she sat down on a stool facing the long counter of the Chili Palace on Columbus Avenue. Balancing her chin in her hands, she ordered a chiliburger and coffee and then lit a cigarette.

She ate slowly, thinking. Tough Theresa. Oh, yes, that was her. She remembered when she was a rookie policeman assigned to her first DOA, dead on arrival. The department was very pristine about that. Male policemen searched male corpses and policewomen got female ones. The first one had been the worst. It was almost as if they were testing her stamina, and probably they were. The deceased was sprawled on a bed in a rat-infested tenement in the slums. Her flesh was black and decayed. Head, limbs, and belly had swollen into a grotesque funhouse parody of a human being. The stench was unearthly. She wished she had had an oxygen mask, but she didn't know enough to bring one along.

There she was, all alone. Men were waiting outside. Then, of all the luck, the body exploded, and a starving cat hidden in the shadows darted forth to nibble on the maggoty remains.

Suddenly, her chiliburger lost its flavor.

The waiter stopped in front of her. "Everything all right? Can I get you anything else?"

"No, I'm fine," Terry said.

That day the body exploded, she had shrunk back, gagging, falling against the plaster wall. She wanted to cry out, to scream, to vomit; but at the sound of the noise, the men had rushed in, and she said stoically: "Better have someone clean up the mess." She made her report without flinching. She felt like fainting. That day she learned how to act, an enormous part of what her job consisted of. She was an actress and a good one. Only now she was acting to her friends and colleagues to protect herself.

Terry sipped her coffee and lit her cigarette. What would really come of all this? she wondered again.

Her thoughts circled and spun just like the smoke billowing from her cigarette. She had found someone once, and she had assumed it would last forever. What would she be doing now if she was still living with Bob? There would be a note on the magic slate taped to the refrigerator telling him she would be late: She was working overtime on a case. Then her note would be gone and the slate empty. No note for her. He would just show up late. She would sniff the particular woman's fragrance that clung damningly to his clothes. After a while, all she cared about was that it wasn't the same scent. Yeah, she was better off a single lady. It would take some adjustment, but who needed a marriage that mocked one every step of the way?

Feeling strangely rejuvenated, Terry paid her bill. She drove down Columbus, which became Ninth Avenue and swerved into Hudson. Down in the West Village she parked and walked around. She had found nothing midtown, and frankly, she was bored. The Village would be a change of pace. She was about to walk a few blocks to Seventh Avenue South when she glanced across Eighth and noticed a tiny flower shop. She crossed the street. Fat pastel mums and two-ninety-nine, prearranged bouquets rested in tin barrels. She took a bouquet of lavender, yellow, and red flowers and went inside to pay for them.

As the florist was wraping her bouquet in paper, she showed him her gold shield.

"I'm looking for a man who buys just white carnations. Do you have any customers like that? I don't know if he buys one flower or a bunch."

The owner was Greek—and where he came from, you kept your mouth shut when the police came asking questions. He liked his customers. But he was a gentle man who loved flowers and plants and whose wife sometimes worked in the store. He didn't like taking rude abuse, and he didn't want her subjected to it. He touched the ear with the gold earring.

"Yeah, we got a guy like that. Lives in the neighborhood, I guess. He comes in here every so often and buys a white carnation. Last time he came in he was in a real hurry. Pain in the neck."

Terry kept her mouth firm. She wanted to cheer like a schoolgirl, but she maintained her poise. This was a dangerous investigation. It could cost her her job.

"When was he in here last? Mind if I smoke?"

He held his hand up. "If you don't mind, no. The plants can't breathe. He was in tonight. That's how I remember him. Bought one white carnation and put it in his buttonhole. He's come in before to buy just that one flower. But tonight he was rude. I don't like that."

"What time did he stop in? Do you remember?"

"Oh, yeah, around seven."

Terry looked at her watch. How had it become so late? Almost ten o'clock. "Which way was he going when he left, uptown or downtown?"

"Listen, lady, I mean, officer. I had a customer."

"On what other dates did he buy just one white carnation?"

"God, I don't remember. I thought he was a musician or went to a lot of weddings—an usher or something like that. Or a waiter. He doesn't stand out in my memory, except he does buy white carnations every once in a while. Other than that, he's not a regular. He doesn't buy other flowers."

When she could, she would interview him more rigorously and get dates and details. "Can you give me a description of the man?"

"Sure, he's between five-nine and five-ten, I would say. Not bad-looking, not especially good-looking—"

"Could you stick to specifics," Terry said, wanting to scream but speaking very calmly.

"Wait a second. Honey?" A woman appeared from the back room. She had a pair of cutting shears in her hand. "This lady's a detective, and she wants a description of the man who comes in every so often and buys one white carnation."

The woman nodded. "Well, he has a sloping nose, you know, like Bob Hope or Nixon. He has no mustache or beard."

"Hair? Is it blond?" Terry asked quickly.

"No," said her husband. "His hair is dark brown. It's not real thick, either."

"Any moles, scars, or marks on the face?"

The husband and wife looked at each other. The woman shook her head. "No. Average-looking guy," she said.

"Yeah," the husband agreed. "Not much stands out about him. Used to wear a black bowler in cooler weather."

"Is there anything else you can remember? Eyes, teeth, eyebrows, dirty fingernails, anything?" Terry was almost begging.

"No," the husband replied. "Not too much stands out. He's not the type of guy who makes a lasting impression, you know."

Tonight. Then there would be another murder coming up. She shook the florist's hand energetically, something she never did, and asked if she could return and talk to him.

She clutched her bouquet and walked back to her car. This was their man. Had to be. Suddenly, she was overwhelmed by a surge of hopelessness. If she was right, she hadn't prevented a murder. Right at this moment there was another woman with a pillow over her face and white petals on the floor. Suddenly, she felt very sad that she was right.

CHAPTER THIRTEEN

Wednesday, April 1. Terry rolled over drowsily and pressed the button on her clock radio. She should have awakened earlier. It was seven o'clock. Then she remembered. She didn't have to work so hard anymore.

In the shower she found herself humming for the first time in a long while. Today was April Fools' Day. She remembered that when she was a kid, she used to switch the salt and the sugar. Her parents would dutifully dump coffee with salt down the sink and suffer through very sweet eggs. They always acted genuinely surprised. Now she wondered if they knew and played along just to humor her.

Outside, the sun was so bright she had to put on sunglasses. As she climbed into the car, she began to whistle.

She would have stopped for an early edition of one of the dailies, but nothing had been delivered to the newsstands on her way. She had a tingling sensation. The murder might just be in the paper.

When she got to the third floor, she found she was in luck. Someone had left a morning tabloid right on her desk. She looked around. The floor was almost empty. She turned the paper around and gasped. What kind of dirty joke was this? They had had the paper printed up somewhere. They must have. As an April Fools' joke.

Across the page in bold headlines that the *Post* was famous for was "FEMALE DETECTIVE ON

LONELY CRUSADE." Somehow they had found a picture of her. It was grainy and blurred. But there she was, her blouse cut a little too low and strained by her shoulder holster. Her lipstick seemed a dark red. Did they touch that up? Her eyes scanned the copy, horrified: "keeping an almost all-night vigil to find the true killer . . . continuing her personal vendetta to find the true murderer of these innocent women . . ." Terry sucked in her breath. There was no mention of the white carnation. Then she read, her lips moving, ". . . the female detective has said of the suspect about to be tried for the slayings, 'That man couldn't kill a fly, let alone make love to a woman. . . .' "

Terry looked around. Men were starting to arrive on the task force floor. They looked away. So they all knew and had left her alone for a few minutes to find out herself how much trouble she was in. April Fool. Her stomach went as sour as if she had mixed sugar with salt. She turned over every page, but there was no murder in the paper.

In horrified fascination she continued reading the story. They had run a miniature biography of her, one of the few female detectives in the department.

She read on, addicted to the soap opera of her life. Her estranged husband was a handsome detective. She had followed in her father's footsteps. Hers was a combination of femininity and spunk that gave rise to her promotion to second-grade detective and got her a gold shield. That she could be seen using her rearview mirror to touch up her lipstick.

My God. This was hardly a bio. It was more likely her obituary.

She squeezed her eyes shut and balled her hands into fists. Who had done this to her? Someone must have followed her. Opening her eyes, she saw a tall, familiar figure lounging against the door chewing on an unlit cigarette.

"Reep!" she cried, and almost lunged at him in her fury.

He ducked.

"You're in enough trouble, lady detective," he said with a sneer.

Terry stayed rigid. The reality of her nightmare became all too clear. Just then, Moskowitz entered. And for once he wasn't smiling at her.

"Terry, Terry, how could you do this? I was so proud of you."

Terry gulped. "Bernie, I did what you and Fazio did years ago. I didn't believe you had the right killer, and I wanted justice. You found the man who killed those ballerinas. They had the wrong man then, too. I just don't believe this guy did it." Terry's voice had gone up higher, and she felt like a pleading child.

"I read the papers," Moskowitz said dryly. "Look, kid, I'm not saying you're right or wrong. I know we went against the department years ago, but we did it together and we didn't make the mistake you did. We never got caught! You're in a lot of trouble, Ter. I'll do my best, but I don't think it will help."

Terry sat down in a trance, her eyes misting.

Moskowitz turned to go and then added matter-of-factly, "You better look sharper than that, Princess. Fazio's on his way over."

She heard a familiar voice in the hallway. She was aware that the few men remaining on the force who were on the floor were watching her little scenario like a sitcom. To her, at that moment, it seemed like a ghoulish reminder of *This Is Your Life*.

"Hello, Bob," she said as he walked toward her.

"Terry, you've gone too far with that ego of yours. Now look at what you've done. Do you realize that this escapade may cost you your job?"

"That ought to make you happy."

"C'mon, Terry, this is nothing to joke about. What made you do it?"

Terry felt all eyes looking at her. Before she had a chance to answer, the squat figure of Captain Frank Fazio appeared in the doorway.

He motioned for Terry to follow him down the hall. They walked into the interrogation room. Fitting. She kept her stomach contracted so that she wouldn't show any emotion. If she took a breath, she imagined that she would scream or cry out from the pain. Terry sat while Fazio paced around, dropping cigar ashes. Terry studied the curly black hair that dribbled upon his forehead.

"A white carnation," he said at last. "That's what made you get into trouble?"

"That wasn't in the story," Terry said feebly. "They left it out."

"I know what you were up to," Fazio replied sharply. "I'm a detective, remember?"

"I don't think that was ever thoroughly investigated," Terry said, using a tone Bob referred to as her schoolteachery voice. "There are certain loopholes in the case—"

"It was me, wasn't it? I was your role model."

Terry shook her head.

"I think it was. Let me tell you something, Detective Morrison, when I solved the Ballet Killer case, I did one thing you weren't smart enough to do. *I didn't get caught.*"

Terry wanted to say it in unison with him, but she wisely kept her mouth shut.

"You know you've cast a bad light on all the women in the department."

Terry thought of her bedroom where she could be alone later.

"I still think I'm right," she said, her voice shaky, but her resolve unshaken.

"No, you're wrong, Morrison," he said harshly. "We have our man. Now let me tell you why you're not going to be fired."

"Why?" Terry managed to inquire in a small voice that sounded, even to her ears, impertinent.

"Because of your father. I knew your dad. One of the finest cops I've ever known. He wouldn't be very proud of you right now, Morrison. The department will keep you on, although I can't promise you'll keep your gold shield. I'll do my utmost. You may have to come up the hard way this time."

Terry bowed her head. After an interminable time, Fazio left the room, and she got up slowly, straightened herself, and walked out the door knowing everyone would be watching. Blindly, she headed for the rest room. There was a hook on the door. She fastened it, sat down heavily on the hard seat, put her face in her hands, and wept bitterly but silently.

The *Times* hardly mentioned the Lonely Hearts Killer. The *Post* and *Daily News*, however, kept his reputation alive. Marty looked again at the stories. Then he rummaged through a drawer until he found a pair of long, thin scissors. He slashed through the paper and clipped out the pictures of her. Then he Scotch-taped them to his refrigerator door. He stood back surveying the black-and-white newspaper clipping of this lady detective.

One woman. A personal crusade for justice. He was going to work when he first spotted the headlines. She knew who he was. But he had forced himself to stay at work all day, wearing a stiff smile. In the evening when he came home, he knew the truth. If she knew who he was, they would all have intercepted him. But they weren't waiting.

This woman had just had a suspicion it wasn't the blond veggie. Smart lady. Almost as smart as he was. But she had been found out. They would make her stop. The newspaper indicated that the police department took a dim view of personal investigations not adhering to official lines of thinking. The chief of detectives had said, in response to what action would be taken with her, "No comment."

He had won again. The gods were favoring him. He went to the wobbly cardboard table in his main room. His list was there. Why couldn't he be as lucky with his mommy numbers? Well, each time was a new beginning. He went to his favorite side of the couch—a little more worn than the rest—scanned his list, crossed his fingers, and dialed the first number.

"Hi, is this Mrs. Freeman?"

"Yes, it is."

She had a nice, warm voice, and she was polite. He took a deep breath.

"Are you the Mrs. Freeman who in 1950 gave birth to a boy and then gave him up for adoption?"

There was a heavy silence on the phone.

"You a white boy?"

"Yes."

"Because I did have a son and never saw the child again, but he was a black baby."

She began to cry. He joined her. "Got a much better home than I could have given him," Mrs. Freeman said. "They paid for him. Not much, but they paid. Oh, yes. Rich black folks. He was a healthy baby. Must be a doctor or a lawyer now. Maybe even a congressman." Marty nodded, tears coursing down his face. He wished he had been her son. He would gladly have painted himself black or brown if that would have helped.

"No," he said stiffly. "This Mrs. Freeman was Jewish."

Neither bothered to say good-bye. Both lines went dead simultaneously.

Marty sat there, one knee crossed over the other, his foot twitching. In his pocket was a pack of cigarettes. The very idea of a cigarette, when he wasn't being Bob, thoroughly nauseated him. He went into the kitchen and stared again at the woman detective taped to the refrigerator. A small picture and the ink had been smudged in a corner. But she had a way of smiling with her face without using her mouth.

Inside the refrigerator he found a fresh tomato. He bit into it, then impulsively pitched it against the refrigerator. A bull's-eye on the picture of the smug detective lady who couldn't leave well enough alone. He watched as the seeds and red juice trickled down the refrigerator door.

The phone rang. Another Princess. He'd have to have two to make up for the last time. His voices had told him that. He had to contribute souls to his harem in heaven.

Scrambling to the phone, he answered cooly, "Hello?"

"Hi, Marty, guess who?"

He made a face and stuck out his tongue. Unfat Phyllis, the girl he almost asked to marry him. The semi-thin skinny girl hiding under the big girl that could have made a nice mommy.

"Hi, Phyllis," he said dully.

"So, what's new? I haven't seen or talked to you in such a long time."

"Oh, I've been a little busy."

"Yeah, me, too. Say, you want to get together? Go to a movie or something?"

He didn't like the new Phyllis. She was taking liberties. He had done the asking. Poor Phyllis. It was so evident. People were just so obvious. She loved him. And to think he even thought *she* was rejecting *him*. Well, he had grown.

"In a relationship, Phyllis," he said somberly, "you have to allow the other person space to grow."

Phyllis was puzzled. That line rang a bell. But what the hell was he talking about? She was calling simply because she felt sorry for him, guilty that she might have ignored him. She fiddled with the tie to her new red jump suit. Her date would be there any minute. Yes, Raoul had called. Later he had told her he had tried to reach her that night of the big binge, but her line was busy or she had been out. She even dated other men. It was like she had emerged from all that weight a new person. But, Marty? What relationship?

She heard her door bell ringing. "Gotta fly, Marty. Call me whenever."

As Marty hung up the phone, he thought that would serve her right. Let her sit home alone night after night wondering who he was out with. She had lost all that weight and deserted him. It was her fault.

It was almost seven-thirty. Prime time for calls. Would the phone ring tonight? Would another sweet Princess want to meet him and ultimately become his? He closed his eyes, trying to recapture the ecstasy of his times with his heavenly Princesses. He concentrated until furrows appeared on his brow. Then he smashed his fist on the couch in frustration. The image was slipping away. He needed a fresh experience so he could live it all again.

At eight o'clock, he padded into the kitchen and opened a cupboard. He found some chunky peanut butter. Spreading it like frosting over a half-decaying banana, he opened the refrigerator and searched for milk. It was important. When he was a kid, he used to have to force down five glasses of milk a day. If not, he would see the back of Sylvia's hand, that was for sure. He closed the door and studied the pink-stained picture of the woman detective. Why had she singled him out when no one else had?

He resumed his alert position and at nine o'clock laughed to himself. Well, a watched phone never rings. He might as well do his correspondence. If they didn't call, he would write to them. Oh, yes, he worked hard.

He took all his recent newspapers and magazines and spread them out on the table. There was a magazine called *Annex,* which had free personal ads. He hadn't found any redheads in there yet. Then there were his weekly copies of *New York* and *The Village Voice*. And his latest *Review of Books* to go through. He could never risk a subscription, and it irked him that newsstand prices were so exorbitant.

He wrote only three letters, slowly and laboriously, his tongue protruding from the side of his mouth. He had varied ways of printing. He had even taken calligraphy once so his letters wouldn't look childlike. His printing was special and elegant. But pickings were slim. He had written to a blonde.

It was after ten o'clock when Terry found her key and managed successfully to enter the front door of her apartment. She fell into her recliner and lit a cigarette, her coat still on. Well, she had done it. She was feeling no pain. She had gone to a remote bar where no one would recognize her. And then she had proceeded to become blotto. All in all, she decided she had done very well. But why was it that whenever she laughed, tears appeared, and she started to shake, realizing she was crying, after all?

She longed to get beyond the pain so she could feel numbness, but it didn't work. Even now she was sobering up. To be so humiliated. Not even allowed to defend herself. To know that Captain Fazio thought of her only as the daughter of a respected detective. Bernie had treated her like a naughty child. Then Bob had to come and rub it in. But, worst of all, she had checked the papers: There was no new murder announced.

Lenny Reep had done this to her. Reep the Creep. Just for a scoop. That stinking piece of garbage. Someday she'd find a way to get even with him. He had been following her. Damn it, why hadn't she noticed? She could have continued her investigation and managed to elude him.

The person she was angriest with, though, was herself. Because they were all right. Her deed had been performed before. Probably many times. But she had made the only unforgivable error. She had been caught. And she would probably pay for it by losing the only thing that mattered to her: her gold shield.

CHAPTER FOURTEEN

Saturday in Miami dawned damp and muggy. But it was always the same in every ward of the Avenging Angel Nursing Home. The same air, the familiar creepy silence, the eternal dogged dragging of time. Benjy Loomus had been awake since dawn. Suddenly his world was different. There were things to do.

Around eleven o'clock, Big Annie appeared and sat down heavily in the chair across from his bed. As luck would have it, she pulled another letter from the pocket of her nurse's uniform. Benjy began blinking his eyes nonstop rapidly, both at the same time. Annie saw him immediately and became alarmed. He never did that. She came up to his bedside and said, "Whatsamatter, baby, something bothering you?"

Benjy continued to blink frantically and even tried to roll his eyeballs upward.

"Should I get a doctor?" she asked.

He blinked twice to say no.

"No? Then whatsamatter? If only you could talk."

If only he could talk! He felt his heart thumping with his urgency to communicate. If only he could make a noise. With every bit of mental power he possessed, he forced a squeaky staccato grunt. Annie stepped back in surprise.

"Something is bothering you," she said awesomely. "Something big going on deep inside you, honey, am I right?"

He blinked once. To answer yes.

"And you don't want a doctor?"

He blinked twice.

"Do you want me to read you a letter from your son in New York, or would that upset you?"

He had been praying she would come. Lying there with a body that was no more than a live eggplant was deceiving to many. His mind was still active. Sharp as a tack. He had figured it out. That lying little bastard wasn't putting anything over on him. He had Marty all figured out, and he would find a way to let everyone else know.

Benjy knew he would get nowhere if he didn't stick to their special code: blinking once for yes; twice for no. One if by land, two if by sea. He blinked once so the old cow would read the damn letter and they could maybe begin.

"You want me to read it, then?" Annie said, sitting down again. She scanned the first part. It was crazy. She could skip that. "There's no end to all the redheaded girls I can get into trouble in New York City. They love me. They call me up and ask me for dates. They even run ads in the paper for me." She looked up. "Sounds like he's having himself a good time." She stared at his face. There it was again. That rapid blinking.

She jumped up. "Something wrong? I'm going to get a doctor."

The blinking stopped.

She looked at the letter in her hand. "You trying to tell me there's nothing wrong with you?"

He blinked once, secretly praying.

Puzzled, she looked down at the letter. "You trying to tell me there's something wrong with . . . your son?"

He blinked once.

"Um-hum, now we're getting somewhere. He in trouble, you think?"

Benjy blinked once.

195

"Nah, you're just worrying, I think. Sounds like he's having a good time there in ole New York." She continued reading the letter, paraphrasing it. "He says he hopes you like it here and to remember he's paying the bills and that he hopes the people who take care of you are nice. Now that's sweet, ain't it, Benjy?"

He blinked twice.

She looked at the signature. He had signed it "Your mistake." She couldn't read him that. The poor old man would worry. Impulsively, she said, "Well, if you don't mind my saying so, sweetie, that son of yours *is* a little strange."

He blinked once, hopefully.

Damn kid, Benjy thought. No good at all, and here was the proof. He always got into trouble and always over girls. He just couldn't control himself. Look at that mess years ago. And now this. He knew—oh, yes, he knew. That Lonely Hearts Killer in New York City. It was really Marty. He didn't care who they caught. It was his dumb son who was the real murderer. He had a sixth sense, and he'd have to convince them. She was studying the letter now. Maybe she believed him. Maybe she saw the clues, too, and read between the lines. He was teasing, playing; but he had always made Marty pay, and he would now.

Annie shook her head almost as if she wanted to deny his thoughts. When a child was in trouble or went wayward, you did all you could to protect and help him. You loved him. The boy *was* strange, though. All this business with redheads and boasting about how he was a big man and how he didn't like his father and all. But, there was the bottom line, he paid the bills. No, it was better for the poor baby not to get himself all riled up. The money might dry up. She patted him on the head.

"Don't worry about your son, Benjy, honey. He'll be all right. You just rest yourself."

She walked away and tossed the letter in a wastebasket. Benjy looked at it longingly. He blinked rapidly, but no one noticed him. Damn her, he thought angrily. Damn everybody. A tiny tear of frustration formed in his eye and stayed there. He'd find a way to prove it. He wasn't giving up. Then he fell asleep from exhaustion.

It was eleven-ten, and she rolled over in bed. She didn't want to think, but the damage was done. She had woken up. Saturday, April 4. So what? The third day of her lethargy. All she wanted to do was sleep. Sleep. The great escape. The only problem was that when you got up, the pain of the real world cut even deeper. Every day it got worse.

On Thursday morning, with a monumental hangover, the phone had shattered what was left of her nerves. She was told by an unknown, chillingly impersonal voice that the department was suspending her for four days. At the end of that time, on Monday morning, she could report to Manhattan South for a different assignment and tour of duty.

Oh, well, she couldn't stay in bed forever. Getting up, she dressed in jeans and a top. She went into the kitchen and opened the refrigerator. Empty as usual. First she'd go shopping for groceries. And afterward, she'd get out the vacuum cleaner and after that she'd go for a long walk and after that . . . she'd just keep going somehow and make the best of it. She was still a cop as far as she knew.

The receiver rested diagonally across the phone, off the hook, but that annoying drone had stopped some time ago. There was no one she wanted to talk to, nothing she had to say.

She tied the sleeves of a cardigan around her neck and left the apartment. Downstairs in the mailbox she found the usual junk mail and assorted bills plus a long manila envelope from *New York* magazine. The ad! There were answers. She had almost forgotten. It had been part of her investigation. Walking to her car, she ripped the envelope apart and found four smaller envelopes addressed to her box number. It was too late now to follow up, but it was fascinating. Curious, half-amused, and strangely flattered, she unlocked her car.

Holding the door open with her foot to take advantage of the April sunshine, Terry sat in the driver's seat reading. She reached into the glove department and pulled out the ad she had scribbled on a paper napkin and read over the phone to that magazine woman.

> SWF, attractive, intelligent, redhead, longs to meet someone with a sense of humor and good vibes. Lonely schoolteacher looking for fun and eventual relationship. Photo appreciated.

It was a conservative, dull ad, admittedly; but she had composed it thoughtfully. She figured that as long as she put in red hair she would be on the right track, and she wanted to appeal to the largest percentage of men without turning anyone off by being too cute. Lousy as she was feeling, she couldn't help but chuckle at the first reply. To begin with, it was handwritten and she almost needed a handwriting expert to figure out a simple word such as *the*. It seemed, if she deciphered correctly, this man wanted to meet his soul mate and live happily ever after. He invited her to call him before seven-thirty A.M. or after ten-thirty P.M. He played basketball or baseball or backgammon, she wasn't sure which, and he liked to cook. He was forty-three years old, of medium height and weight, and he had never been married. Nothing else. He was not a lawyer, and there was no picture attached.

Fascinated, Terry ripped into the next envelope, which was a little thicker. Inside she found a tape cassette and a snapshot pasted over it. It had "Play

Me" written across it. How clever. She had a tape deck in her car, though she never used it. Then she found herself laughing. It was preposterous. The tape didn't fit. And her recorder was a standard size. Some poor man had all those tapes made to fit a one-in-a-million recorder! It sounded cheering to hear her own laughter again.

The third letter was carefully typed. Probably on an electric typewriter. Under the heading "ME" it had a simulated personal ad.

DWM, good-looking, soon-to-be-divorced father of two twin boys, very available, teacher of high school geometry, loves to cook, really a klutz at sports but swims a little. Write "ME" back because it takes so much more of "YOU" when you write a note about yourself.

There was no phone number. Only a box number. Soon-to-be-divorced? She doubted that. She found herself getting angry. Who did he think she was? She wasn't some gullible, impressionable, desperate woman who needed someone called "ME." And then she reminded herself that she didn't run the ad as herself. Oh, yes, she felt a little better already. Not great, but living. Her stomach began to rumble, and she invented a mushroom and cheese omelet, one where she would shred the cheese into the scrambled eggs and pile the mushrooms in the center of the frying pan.

She opened the fourth letter, which was carefully printed in a script style.

Hi. My name is Bob. I never think last names are important, do you? I am a CPA and I work in the midtown area. I have a weakness, you might say, for redheads. I'm 34, 5'10", and my hair is thinning a little, but people say I'm fairly attractive. I hope you will want to discover if I am.

I like to cook, like to clean up, too, and respect the independence of a woman. But I also feel protective at times if you don't mind. I guess I'm just old-fashioned that way. Why not give me a try? I'm sure you have a lot of letters, an attractive redhead like yourself.

Terry's hand was trembling when she finished reading, and she realized she had lost her appetite. Was that him, or was that him? He was charming. She would pick him. Honest, sweet, all the right answers. He wasn't a lawyer, though. She bit her lip. She had never run into a letter like this in any of the victims' files, so maybe her theory was right. He took them with him, this Bob fellow. And if that was the case, maybe he changed professions as a cover-up of sorts.

The big clue was that he was crazy about redheads. And like Candice Klein had said, his hair was thinning. Glancing over the letter again, she read it with the viewpoint that he was a very slick man who knew what he wanted and how to get it.

Terry leaned back and rested her head on the seat cushion. It was starting again. That obsessive desire to solve this case and prove herself. There was that very real-looking red wig that had cost her sixty-five dollars. Then she sat straight up. If she got caught and got into more trouble, she wouldn't get a second chance. She'd be through, finished, washed up in the department. Maybe she had better forget about it and bide her time. She looked into her rearview mirror and began to start the car. It was her reflection that made her think twice. She *was* a woman and she *was* single. Hell, the department couldn't stop her from dating.

She backed out of her parking space slowly. Probably she was wrong, and it would be just that, a date. She'd amuse herself for a few hours. After all, it was time she started going out. Then again, if it was the killer, she'd have her man. She had a gun and he didn't. How many times did she decoy when she was a policewoman and then take some man by surprise before her backup even got there. So it was settled. Now she felt better. More like herself. Like a homicide detective. She'd wear her green silk. And the red wig.

The coffee machine sat on a hot plate in the nurses' station at the Home. Next to it was a little kettle of hot water for the tea drinkers. Every once in a while someone would leave an open box of assorted doughnuts or cookies from the bakery. This afternoon, there was an already butchered homemade coffee cake. The nurses were taking their break next to it. And they were doing what they ordinarily did when they congregated. They gossiped about the patients.

"Mrs. Murphy regained the use of her right hand. She's so thrilled. Dr. Gottfried came to see her today and said maybe there will be more improvement."

"She the one whose children hardly ever come to visit?"

The nurse made little clucking sounds with her tongue. "They come. But only every few months. Poor thing."

"And what about poor Mr. Loomus," Annie said, reaching for another chunk of the sugary cake. "Poor baby. He's so agitated. You know what he tried to tell me by blinking his eyes like mad and giving out a little frog sound? Benjy thinks his son is in some kind of trouble."

"They lie so long like that, their minds sometimes play tricks on them," another nurse said.

Not many nurses took to this special line of duty, caring for the almost hopelessly paralyzed. It was depressing and required a certain kind of attention and intuition. The rewards were few, and the work was difficult. But those who did it had an extraordinary gift for caring and a deep compassion.

"I've been reading him those letters his son writes from New York," Annie said, licking frosting off her fingers. "I have to admit, that boy is a mite peculiar. But he seems to be having a good time. I don't see where he's in trouble, though. I just don't know what to do for Benjy sometimes."

"Maybe he would like his son to be in trouble. Maybe he would like to punish him for not visiting." Everyone looked up as Dr. Gottfried entered the room and walked toward the small mound of cake. They all nodded in agreement. That was a very smart observation.

The phone woke Marty up. The window over the fire escape was open slightly, just enough to bathe him in a shaft of warm air. A newspaper was resting on his face, and his ankles were crossed. He had dozed off. Just a little Saturday afternoon nap. On the weekends he slept days and became a night owl.

"Hello?" he said fuzzily, reaching for the recently polished red phone.

"Hello." A female voice. A Princess-in-Waiting. Instantaneously, he was awake and alert. Be cool, he reminded himself.

"Who's this?" he said in a low, curious voice.

"I ran an ad in *New York* magazine and you answered it."

Silence.

The voice at the other end faltered slightly. "It was Box C267."

"Oh, yes," he said vaguely as if she were applying for a job. "Could you tell me more about yourself? Not that I answer so many of them, it's just that the box numbers are hard to get straight."

"Well," said the voice slowly and distinctively. "I'm a redhead and I—"

"Oh, yes," he replied. "Now I remember your ad."

Marty wouldn't bother to search for the ad. This was pay dirt. A winner. It didn't matter what the ad said. And the timing couldn't have been better. This must have been one of the new letters he had written.

"What do you do, Bob? I forgot."

Marty was about to open his mouth and then he closed it. He had forgotten, too. What was the last batch of letters? He hadn't used dentist. Doctor . . . well, that wasn't such a good idea anymore. Bad luck. Was it lawyer? No, he had used that a lot. Must have been CPA.

"I'm a CPA," he said somewhat tenuously.

"Oh, that's right, now I remember. That was in your letter."

"What's your name?"

"Sharie."

"Have you done the personal ads a lot?"

"No, not really."

"Well, it's safer all around to meet in a public place."

"Yeah, I guess it is."

"Name a place around you."

There was a pause, and he thought she was deciding. "There's nothing around me. You name a place. It would be more fun."

This had never happened to Marty. This one was supercautious. But after what had happened to him the last time, beggars couldn't be choosers.

"There's a bar on Fifty-third Street. Whistler's Mother. Between Eighth and Ninth Avenues." He had stopped in there once when it had started to snow. He hoped it was still there.

"Fine."

"Tomorrow night? Is that okay?" He didn't want to sound too eager.

"Yeah, but let's keep it early. I have to go to work in the morning. I teach school."

"Hey, how will I know you?"

She thought a minute. "I have red hair, and I'll probably be wearing a raincoat."

"What if it's too warm? Hey, I got it. I'll be wearing a white carnation."

The voice on the other end seemed to be silent for so long, Marty was afraid he'd said something to offend her. Damn. He hated this. But he couldn't afford to lose her.

Finally, she said, "That's really very clever of you."

"Okay, see you in front of Whistler's. Say, around six o'clock?"

"Fine. I'll be looking forward to it, Bob."

When he hung up, he chuckled. Did he notice a little flirty-flirt at the end of that? He went to the wall. With his red magic marker he had written Laura, Debbie, Doreen, Martha, and Heather, all of which he had crossed out. He wrote Sharie's name below that.

Terry felt as if the phone might explode. So that's how he did it. "How will I know you?" And then the wonderful "I'll be wearing a white carnation." But the petals on the floor. How did that happen? She would find out tomorrow night. Because she would have to catch him in the act. This would require all the acting ability she could summon.

CHAPTER FIFTEEN

The phone rang four times Sunday, and Terry decided to take it off the hook again. She **didn't** want to speak to anyone at all, and she didn't want to listen to the constant ringing. Over and over she rehearsed how she would take this man. She couldn't get him solely on the white carnation or the fact that he answered ads or that he dug redheads. She would have to trick him until she was positive.

Around noon she made herself a ham sandwich, but she was too nervous to finish it. The clock seemed to stick at each hour. Years passed between the numbers three and four. She filed her nails and polished them with beige almond. Cherry red would look too gaudy with her outfit. She switched back and forth from beads to a simple strand of pearls. Pearls were so feminine and old-fashioned. But the beads... Suddenly, she regained her sensibilities. If this was her man, he wouldn't give a damn *what* she was wearing. The other women were found dead with nothing on.

She kept that in mind as she applied her lipstick. Her hand slipped so much, she missed her lip line by about a fourth of an inch and had to reach for the cold cream, soap and water, and powder, and start all over with a lipstick brush.

She wore her green silk dress. She finally decided against both the beads and the pearls. It was way too early, but she was so nervous, she decided to drive into the City and wait in her car. The air was light and summery, and the sky had darkened over as if it might rain.

Walking out the door onto the street, Terry met a woman she recognized from the laundry room. The woman did a double take. Terry winked, but the woman still looked confused.

The red hair was a great disguise. In fact, this wasn't her first experience with a wig. Once she and Bob had gone impulse shopping. She had tried on wigs in a department store. Frosted, blond, brown, and red. Bob had bought her the red wig because he thought it looked sexy. Later he had insisted she wear it to bed.

What happened to that wig? Oh, yes, she had put it in a plastic bag and stored it away. Then when they were dividing the spoils of a moribund marriage, she had thrown it away. It was a memory she had wanted to ruin. And she did. It ended up in the big trash can in front of the house, and the lid slipped off. The wig fell out of the bag. She was driving down the driveway in the rain when she saw it. First she thought it was a dead rat. A fitting tribute to their marriage.

Her car windows were rolled down as she drove across the Fifty-ninth Street Bridge. Her eye caught another car. A man was definitely looking at her. She glanced into the rearview mirror. Yes, it was believable. But really, she had never liked wigs. They itched—and either slipped or cut off circulation.

When she got to Eighth Avenue, she found a parking spot immediately and sat there waiting, smoking. She was carrying a camel clutch bag. Though large, it fitted perfectly under her arm. In it were all the usual paraphernalia, including—wrapped in a geometric-patterned scarf—her gun.

She looked at her watch again. Ten to six. She'd sit five minutes longer, then stroll over to the bar and wait outside. She saw a lot of couples walking around. They were holding hands and laughing. There were squeezes and quick kisses. She thought of four young women who would never have that kind of fun on a spring evening. Slowly, she got out of her car. Either Bob was her man, or he wasn't. And she thought he was.

As she walked toward the bar, her eyes looked for only one thing: the white carnation. She moved regally, confidently. She was so in control, she thought she'd go mad.

Then she saw him. Time to go into her act. She slouched a little to appear shorter. As she crossed the street, she looked down shyly. Then she stepped up on the curb and into the eyes of the only man, around five foot ten, who was waiting in front of the bar and wearing a white carnation in his buttonhole.

"You must be Bob," she said, touching her hair self-consciously. "I'm early, I think."

"And you must be Sharie. So am I."

She giggled. Her laugh was high-pitched, a reasonable facsimile of one she had heard from prostitutes when she had been a police matron. A job she might have again if she didn't deliver. She mustn't make a slipup. She couldn't even think as Terry. She had to be Sharie Somebody, the teacher who wanted to meet a nice eligible bachelor.

"I hope you don't think I'm a male chauvinist, but you're a knockout."

Terry feigned shyness, tossing her head, not realizing it wasn't her own long hair but instead, a wig fastened by hairpins. As they moved through the door and into the bar, she met his twinkling eyes and felt a deep chill running through her. My God, he looked like the boy next door. No wonder those gullible women were taken in.

The waitress came up. Terry was dying for a stiff drink but knew she couldn't. "Coke," she said lightly. "I've had a stomach virus."

Bob ordered red wine. Wine. The wineglasses that were free of fingerprints.

They exchanged smiles. Two lonely strangers brought together by a fad.

"What grade do you teach, Sharie?" he said politely. His white carnation was fastened in the buttonhole of a navy jacket. He wore no tie, just a white shirt and gray pants.

"Second. I teach second grade."

"Where?"

"Where. Oh, at The Little Red School House. On Bleecker."

"And do you like it?"

"I love it. And you?" Oddly enough, she found him attractive. And normal. For one panicky moment, she wondered if she was wrong. She desperately wanted to be right. Her career, her life, was at stake.

"Yeah, I love my job. I work for Sullivan and Shawn." Their drinks came, and she bobbed forward, sipping her Coke from the straw. When she met his eyes again, she felt he was looking at her strangely. It was just a flicker, and then it passed.

I bet he lives in the Village, too, Terry thought. He didn't question the school. Maybe he passed it all the time. That would put him in the West Village. And he bought his carnations at that little flower shop on Eighth Avenue.

He studied her face. He was beginning to have the funniest sensation that they had met before. Where? At a singles mixer a long time ago? Maybe she lived in the Village.

"By the way, where do you live?"

Funny, she was just going to ask him the same question. "I don't know if I should say. I hardly know you."

Again Terry bobbed down for her Coke, and his eyes grew wider.

When she lifted her head, the face he presented was fully composed, smiling.

"I think you don't live in Manhattan," he said simply. "And you feel reluctant about it."

She studied him. That was uncanny. Her hand moved to her clutch bag. She opened it and fingered around for her cigarettes. She offered him one, and he took her lighter and lit their cigarettes. Damn wig. It was starting to itch. Well, she'd just have to live with it. She tossed her head again, unconsciously, like she did with her own long hair.

"Where did you get that beautiful red hair from?" he asked pleasantly.

"My mother," she said.

He stared at her hair. Underneath the red were a few tiny strands of pitch-black hair. No, they weren't roots. She was wearing a wig. She was a fake Princess. Why? He couldn't figure it out. He would kill her, anyway, but why the ad, why the trick? Then he blinked. And when he did, he saw a picture. A small, grainy black-and-white photo in the clipping he had pasted to the refrigerator door. And he saw a face. Not a clear face. A small tomato-stained newsprint face. Not unlike the one he was sitting across from. And when he squinted, he could imagine black curly hair and not the fake red wig. But then he had known when he guessed she didn't live in Manhattan. Most cops working in Manhattan lived elsewhere.

Clever. So he had been caught. He looked around. Were the people at the tables all plainclothes policemen waiting to arrest him? She was too feminine to be a cop, with the pretty dress and the fluttering eyelashes. Didn't cops carry guns? Where was hers? In her bra?

"So, where *do* you live?" he asked casually.

"You were right. I don't live in Manhattan. Queens. Men don't like to go out with girls who don't live here, so I don't like to say it right off. But the rents are so cheap. I have a beautiful apartment."

"I'd like to see it. I don't mind traveling for someone I think is special."

Again that gesture of sipping her Coke and this time he saw the wig slip. He had to play it cool. She could ruin everything. It was either kill her, or he couldn't live.

"How did you get here?" he asked.

"I have a car."

That figures, he thought. And she's probably got the gun in her car. Still, he had to take her somewhere. She couldn't come to his place.

Terry was thinking that she still didn't have anything on him. She would *have* to bring him home.

"Do you have to go right home?" he said. "I was thinking it's such a great night. We could go for a ride if you have a car."

"Why not ride over to Queens? I have wine," she said.

"I could take the subway home," he said innocently.

"Well, don't expect to stay over," she replied, laughing self-consciously and then ducking again. She had no script for what was to follow, only the knowledge that she was smarter than he was, because she was a cop and she had a gun.

"Nice night," he said crisply when they emerged from the bar.

"Yep."

When they got into the car, Terry put her bag between the door and the seat on her side. She would lose control of the car if anything happened, but she would have her gun.

As they drove to Queens, he told her his name was Bob Freeman and that he had been born in the New York area but had lived in the South for a while. He liked New York, especially the snow.

They were still chatting as they took the elevator up and, knowing what she had to do, Terry unlocked her door. Anything related to the police department had been cleaned away, shoved under something or camouflaged. Her handcuffs were under the couch. She'd need those quickly. To the eyes of a single man, it was a simply furnished apartment in a highrise in Queens. An apartment you couldn't get for that price in Manhattan. There was a tweed couch with fat cushions and bright throw pillows, a black reclining chair, a bar with one stool, reprints and photographs on the wall.

"Nice place you have here," he said, and sat down on the couch.

Terry was standing. "Can I get you some . . . coffee, tea, wine."

"Coffee, tea, or me," he joked. "Wine. Any kind is fine."

Now she had a problem. She was still clutching her bag under her arm. If she could get him off the couch, she could slip it between the cushions and pull it out if, and when, she needed it. Instead, she took it into the kitchen with her. Awkwardly. Realizing she was shaking. And then she had to carry her soft drink and his wine, still with her bag under her arm.

She sat on the couch next to him and placed her bag to the left. To the right was a crack where the pillows joined. That's where she wanted her gun. Maybe he'd ask to use the bathroom.

Where another man would have flung his arm on the back of the couch behind her, he sat with his hands folded. She was tense, waiting for his next move. How did he do it? He must take them by surprise. Her hand fiddled with the snatch of the clutch bag. Too soon.

He smiled at her innocently. He sipped his wine, then rested his glass on the floor. "That must be some commute you have every morning."

"Well, I used to teach in Queens, but I got a job downtown. The car makes life easier."

"Say, I was wondering," he said, casually, "do you have the letter I wrote you?"

Every nerve in Terry's body was tingling. So this is how he did it. The white carnation so they would know who he was. The letter . . . he pocketed the letter so no one would find it.

"I think so, why?" She smiled back at him, but her knees were trembling. Something was going to happen.

"Oh, just because I forgot what I wrote and I'd like to see it."

Had any woman ever said no? It was such an innocuous question. This lady wasn't that smart. He was one step ahead of her.

"The letter is in my bedroom," she said, but didn't move. She could pick up the clutch bag and say she had to touch up her makeup, which sounded phony. Or she could make it fast. And come right back to the couch. She debated for a second, stalling by lighting a cigarette, trying to tease him. Deftly, he took the cigarette out of her hand and began smoking it. This was it.

She slipped off her heels so she could move faster. Get the letter. Come back. Lean over for another cigarette. He'd probably make a move. Get the gun. But you couldn't choreograph it. That's why she was a cop.

She walked slowly into her bedroom and dashed to the dresser. She had saved only his letter. Scrambling out, she walked slowly again toward the couch.

"Here's the letter," she said.

He was smiling.

She sat down and reached into her bag for a cigarette, fumbling under the silk scarf for her gun. She could feel only lipstick, comb, lighter. It had shifted to the bottom. Damn. Trying not to look conspicuous, she wiggled her hand around, her fingers frantic to touch the metal. She heard him laughing. Must have been something in the letter. Then she turned. Her hand was still flapping around in her bag behind her, feeling for her gun, when she realized she was looking at it. She was right about him. He was very clever. He had found her gun and he was pointing it at her.

The third floor of the Twentieth Precinct that had housed the once-frenetic task force was now nearly empty. The suspect had confessed. The hotel clerk had identified him. Top psychiatrists had diagnosed him and believed him to be the killer. Where there had been frequent murders, there were none.

It was late Sunday night, and Bernie Moskowitz should have left long ago. Instead, he took the elevator to the third floor. But he couldn't get Terry off his mind. He was concerned.

Feeling slightly guilty, he walked over to Terry's desk and looked around. Slowly, he opened the drawers, searching for something, anything, that gave her real justification for her mistake. In one drawer was a box of tissues. In another drawer were some papers. He seized them. But the top one had only five lines written on it—all in capital letters. FLORISTS, WITNESSES, LETTERS, FAMILIES, MURDERER PROFILE. But nothing had been written under those headings.

She must have something with her. There must have been a solid reason to launch a whole case that ran embarrassingly counter to the department. He studied her list again. FLORISTS. That was unusual. The white carnation. They had held that back from the press as Terry had done first. For some reason it hadn't been in the exposé article. So that had bothered her. But to do a one-detective search of every florist in Manhattan? He rubbed his chin. Yablonsky had cased every hotel on his off hours. Well, that was different.

He pounded his fist on the hard steel table, and then he sucked his knuckle because it hurt. She could have been more subtle about this. That was the trouble with Terry. She could be jugheaded. He knew he wouldn't get any sleep until he found a way of helping her.

Detached, she watched the ceremony. Her dress was starched so much that it stood out like a white cloud. Her white anklets were spotless, and her new white patent-leather Mary Janes were her pride and joy. She wore lacy white gloves and carried a bouquet of flowers. A white filmy veil followed her whenever she moved her head.

"Just think, Terry, we look like brides. When we get married, we'll have longer dresses and wear high heels. Oh, and we'll have handsome bridegrooms."

"Shhhh. I'm not getting married."

Her friend kicked her in her white, almost-identical shoe. "That's dumb. Every girl wants to get married."

"I want to be a detective. Like my father."

The little girl next to her chuckled. "You mean a policewoman, stupid."

A nun was watching the two little girls and gave them a severe, reprimanding look. She put her finger to her lips in warning, and nothing else was needed to silence them during the confirmation ceremonies.

But of course they couldn't keep quiet. "Will, too," whispered Terry hoarsely, her lips barely moving.

"Will not," hissed the other little girl.

"Will."

"Won't."

When the children filed out of the pew, Terry looked up and saw three familiar masculine faces beaming back at her. They were her father's old partners, and they had come because her daddy couldn't come. He was dead.

There were smiles and more smiles. And Terry was wearing a long white dress and white sling-back heels. She could barely see through the white, filmy veil, and she carried different flowers. Orange blossoms and baby's-breath that seemed to be growing out of a shiny white Bible with gold lettering.

Next to her was a tall, handsome man in a dark suit. She was watching his mustache move with his lips as he said his vows. She watched as he slipped the wedding band on her finger.

Then they were seated, and one of the old familiar faces, her father's partner, his hair graying now, was toasting them with champagne. A voice said, "You'll be wanting to start a family and give up your police work." Terry watched herself. No words came. "Tell them," she wanted to whisper. "Tell them you're going on to be a detective. Like your new husband. Like your father. Tell them. Tell them."

But the figure said nothing. She just smiled like the bride that was sitting on top of the beautiful tiered wedding cake. She watched the cake sink and crumble and turn into little pieces of dust, and then she was in a drafty room. The stench was so bad she wanted to float down and put a clothespin on her nose. And then she melted into herself, and she was the one who took out her notebook.

"Who found her?"

"The super."

"Where does she work?"

"They're checking."

Cameras clicking. Voices low and respectful. And that putrid smell. Forcing herself not to gag. Being professional. She looked down toward the floor and saw that she was wearing brown pants and a tan vest and blazer. Her blouse was cotton, businesslike.

Her tan boots were highly polished. Under her jacket, her gun nestled in the holster.

She had to be perfect. She was a homicide detective and a woman.

Embarrassed, she covered her body as her sharply tailored clothes disintegrated on her. She was wearing a gauzy, gray-white gown and she was barefoot. She stepped outside her body. Why were the people crying? Then she saw. She lay like a queen, rigid, resting in a coffin.

Two of her father's partners were there. They weren't crying. They were whispering. Soon the whispering had become so loud, it sounded like a hum, like a hymn. "Own fault." "Not the cop her father was." "After all, she let herself get caught."

Terry put her transparent hands over her ears, crying silently, No, no. She looked at her own corpse.

"No, no," she kept crying as she tried to make her voice heard. "No, no." She was swimming, crawling, struggling out of the dream world. And then she blinked. She was awake. Her eyes were open, but it was still dark.

She was breathing heavily now and shaking all over. And she wasn't watching herself. She was herself. The pain. She felt the pounding, relentless pain. It felt as if her head was split in two. Someone had hit her with a brick. Or a gun.

She was lying down, but her hands and feet had been tied together, and it was dark. She screamed, but no sound came out. Something was pressing on her face. Of course. She was gagged. Bound and gagged.

And she remembered it. All of it. The red wig. The green silk dress. The gun that was pointed at her. And then she remembered that she had made a big mistake. The biggest of her life. And it was something fundamental. Something she had thought she had learned as a policewoman. Just because she was a cop didn't mean she wasn't female, and you can't expect to overpower a man who is, most likely, physically stronger. She had thought she could take him. Her ego again.

She shivered in the dark, though it wasn't cold. Struggling, she somehow swung her legs to the side, bent her knees and, lifting from her diaphragm, managed to sit up. She felt objects assaulting her in the face, and she ducked a little. He had put her somewhere. But where the hell was she?

CHAPTER SIXTEEN

At seven o'clock on Monday morning, Moskowitz was at his desk. He hadn't slept well. All he could think about was Terry and her stupid move. He looked at the clock and took a sip of his coffee. What was she doing this morning?

Did they reassign her? He had heard she was shelved for a few days. Poor Terry. His anger at her recklessness gave way to fatherly concern. The least he could do would be to call her and give her some support. Tell her she'd win back her shield, even if he didn't believe it. Though, knowing Terry, she'd spend half her life trying.

He dialed, eager to be of help. No answer. Well, she was probably still sleeping. For her sake, he hoped she wasn't even home. He hoped she was waking up somewhere else with someone who could replace some of what she was going to be missing now that she wasn't a detective anymore. Though, knowing Terry, he knew that wasn't what was happening.

He tried to push it out of his mind until an hour later when he saw Detective George Yablonsky move into what had been Terry's desk. When he saw Yablonsky pitch her coffee mug with the rainbow on it into the trashcan, he dialed her number again. Eight o'clock. It rang ten times. He went back to work, but it was bothering him.

There was no night and day, only darkness. She thought she saw little flickers of light that danced like dust motes, and then she seemed to lose them again. Her head still pounded, and it helped to close her eyes and sink into sleep, though every nerve in her body was aware of noise, change of light, anything. She was on guard, yet asleep. She woke up to a ringing. A phone. For who?

She fought down the panic that bubbled in her throat. Patience. Something would happen, and this nothingness would end. She recalled nursery rhymes and sang popular songs in her mind. Exercising almost inhuman control, she tried to hold back the pressure that had built up terribly in her kidneys.

She rolled as far as she could to the right and then back to the left, feeling about with her hair, her nose, her eyelashes, for something, anything. She rolled into something cold and clammy. It clung to her like flypaper, and she thrashed around, repulsed, frightened, trying to throw the substance off. She couldn't breathe. But she did. And there, gagging in the dark, she realized to her disgust that the dampness under her and the relief in her lower abdomen were connected. She had been so scared, she had just peed in her pants.

Later that afternoon, an angry Frank Fazio phoned Moskowitz.

"I just got word that Morrison didn't show up for her new assignment. She's lucky to be a policewoman again. What's the matter? Not good enough for her? Maybe something's wrong. Do you know anything?"

"No, Frank, I don't," Moskowitz said sadly, now more concerned than ever.

"Well, I thought you'd know," Fazio said. "Listen, I'm busy. If she shows up, tell her to report in."

Moskowitz was beating the eraser tip of a pencil against the desk. "Sure, Frank. I'll do that."

Against his will, he picked up the phone and dialed the Sixth Precinct. He let it ring, and when someone answered, he hung up fast. No, he couldn't do that. He owed it to Terry not to call her soon-to-be ex. Yet this was beginning to worry him.

Terry was lying on her back on the floor again. She was in a cage of some sort. Maybe if she rolled diagonally she could figure it out. She started but didn't get far. There was a soft square like a base in a baseball game. Her nose touched and sniffed the fabric. Odd. With all the strength she could muster in her abdomen muscles and the back of her thighs, she rose up. She waved her nose in the air. Then she felt that clammy, sticky substance again. It was paper-thin and clung to her nose and mouth. All she could think about were dead jelly fish lying on the beach. She pulled away, nauseated. Was she just going to be left to die? When was the last time she had eaten or had any water? Now she had energy and she was angry. Angry at herself. Would he come back and kill her or leave her like this? Panic made her dizzy, and she forced herself to regain that anger. It gave her courage. Through her gag she said with all the force she had, a very muffled, "God damn it!"

"God damn it!" Moskowitz shouted. He was tired of not getting an answer. And why didn't she show up for her new assignment? It was none of his business, and it was all of his business—because she was a friend and he cared.

There was one possible answer, though he wasn't sure he would be doing the right thing. He put on his raincoat and left the building.

In his pocket he was fingering his key chain. Three keys didn't belong to him. They were Terry's apartment keys: outer door, top lock, bottom lock. When she moved in, she had said to him, "Bernie, what if I'm ever locked out? You're the only friend I trust with this. Keep my extra keys in case of an emergency."

He still had the keys. And now he was going to use them to enter her apartment. Because, if she was sitting there chain-smoking and not answering her phone, she was going to get the lecture of her life.

Terry's stomach started to rumble violently. She had to think of something else. Him. The boy next door, that's what he looked like. Maybe not as attractive, but charming in a shy, sweet way. Some decent man you might chat with as you went down to get your mail. You could talk about the weather or junk mail or the latest tenant meeting. Then he would go to his apartment and you to yours . . . and he would figure out what innocent woman he was going to kill next.

She heard a noise. A distinct noise . . . like a door slamming. He was back! What time was it? Night or day? He had come back, and he would open her cage and kill her. She curled into herself, not making a sound, afraid to breathe.

Words. Screaming. She heard a voice.

"Terry? Terry!"

She shot straight up and then crumpled back down again. Moskowitz? It was Bernie. He caught the killer and had come to rescue her. Smart, smart Moskowitz. She loved him.

"Terry? Are you there?"

"I'm in here," she shouted, but of course it came out no louder than the drone of summer mosquitoes.

Bernie Moskowitz, feeling almost criminal, tromped through the living room, dining area, and into the empty bedroom where the bed was made and stood at the door of the bathroom.

Terry began to shout and cry as loudly as she could, banging her head against the wall and thumping her bound feet on the floor. Moskowitz was in the kitchen getting a drink of water. Carefully, he rinsed and dried the glass. Should he write her a note that he had been there? Nah, she was going through a bad time. She'd turn up. Besides, she might accuse him of being overprotective.

Passing the big front closet in the living room, he left the apartment, slamming the door again. Hands in his pockets, he went down the hall.

Terry was trying to fight for breath. The door had slammed. He had left! Just like that. And he could have rescued her. Tears of frustration rolled down to the tip of her gag, and she began to hiccup. Damn it! How stupid could she be? Where was she? "Oh, Terry, look at all the nice closet space in the apartment. I'm so envious. You could put another bedroom in that front closet. A walk-in closet, practically. And a key. It locks. How lucky." Oh, it was humiliating. She was locked in her own front closet.

That clammy stuff was the plastic from the dry cleaners. The base was the bottom of her vacuum cleaner. He had dumped her, gagged her, tied her up, and imprisoned her in her own apartment. She wasn't frightened anymore. It was home. But she was so furious, she would get herself out of there even if she had to ram the door down with her head.

Phyllis Samuels liked to have a cocktail before starting dinner, which she ate around seven-thirty. She poured a Chocolate Alba Fit 'n' Frosty 77 into her blender, then she added some bubbly chocolate diet soda up to the two-ounce level and one plunk, blend, ice cube; two plunk, blend; three plunk, blend, ice cubes. Then she turned off her blender and poured the low-calorie milkshake into a glass.

She would be on maintenance soon. All she had wanted to do was get down to a skinny size, but there had been so many personality changes that accompanied her weight loss. She was more confident now. She had Raoul, and there were others. Pretty soon she'd start looking for a job in public relations. Six months ago she couldn't have acted or thought this way. Six months ago, if Marty Loomus had rejected her, she would have abandoned her diet. She would have cheesecaked herself steadily downhill.

Marty, what was he doing now? Not that she really cared, but she felt sorry for him. She had just outgrown him. She walked her drink into her tiny living room and sat down.

She reached to an end table and picked up her big envelope of letters. They had been set aside during those awful Lonely Hearts killings. But now it was safe. Probably safer than picking up men in a bar. And making up for lost time, she was always looking for a new man to date.

Some of these letters she hadn't had time to read. She picked one up. Funny, this one had looked good to her when she first started. She put it down listlessly. No, she didn't want to come over and have breakfast in bed with him, and she resented being called "my darling" by a virtual stranger.

She picked up another letter and read it through and then smiled. Now that was sweet and sincere. She didn't have to go out with every kook in the world just because she had lost close to thirty-seven pounds. She liked genuineness and gentlemanliness and, yes, humility.

Why not? She picked up the phone to dial and then dropped it as if an electric current ran through it. The number. That creep. That hypocrite. Marty had answered her ad!

He swayed to the left, and he swayed to the right, his arm holding on to the strap. A young woman sitting practically under him looked up from her paperback romance. He was kind of good-looking in a nice way. Well dressed. Nice tie, although it was loosened now because of the heat in the rush-hour subway. Then she went back to her book. She wasn't much good at picking up guys if they were strangers.

Marty was oblivious to the young woman's subtle

attentions. He was thinking of how great it was to have two apartments. His fingers rummaged around in his pocket, and he found her keys. All that power in one piece of metal. He could have killed her last night and made her a cop Princess, but he couldn't do it. This was smarter in the long run and more fun. Even now she was thinking of him, analyzing him, waiting for him but not knowing if he would rescue her. He smiled broadly, and his chin dimpled.

He was aware of a woman speaking to him. "Excuse me," said a face almost directly below him. "Haven't we met before . . . somewhere?"

He looked down, startled, frightened. He wanted to run, but it was an express train. "N-n-no," he stammered.

"Do you take the A train often?" she said, still looking up at him.

"Never," he said abruptly. He didn't trust strangers. Why did she have to pick on him? But he wasn't stupid, not Marty Loomus. She could be one of those lady cops or someone his voices might be tricking him with. When the train stopped, he'd mingle with the crowd and lose her. They continued the trip in silence. She went back to her book and thought how bad she was at that sort of thing.

Marty continued reading the subway ads in English and Spanish, moving his lips. He had come from work like any other commuter going to Queens. It was no trouble finding her apartment, and once outside, he stood in front of an art store diagonally across the street. There were too many people going into the lobby. It was a doorman building. He wanted to wait for a minute until the doorman stepped away. Then he could sneak past.

He came closer to the apartment and watched carefully. The doorman vanished, and Marty stepped into the elevator. There was low, tinny Muzak in the elevator. He shut his eyes and heard applause. He saw hot pinks and vivid greens and was with his

Princesses for a minute. Then he opened his eyes to the muted, weather-stained carpeting, and the elevator opened on her floor.

Striding out, careful to look in both directions, he took out her door key and the long, skinny closet key. This, he thought, was the most intimacy he had shared with a woman, other than his Princesses, since Fat Phyllis.

He thrust the key in the lock and then took a deep breath as the door opened. A funny smell greeted him first. The type of odor you smelled sometimes in the subway. Whoops, he'd have to do something about that.

In the bedroom he found what he wanted. On a little glass tray were cologne and perfume bottles. He sprayed and sniffed and dabbed until he found a sweetish, lemony one that he liked. He couldn't pronounce the name. He'd probably use the whole bottle.

Terry had fallen into a fitful, nightmarish sleep, and when the closet door opened suddenly and the light poured in, she blinked uncomfortably. All at once he was spraying perfume into the closet. She couldn't catch her breath. He kicked her then and took both of her arms, yanking her up and out of the misty closet.

Trying to adjust her eyes to what seemed like glaring light, Terry managed to stand with her feet bound together. When he let go, she felt like a wobbly colt sagging in the middle. She looked down at her expensive green silk dress. It looked like dirty, wrinkled wrapping paper.

Terry glared at the man hatefully. He reached into his jacket pocket and pulled out what no one on that subway had suspected he had. It had given him a thrill to carry a gun all day. He could see by the look in her eyes that she expected him to use it. That was just like a cop. Everything was guns and violence. He abhorred it. The gun was power, that's all. This was a play, anyway. And he was writing the script as he was going along. He chuckled. Though he did know what the last scene was.

He untied her hands and feet carefully using wire snips. It had been her idea, of course. In her broom closet, on the shelf above, he had found a carefully lettered cardboard box. TOOLS. There was everything he needed for her captivity. Wire, shears, and in the linen closet, a dishcloth that was just the right size for a gag.

"Want to go to the bathroom? God knows you're not good at controlling yourself."

Terry nodded. Maybe there was something there she could find to free herself. He pointed her in that direction, marched her down the hall, and took great delight in jabbing the gun in her back.

Woodenly, Terry went into the bathroom. She mustn't start thinking like a hostage, which she might be, or like a victim, which she definitely was. She looked at her things differently now since she was a prisoner in her own house. Quickly, she scanned her hand lotion dispenser, her dusting powder, her collection of nail polishes . . . her nail file.

When she came out, he pointed the gun in the direction of the kitchen.

"You must be starved," he said compassionately.

She turned sharply to see if he was smirking. But he wasn't. He was honestly concerned. Was it a trick? "Yes," she said tonelessly, keeping her eye on him.

He went to her refrigerator and opened it, indicating with the point of her gun that she should look inside. Carefully, she clutched onto the door while he held her at gunpoint. Then quickly, she let it slam back as far as it would go, hitting him in the chest and getting him off-guard for a moment. Sure enough, the gun fell to the floor. There was no contest; the gun fell on his side of the door. Besides,

Terry was too weak to bend this quickly. He snatched the gun. Next time she would.

And then she saw it. Shining on the floor. The file had dropped out of the top of her dress. They faced each other as before on either side of the refrigerator door. She expected fury, recriminations. "Nice try," he said evenly. "I think you'll find some ham in there."

Terry shivered. Talk about having your privacy violated. He was raping her apartment. Yes, there was ham. It seemed years ago that she had gone to the deli and watched him slice a pound of ham and then bought fresh Swiss cheese. That was gone. There was a loaf of whole-wheat bread she kept in there so as not to entice the roaches. She felt a pang for a life she was being deprived of.

Not that she felt her stomach could handle it but she took out the cole slaw and olives. She started to reach for some cold beer, but he stopped her. Instead, he handed her a jar of mustard.

Terry slapped the ham on the slices of bread and slathered the top piece with mustard. All the while the gun was pressing into her back. She plopped the cole slaw into a small dish and kept telling herself she was sane—he was the psycho.

They carried the plates of food into the dining room and put everything down on the table. He walked into the living room, stopped at the bar, and walked back. She was dying of thirst. "Drink this," he said. "It will relax you." He handed her a bottle of whiskey, no glass.

"What do you want with me?" she said against her better judgment. "Why are you going to so much trouble to keep me alive when you killed all those other women?"

"Always the cop. Trying to get a confession from me."

Terry said nothing. She finished her sandwich and tried not to drink too much whiskey. Demeaning.

The man was making her drink it straight from the bottle and at gunpoint. He never relaxed his hand, and he was eating, too.

"I need a cigarette," she said.

"Nope. You should quit. It's bad for your health."

So is that gun, she mused. She wanted a cigarette so badly she could have screamed or begged. But she sat there mute.

"You know, lady detective," he said, laughing, enjoying her dilemma and his new assertiveness with her. "You could be of real use." He wasn't Marty the schlepper or Bob the cool guy. He was everything he had always wanted to be. He was a walking Humphrey Bogart movie, and he could turn it all on or off at will. And Benjy said he wasn't very smart. "Don't go to computer school because you're not a very bright boy." Hah.

Lady detective. God, how she hated that. Reep the Creep. He had called her that. It was all his fault. She was right. All along, she was right. And she was being punished for it. What did they want from her as proof, this?

"Have another olive," he insisted. She stared at him. He was congenial again, as if they were at a picnic. The man was a maniac. She had to keep trying to think of ways to save herself. He hadn't used the gun so far. He would probably put her back in that smelly cage. She was right. She was a hostage of sorts. What were the terms? Did Moskowitz know? Did Bob know? Bob. Suddenly, she missed her soon-to-be ex-husband. Suddenly, if she never saw his face again . . . it mattered.

Bob. He had teased her about so many things. Like this tablecloth on the dining room table. With that recollection, an idea was born. Bob had made fun of the little white tassels, tiny balls hanging like fringe. But those prissy little white balls could be ripped off one by one. She began storing them in her hand. Because if Moskowitz was here once, they must have missed her. He'd come back. Her fingers worked deftly, winding and ripping the little balls off the strings. Then, using Hansel and Gretel's ruse, she would leave a path so someone could find her. Brilliant.

"Eventually, I will have to kill you, you know. It gets easier for me. I like it."

Terry nodded silently, ripping off balls and remembering bits and snatches of the rosary.

He looked at her, lifting the gun, her gun. Carefully, she got up. Now what? Had she been correct, or would he just pull the trigger? Would she live or die?

"I'll do the dishes. Don't worry."

She had to struggle to keep her wits. What did that mean? He'd kill her and clean up. No, they were walking into the living room. It was back into the closet. Her white, furry balls. She let one drop every three inches as she walked, thank God, behind him. When he turned, he was reaching for the wire, the wire snips, and the musty washcloth. She gagged before he fastened it and hopped a little as he pointed her into the closet. It was too crowded to stand up. She crumpled over into a ball, knees against chest, and watched wide-eyed as the light got smaller and smaller and the door closed.

Marty locked the closet and then took off his jacket and rolled up his sleeves. He carried the dishes back to the kitchen sink. Emptying the garbage, he figured he could carry it with him as he left. Humming a little tune, he washed and dried the dishes. Then he took one of her sponges and carefully mopped up all the damp surfaces so everything was spic and span. He couldn't stand roaches.

Coming back into the living room, he fastened his cuffs and got into his jacket. He saw them. A trail of little white balls. He picked one up. Then he looked toward the tablecloth. So she had tried to outsmart him. Very funny. They stood out on the dark blue carpeting like a dotted line. He went over to where she had been sitting. The bottom of the tablecloth was de-balled. Clever lady. But not as smart as him. Quietly, he picked up each ball that led almost to the closet door. He deposited them in the garbage bag and walked out the door.

On the subway going home, Marty saw that the train was half-empty. A drunk slept with his knees curled into him, hugging a ragged jacket. People had moved away because he smelled like he hadn't had a bath in months. Marty was staring at one of the tabloids someone had left behind. The headline was "AX KILLER SPLITS." Hello, Ax Man; farewell, Lonely Hearts Killer. New York had forgotten. And no wonder. Everyone thought he was safely tucked in at Bellevue. It was beautiful, really it was. He laughed to himself, and a lady looked at him reproachfully. He quickly shut up and put on a sober face.

Staring into space, he appeared to be studying a beer ad, but he was looking through it, seeing, instead, pictures in his mind. A closet. It had been a long, long time ago. Sylvia had locked him in a dark, musty closet in the cellar of the old house. Benjy had told him that he was a bad boy and threatened him, again, with the warning that they would send him to the orphanage if he didn't behave. He could still feel the smallness of the space, still smell his own sweat and the odors of the storage closet. Once he got so hungry, he killed and ate a water bug.

What were his crimes? Sylvia kept money hidden in her underwear drawer. Quarters in a tiny, silken, red change purse. He had stolen the quarters to buy his friends ice cream. Or buy friends. Because they weren't really friends. He wasn't allowed to play like all the other kids because he had to help out in the shop, pay them back for adopting him and raising him. And even after he bought Eskimo Pies or frozen custard or popsicles, his so-called friends ignored him. Sylvia found out about the quarters and put him in the closet to punish him. And another time he had been a very bad boy. He had torn pages of the female reproductive system right out of an old textbook he had found in a secondhand store. He was twelve then, and they had told him nothing about sex. Only that he was bad and would get girls into trouble if he did "things" to them. He had spent a week in the closet then, with food and water brought to him. Then he took a note to his teacher, saying he had a cold. He had never told anyone about those incidents. Hadn't he deserved the closet and the other punishment—when they dipped his fingertips into the gas flame on the stove and they wouldn't let him run them under cold water?

He could still see Sylvia with her red hair flying out from under her tight bun, and Benjy, never showing emotion, only blind fury. They had bought him from his real mother and even when she had come back and appealed to them that she had made a mistake, they wouldn't give him back to her. Now Sylvia was dead, and Benjy was as good as dead. But sometimes he thought Sylvia was still alive and was one of his voices. Benjy, too, could talk from a long distance. He had told him to put that woman in the closet.

The train flew in a streak past the local stops. In a flash they were at Forty-second, then Thirty-fourth, then Twenty-third, and finally Fourteenth Street.

His spirits sank as they so often did when he approached his apartment. Maybe food would cheer him up. There were so many Chinese restaurants in the neighborhood, it looked like Asia was infiltrating Greenwich Village. He could get that dish with the little noodles and the tiny shrimps. Nah, he wasn't in the mood. Maybe he should have stayed in the apartment in Queens. He could have slept in her clean bed, knowing that she was locked in that stuffy, smelly closet. Just as he once had been.

He walked slowly into his building. As he neared his own door, he heard the phone. Hurrying inside, he grabbed the bright red machine with its inches of curlicued, knotted red cord.

"Hello?"

"Well, hi, is this Bob?"

"Yes," he remembered to say. He knew he must play it cool, though he was terribly excited.

"My name is Audrey, and you answered my ad in the *Voice*."

"Uh-huh," Marty mumbled. Oh, please, God, let her have tangerine-colored tresses.

"Do you remember my ad?"

Marty felt more relaxed now. She was obviously inexperienced, which was infinitely more fun. He could play the game. "Did you use your name?"

"No," she said. "Don't be silly." And then she laughed harder. "Oh, I see what you mean." He liked that high shrieky laugh. So like lovely Doreen and her horse's neigh.

"Read it to me," he begged. He would have another Princess soon. To make up for the one he lost. Even now he thought of what's-her-name with the roommate distastefully. As if he had been tricked by his voices.

"Well, it ran in the *Voice*, and it was about the third column in and the fourth ad down. It said, 'TAURUS, unattached and attractive, 30s, female, desires to lock horns with male who doesn't throw the bull and who isn't a Libra.' Taurus is the sign of the bull, get it?" That high, shrieky laugh again.

He scrunched up his nose. When had he answered that? Was it recently?

"Maybe you could give me a description of yourself? And it's not that looks are important, mind you, it's just that I was burned very badly in a marriage. My wife was overweight and let herself go completely, and I'm kind of sensitive about that sort of thing."

"Oh, don't worry, I'm slim. And everyone says I'm very attractive. I liked your letter."

He waited for more. Now he was afraid of losing her. Well, he didn't have to marry her; he could just go out with her. If she wasn't Princess material, it was only a loss of a few hours. But he would be frustrated. And he had no time to waste now.

"I'm . . ." he began.

"You explained everything in your letter."

"Hey, let's get together and—"

"Let's. Are you free tonight?" she interrupted.

"You want to meet tonight?"

"Well, I don't want to make a big thing out of this. I usually meet men at the Blue Elephant for just an hour. Then, if we're attracted, I make a date. It's beautiful out tonight, and I have some free time. I thought maybe you'd go." She was thinking how many more names she had to call. Now that it was okay to do this again, it was hard to fit them all in.

He was wrong. She was experienced, after all. "Wait a second," he said. He needed time to think. At the window the blanket he used for a curtain was flapping in the warm breeze. The Blue Elephant. Then he gave her his attention. "Do you live below Fourteenth Street?"

"That's another rule of mine. I don't tell my address or my last name until I get to know the person. And after what's happened, can you blame me? What's your sign?"

"Oh, that. I'm Leo. It's just that I live in the Village, very near the Blue Elephant. I could meet you in a half-hour."

"Oh, really?" Her voice rose provocatively. "How will I know you? You didn't describe yourself."

Like taking candy from a baby. "Well, tell you what—I'll be wearing a white carnation."

She screeched even louder in laughter. "I like you. You sound nice. Only about an hour, now. I have long brown hair, and I'll be wearing a lavender top."

Marty made a face. How depressing. At least she could have been blond—but mousy brown hair? It would be a waste, and yet she was like Doreen in so many ways. Maybe his voices were trying to tell him something. And there was that other thing. Before he had been driven to kill for an urge. Now he knew he liked it. He craved it. Otherwise, his head pounded, and he saw Sylvia and Benjy making fun of him and punishing him.

Quickly, he stepped into the shower and sprinkled some Chanel for Men all over his chest. He bought that at Saks with his employee discount. He had overheard a woman customer saying the scent drove her wild. Very carefully, he selected a white shirt and navy pants. Bob dressed differently than Marty did. It was a disguise of sorts. There would just be time to dash off a note to Benjy, mail it, and stop at ye old corner flower shop for his favorite posy of all time: one snowy white bridal carnation.

As he left his apartment, his spirits soared to a welcome high. Everything was right again. Maybe her hair had reddish highlights. The stars in the sky were twinkling back at him from a blanket of black. Or were they winking? Maybe one was Laura; and another over there (hi, Debbie), and cute Doreen and sensitive Martha.

He was all powerful. He was omniscient. New York's Stupidest had the wrong man in the nuthouse. He had the famous lady detective locked in her own closet, praying her little white balls would bail her out.

He stood still, looking up at the glorious sky. Anything was possible. He was on top for the first time in his life. Finally proving that he was smarter than

Benjy or Sylvia imagined. And that was when his plan came to him. It was so simple. He could have anything he wanted. Why not let the City of New York give it to him?

Dear Benjy,

Just a note. I have another date tonight. Not a redhead but she'll do, I hope. You were wrong, Daddy dear, I am smart. And famous. Have you guessed how? Do you read the newspapers and watch television and listen to the radio? I am the man they all want. Everyone will want to talk to you, and what will you say? Nothing.

All kidding aside, everything's great. I hope to be in Miami soon, and I'll bring Oreo cookies. Remember how the only cookies we ever had in the house were Oreos? You wouldn't take anything else out of the store. You know what, Daddy dear? I hate Oreo cookies.

Be well,
Your son, the ladykiller,
Marty Bob

CHAPTER SEVENTEEN

Her sandals clacked against the pavement as she pretended to walk up and down the street. The hardest thing in the world, Audrey thought, was to wait for a man to meet you. Actually, he wasn't late and *she* was a few minutes early; but every second seemed like an hour when you felt self-conscious. It seemed everyone knew she was all alone and was looking at her and felt sorry for her. All eyes were on her. But not one person sitting at the outdoor tables was even looking her way.

Finally, she saw a man in a white shirt and navy pants on the next corner. She squinted. Yes, it was him, and he was wearing a white carnation in his buttonhole just like he had promised. She walked toward him.

"You must be Bob."

He smiled broadly, and his eyes were bright. "None other," he said merrily.

She liked him. She knew right away. It was the smile. It said a lot, and she was good about reading people. It said he was an unusually happy man and that he was just a little shy. It would be a challenge putting him at ease.

Terry had rolled herself to the back of the closet. The phone again. She could hear it ringing. It perked her up. Someone was trying to reach her. They missed her. Was Bob calling?

That's what she would do to keep from going mad,

from counting the seconds until that killer came back to torment her. She would think of her husband. How had they met? Funny, women were supposed to know those things. But she had met him a few times. Once in the police academy. He was a detective, but he had come back to meet a friend and they had been introduced in the hall. She thought he was tall, blond, and handsome, but if she had a dime for every good-looking male cop she had met, she'd be rich.

It wasn't until he was a detective and she was a policewoman in Brooklyn that they met again at a party for somebody or other. They were standing by the cheese dip or at the makeshift bar, and he said, "Too bad all women cops are so unattractive." She had looked up, trained to pounce on any sexist remark. But all she saw were crinkly eyes and a merry smile. What had she said then? Something. Oh, yes, she had replied—not something sexy and cute, but simply—"I intend to be a detective."

She rolled and bumped into the tall pole that was merging from her old-fashioned vacuum cleaner. She let out a sigh, and it turned into a silent, restrained sob. It wasn't fair! Where was the anger that had made her seek a divorce lawyer? She missed him. Why did he have to change? Why had she . . . why? Why? *Would* she ever see Bob again to tell him she had been held captive or hostage by a raving maniac? Suddenly, life seemed very short. And her tremendous ego? Sitting in the dark in a closet did wonders for one's humility.

They each had a glass of chilled Chablis and talked twenty minutes past Audrey's deadline of only one hour. Because she knew after ten minutes that he was sweet, and she loved it when men asked her questions instead of only talking about themselves.

"You know," she said, "if you're that interested in

seeing the slides from my Japanese vacation, you could come up."

"I might go to Japan this summer," he said, looking at his watch. "What about right now? Do you have other plans?"

"Yes, no—actually, we just met. I thought we might make a date."

"What's the difference, Audrey, if I see your slides from Japan now or next week. We both have time."

"Yeah, I trust you," she said simply.

"Of course." He smiled. "Why wouldn't you?"

"Oh, well, you can't be too careful. Weren't those Lonely Hearts murders the worst?"

"Yeah. But the killer is under lock and key. And besides, do I look dangerous?" A boyish grin spread across his face.

He paid the check, and they walked the short distance back to her apartment on Bethune Street. Audrey was beginning to feel that special magic when, after twenty boring blind dates, she found one that was . . . right.

"Well, this is where I live," she said as they approached a building with a canopy. "It looks modern but it's renovated."

"No doorman?" he inquired, somewhat critically, really relieved.

Apologetically, she said, "No, we have a special buzzer system, for talk and listen, before you buzz back. I think it's just as safe."

When she unlocked her door, he couldn't help but gasp. Everything was done in red and black. Tall plants lined the front windows resembling a strip of African jungle and everywhere, in every free space, were paintings.

He was impressed. "Are those all yours?"

"All mine," she said somewhat discouraged. "I sold one at the Village Art Show last year. I'd love to paint all the time, but how would I support myself? So I'm a layout artist for a boss who treats me like his secretary and an office full of people who think of me as one of the girls. But in my heart I'm a painter. Probably be famous after I'm dead. Gee, you're so easy to talk to."

"These are really good." She was better than Laura, who had just dabbled.

"I know," she said simply. "Maybe one day I'll get married and then I can paint." She stole a look at him. "I'm just joking, of course. Some wine?"

"No, I've had enough."

"Yeah, I've had enough, too. Let me get out my projector."

He took out a cigarette. "Mind if I smoke?"

She got up quickly to get an ashtray. There was a shell one around somewhere. Actually, she did mind the smoke, but she could live with it. As long as he wasn't a chain smoker.

"Hey," he said when she returned with the ashtray, "this is stupid, but I've been racking my brains trying to remember what I said in my letter."

"It was a nice letter. As I remember, you said you were a lawyer, you liked to cook and clean up, and you hoped I replied. I liked it. I would have answered you sooner but for . . . you know."

"Did you save it?" he asked shyly.

"Yeah, I save everything. Look at what a mess my apartment is."

"I'd like to see it if you don't mind."

"Oh, sure. No problem. I'll get it in a second."

At ten o'clock Bernie Moskowitz lay propped up in the double bed chasing channels with the remote. There was nothing he really wanted to watch on television, so he decided to switch it off. But he couldn't fall asleep.

His wife, Blanche, walked into the room. He was sitting straight up in the dark, smoking. She saw the tiny dot of fire and the smoke.

"Can't sleep?" she asked.

"Nope."

"Terry?"

"Yeah," he said, letting her solve it for him.

"Maybe you should keep trying," she suggested.

He turned on the light and dialed Terry's number. Then he hung up. "It rang maybe ten times. No answer."

At eleven, he had unsuccessfully tried to fall asleep on his stomach, side, and back. Angrily, he switched on the light. He reached into the night-table drawer and got out a little book of addresses. The Sixth Precinct. Even as he dialed, he wondered if he was butting his nose in other people's business too much.

The man who answered the phone took a message. Detective Morrison was out. Moskowitz turned off the light and rolled over on his side. In a few minutes, he was asleep.

Just as a touch, after it was over, he took his white carnation and planted it firmly, straight up, between her legs. Then he stepped back to enjoy his rather reckless effect. That's how they would find her, sprawled on her open Castro couch, a pillow over her face, the wrong color hair, and his trademark.

He had left some snowy petals on the carpeting also. "She loves me, she loves me not, she loves me . . ." He always stopped there. Just enough time for their souls to slip out of their dead bodies. That way they knew who they belonged to. Years ago he used to sit plucking daisies in a meadow—before an apartment complex was constructed over it. "She loves me, she loves me not, she loves me . . ." He had always stopped there then, too. Nobody had ever loved him. He just sat in the lonely field and daydreamed about a Princess all his own. Now he had five. In that green pasture in the sky.

She had been a vixen, this Audrey with the long brown hair. It had excited him up to a point. But when she slammed down the shell ashtray, breaking it, the spell had been over.

He looked around. Everything was wiped, and everything was accounted for. He never made mistakes. There was no trace of him but the flower, and he could afford to do that now. After all, he was going to be famous.

At the door he waved and blew kisses to the sprawling corpse. "Good night, Sweet Princess." He had gotten lucky, and the sweet, familiar euphoria had him floating on a cloud. Today was April 6, and he loved the number six. A near-neighbor of sex.

When the phone rang, both men jumped. Bernie scrambled for a cigarette and a light with one hand and the phone with the other.

"Morrison here. You called?"

Moskowitz was fuzzy for a second. He knew he called, but he couldn't grasp what the time span was. "Is Terry with you?" he said bluntly.

Detective Morrison laughed sardonically. "Not for about six months, you know that, Bernie. Why?"

"Because—"

"Is something wrong? Is she in more trouble?" Moskowitz could hear the concern in his voice and wondered once again how two people so obviously in love with each other could be so pigheaded. Why? Stupid question. Because they were cops.

"Well, she was given a new assignment, actually demoted, and . . . she didn't report. She's been missing ever since. I can't find her anywhere. I even broke into her apartment with this key she once gave me."

"That's not like her," Morrison said.

"Probably nothing, huh?"

"What?" said Morrison. "Oh, yeah, nothing. But keep me posted." Morrison hung up. He wondered if she was in trouble or with another man. He couldn't blame her if she was, but he was ashamed to admit he would rather have her in more trouble than with someone else.

Moskowitz smoked another cigarette before he went to bed. It was too early to file her with Missing Persons, he knew that. Usually, it took five days. But, hell, she was a cop. He'd do it first thing in the morning.

CHAPTER EIGHTEEN

The afternoon sun was still strong, and the whole neighborhood turned out to watch the display. Four turquoise-and-white patrol cars came in from the Twentieth Precinct's nearly defunct task force. Eight unmarked cars filled with detectives pulled up behind those. The ringing sound of sirens could be heard in the ears of everyone who lined Bethune Street and the surrounding streets in the West Village. People came out and sat on their front stoops to get a better view.

A car drove quickly down the street and stopped in front of the apartment house. Joel Fenster, the erudite-looking, unsmiling chief medical examiner, stepped out of the car and looked through the crowd. He walked past skinny apartment buildings with flower boxes in the windows that had been painted red and pink and orange, and progressed quickly to the newly renovated apartment building on the corner.

Following the medical examiner were a single file of officers and detectives. Following them were the members of the press. A car bearing the mayor had just parked unobtrusively on Eighth Avenue, and the mayor was telling the *Daily News* that he was especially outraged because the murder had taken place in the peaceful, sleepy West Village. In addition to his residency at Gracie Mansion, he had a little apartment in the Village.

Like a badly drawn cartoon of too many men stuffing themselves into an undersize car, all those people tried to cram into Audrey Lipson's studio apartment. Already in the small space were the chief of detectives; the Deputy Inspector; Zone Captain Frank Fazio, who organized the Valentine task force; and Detective Bernie Moskowitz, who had, in the last frenzied hours, whipped it back into shape. In the apartment, also, were three men from the crime scene unit flashing pictures. There were more people than Audrey had ever invited to one of her intimate parties. And she certainly would have never invited her mother, who stood cowering between two of the huge plants by the windows weeping loudly into a tissue that resembled Swiss cheese.

They were waiting for the pictures to be taken and the men to get their memorabilia. They were also waiting for Joel Fenster, who was coming in person to attend to this surprise murder in a case that was considered closed. The apartment was unbearably airless.

"I can't stand to see her like that," Mrs. Lipson whispered. "Can't anybody do something. Like cover her?"

Moskowitz went over to her and touched her arm sympathetically. "We can't do anything until the medical examiner gets here, Mrs. Lipson." Then he added tactfully, "Wouldn't you be more comfortable waiting outside?"

"No," she said sharply.

Moskowitz knew she would be outside shortly, but he didn't want to upset her.

Just then, Joel Fenster marched in with his tiny entourage and demanded that the room be cleared. Everyone crowded into a huddle and stuffed themselves into the mini-kitchen. The crime scene unit went into the bathroom.

"We were supposed to meet for lunch," Mrs. Lipson announced, wanting to tell her story. She had a ready audience. Where could they go? "She didn't show. We were going to meet by the perfume counter and have lunch in B. Altman's and then do a little shopping. But she was late. So I called her office, and they said she hadn't come in, hadn't called in sick, nothing. So I phoned the apartment. No answer. What mother wouldn't worry? I had a key to her apartment in case she got locked out or there was an emergency. So I ran back to Port Authority and caught the next bus to New Jersey. I found the key, you know where? In my sewing box, that's where. Audrey made me a button box when she was in the second grade. A painted oatmeal box covered with sequins and sparkles."

The men nodded, feeling increasingly uncomfortable, wishing she would shut up so they could think. Most of all, they wanted Fenster to finish and give them his report. He was the most temperamental examiner they had ever known.

Eyes wide, Mrs. Lipson finished her story. "My heart was pounding, you can imagine. I turned the key and—" Mrs. Lipson stopped and privately relived the horrible scene of discovering her daughter's body.

A voice they identified as the chief of detectives said quietly, "Mrs. . . ."

"Lipson," said Moskowitz.

"Yes, well, it would be better, I think, if you let us go about our work and waited in the hall. I'll have a policewoman sent to help you. Have you called Mr. Lipson?"

"He died last year."

There was a collective sigh. Moskowitz gently led her into the hall. He thought if Terry were here, she would have known what to do; she'd have just the right touch. Where the hell was she?

The medical examiner replaced the pillow, which Audrey's horrified mother had accidentally removed. It was as if covering her face made her sprawled-out naked body more anonymous.

The mayor and his deputy stepped briefly into the apartment to make an appearance. One look at the scene and they stepped quickly out into the hall.

Then one of the photographers from the crime scene unit shouted, "Here's something!" Everyone crowded in. There on the carpeting was a little smashed stub of a cigarette. "I wonder if she smoked," Moskowitz said.

Mrs. Lipson was just going down the hall steps with a policewoman who was going to drive her back to New Jersey.

"Mrs. Lipson," shouted Moskowitz after her, forcing himself through the crowd. The woman turned on the steps, her eyes searching for a voice.

"Did your daughter smoke?"

"No. Never."

Moskowitz rushed back in. "It's not her cigarette. She didn't smoke."

"Here's a broken ashtray," someone else said. "Maybe she tried to fight back."

"She didn't make it. Bag it," Fazio said.

Joel Fenster had pronounced the time of death less than twenty-four hours ago; the method of murder, asphyxiation; and obvious intercourse before death. The rest would have to be done in his offices. It was the modus operandi of the Lonely Hearts Killer. With minor variations.

The medical examiner was leaving. He turned. "I think you should know that one of our lab technicians was fired. We believed him to be selling information to reporters. Unfortunately, I think the part about the white carnation might have leaked."

All the men looked over at the body, trying not to stare at the defiant positioning of the carnation. "He never did *that* before," Fazio commented, beginning to feel the case take shape. "He never left a cigarette, either. The woman has brown hair. Not a red hair on her body."

"Look," a sergeant said, coming into the room. He

shoved a *Post* in front of Fazio's face. A small story but it was a priceless piece of the jigsaw puzzle. "THE KILLER LEFT A WHITE CARNATION." There was a picture of Krueger, his hair still looking mowed. Fazio turned to his men. Wait until the press got *this* story!

"How old is that paper?"

"Came out last night, captain," the sergeant replied.

"Could have been enough time. Yes. This is the work of a jealousy killer, men. That's what I think. I've seen it before. Look, a cigarette butt. No wineglasses. She has brown hair. Don't touch anything, no mistakes. I don't think this is the same killer, and he may not have wiped like the last one."

Instantly, there was a buzz in the room.

"Can't find those personal ad letters anywhere, captain," Moskowitz said. "Her mother doesn't know anything about her love life—they didn't have that kind of relationship. Doesn't even know if she ran an ad."

Fazio's eyes narrowed. "It's a different killer. Now, I may be wrong, but this is a man who has read those damn papers and wants some attention. Shouldn't be too hard to catch, huh, men?"

Frank Fazio was the most respected homicide detective on the force. No one disagreed with him. Moskowitz kept quiet, studying a man whom he revered. Funny about people. When the two of them had worked together, Fazio's motives sprang purely from honesty and justice. But no cop was that way forever. That was for the movies. Now Moskowitz detected ego for the first time.

"You're saying it's another murderer altogether?" piped in the mayor, who had returned.

"Your honor, that's my opinion."

"Well, you're the head of the task force. Add more men. Triple the force. Only find this new man." He took out a handkerchief and mopped his shiny forehead and the dome of his almost bald head. He needed to use the bathroom desperately, but no one could disturb the crime scene unit. Not even the mayor.

As they began to walk out of the apartment, Fazio said to Moskowitz, "I'll be at the helm full-time until we crack this. Put up cots on the second floor for the men." He slapped Moskowitz on the back. "We're going to crack this case. Just like we have before." Moskowitz nodded.

Outside, representatives of all the dailies were waiting with the camera people and TV journalists from the local and network stations. The mayor had said that another murder had been committed, but now the media wanted a statement from the police.

Captain Frank Fazio, who had appeared on television many times, squinted into the cameras. He announced that the City of New York had what was known as a "jealousy" killer on their hands. It wasn't the same man killing for the same reasons—but an imitator who wanted the glory. The worst thing the press could do was to publicize it in such a way that the man got his wishes.

Moskowitz was just getting into his car. He slipped an antacid tablet into his mouth. The whole thing had happened like a circus. And yet two things bothered him. Terry was missing, and perhaps this last murder had something to do with her disappearance. Also, she had insisted that the fruitcake in Bellevue wasn't the killer. Fazio was insisting he *was*, but that there now was a copycat killer. The important issue was to catch this killer. But Moskowitz wondered about the motives behind Frank's insistence.

Lenny Reep sat in a neighborhood bar under a wooden-beamed ceiling. They were all filing now. Big story. Another murder. New killer. The White Carnation Killer.

Yeah, well, he could take credit for finding out

about the flower first. It should have been a bigger story, but you never could tell. At least he picked up a few more bucks for withholding it. And what timing! But *he* didn't need this latest twist. He had a bigger and better scoop. Because it was an exclusive.

He'd wait a little while longer to sell it. Let them have their fill of this new headline breaker. Then he'd follow it up with something only Lenny Reep could do.

He ordered another drink. He loved it when the City was brought to its knees in a panic. He didn't care if it was a snowstorm, hurricane, mass murder, or the threat of a transit strike. It was news, and people forgot everything except what was in the headlines.

And that was something Lenny Reep was notorious for. Creating headlines. Yep, they expected something unique from Lenny Reep and they got it because he was a pro and he delivered. He took everything one step further, that's why.

While everyone was covering the murder, he was noticing that the lady detective was not there. Had she been demoted? That was a story. But as he hung around the Twentieth, when the task force was a dying ember, he had picked up on the conversation. The lady detective was eluding them. She didn't show up at the murder scene because she hadn't shown up anywhere for days. She was . . . missing.

There was a long, pink bath brush hanging from a hook. He lifted it off and began scrubbing his back awkwardly, singing. On his head was a pink shower cap. He was taking a shower in her spic and span apartment that was part his now.

They had found his latest Princess. He had bought the latest editions before taking the train. Now they were looking for *him.* But not really him. A new him. He had tricked them once again. This time he had taken all the letters so that there was no trace of a killer who struck through the personal ads. And they had taken the bait. He chuckled and scrubbed under his armpits.

Careful to step on the round, pink-fringed bath mat, he yanked off her bouffant cap and placed it where it should be. Then he dried off with one of her red-and-gold towels. Padding barefoot into the kitchen, he reached into the refrigerator and took out some fresh cherries he had bought. They were washed and in a small white bowl. He ate them hungrily, spitting the seeds perfectly into the lined trashcan. He was on a holiday. He had told them at work that he had to return to Florida. Daddy was sick. Daddy would always be sick. And had always been sick in the head.

He started to wonder if it was time to look in on her, thinking of her rather like a cake baking in the oven. She would be beginning to smell more by now. Like one of those odious bag ladies. Then, too, he was squeaky clean and freshly powdered in contrast.

Sylvia had pounded cleanliness into his head until he had become fastidious. How many times had she warned him, "Wash your little bird. If it gets dirty, it will fall off." He squeezed his eyes shut, knowing that one of the bad memories was seizing him. The time he had been taking a shower, fooling around the way guys do—or so he had heard—and he looked up to find her staring peevishly at him through the separation in the shower curtains. Startled, he had fallen back against the wet tile wall trying to cover his naked body with his arms.

"You touched it that way, I saw you." He shook his head fiercely, water dripping into his eyes. Benjy came into the bathroom. They pulled him out and dried him off roughly. He had been about thirteen at the time.

"If you touch your little bird like that, it will fall off!" Sylvia shrieked.

"If I catch you again, I'll cut it off," Benjy shouted.

He had had the misfortune to take that shower on a Friday night. They threw him in his room, which had a padlock on it, and they left him there until Monday morning, when it was time to go to school. He had spent the weekend throwing a pocketknife into the wall and swearing to get even with them. All he had had to eat were two stale cookies he had found in his lunch box. Whenever he wanted to, he took his "little bird" and aimed it out the window into the snow. Another childhood scene. Not exactly Currier and Ives.

Angry now, he stomped over to the closet and got ready to hold his nose. Time to let her out. And he had dinner prepared for her. He unlocked the closet door, which smelled like a dark corner of a subway station that had been used for a urinal.

"Phew," he said.

Terry didn't hear him. She had fallen into a sleep that was calm and peaceful, where she wasn't jerked awake by the nightmares. He kicked her, and she opened one red-rimmed eye. Then, as if rolling a tied-up rug, he inched her out of the closet. She couldn't fight back. It was the return of a nightmare. She woke up when the smell of his powder and the fresh air from the window made her aware of the fetid box she had just rolled out of.

He clipped the wires around her wrists and ankles. Crawling first on all fours, Terry managed to stand. She swayed and tried to adjust her puffy eyes to the bright light in the living room. Her living room. It had been her cozy home in the past, and now it was a frightening prison. She was able to open both eyes now, and she saw a frightful sight. Herself. She was standing in front of her oak-framed oval mirror. That lady with the haunted look; the matted, sticky hair; and the sallow skin was . . . her.

Don't let him do this to you, she warned herself. Don't let him crush your spirit. She remembered quickly all that she had read about what they called hostage mentality. A person turned into a victim totally dependent on a tormentor. Some hostages, upon being freed, even praised their captors. Not me, Terry vowed. She would hate him, and that would keep her alive. Or at least she hoped it would keep her alive.

Then she gasped. He had stepped in front of the mirror, and she could see very clearly his big grin and wide-eyed stare. They were both standing like a hideous tableau from one of her fitful nightmares. In his buttonhole was a white carnation.

Well, it was worth a try, Phyllis thought. She had never been very devious, but she was a lot looser nowadays. And she knew she had developed a sense of humor. She could phone and say, "Hi, I'm calling in response to your ad. Is this Bob?" Bob. That's what puzzled her. Why did he use a phony name? Well, Marty was strange.

She would lead him on in a false voice and finally take him by surprise and yell, "Dummy. It's me." Then they would both have a laugh.

She dialed Marty's number, ready to play. He was usually home in the evenings. No answer. He's probably out on a date, she thought wistfully. Maybe he's changed, too. Just when she thought she had Marty Loomus all figured out for a loser. The surprising thing about finding the letter and knowing that he was answering ads was not her anger at being deceived. No, oddly enough, now, because of all that, he really interested her.

Each ankle was strapped with wire to a leg of a dining room chair. Her arms were pulled behind her, and her wrists bound with the same cutting wire. In front of her place above the shorn and de-balled tablecloth were three grapes, but, of course, she couldn't eat them.

He was pointing her gun toward her. With his free

hand he tipped a piece of pepperoni pizza into his mouth and then lifted it away, letting the string of elastic cheese drool tantalizingly. Terry thought to herself, I will not let him make me go mad. She kept her eyes fixed on a patch of blue tablecloth. But she was fully aware that three more slices of pizza remained and that the heavenly aroma would linger in her memory for a long time.

He had fed her three grapes, which she all but gobbled. He had also read aloud all the news stories about Audrey. She felt a rising triumph that another body had been found. And then a crashing letdown when he read the worst part. No, it didn't prove her right. Everyone thought it was a new killer, a "jealousy" killer. That was worse torture than any little scenario of sadism he seemed to delight in staging for her. Well, she would play the victim; but she wasn't one, really. The only thing that terrified her was the white carnation. Was that a signal that he was through playing games? One reflex movement of his finger and she would be murdered in her own apartment. And he would get away with it, too. Another case unsolved for decades—somebody stumbled across dried-out bones a flood washed up with an earring or a watch or some odd thing a crackerjack detective could trace.

He tore off a circle of pepperoni, ragged with sticky cheese, and held it under her nose for so long, she could feel her nostrils quivering. Then he popped the pepperoni in his mouth and made a great to-do out of chewing. He remembered those three nights and two days in that box that became his room. Downstairs, Sylvia was baking a cake, stirring chili, roasting a turkey. All of those tantalizing smells had seeped through the cracks in the wall.

He left one wedge of pizza in the box and seemed to stare at it with relish. Licking his fingers like a cat cleaning up, he left that last slice. Terry thought of that advertising cliché—mouthwatering—and then murders. He wrote these letters. And the man is paralyzed, so he—"

"So, why are you asking me?" Fazio said. His nerves were brittle, his patience at the breaking point. This looked to be the last straw in an impossible day.

"I don't know what to do. We can't send a team to Florida."

That was it for Fazio.

Very crisply, enunciating each word, he lashed at the youngster. "What do they teach you at the police academy nowadays? I hear you have to go longer than we did. It's simple. What's your name?"

"Johnson," the young man whispered.

"Detective Johnson, the son lives in the City. Send a team to his address. You got his name and address, didn't you?"

"Yes," the young man lied.

"Then follow it up," Fazio snapped, and he walked toward his office.

Johnson sat back down. He stared straight ahead. First of all, he didn't have the man's name and address. He only had the nurse's name and the address of the nursing home. But that wasn't what bothered him so. What good would it do to send a team to follow the suspect? If he were really guilty, he would be covering up his tracks—or worse, a team wouldn't stay with it that long. There were hundreds of suspects, and a lot of teams following up.

Then he remembered something. Somewhere there was a directory of area codes and out-of-state numbers. He located it on the rack with other directories and reference books. He thumbed through until he found Miami, Florida, Dade County.

He picked up the phone, wondering if you could make a long-distance call on the task force, and dialed, anyway. When he had reached his party in Miami, he lowered his voice and said as maturely as he could, "Now, listen up, this is Captain Frank streets that will keep them off the streets. If you know what I mean . . ."

Nothing more need be said. Everybody understood the mayor's message. If the killer remained at large much longer, people could start kissing their jobs good-bye.

It was almost midnight when the young detective who had taken the call from Florida started to leave. Who the hell knew when Fazio might get back? There were cots set up toward the back of the room, but Detective Timothy Johnson wanted to go home. But that phone call from Miami troubled him. It was the most unusual he had taken all day, and it had the ring of truth about it. He didn't think it was an intentional crank call. The old guy may have been making up a tall story for attention, though.

Just as Johnson was starting to leave, thinking he could try again the next morning, he bumped into Captain Fazio. His raincoat was draped over his arm, and his hat was pitched low over his forehead.

"Captain Fazio," the young man said, marvelling at his luck.

"One and the same," Fazio grunted. He looked at the young blond man and wondered: Was anyone ever that young? The kid was growing a mustache, and in the light it looked as if he had just drunk a glass of milk. Fine little hairs.

"Sir?" the young detective began.

Fazio felt beat. A weary detective trying to hang on to his reputation or, maybe if the mayor made good his threat, even his job.

"What do you want, detective?" he practically barked.

The young man cleared his throat. "Sir, a kind of offbeat call came in from Miami. This nurse—she called long-distance to say there was a man who thought his son in New York had committed the able to pick up fingerprints at the scene of the other crimes. And a white carnation was left, uh, behind. Two different killers."

All the men nodded again in agreement. "And, anyway," said the chief in his harsh, gravelly voice. "We're still looking for a killer. Does it make any difference?"

"No," said the mayor, "but people are asking me to protect the civil rights of that man in Bellevue now that a new murder has been found."

"If you don't mind, Your Honor," chimed in the deputy inspector, "that's the least of our worries right now."

"Before, we had a clear profile of a psycho," Fazio said. "Now I think we're looking for a more playful killer. One who feeds on headlines—"

"He's got 'em," interrupted the mayor wearily.

"Yes," continued Fazio, absorbed in his theories. "This one likes to ride on the coattails of the other's fame. This one is insidious to a degreee. This one—"

Joel Fenster had been looking from side to side as if he were following a video game. If he didn't get to speak, then what was the point of his being brought to this meeting. For display? He felt foolish. Without thinking, he interrupted Fazio with the comment ". . . smokes Kent IIIs. I mean, that's what the lab found the cigarette stub to be." Everyone looked at him and noticed he was blushing.

Then the mayor said, "It's April."

No one moved to agree or disagree.

"We still have a killer on our hands. Whether it's the new one or the old one or whoever. Toward the end of spring, people start coming here to take their vacations. They come from all over. They come from Iowa, from California, from Europe, and from Japan. New York thrives on that tourism, and we welcome our visitors with open arms. They're not going to come, though, if there's a maniac loose killing women! So we'd better not have a killer on the

They all sat around an enormous conference table in City Hall. Frank Fazio would have been more comfortable had the meeting been held at One Police Plaza, his turf. Dusk had shadowed the windows long ago, and now it was dark outside. A tray on the table revealed half-chewed crusts of bread, a few folded cold cuts, a tiny mound of potato salad. Limp, shiny cheese hung over the platter, and you could still hear the crunch of a pickle as the men finished their makeshift deli dinner.

The mayor sat at the head of the table. He was flanked on one side by his deputy and on the other by a stenographer. At the other end of the table, like an opposing camp, sat Captain Frank Fazio, the deputy inspector, and the chief of detectives. Joel Fenster, the chief medical examiner, who wasn't sure why he had been summoned to this after-hours meeting, sat somewhere in the middle, isolated, on the side facing the now-dark windows.

While the young woman at his left scribbled away, the mayor asked, "Just for the record, again, you do believe that the killer we have in Bellevue, uh, what's his name . . . ?"

"Krueger," his deputy supplied.

". . . right . . . is the killer of the first four women, but the fifth woman is the victim of a new killer."

"Yes, that's correct," Frank Fazio said.

The other two men with him nodded.

"And you do not believe that perhaps one man did all the killings, making the man in Bellevue—though I understand there's a strong case against him—merely your average schizophrenic?"

Again Fazio spoke up. "I've given that close scrutiny, Your Honor, and, no, I do not believe that to be the case. The M.O. is entirely different, you see. No personal ad letters were found in this last murder. A cigarette stub was found." He smiled, saving the best for last. "We have a fingerprint whorl on the cigarette stub we are trying to trace. We were never mented that it was like untying your skates and feeling for a few seconds as if you were still on the rink.

"You say you're a psychic . . . no, I'm not doubting you, ma'am. We use psychics a lot . . . you think the killer will strike at midnight near a body of water . . . yes, ma'am . . . you think the killer is a Gemini. . . ."

"Your name . . . Sue Ann Hendricks . . . your next-door neighbor? . . . well, what makes you suspect he's the killer? . . . um, hum, he answered the personal ads . . . yeah, he goes out late at night . . . well, yes . . . oh, I see, he told you he was the killer . . . yes, let me take your name and address, and I'll send someone over. . . ."

"You're calling from where? . . . Miami, Florida? . . . yes . . . yes . . . yes . . . let me get this straight. You have a patient that can't talk but blinks yes or no . . . and he blinked that his son was the killer after you asked him questions to find out what his problem was . . . yes, I know you're paying for this phone call but . . ."

The detective hung up and stroked his chin. That took the cake. Definite borderline. It sounded like a crank, but then why would a nurse call all the way from Miami? This was something he'd have to bring up with Captain Fazio. He got up from his desk and went to the office. Empty. He turned around.

"Captain Fazio went to a meeting with the bigwigs," a detective informed him.

He turned and saw the captain walking out with his hat and raincoat on. He shrugged. It would have to wait. He couldn't send anyone to Florida, anyway. He went back to his phone.

"No . . . you don't have to say *your* name . . . well, I wouldn't worry about that . . . yes, I know killers sometimes get free on parole and come back to haunt the people who put them behind bars . . . No, sir, I didn't see that movie. . . ."

* * *

understood the phrase for the first time in her life. Humans were basically primitive animals, she realized, but she would never beg; she would never even ask. But, God, she wanted that slice of pizza.

Just then she felt something wet underneath her. She had tried to practice control, and he hadn't let her use the bathroom at all. She bit her lip.

"I smell something," he said. "Shame on you," he scolded, turning into a deranged mommy figure. He came closer, and she instinctively pulled back. The back of his hand came crashing against her jaw. Terry pulled at her restraints. She desperately wanted to wallop him, to send him flying into her china cabinet. Her tongue reached around her mouth, and she tasted blood.

"Naughty, naughty," came that falsetto woman's voice. Then he was himself again. "I'm going to have to put you back. If you hadn't done such a bad thing, you could have had that last slice."

Terry blinked. As if making that naughty mess had been her fault. Tears began streaming down her face, and wracking sobs accompanied them. He smiled at her with approval. This was what he had wanted. She had lost control.

The task force floor was jam-packed. Extra phones had been installed in no time, and all of them seemed to be ringing at once. There weren't enough chairs and desks to go around.

The instructions were to follow any lead unless it was an obvious crank call. If there was a hairline of doubt, follow up on it. There were two hundred and eighty men on the Valentine task force, and two female police officers.

Frank Fazio sat like a teacher grading papers in a separate office. Officers lined up outside his door with questions about procedure. Some members of the task force, when they left the building, still heard the hum of voices in their ears. Someone com-

Fazio of the Twentieth Precinct here in New York City, and I wonder if you could do us a little favor . . . ?"

It was very late at night and early in the morning. Marty hid behind a car until the street was clear. In his hand was a flower, a strip of Scotch tape, and the plain white envelope. It just happened to be the most important letter he had ever written.

After a while he decided he had to make a run for it. No one had come in or gone out in an hour. All he had to do was stick the whole thing onto the glass front door, and it would be found. He would then be able to correct any mistake fate had made. Which is, of course, what his voices were always telling him to do. Except when the Sylvia and Benjy voices tripped him up. But they were far gone now. When someone found the note he had taped to the door of the Twentieth Precinct, it would be his crowning moment. Carefully, he taped the envelope to the door. Then he stepped away to appraise his work. They would know immediately. He had taped a white carnation to the envelope. And then he had to laugh. Who would have thought it? Mild-mannered Marty Loomus holding the City in the palm of his hand.

CHAPTER NINETEEN

Light was just coloring the City when a drunk stumbled down Eighty-second Street, passing the brick house that was the Twentieth Precinct. He cocked his head. Darned if there wasn't a flower pinned to the door. Or was he hallucinating? Weaving in and out, he made it to the door for a closer inspection. It was real.

Tittering, he looked around, yanked up his pants, and then pulled the white carnation right off the door. An envelope slipped sideways, still clinging to the door, but he paid no attention to that. He placed the flower in the buttonhole of his ragged jacket and continued his broken path down the street, stopping to inspect open trash cans for discarded bottles with a half-inch of good stuff left.

He was way past Columbus Avenue and stumbling toward Central Park West when Detective Hank Kelsin put his hand on the glass door to open it. He realized there was a white envelope hanging precariously from a strained piece of tape. Curious, he pulled the envelope down and carried it into the Twentieth. He took out the single white page and emitted a low whistle.

The men on night tour were startled by Kelsin's shouts when he reached the third floor. When he ran to the nearest desk, he dropped both envelope and letter, as if they were pictures wet from development.

"What's up?" said a drowsy detective.

Hank Kelsin groaned.

Someone reached to pick up one of the papers, and Kelsin smacked his hand. "Don't touch that!"

"Why, is it contaminated?" came a quick reply.

A group of men gathered around the desk, craning in with their necks, trying to see the letter. One man began reading aloud.

To the task force:

I have in my possession something you want. A detective, female, known as Terry. I am keeping her in a special hiding place. If you want her back alive, you must follow my instructions.

I am adopted. It's a mistake. I'm looking for my real mother. Her name is Mrs. Freeman. You have the power and the force to find her for me. Bring me my mama, and I'll give you back your number-one female detective.

You have forty-eight hours to deliver. And I mean what I say. If I don't get what I want, if I don't read it in the newspaper, I won't call you, and you won't get Theresa Louigi Morrison back. You know who I am. I left my calling card on the envelope.

"What's he mean by that?" someone asked.

"Don't touch the envelope."

Hank Kelsin groaned again. "I don't know if it matters anymore. I have my fingerprints all over it. I didn't know." He smashed his fist on the desk, and the papers jumped.

"How do we know he has her? It could be a hoax," a voice from the rear shouted.

"I thought she was reassigned," someone said.

"Didn't you hear? She disappeared."

"Louigi? What's that? Her middle name?"

"She's married, you dumbass," one of the policewomen said. "That's her maiden name."

Frank Fazio stepped through the little crowd to see what new development had taken place. He was stiff, cranky, exhausted. He had slept in his chair with another chair supporting his legs.

Quickly, he scanned the letter.

"Damn her," he said aloud. They had a killer to catch, and she was screwing up again.

"What was on the front of the envelope?" he demanded. "What's this about his calling card?"

Kelsin shrugged. "I didn't find anything."

"But, captain," someone interrupted, "do you think it's authentic?"

"What choice do we have? We can't debate it. We have to do something. Her life is in danger." He cursed again but this time under his breath.

Fazio sighed. "Turn it over to the lab. Maybe there will be a trace of a fingerprint other than Kelsin's." Kelsin looked down at the floor guiltily. Fazio glanced out the window. It was getting light. A detective was brushing his teeth with ginger ale and spitting out the window. Another day. A detective missing. A mother to find. A killer loose. He had two hundred and eighty on the force, but frankly, he didn't think it was enough to handle it all.

At eight o'clock a detective appeared at the Avenging Angel Nursing Home in Miami. The sun was beginning to glare, and it looked like a nice day for the tourists. The detective had been told to interview a man with a lead on that big Lonely Hearts Killer case up in New York. A glamour assignment, for a change.

He had stayed up late reading a detective novel to sharpen his interrogation skills. There wasn't much call for that on his beat. He encountered a lot of stabbings, pistol whippings, racial feuds, but no mysterious mass murder to unravel.

An ample-bosomed black woman came into the

lobby and beckoned. He then followed her out of the vestibule and down a long corridor.

"Did anyone tell you about our Mr. Loomus?" she asked.

"Just that he was to be interviewed about the singles killing in New York."

She turned to look the young man over. "He thinks the murderer is his son."

The detective let out a low whistle. This was better than he had thought.

"But you know all about Mr. Loomus, then?" the nurse continued.

"No, just what I got. What I told you."

She sighed. They were approaching the ward, and she stopped the man with her hand to slow him down. "They didn't tell you. See, Mr. Loomus can't talk."

"He writes notes, then, is that it?"

She shook her head. "No, sir, he blinks. One blink means yes, and two blinks mean no."

Before the startled man had a chance to reply, they were both standing at the side of a withered man with silky white hair. He seemed, to the young detective, all wired up and plugged into machines. Eyes were glowing like marbles in the sunken face. The detective tried not to shudder, but he couldn't fail to notice how like a living skeleton the man looked.

"How do you do. I'm Detective Ralph Yarborough, Dade County Police Department," he said, his voice seeming to trail away. Was this doing any good? He was greeted by a silent stare. Then came one blink.

He coughed lightly behind his fist, a nervous habit. "Well, then, let's start right in, Mr. Loomus. What is it about your son you would like us to know in connection with the killings in New York?"

Again there was a measured silence.

The nurse, Annie, said, "You don't understand.

See, Mr. Loomus can't reply to anything complicated like that. You tell me what you want to know, and I'll figure out a way to change it to a yes or no question."

The other patients seemed to stare at this scene with the detective. Actually, most of them stared most of the day at something. Benjamin Loomus could only see directly in front of him. He had no peripheral vision. What he saw day in and day out were mirror images of himself. Other shadowy old men, who reminded him that time was running out. But now, he thought, joyfully, he had a real mission. Alert the world about his maniac son. The boy was no good from the beginning. He always knew that. They should have returned him to the mother when she came back to claim him that day. How many times had he wished they had? But Sylvia had her heart set on a son and heir. Someone who would carry on in the grocery store.

"Find out why he thinks it's his son who's the murderer."

"Oh, I can tell you that, detective; he got these weird letters."

"Then you have the son's name?"

"It's on the letters."

His illusions dashed, the detective began to get slightly angry. What was this? Some form of crank theatrics designed to steal time from his caseload? So much for glamour. He had an overactive imagination.

"You don't need me," he said to the nurse. "Just get me the letters, and I'll forward them to New York."

"Well, I can't get you the letters," she said, growing impatient herself. "Because I never saved the letters. Just lately I began to realize what poor Mr. Loomus was so agitated about. He thinks his son is the killer they want in New York. His son uses crazy names. I'm not much good at remembering things, and I don't recall what his real name is."

The detective stared at her. There were so many questions he had planned to ask. Occupation, age, personal habits, sexual quirks, childhood patterns, and—because he had followed the case avidly—preference for flowers.

But he was a detective, and this is what he was stuck with.

"Mr. Loomus, I'm going to go slowly through all the letters of the alphabet. Do you understand that?"

Benjy blinked once for yes.

"We are going to attempt to spell out your son's first name, okay?"

Benjy blinked once.

"The way we are going to do this is to start with the letter *A*. If his name begins with *A*, like Alan or Albert, then you will blink once. If that is not the first letter of his name you won't blink at all. Understand?"

Benjy blinked once.

"Okay, now, Mr. Loomus, this is the first important question we need answered. What is your son's name? Does it begin with *A*?"

The detective waited. Benjy stared.

"*B*?"

Benjy stared.

At *F*, the detective had a yearning to just walk out, but when they reached *M* and it happened, he became fascinated. Just the simple, quiet sincerity of one blink. He began to repeat the alphabet while the nurse ran for a pad of paper to write it all down.

"Okay, now, Mr. Loomus, that was very good. We need to know the second letter of his name. Is it *A*?"

Benjy blinked.

Miraculously, they watched his first name materialize on the pad. "M-A-R-T-Y."

"Your son's name is Marty. Is it also Martin?"

Benjy blinked.

"Your son's name is Martin Loomus, called Marty, and you think he murdered a woman in New York City?"

Benjy waited for a second. This was a dilemma. He believed Marty killed them all, but there was no way of communicating that. Finally, he blinked once. That would have to do.

Three hours later, wiping his wet face with a handkerchief and knowing his deodorant wasn't holding, Detective Ralph Yarborough left the Avenging Angel. He carried away eleven pieces of note paper with information about Marty Loomus that the New York police would want to know. What an interview that had been! What a story for a reporter who wanted to study a day of a detective! That old man had really enjoyed informing on his son. When they finished, his face sparkled, and some of the wrinkles seemed to be ironed out. He said good-bye to the nurse and noticed that Mr. Loomus had dropped off to sleep.

There were those who thought that Lenny Reep didn't have a home. That he hovered at corner newsstands or camped out in his car or inhabited phone booths. Early that morning he was in his favorite pose—hat tipped rakishly low, ankles crossed, leaning against a building, reading a newspaper.

One corner of his mouth inched outward into a smirk. The headline on the *New York Post* was perfect. It read only, "WHERE'S TERRY?" Beautiful. He had manufactured the story, embellished it, and he was getting paid for it. Unfortunately, no byline—but that was a thing of the past. He didn't like to be tied down to any one paper.

"WHERE'S TERRY?" It was even the headline he had suggested. Personally, he didn't care diddlysquat where the dumb broad was, but the longer she stayed there, the more money Lenny Reep would make. He would milk this story for all it was worth. He loved it when he created news.

He decided to go somewhere for coffee and to read the entire story, savoring every word. In a little coffee shop on Ninth Avenue, he cracked open the newspaper again. The waitress brought him coffee. Within a minute, he had knocked the cup over, and coffee was streaming across the floor mixed with jagged china pieces. Shit! The rest of the story wasn't his. He didn't give them any letter. He didn't know she was being held hostage until the cops produced the mother. What reporter had aced him out of that? The letter was right in the paper. They wanted the mother to call the Twentieth.

He put his hat back on and ignored the waitress's shouts for money. He would have to be on top of this story now. If all he could give the press was that she was missing and someone else had invented that letter, he had better create a new angle. His reputation as a reporter was at stake. On second thought, screw his reputation. His paycheck was more important.

A small plastic container of cottage cheese and a slice of whole-wheat bread on her desk, Phyllis ate breakfast with the *Post* spread over her typewriter. Usually, she paid no attention to the dailies, which she thought of as reporting a murder a day to keep the City at bay. But, with the onset of the Lonely Heart killings, she had begun to buy the *Post.* Lately she had been picking it up on her way to work.

Her eyes on the newspaper, she spread a layer of cottage cheese onto her bread. Then she stirred Sweet 'n' Low into her coffee. Outside, the weather looked iffy, and she hoped another drizzly April shower wasn't coming their way. She had a lunch date with another man from the personal ads. Friends had told her you had to go through about twenty blind dates before you found one live one.

Then the ratio changed: You just tried to stay alive. (A little black humor there.) She chewed her high-protein breakfast and tried not to look at the doughnuts someone had donated. Honestly, how could they get through the morning on all that white flour and sugar?

For lunch she would order a salad. She had made that date before the last murder. Besides, they said the last murderer was an imitation, didn't even answer a personal ad. And, anyway, what could happen in a coffee shop? She wouldn't tell him her last name or address or phone number or anything.

Suddenly she began to choke, and her plastic coffee container flew in the air. Her cottage cheese plopped on the floor. Two women from across the room ran to her and started slapping her on the back.

"I have to go," she sputtered. "I have to go home."

"Should we tell your boss you got sick? Do you want us to call personnel?"

Phyllis wasn't listening. She was running out the door, newspaper in hand, her coat half on, searching in her bag to see if she had enough money for a cab. At the curb she lifted her arm, and a taxi slowed down. It screeched to a stop, and she got in.

"Thirty-fourth and Third."

When she got to her door, she fumbled blindly for her keys. Carefully, methodically, she removed each item in her purse until, at last, at the bottom she took out her small key case.

"Oh, God," she whispered. She tossed her coat on a chair but clutched the newspaper, running into her bedroom. She held her breath for a second, rummaging through the drawer. She dumped all the letters in the envelope on her bed. It was there! She put that letter next to the one reprinted in the *Post*. There it was. The same unusual printing. The *m*s were all skinny, the *t*s looked like backward fours, and the *g*s looked drawn, like a child's caricature of a cat. The two letters were obviously written by the same person.

Just to make sure, she got out her address book and checked Marty's number against the letter from her personal ad. It was the same. Then she reconfirmed the printing on the two letters. It was the same.

Marty kidnapped that detective! And if the letter was what she thought, then maybe Marty was the killer as well. The police should know about this. It was her duty, friend or no friend. She grabbed the newspaper, folded the letter into her bag, threw her coat back on, and dashed into the bathroom where she kept spare cash in a Band-Aid box. Extracting a twenty-dollar bill, she folded it into her purse and ran out the door, hastily double-locking it.

On Third Avenue she raised her arm. It was nine forty-five, but it seemed to Phyllis that everybody must be late for work. There was not an empty cab for blocks. Finally, a taxi pulled up, and she announced, "I want to go to the Twentieth Precinct." Then she muttered, "Damn it!" She should have looked up the address in the phone book.

"I know where it is," the cabbie said. This was his favorite fare. Someone who didn't know where they were going. Almost as good as a tourist.

"It's an emergency," she said, knocking on the glass partition.

He nodded in acknowledgment. On the other hand, he told himself, this might be something important. Maybe he wouldn't take her for the usual joyride. Considering the destination.

Bob Morrison took exactly five minutes to pack up and inform his lieutenant at the Sixth Precinct that he was defecting to the task force at the Twentieth.

"You can't do that!" the lieutenant shouted.

"She's my wife, man!" Morrison shouted.

Ten minutes later he was uptown, out of breath, and facing Moskowitz.

"You want to tag along as a volunteer, okay with me. Fazio won't mind."

"Good," said Bob emphatically.

"Just one question. What took you so long to get here?"

At the Two-oh Fazio called for order, and the big room quieted. Phones were taken off their hooks. Fazio was wearing yesterday's shirt, and his eyes looked redrimmed and slitted. An unlit cigar hung from his mouth, and he didn't bother to take it out while he spoke.

"In regard to the disappearance of Detective Theresa Louigi Morrison"—everyone was quiet—"the case assumes equal priority with the existing case now before the task force. More detectives are being added for the forty-eight-hour deadline given us. Half the task force will be delegated to the tracing of the kidnapper, the location of the supposed adopted mother, and the rescue of Detective Morrison. The other half will continue to work on the case of the White Carnation Killer."

Fazio began reading off a list of names. Those who would work with the computers and telephones and leads, trying to trace the man's natural mother. Those who would reconstruct Terry's every move before her disappearance. Others who would continue tracking the killer.

"I'd like to work with Moskowitz," Morrison volunteered.

"Who are you?"

"Detective Robert Morrison, captain."

Fazio quickly scanned the list. Morrison. Morrison. Odd. Her name was Morrison.

"You're not even on the list!" He looked up at the man.

Morrison shrugged.

"He's her husband, captain," one of the policewomen yelled.

Fazio threw up his hands, papers rattling, like a father dismissing precocious children. He was losing control of this case, and he didn't like it. Every day there was a new crisis, an unexpected complication. The pressures increased, and there was no progress. Now they had a hostage situation. It seemed like a treadmill, and he was dog-tired.

Downstairs, Phyllis Samuels had arrived and stood trembling with urgency in front of the long precinct desk.

"I have evidence you need," she told the policewoman on duty.

"I'll take it," the officer said. "They're awfully busy upstairs." The woman was accustomed to almost anybody walking in, making demands, having all the answers, and generally wasting everyone's time.

Suddenly, Phyllis felt like a traitor.

"He was my friend. I want to talk to someone on the task force—like it says in the paper."

"Sure, okay," said the policewoman. She picked up the phone and dialed the floor. There was so much noise and commotion, she could hardly hear. She reached Detective George Yablonsky and explained that there was a lady who had evidence pertinent to the case and that she was downstairs.

"Should I send her up?"

George Yablonsky had about five people milling around his desk. "Tell her to wait. I'll send someone down to get her."

Upstairs, five minutes later, Yablonsky was called into a meeting in Fazio's office. Five minutes after that the phone conversation had completely slipped his mind.

Fazio said, "Listen, George, the lab just called. That small whorl we found on the cigarette stub.

Well, there's a partial whorl on the envelope from the kidnapper and . . . they match."

"It could be that the killer is the kidnapper," said Yablonsky, the possibility just occurring to him.

Fazio waved away the obvious with his hand, as if Yablonsky were a student at the academy. "We have something more important to check out first. A lot of our men touched the envelope, and the cigarette stub was handled, too. Fingerprint all the men at that crime scene—and the men around the envelope. This is very important because it could save a lot of investigating time. We have a deadline here. Tell no one, Yablonsky, not even your own mother. Just get their fingerprints quickly and don't say anything."

"You can trust me, captain."

"That's why I chose you." In one swift motion Fazio picked up the phone, which was a dismissal signal—and Yablonsky left. He was trying hard not to grin. He had always suspected that the captain liked him. That he would help him along. George Yablonsky had never thought of himself as just another cop. No, he had a big career in mind.

Someone touched him on the shoulder.

"Call from downstairs. There's a woman waiting for you."

"What?" Yablonsky said. "Oh, yeah. Listen, I'm real busy now. Turn it over to someone else. Give it to Moskowitz. He'll know what to do with it."

Assuming it was something that only Moskowitz could handle, the detective—not being able to locate him on the floor—left a note that eventually slipped in the middle of a pile of papers that had accumulated on his desk.

Moskowitz and Morrison were at that moment leaving the building. Somebody had kidnapped Terry, and her name was in the papers. They were going to the streets to find out if an informer knew anything, get a feel for the street talk, find out if any money was riding on this.

"Know what I think?" Moskowitz said to Morrison. "If there *is* a mother, she won't even admit he's her son." Morrison grunted.

"Know what I think?" Morrison said to Moskowitz. "Your Captain Fazio's got a bug up his ass. The person who sent the letter is the man who's been doing the killing."

"You mean the woman in the Village. The last one?"

"All of them. I think Terry was right. You caught the wrong man. And she's paying for it." He clenched his fist in anger and said nothing else.

Moskowitz gave a grunt that was somewhere between "you may be right" and "I don't know."

In disgust, Detective Ralph Yarborough placed the receiver back in the cradle and lit another cigarette. He didn't have all day. Every time he dialed the Twentieth Precinct, the same thing happened. One continuous busy signal. The eleven little slips of notepaper were smudged from the sweat of his fingertips. He had to leave the office soon. He couldn't neglect his job. And yet he was compelled to forward this information.

"Operator!" he shouted into the phone. "Can't you say it's an emergency and cut in?"

There was a pause.

"I'm sorry. But they have other emergency calls waiting."

Yarborough slammed the phone down, grabbed his jacket, and went out. He pitched his cigarette into the street and watched the ember die out. New York's Finest, yeah, sure. He had the biggest lead of all, and they couldn't even come to the phone.

* * *

At noon, Phyllis, who had asked the policewoman to call upstairs once again, realized Marty had done it to her again. He had screwed up her life. She was missing work, and she would be late for her lunch date. And for what? The hell with it. She didn't think he had the brains to be a murderer, anyway, much less the sex appeal to get all those women. Worse, she was hungry. And when she got hungry, she got mean.

With a gesture of annoyance she scooped up her belongings and returned to the huge desk.

"I can't wait any longer." She reached in her bag. "Here, take the dumb letter and give it to whoever you want. I don't care anymore. I know who wrote it, and it matches the letter in the *Post*. My name is Phyllis Samuels. Call me when you wake up."

The policewoman's hand was on the phone. "Wait just one minute. Hey, someone, stop that woman."

Phyllis was walking as fast as she could out of the Twentieth Precinct. She turned around. No one was following her. No one had tried to stop her. So much for justice.

The weather forecast had predicted rain, and they had almost called it off. But at four that afternoon, the sky was blue and the sun was still shining. The rain passed over; God had given His blessing to the candlelight demonstration.

This was one of the biggest demonstrations New York City had ever seen. Like the suffrage and women's rights parades, it began in late afternoon near the Plaza Hotel and wound slowly down Fifth Avenue where a speaker's platform had been erected in Bryant Park. The principal speaker was the mayor, who televised so well. Then there were the editors of the personal-ads sections of the major publications, and representatives from singles groups, ranging from videotape services to neighborhood church social clubs. The demonstration had been called to make the City safe again for single women. A few feminist leaders were on the podium. The nearby families of the victims had been asked to speak out for the cause, but all had declined.

Banners in the candlelight ceremony were held equally by men and women who chanted, "Make the City safe for singles." Slogans proclaimed, "We're lonely since the Lonely Hearts Killer," "Roses are red, violets are blue, I'm afraid and so are you."

The speakers' voices filled the park, and the attentive crowd heard every word. The freedom of New York's singles was being violated. Even men were actively involved in this demonstration—because they were so often being perceived as potential killers. They couldn't approach a woman easily.

Emotions escalated to a fever pitch when a shouting woman voiced what they all felt. First it was the personal ads, then it would be a killing outside of the ads; soon every other singles activity would be suspect. Outraged singles applauded and cheered, and more than a few made tentative dates.

Marty Loomus turned to the woman beside him and said with a poker face, "Come here often?" The woman, sporting shoulder-length red hair, appraised him in one swift glance. Then she turned away with no comment. Honestly, she thought, she got so tired of some of the dumb things men could say.

Marty kept staring at her hair. No, it didn't work. It never worked. He couldn't come on to women. But it worked when he was Bob and he answered ads. Then they wanted him and they heard his voice and they made a date and he was different somehow. Because he knew he would have final control. He would kill them.

It was after eight that night when the phone in Fazio's office rang. Fazio picked up the receiver, mumbled something, then rubbed his burning eyes.

"Is this Captain Fazio?"

"Yeah, I just said so." He was picking at the crumbs of a stale danish. Soon it would be time to order out again. Maybe pizza this time. All he could think of was Connie's pot roast and hash brown potatoes and her coffee. God, he loved her coffee!

"This is Detective Ralph Yarborough, Dade County Police. I have that information you wanted."

"What information?"

Yarborough, whose nerves were frazzled and whose ego had taken a spill since his innovative but successful interview with Benjamin Loomus, crunched his fist. "Goddammit, man, listen! You asked us to do you a favor. Now I have an overload of cases, and I've been trying for almost seven hours to get through to your damn precinct."

"What's on your mind, Detective Yarborough?" Fazio asked dryly.

Phones were still ringing everywhere on the floor, and he had to connect with this lunatic.

"Look, I went to the Home and interviewed him like you wanted and I have some info. But just remember where you got it from and remember, it's Y-A-R-B-O-R-O-U-G-H."

Fazio felt his face turn what his wife called boiling-point pink. He sat up straighter in his chair. "Listen Detective Y-A-R-B-O-R-O-U-G-H, you are talking to a man who has gotten maybe seven hours of sleep in the last three days, and you are talking to a captain who doesn't know what the hell you are talking about and who is going to hang up if you don't explain why you have me on the phone!"

The Florida detective bit his lip. Well, what did you expect from New York City, huh? He wanted to say, "Listen, pal, you called me," but he knew that imparting his information was the top priority. The man was obviously under unbearable pressure.

"I believe, Captain Fazio, sir," he replied, trying to leave out any touch of sarcasm in his voice, "that I interviewed the father of the Lonely Hearts Killer, and I have information that would be very beneficial to the case."

"What kind of information?" Fazio said cautiously, afraid to get his hopes up.

Yarborough looked wistfully at the eleven pieces of notepaper. "A man in a nursing home here in Miami has been getting letters from his son. The man believes his son is the killer. The son's name is Martin Loomus. I think you'll be sorry, sir, if you don't check this out. I might add, I went to a lot of trouble to get this for you."

Fazio was writing the name down. Yarborough gave him the address and decided not to add that it had taken just about one hour to get it.

"He thinks his son killed that woman in the Village, is that it? The address is nearby." Fazio was lighting a cigarette.

"No, captain, this man believes his son was responsible for *all* the killings."

Fazio thanked the detective. Just then, a man appeared to report on the Freeman thing. He had talked to a Mrs. Freeman who had had a son and gave him up for adoption, but she refused to see anybody until nine o'clock in the morning.

"Did you tell her that it was an emergency?" Fazio shouted. "A woman's life is at stake, for chrissake."

"We have others, captain. We'll keep calling them."

"Make sure you and the men get some sleep, at least a few hours, or you'll all make mistakes." They regarded him with the respect due a general. They knew he would work through the night. They all knew they wouldn't sleep, either.

"Send Yablonsky in," he said, dismissing the men.

"Captain, sir, some of the men are out, and I can't get all the fingerprints but—" Yablonsky said, walking into the office.

"Never mind, Yablonsky, just sit down. I got a call from Florida just now. Do you know anything about that?"

Yablonsky shook his head.

"Okay, never mind, don't worry about it. Here." He shoved a piece of paper towards him. "Send a team to this address. A suspect." He was too tired to add the word *important*, and too tired to explain why the man was a suspect. "See that he's followed. Don't let him out of sight. Call in if anything unusual happens."

Yablonsky nodded and disappeared. He had sent a few teams out that afternoon to tail various suspects. There were four in all. The task force was leaving no stone unturned. Fazio hoped, though, that the killer would turn out to be one of the suspects he had so skillfully discovered.

Moo goo gai pan sat like a tantalizing topping over the fluffy steamed white rice. Marty had heated up a takeout dinner from a Chinese restaurant near Terry's apartment. A dinner for one. Near his plate was a frosty, refreshing Coca-Cola. He shoveled in his dinner with heavily buttered slices of French bread.

In front of Terry was a small plate containing three radishes. She wasn't even looking at him anymore. Her eyes were closed, her head lolled to one side. The best way to keep her sanity was to sleep. She thought she had mastered the trick of being a nonperson, but it was tough to keep her eyes closed when her hands and feet were bound with wires, when she was almost crucified to one of her own dining room chairs, and when her very own gun rested less than a foot away and she couldn't grab it.

If she opened her eyes she could see a big chart. It was a forty-eight-hour clock. Yes, he had told her everything. She knew that hours had ticked by. That everyone knew she was missing. That when they presented him with his real mother, he would give her back. That's what he had told *them.* But she knew the truth. She would never be free again. She would never do the work she loved. She would never be able to tell Bob that she had been a damn fool and that she loved him so. This madman was going to kill her. But first they would find his mommy for him.

Cheryl Lee Hunter tossed and turned. It was one A.M., and something was keeping her awake. "For God's sake, darling, make yourself some warm milk," her husband said.

"No, I'm not tense. It's more like something I can't remember. And it's important. Something on the news. I had it, and then it slipped my mind. I can't fall asleep."

"The thing about the president's trip—"

She interrupted him. "No, that's not it."

"That pathetic story about that little boy they found. . . ."

"No!" she cut him off. "I remember now. It was that detective who's missing. The hostage. They were looking for the mother of the kidnapper."

"Yeah, what about it?"

"I can't remember—"

She heard his fist pounding the pillow. "You're impossible."

"Do you remember her name?"

"No," he said, talking into the pillow.

Cheryl got up and reached for her bathrobe. What had they done with the newspapers? Oh, yes, they had put them in the incinerator room with the garbage. In house slippers and robe, she looked both ways, then ran down the hall. No newspapers in the incinerator room. She padded back. Then she discovered a book on the shelf. A silly thing her mother had given her: *What to Name the Baby.*

Yawning, knowing she had to solve the mystery that was keeping her awake, she settled back in a recliner and thumbed through the names. Maybe one would spark her memory and link it to that poor woman whose life was in danger. If only she could remember the name. . . .

CHAPTER TWENTY

At exactly six A.M. on the second day of the forty-eight hour deadline, Fazio sat back in his chair, shoes off, with his feet on his desk; Moskowitz was putting Murine in his bloodshot eyes; and Morrison seemed to be in constant motion, fidgeting, squirming, and scratching.

"I think we should just arrest all those suspects who are being followed," Morrison said too loudly.

"On what grounds? They'll throw us out of court later," Fazio said.

"Who cares!" Morrison shot back. "Rough them up. Maybe they can tell us something, anything. Her life is at stake, don't you understand that?"

"This whole thing could be a crank, too," Fazio said, his voice heavy with exhaustion. "Just remember, we've got the City of New York spinning when your wife or ex-wife might be somewhere else having herself a great time. We have no proof he's got her."

Moskowitz barely managed to restrain Morrison from slugging the captain.

"It's the deadline that's doing it," Moskowitz said softly. "We're not thinking clearly. Everyone's pressured."

The phone rang. Fazio picked it up. Moskowitz noticed that Fazio's hand was trembling. He had never seen that before. "No, not yet," he said into the receiver, replaced it in the cradle, and pulled a cigarette from a pack in his pocket. Moskowitz noted that Frank usually smoked cigars.

"That was the *Post*," he said. "They're going with a countdown headline. But they can change it at the last minute."

Another call. "Can't give that to you. No comment." He slammed the phone down. "The *Today* show." Savagely, he took the phone off the hook.

A detective came in with a slip of paper. "Seems a call just came in. A woman who works in the personals section of *New York* magazine remembers a lady who placed an ad, and she had the same name as the woman detective she heard about on TV. The woman's name is Cheryl Lee Hunter. Should I send someone out? Says the transaction is on Visa, and they have records. Also, she remembers the woman said she was a redhead, but the picture on TV showed a brunette."

"Damn it!" Morrison was shouting. His voice boomed so loudly that men in the big room turned their heads toward the noise. "What more proof do you need? She ran an ad. Don't send someone to talk to that woman. *I* know Terry's Visa number. She was trying to catch a killer, and he caught her. Don't you see? The killer and the kidnapper are one and the same, and he's the one who did *all* the killings. She was right!"

"He has a point, Frank," Moskowitz said in a soft, respectful voice.

Another man appeared in the doorway. "Okay, we found the man's mother, this Mrs. Freeman." All three men stood up. Fazio ran his hand through his hair. Moskowitz let out an audible sigh of relief. They didn't have to wait for the nine o'clock interview with the other Mrs. Freeman. They could phone the media, and things could start moving.

"Good work," Fazio said, whistling under his breath.

The detective in the doorway didn't feel he should step into the office. "She's dead, captain. Her name was Rose Freeman, and she died six months ago. On her insurance papers she listed the next of kin as Robert Martin Freeman, adopted as Martin Robert Loomus. That's how the computer traced it. He was listed as beneficiary. Letters had been sent to a Miami address in care of a Benjamin Loomus, but the letters were returned."

"Son of a bitch!" Bob Morrison cried.

Another man stuck his head in the door. "The *News* keeps phoning. Like every five minutes, captain. It's annoying."

"Tell them to wait till they hear from me. They'll get something soon!"

They remained in the doorway. "Shut the door behind you, sergeant," Fazio snapped.

He sat down. Moskowitz sank into his chair. Morrison remained standing. "If the mother is dead, then we invent a mother," Fazio said briskly, and Moskowitz was immediately aware this scheme had been brewing for some time. "If we don't give him something, Morrison, he will kill your wife. We'll use a policewoman. A decoy. Set her up in someone's apartment. Put it in the papers, special edition maybe." Fazio was stabbing his watch with his forefinger. "It's twenty after six. We're sliding into the final twenty-four hours. We can't take any chances."

"It's perfect," Moskowitz said. "I agree. How's he going to know who his real mother is? He's adopted."

"Get the shrinks on the phone. Get a profile of the type of woman we need, and let's get her started," he said to Moskowitz.

"I'll phone the papers," Fazio continued. "And, Morrison, I want you to make a plea to the killer. . . ."

"No. It won't work."

The two men looked at Bob as if he had taken leave of his senses.

"Don't you see? You're going to all this trouble for nothing. He's going to kill her, anyway. You're going about it all wrong. You have to close in on the

285

killer. It doesn't matter what you give him; he's going to kill Terry! Don't you understand?" He looked wildly from one man to the other.

Fazio's stare was direct and chilling. "Morrison, you're off this case. Go back to your precinct. You're not a valid member of the task force."

Moskowitz touched Morrison's shoulder sympathetically.

"You're too emotional, man," Fazio said. "Let us find your wife, and get out of our way! Now let's get this show on the road." He picked up the phone to call the papers. Morrison turned, shaking his head. Hands in pockets, he stalked to the elevator.

When he reached the ground floor, he realized that in his fury he had forgotten his raincoat. The elevator had disappeared. Cursing, he punched the up button again. A policewoman stood beside him. "Listen, are you going up to the task force by any chance?" she asked.

"Yeah."

"Would you do me a favor? We are *so* overloaded." She pointed to the precinct room, which was truly standing room only. "Could you just messenger these papers up to Detective Yablonsky? If he's not there, Detective Moskowitz. Or Captain Fazio. I don't care." She pressed the papers into his hand and ran back into the precinct room.

The elevator came, and Bob Morrison, feeling impotent, like nothing more than a go-for, really, idly cast an eye to the papers. On the second floor he punched the button again for down, realizing that, yes, there was a God. So much for Fazio's task force. It couldn't be trusted to do anything right. It was too big and unwieldy.

He looked down at a handwritten letter signed "Bob," notes that said the handwriting was supposed to match the kidnapper's as it appeared in the paper, and the name of the woman who had tried to give them a tip. He slipped the whole thing under his jacket, and when the elevator touched the ground floor again, he walked out quietly.

"It's all set," Fazio shouted to the men gathered in his office. He was getting his second wind now. "When he calls, it will come directly into my office. Tape working?" Men were hovering around his phone. "Yeah, captain," someone replied.

"Great. Make sure all those phones out there are quiet after the second edition of the *Post* comes out. They'll have the story first."

"Mayor's on the phone, captain," Yablonsky called in. "Said he can't reach your direct line."

"I'll call him back," Fazio shouted. Two officers were escorting a rather dazed police matron into the room. She had light brownish-gray hair that fell in soft waves around her face. When she smiled, it was warm, motherly. Her voice was soothing. Fazio felt like kissing his thumb and forefinger. Perfect. Only the clothes would have to go. The navy blue uniform, skirt, jacket, cap, and the club would be replaced by a housedress and apron and perhaps some knitting. Fazio stood up, extending his hand. In about an hour this woman would be Mrs. Freeman, their decoy mother.

"Are you Phyllis Samuels?"

She pressed her face, one eye closed, closer to the peephole and saw a distorted fishbowl face.

Phyllis gripped her robe tighter around her neck. "Yeah."

"I'm Detective Robert Morrison of the New York City Police Department."

"Prove it," she yelled. Weren't they supposed to go in pairs?"

"Do you have a chain lock?"

"Yeah."

"Open the door an inch, keep the chain on, and I'll show you my shield. Fair enough?" He had to watch himself. He was standing outside the door of a woman who had his wife's life in her hands.

The door was open a crack, the identification scrutinized. Then the chain slid across the latch, and he was looking into the face of Phyllis Samuels.

"Did you leave this at the Twentieth?" he asked, producing the letter.

"Yeah. And after waiting almost three hours and coming close to losing my job."

"How well do you know this man?"

"Pretty well, I guess."

"Did you run a personal ad?"

"Yeah," she said defensively.

"And this Bob answered it."

"He calls himself Bob. His real name is Marty Loomus."

Morrison had to control himself. That was the name he had heard in Fazio's office. "And you think this letter matches the writing in the paper?"

Phyllis crossed to a small table and showed him a folded, open copy of a newspaper with the letter. "See for yourself."

Morrison cleared his throat. "When would you say you got this letter. Recently?"

"It wasn't recent. I stopped answering the letters when there were all those unsolved murders."

"So he wrote it a little while ago?"

Phyllis shrugged. "Must have."

Phyllis remembered later that she had never seen a man plead so with his eyes. "Ms. Samuels," he said, "I hate to disturb you—a woman's life is at stake and . . . may I just step in and talk for a little while longer?"

Phyllis opened the door wider, and Morrison came in.

He stopped and bought a box of Jujubes along with the newspaper. Carefully counting out the change, he looked around the little candy store. It was just like the little stores they had in the Bronx where he grew up. The smell of vanilla ice cream at the tiny counter, the overlapping potato chip bags, and even the magazines with naked women in them. It gave Marty a good feeling.

He paid the clerk. "Have a nice day now."

"You, too, buddy."

It was a glorious April day, and Queens looked like a sun-drenched village. He rather liked living there. Last night he had watched television in Terry's big bed before falling asleep. Of course, she had slept in the closet. Like an animal. He chuckled. He wasn't so sure she knew the difference anymore.

Reading the headline as he walked down the street, he felt mounting excitement. "PLEA TO KIDNAPPER: MOM FOUND. CALL 20TH PRECINCT." They had actually found his mother for him. Here was her photograph. Only one thing he couldn't understand and it frustrated him. Early on they had left out any reference to a white carnation, and then he had pinned it to their door so they would know. Oh, well, they didn't give him credit for being the smartest killer in the world, but they were going to give him his mommy. Or were they? He studied his mother's picture carefully.

Suddenly enraged, he tossed the paper in a wire wastebasket on the corner.

Rushing down the street, his cheery mood evaporated. They had tricked him. That dumpy woman with the ass-kissing smile wasn't his mother. He had seen his mother that time when he was five; she had come to plead with Benjy and Sylvia: she wanted him back. They had thrown her out of the house. But he had been hiding behind the couch, and he had seen her. She was slender. She didn't have mousy hair. Hers had been long and black. Even if she had grown stout and gray, she couldn't be this woman in the paper. No, his real mother had been tall. He remembered that. Even Sylvia had remarked several times that he might turn out to be as tall as his mother. He hadn't. It was Sylvia who was short and fat. Sylvia looked a lot like Phyllis, now that he thought of it. The woman in the paper, the fake mother they had found, was a joke.

Well, the joke was on them. Did they really expect him to fall for a stupid trap like that? Just let them wait for that phone call from him. They would wait forever. He had other plans.

What time was it? What day? She had slowly recited the alphabet thirty times and panicked because the last few times she had forgotten how it ended. The hunger pains stopped long ago. Vaguely, she remembered there might be a pack of half-opened Life-Savers in a coat pocket. But the effort didn't equal the reward. That was for sure.

She was lying on her stomach, her hands bound in back of her, her feet tied together. When she opened her eyes, there was darkness. But when she closed them, she saw wisps of clouds that looked like cotton candy. She was just below the stratosphere, but she wasn't on a plane. And then she was in the misty moors and Bob was waving. Earth wasn't a substance anymore. She felt light and weightless. She was her body, and yet she wasn't.

That's how it would happen. She would close her eyes and float among the mists and the drifts of white cloud and never have to open her eyes to the eerie darkness of her closet home again. It would happen naturally, as though she were fifty years older, dying peacefully in her sleep. No need to fight it. It was meant to be.

Quickly, she jerked herself awake and forced her legs to fold under her so she could sit up. If she died like that, Bob would never know how she had come to her senses. If she gave in . . . she *couldn't* give in. The closet floor was suddenly like a deathly claw pulling her in. Forcing herself to stay upright, she ran through the multiplication tables.

Sometime after lunch, he took his place behind one of the portholes in the credit department at Saks. A few of the workers noticed he was back. Some hadn't really known he had been away. Or why.

One woman clapped him on the shoulder. "How's your dad?"

"Oh, you know, lingering."

"Yeah," said the woman sympathetically. She didn't know, but she thought someone should be nice to him.

Marty had come straight from Queens. On the subway ride in, he had decided to continue his own search for his mother. As for the cow in the closet, he'd just leave her there. One day someone would find her rotting carcass—but there would be nothing of him there.

"Phone call, Loomus," came the shout.

Marty was at the computer. He turned, momentarily confused. All he could think of was, Had they found out about him? Woodenly, he marched into the office and picked up the receiver.

"Hiya, Marty."

For a second he couldn't think. It sounded like Laura, his first Princess.

"Phyllis?"

"Yeah, that's me. Why? You sound funny."

"I'm busy. Why are you calling me here?"

"Well, to tell you, Marty, that you were right." She kept her voice low. "About my weight, I mean. I've gotten too thin, you know? So, I decided to make a fat meal tonight, say, chicken with sour cream sauce over egg noodles. You like that, don't you? And maybe I'll have time to make one of my quick chocolate cakes with the frosting that tastes like whipped cream and—"

"Phyllis I have to get back to work, I—"

"Marty, for God's sake, I'm inviting you to dinner. We hardly see each other anymore. What about seven? Tonight."

"No, I can't, I really can't, Phyllis." He had to wait for Princesses to call and he had to listen to the news and he had to zip back to Queens. No, he didn't have to do that. Come to think of it, he hadn't eaten since that box of Jujubes earlier. "Okay, Phyl, I'll be there." She was in love with him. It wasn't his fault. "But I can't stay late." He could still get a phone call.

"Whatever." The thought of all that food sickened her. But she had to know. Had she been to bed with a killer? How could that be? Since he had never killed her.

In offices and homes throughout New York, radios and televisions were turned on, awaiting a special bulletin. Everyone had been following the citywide soap opera, "Where's Terry? Will We Find Her in Time?" So far the kidnapper had not stepped forward to claim his mother. The killer had not been found, and hour after hour, no new news was forthcoming. By evening rush hour, most New Yorkers became involved with their own problems. Like a snowstorm that hits the suburbs but misses the City, the Terry case was fast becoming yesterday's news.

Moskowitz sat in the chair opposite Fazio's desk. They were both staring at the phone. It had rung off the hook earlier in the day, but all the calls had been cranks.

Fazio was at his edgiest, prowling his office, his nerves on a very short circuit, his patience nonexistent.

"We're getting too old for this kind of case," Moskowitz muttered pessimistically.

"That suspect that was called in from Florida . . . nothing," Fazio said almost to himself. "I've got three cars outside his apartment building in the Village, waiting. He doesn't come in, he doesn't go out. Time's not on our side. I'm getting a search warrant. They'll have it in an hour. They can break into his apartment. Who knows? If we're lucky, we might find something connected with the case."

"And what do we do about Detective Theresa Morrison?" Moskowitz said sadly, feeling more tired and disillusioned and depressed than he ever had in his whole life.

"What more can we do?"

Moskowitz nodded.

"In a way it's her own fault. We did a check on that Visa card—well, you know that. Pisses me off. She ran an ad in *New York* magazine. Can you believe that? After all the trouble she got herself in, she was going to continue her little ego trip. You know what I think?" He was pointing his finger at Moskowitz. "I think the whole thing, the letter, the demands, everything . . . it's a hoax. She's already dead, and we're spinning our wheels for nothing."

Moskowitz stared at him.

"Say something, Bernie . . . I tried."

Six forty-five. Moskowitz was thinking that he had been in the building all day. Cigarette smoke was burning his nostrils, his ears were ringing from the constant noise and nonstop phones. His spirit was at an all-time low.

"I'll guess I'll go out for some air, Frank. Just take a little walk, you know, around the block. Can't help thinking about a spunky lady who was the only woman detective friend I ever had."

"C'mon, Bernie," Fazio called after him, but Moskowitz had already walked across the floor to the elevators. Fazio angrily reached for the phone.

When he got outside, Moskowitz found he didn't relish walking, after all. He just sat in his car with the window open and watched people pass by until he regained his sanity. He didn't care anymore. And that frightened him.

The window above Moskowitz's Pinto looked out over Eighty-second Street. Frank Fazio heard his name being called, but he stood watching the almost toy car, fascinated. As another car pulled alongside Moskowitz's car, Fazio stepped reluctantly away from the window to answer the voice. It was coming from the chief of detectives.

Phyllis ripped apart the lettuce into a huge wooden salad bowl. Methodically, she sliced a cucumber as if she were chopping off heads. Coring a tomato, she knicked part of her thumb and sucked the tiny spurt of blood. She reached for the scallions, calling out, "Everything all right in there?"

The television set was on, and Marty sat quietly in front of it. They were running a special on Metromedia, Channel 5, and Phyllis had had it on when he came.

"It will be ready soon," she said, suddenly in front of him, peering down. "More wine?"

Marty shook his head.

"I like your yellow sweater, Marty. Did you get it at Saks?"

Marty nodded.

"Cashmere?" she asked, rubbing the material between her thumb and forefinger.

"Nah, lamb's wool," he replied. Marty's eyes were glued to the TV. Footage shot by an enterprising team of reporters was being telecast. There were bits and clips of Terry, the missing woman detective.

"Pretty, isn't she? It's a shame." Phyllis watched his expression.

He took out his pack of cigarettes and lit one. Phyllis's mouth hung open. "When did *you* start smoking? I thought you absolutely hated it."

Marty looked at the cigarette in his hand as if someone else had put it there. He had, for the first time, become one with Bob. He was Marty *and* Bob. What could he do?

"About once a month I have a cigarette, Phyllis. But the smoke from other people's cigarettes disturbs me."

Phyllis heard the buzz of her timer and went back into the kitchen. She had tricked him by wearing an overblouse and full skirt. He must think she had gained weight. She dipped her finger in the sour cream sauce and tasted it. Oh, but he looked so earnest and vulnerable in his sweater and tie and shirt, maybe she had made a mistake. He was just Marty. She took out two plates and dropped one, watching it twirl like a top and stop, unbroken. Shaking, she picked it up. He smoked?

"Well, then, dinner is ready," she announced, her voice high and near cracking.

She brought over two plates heaped with chicken and noodles. Then she carried in the salad and wine. She refilled Marty's glass ceremoniously.

"So, here's to our continued friendship, Marty," she announced, clinking her glass with his. She reached over and lit the tapering candles in the center of the table. "Well, dig in," she said enthusiastically. "What have you been up to since I saw you last?"

"Nothing much."

He smiled across the table at her, and she caught a glimpse of the essence of Marty Loomus. No, it couldn't be true. She had to be wrong. There was that quick, shy smile, signaling a put-down couldn't be far behind. His clothes were sharper. No doubt about that. Maybe he had dated someone who had advised him to leave his plaids and checks behind. She felt a lump in her throat. He was the man who went out with her when no one else wanted to. Oh, it was all a horrible mistake. It had to be.

"You're not eating, Phyl," he said reproachfully. "Anorexia doesn't become you."

She stopped eating and smiled back. See, there was the controlling remark, as predicted.

He smiled merrily back at her. That sacklike outfit didn't fool him. Fat Phyllis had changed into a Princess type. She didn't look like Sylvia anymore. Phyl wasn't Syl. Well, he'd warned her, so it wasn't his fault. He'd have to kill her. Why not? Talk about convenience. But he'd have dessert first. It wouldn't be exactly the same as the others, but he could do it because she had changed. And because he had changed.

Frank Fazio paced frantically in his office, drumming one fist against the palm of the other hand. The chief wanted him to do more, though he couldn't say exactly what. The mayor wanted him out, which came as no surprise. The men who had worked straight through double tours and who walked the floor like haggard, unshaven gray ghosts wanted more direction.

He couldn't give anymore. God, he was tired. But he felt like he'd never be able to lie down on a bed and fall asleep again. He wouldn't be able to unwind. And if this wasn't solved, he would never sleep well again.

"More coffee, captain?" Yablonsky asked, stepping into the doorway. "No," Fazio replied, waving his hand. "Where's Moskowitz? Did he come back up?"

"No, captain."

"Any calls on the floor? Anything interesting?"

"No, captain. Nothing else."

"Yablonsky?"

"Yes, captain?"

"It is not necessary to address me as captain every time you open your mouth." Then he muttered, "Oh, what the hell," and ran his hands through his hair. If only the damn phone would ring. If only the man would call so they could begin. Now he knew what a condemned man on death row felt like—knowing that a single phone call could save his life. He walked listlessly over to the window. The toy cars had changed positions. Now he couldn't find Moskowitz's Pinto. Where was he? Pretty soon they would have the search warrant on the man in the Village. At least that was something.

"Someone to see you, captain. Important."

Fazio didn't turn. "Okay, Yablonsky."

When Fazio faced his visitor, he saw a man with an unzipped jacket holding an unlit cigar. Fazio was too tired to shake hands.

"I'm a cabdriver. But I have a memory like an elephant, you know. I never forget a name or a face. That white carnation you found at that there murder in the Village. I read about all that in the papers. I'll never forget; see, I had this fare, and he left the lowest tip I ever saw, and it made me mad, you know?"

Fazio stared at the man in such a way that he came to the point fast. How had this jerk slipped by?

"He was wearing a white carnation in his buttonhole."

Fazio tossed a pencil around in his hand. "Was it around the night of the murder?"

"No. Way before. And he was going uptown, East Side."

"Before . . ." Fazio said half-challenging, somewhat sarcastically.

"Yeah."

"Yablonsky!" Fazio shouted. He looked up at the big circle with black letters on his wall that was his clock. He wanted to shove back the hands. Now this man would meet with an artist to get the sketch right. Then the sketch would be put on the air. Ten hours ago he would have cared. But the case was like an ocean. Waves washed ashore and rolled back into the same body of water.

And the cabbie had seen the man who wore the white carnation *before* the last murder. Long before. His shoulders sagged, and he beckoned George Yablonsky in. Why, he wondered, when he had a floor full of unshaven zombies, did Yablonsky look like he just stepped out of a deodorant commercial.

"Sit," he commanded.

Who did the man remind him of? Fazio questioned himself. Someone. Search what was left of the old memory bank. Oh, yes, he must be getting senile. It was right there up front, couldn't miss it. His old boss, Captain Bill Hogan, who would have sold his grandmother to the Mafia to be promoted. When he had captured the right killer who was murdering all those ballerinas in Lincoln Center, he had revealed Hogan for the schmuck he was. Now he was all but knitting scarves somewhere in Manhattan South. Yablonsky looked like a young Hogan. That was it!

"Tell me, Yablonsky . . ."

"Captain?"

"Right . . . listen, if I told you to let this cabdriver go because we already have a suspect, even though you knew in your heart he had valid information that might lead us to believe that he had seen the real killer, what would you do?"

"Could you repeat the question, captain?"

Fazio did just that.

"Well, I'd dismiss him."

"But he might be able to give us a clue to the man who's been doing all the killings."

"But as you said, captain, we already have a suspect. You've said he was the killer and that there was a jealousy killer."

"And you believe that to be the truth?"

Yablonsky's voice had an unmistakably cold edge to it. "That has nothing to do with it. You're my superior officer and you reflect the department."

Fazio nodded his head. "Good man, Yablonsky."

"Thank you, captain," George Yablonsky said. Fazio got up and put on his raincoat.

Yablonsky looked at him.

"I just remembered something, Yablonsky."

The detective's voice was peevish and nasal,

though he gave no outward evidence that he might be annoyed. "Well, captain, if it's something you want, I can send someone."

Fazio put up his hand, smiling amiably. "No, no. I'll attend to it." He clapped Yablonsky on the shoulder and shook his hand. "Keep things moving along, Yablonsky. You're in charge."

"Right, captain."

Fazio turned before he walked out the door. "You forgot to say captain, sir, Yablonsky."

The dishes were stacked in the sink. The candles still flickered, and only one little lamp was on in a corner. Marty and Phyllis were sitting on the small print couch drinking coffee.

"Marty, now that we know each other again, I have to tell you something really funny."

She reached over and cut him another little slice of her famous chocolate cake. "Boy, no one cooks like you do, Phyl," Marty said contentedly.

"The thing is, Marty, you answered my personal ad and signed your letter 'Bob.'"

Marty nearly choked on his coffee. He wiped his face with a napkin. "How did you know it was me?" he asked smoothly.

"Marty, your phone number! C'mon, you told *me* not to run a personal ad; now you're answering them. Then I try to call you and you're never home."

Marty smiled, his teeth darkened with chocolate cake. Now it wasn't passion that would force him to turn Phyllis into a Princess. He knew then that, just to protect himself, he had to kill her. He had made the one mistake he was fearful of, the one that would be beyond his control to stop. Whatever she knew was too much. Phyllis had always caused him trouble. He hugged one of her throw pillows close to him and began inching slyly, shyly closer. His arm went around her shoulder. He was definitely Bob.

"So you discovered me. Can I see the letter?"

"You want to see the letter you wrote to me?" A moment ago Phyllis was accepting compliments on her cooking and now suddenly there was an aura of danger in the room. Marty had changed. She looked around the room, panicking, and then said, simply, "I don't have the letter."

"You're not lying?"

"I never lie. Why would I lie? I—I threw it out."

Okay, he'd check her story later. This one would be easy. But he couldn't wait to maneuver her into the bedroom. Phyllis might plead one of her headaches. It would have to be now. He looked at her as she edged to the other side of the couch. Her face changed shapes and colors like the end of a child's kaleidoscope. She was Laura and Debbie and Doreen and Martha and Audrey. She would be number six.

Marty's lips came crashing down on her composite face. Phyllis pushed him away. "C'mon, Marty, there's time for that later." He pulled her blouse and ripped it. She jumped away, but he was stronger. "No, no," she whimpered, "you don't know what you're doing, Marty. Don't." When she saw him pick up a throw pillow, she screamed loudly before her sound became muffled. Marty was on top of her when he heard the noise. He looked at the ceiling. Sounded like the creak of a floorboard. Then he looked down a little, into the barrels of two guns. As Phyllis slithered out from under him and onto the floor, he saw, as if in a nightmare, the faces of two men—a short, redheaded fat guy and a tall blond with a mustache. How . . . ? She had tricked him.

Phyllis was sobbing so loud he couldn't think.

"Police," Moskowitz and Morrison had said in unison. *But for what?* They both had been thinking while hiding in Phyllis's bedroom closet. What were the charges? Heavy petting after dinner. They didn't care. They'd just rough him up a little and find out where he had stashed Terry, then they'd worry.

Marty reached in his pants quickly, and before

Moskowitz and Morrison could even guess what he was doing, he pulled out a gun and pointed it at Phyllis's forehead. He stood up. "I'll shoot her if you don't drop your guns."

"Shit," said Morrison quietly. Both men lowered their arms, but neither let their guns fall to the floor.

"Get up," Marty ordered the hysterical Phyllis. He put the gun in her back and marched her quickly to the door.

"Please, Marty, don't kill me. I didn't mean to trick you. I was trying to help you. You didn't do anything. Don't kill me. You might go to jail or something." She fell, and Marty yanked her to her feet. At the door he turned and faced the two shocked detectives. Morrison lifted his hand and fired. Marty saw it coming and swayed toward Phyllis. Phyllis passed out from fright. Marty stepped over her and fired twice. There was a shout. Then Marty opened the unchained door and dashed into the hall. The elevator had stopped at her floor, and he leaped in.

Moskowitz and Morrison practically slid across Phyllis's body. Morrison's wrist was leaking blood, and when it dripped on Phyllis, she started to scream, thinking it was hers.

Bumping into each other, the two detectives took the steps two at a time. "He got away," Morrison shouted, in the street, the pain in his hand almost forgotten.

"No!" Moskowitz screamed. "There he goes. See that yellow? He's heading toward Thirty-fifth Street to the left. You okay?"

Morrison didn't answer. Their guns pointed, the two men ran up Third Avenue. A few people screamed and abandoned the street to hide behind parked cars. The men kept running. "He's just ahead. Look for the yellow," Moskowitz yelled, gasping for breath. Morrison started firing, aiming at the yellow. All along the street people were flying into restaurants and shops. There was a chorus of screams. Then the yellow turned a corner and, cursing, they saw they had lost him.

Morrison was leaving a trail of blood on Third Avenue. The two men, their chests heaving, turned the corner and saw there was a crowd. "Call the police!" someone shouted. They stopped, breathing heavily. There on the ground was the yellow-sweatered Marty, facedown on a sidewalk slippery with his blood.

"You must have gotten him back there."

"No, I missed. I thought you just fired a second ago."

There were sirens in the distance, and out of the crowd stepped a short man wearing a black raincoat. His gun was still pointed at the body lying stomach down, cheek to the side, palms on the pavement.

"He dead?" Fazio said.

Morrison stared at the captain, his mouth falling open. Then, quickly, he kicked Marty, the blood from his wounded wrist making new spots on his yellow sweater. The body twitched.

"Find out where she is," Fazio ordered.

Morrison felt his knees buckle. He staggered backward. Moskowitz bent over the body. He whispered in Marty's ear. "Where's Terry?"

Marty smiled on the inside. He no longer had the strength to do anymore. His Princesses were dancing in front of him like twinkling stars in the heaven. Terry. They would find her, and she'd be dead. Dead. Like him. But the last laugh was worth it. It had worked out after all. He was a star now.

With all his energy he slowly brought his right arm to his pocket. Some people in the crowd gasped, horrified. They thought the poor man had to be dead. Moskowitz reached in the pocket and pulled out a set of keys. "Terry's," Morrison said, holding his wrist. The keys were attached to a chrome-and-black key chain that was in the shape of a *T*. Someone in the crowd passed him a handkerchief for his wrist as Morrison screamed, "Let's go."

It was then that the sirens became deafening. Squad cars pulled up one by one to Thirty-sixth Street. Phyllis Samuels, buried in the crowd, had recovered and was screeching, "Marty! Marty!"

"Get these people away," Fazio shouted to officers now on the scene. "Move, move."

Morrison, together with Moskowitz and Fazio, climbed in a squad car. Then he stepped out. "You!" he screamed to a man with a camera. Lenny Reep, the first reporter on the scene. He was clicking away, getting all the angles of the dead man still sprawled on the street. With his good arm, Morrison snatched away the camera, threw it on the ground, and jumped on it. Two seconds later he was back in the car. Lenny Reep yelled after him, "Violation of the First Amendment. I'll take you to court. . . ."

The car, sirens screeching, roared away, leaving Reep waving his arms at nobody. Morrison and Moskowitz sat in the backseat.

"How did you do it, Frank?" Moskowitz shouted.

Frank Fazio stared straight ahead. His mind was on a dozen threads and fragments, too. He lit a cigarette, rolled down the window, and threw his match out.

"The guy in the yellow sweater . . ." he began awkwardly.

"Marty Loomus," Morrison supplied.

"Yeah. He was a suspect. I had a search warrant issued, and they broke into his apartment. They found the letters he had taken from the women, found a list of suspects on the wall, and Terry's picture pasted on his refrigerator. Incriminating evidence."

"Just a suspect, huh?" said Morrison, almost bitterly. "For *all* the killings and the kidnapping, is that it? Is that how you're playing it now? Now that it's obvious?"

Moskowitz turned on Morrison. "Hey, watch it. This man single-handedly got that killer. I don't care how he did it. Frank Fazio solved the case again." Moskowitz whistled low. "Gotta hand it to you, Frank. We would have lost him. Morrison found out through his girl friend, and then I joined him, but *you got him.*"

Frank Fazio cleared his throat. He rolled down the window again, and tossing his cigarette stub through the small opening, said, "Yeah, well, Bernie, I got lucky. The ugly truth of the matter is . . . I had you followed. That's right. I didn't trust you, old buddy, when you walked out, and I guess my self-confidence was slipping, too. I knew where you and Morrison had gone. And then something happened to me. I realized I was wrong, and you guys were, no doubt . . . right. I radioed in and found out about what was uncovered. Figured the guy in there must be this Marty Loomus. Then I saw a man running out the door with a gun. He was running fast. I chased him in the car, but I was driving slowly, following him down Third, going against traffic. At Thirty-fifth Street, I jumped out. I shot him. Same guy, huh? Marty Loomus?"

"Yeah," Morrison said, looking out the window. They were on their way to Queens. To Terry's apartment. Didn't anyone care that she might be dead already?

"You had me followed, Frank?" Moskowitz said softly.

"I'm being honest, Bernie. Know what finally brought me around?"

There was silence.

"Kid by the name of Yablonsky. Detective George Yablonsky. Like a clone for Hogan. Remember Bill Hogan?"

Moskowitz laughed in spite of himself.

"Suddenly, Yablonsky, that phony ass-kisser, reminded me of Bill Hogan and how he put himself before the case. Then I realized, Bernie, the kid didn't remind me of Hogan. I did."

No one said anything.

The driver said, "We're just about there."

"Record time," muttered Moskowitz.

And then there was quiet as each man said a private prayer that Detective Theresa Louigi Morrison, who had known the truth all along, would still be alive to give them hell.

CHAPTER TWENTY-ONE

"One hot corned beef sandwich coming up, hold the pickle. Hey, if you had any more flowers crammed in here we might think you didn't pull through."

Terry laughed and accepted the warm, fragrant bag from Captain Fazio. A hand snatched it from her. "Not right now, honey. Take it easy. We almost lost you."

Terry made a face at Bob and caressed the hand that was wrapped in bandages. She looked out the hospital window at the sunshine flooding in. It was the most exquisite sight she had ever seen. "See how I've become a docile little wife," she said, laughing. "I'm not even smoking. I guess I cut down, after all."

Neither of them laughed at that. Bob was thinking of the smell that came from the closet. He thought for sure they'd find a corpse.

Moskowitz burst into the room holding a bag of plump, sugary cookies that his wife had baked. He was carrying the latest newspapers. Today's headline, five days after Terry's ambulance transport to Flushing General, read, "KRUEGER RELEASED FROM BELLEVUE." "Listen to this, Princess. Turns out his real name was Krueger Ashworth Edgerton Galladoit. He's from Boston and real upper-crust. Shrinks say he was running away from his wife. She was pregnant, and he freaked out. Didn't want to be a father. But he was no murderer. His stay in Bellevue was a godsend. Otherwise, he might never have remembered who he was. They finally contacted his family, and he went home."

Terry saw Captain Fazio look away. He was embarrassed. She had always known Krueger was the wrong man. Her surprise was that the captain was human enough to admit defeat.

"And some bad news of a sort," Moskowitz continued. "Marty's father died. Just seconds after Marty, I'm told. They'll be buried side by side."

Fazio said, "Well, I'd better get back." He took Terry's hand. "You're a damn good detective, Morrison. Your father would be proud of you."

Terry nodded. Then something unforeseen happened. She heard a sob; only a split second later did she realize the sound came from her. "The hell with it," she said, half-sobbing, half-laughing. She asked Bob for a pencil and scratch paper. She scribbled quickly, then handed the pad back to her husband.

He read it aloud. "MWF . . . I guess that means married white female . . . looking for adventurous affair with man who is happily married but wants fun and games. Preference for good-looking man, blond with mustache."

Moskowitz, who was now demolishing half the corned beef sandwich said, "Good-looking? That leaves you out, Morrison."

The cemetery wasn't in Miami proper. It was in a tree-clustered community known as Coconut Grove. The Florida sun beat down on the small group in the grassy knoll.

The funeral was over now. Some *Miami Herald* reporters had come. And a detective, Ralph Yarborough. Phyllis Samuels stared long at the two markers on the graves. Benjamin Loomus, Martin Robert Loomus, and the gray tombstone in the middle for Sylvia Loomus. Phyllis had used the insurance money from Marty's real mother to give him a decent funeral, but no one had shown up. There were no other mourners.

Phyllis wiped away the tears that threatened to unleash rivers of mascara. Everyone had said that Marty wasn't an evil person, just a sick boy who had grown into a very twisted man. It was all so sad and futile.

She wept openly, though, as she placed something on the mound that represented his fresh grave. Stepping back, she smiled, thinking how happy it would have made him. Sprinkled like a ceremonial garland was a cluster of white carnations.

She turned to go, looking down so as to avoid the glare of the sun. But she stopped and turned to look once more at the marker for the man she had known. She would never come back to visit.

In ten years everyone would forget about Martin Loomus and the terror he had created. Everyone except her. She would never forget. Because it had been her idea to plant the detectives in her apartment the night he was killed.

"Marty?" Phyllis whispered. "One more thing. All of the women you killed were so pretty and thin. I saw their pictures in the paper. But in the year I knew you, you never tried anything." She closed her eyes, and a little tear escaped. "Thank you for thinking I was pretty enough at the end."

THE ADVENTURES OF SKIPPER GOULD

BLOODRUN Robert Kalish 88021-0/$2.75 US $2.75 Canada
Skipper Gould said his goodbyes to Asia after Vietnam. There he had become a man, but like the lover who never forgets his first woman, when Asia called to him again, he came, came back to find out who killed his brother Ricky. Skipper's only link to the killers was a sensual Oriental beauty—a link strong enough to lock Skipper into a spiraling game of oil politics, KGB intrigue and corruption.

BLOODTIDE Robert Kalish 89521-8/$2.95 US $3.75 Canada
The second novel featuring tough, ex-navy fighting man Skipper Gould is an explosive, high-voltage thriller of murder, intrigue and atomic espionage off the coast of Maine.

Skipper was the editor of a small town newspaper now. But the woman came to him because of what he had been. And finding a dead man's body floating in the bay was enough to sweep him toward a giant maelstrom of evil and violence.

BUDDHA'S RETREAT, the third Skipper Gould novel, will be published in August 1985.

AVON Paperbacks

Buy these books at your local bookstore or use this coupon for ordering:

Avon Books of Canada, 210-2061 McCowan Rd., Scarborough, Ont. M1S 3Y6
Avon Books, Dept BP, Box 767, Rte 2, Dresden, TN 38225
Please send me the book(s) I have checked above. I am enclosing $ _____
(please add $1.00 to cover postage and handling for each book ordered to a maximum of three dollars). Send check or money order—no cash or C.O.D.'s please. Prices and numbers are subject to change without notice. Please allow six to eight weeks for delivery.

Name _____

Address _____

City _____ State/Zip _____

KAL 10-84

SLEAZE
By L.A. Morse
89227-8/$2.95 U.S. $3.75 Canada

From Edgar Award-winning author, L.A. Morse comes SLEAZE—a tough, fast-paced novel of the seamy L.A. underworld, featuring steel-fisted detective Sam Hunter in a case where Hollywood's sex-for-sale is X-rated with blackmail, blue movies, and the deep, dark red of murder.

"Next to Sam Hunter, Dirty Harry looks like Mother Teresa."
New York Daily News

"I'd cross the street to avoid him." *Los Angeles Times*

"One tough hombre...Hunter's excursions into bone-breaking and face-crumpling are frequent and explicit—so for that matter, are his sexual exploits." *Toronto Star*

The call for help came from *Sleaze*, a trashy Hollywood magazine. Los Angeles private eye Sam Hunter didn't get his kicks from 8 x 10 glossies, but when editor Natalie Orlov turned out to be a living doll with curves that stopped traffic, he got the picture and took the case.

THE BIG ENCHILADA
By L.A. Morse
77602-2/$2.50 U.S. $2.50 Canada

THE BIG ENCHILADA introduced Sam Hunter, the L.A. private eye who likes his women wild-eyed, and his cases big, bad, and brutal.

Hunter has three cases to crack: a woman who wants to know exactly *what* her husband is up to; a man who wants to find a missing daughter; and a father trying to hide from his murderous son.

THE OLD DICK
By L.A. Morse
78329-0/$2.25 U.S. $2.25 Canada

Edgar Award winning novel, THE OLD DICK features Jake Spanner, a 78-year-old, wise-cracking private eye who is dragged out of retirement by an old enemy and galvanized back into action to become embroiled with a bunch of senior citizens, hardened criminals, old cronies, and a ravishing young lovely.

AVON Paperbacks

Buy these books at your local bookstore or use this coupon for ordering:

Avon Books of Canada, 210-2061 McCowan Rd., Scarborough, Ont. M1S 3Y6
Avon Books, Dept BP, Box 767, Rte 2, Dresden, TN 38225
Please send me the book(s) I have checked above. I am enclosing $ _____
(please add $1.00 to cover postage and handling for each book ordered to a maximum of three dollars). Send check or money order—no cash or C.O.D.'s please. Prices and numbers are subject to change without notice. Please allow six to eight weeks for delivery.

Name _____
Address _____
City _____ State/Zip _____

MOR 10-84

"The finest thriller writer alive." *The Village Voice*

Elmore Leonard

LABRAVA 69237-6/$3.95
A fast, tough suspense novel of the crime beds of Miami, where a favor for a friend casts an ex-secret service agent and a once-famous movie queen together in a scene of sex and murder where this time the fade out...could be final.
"LaBRAVA is pure pleasure." *USA Today*

STICK 67652-4/$3.50
Just out of the slammer, Stick is caught between drug dealers, high-flying financiers and lovely ladies. Will his scam make him a rich man or a memory?
"Jumps right off the page." *The New Yorker*

UNKNOWN MAN NO. 89 67041-0/$2.95
When a process server with the reputation for being able to find anyone is engaged to track down a missing criminal, he finds himself caught in a treacherous labyrinth of deception, betrayal and murder.
"Will keep you on the edge of your chair." *The New York Times*

52 PICK-UP 65490-3/$2.95
This chilling tale unfolds a ruthless game of sex and blackmail—in which the only way an angry man can win is murder.
"A tightly wound thriller with a smash-up climax." *Village Voice*

CAT CHASER 64642-0/$2.95
An ex-Marine intends to live life peacefully in Florida, but a sentimental journey leads him to Santo Domingo: a hotbed of intrigue, double-dealing and violence.

SPLIT IMAGES 63107-5/$2.95
A Detroit homicide detective and his beautiful journalist lover track a rich playboy killer and his accomplice.

CITY PRIMEVAL: HIGH NOON IN DETROIT 56952-3/$2.50
In pursuit of a murderer, Detroit cop Raymond Cruz finds himself face-to-face with a wily, psychotic killer.
"One can hardly turn the pages fast enough." *Miami Herald*

Buy these books at your local bookstore or use this coupon for ordering:

Avon Books, Dept BP, Box 767, Rte 2, Dresden, TN 38225
Please send me the book(s) I have checked above. I am enclosing $ _____ (please add $1.00 to cover postage and handling for each book ordered to a maximum of three dollars). Send check or money order—no cash or C.O.D.'s please. Prices and numbers are subject to change without notice. Please allow six to eight weeks for delivery.

Name _____
Address _____
City _____ State/Zip _____

Leon 11-84